DAMOCLES

DAM●CLES

S.G. REDLING

Text copyright © 2013 S. G. Redling

Published by 47North
PO Box 400818
Las Vegas, NV 89140

ISBN-13: 9781611099652
ISBN-10: 161109965X
Library of Congress Control Number: 2012954517

DEDICATION

*This book is for my first tribe,
my siblings—Mary, Monica, and
Matthew. You made me brave.*

O N E

MEG

Meg decided that any word that started with *re* was evil. *Reanimation, rehydration, recalculation, restabilization, reatmospherication*—okay, maybe that last one wasn't really a word, but that endless drone of the computer over every loudspeaker on the ship made her brain start to tack *re* onto every sound in her aching head. If the computer wanted to throw a few applicable words onto the list, why not discuss the urge to *regurgitate* her *reconstituted* meal of *reengineered* proteins? She pressed the heel of her hand into her left eye where an especially intense hammering had begun.

"Feel any undue pressure, besides the usual readjustment?" Elliot Cho, the bioscience officer, scrolled through several data screens beside her head. He had been the first roused from deep sleep to oversee the rest of the crew's awakening.

"How long have you been up?" Meg's lips felt thick and gummy.

"Couple hours."

"You look like shit."

He turned a bleary eye to her. "Want a mirror?"

Meg shook her head and reached for the water tube hanging beside her sleep sling. The water tasted like warm iodine with an undertaste of rock salt, but she sucked it down greedily. When the thin stream trickled out to only drops, she groaned.

"Pace yourself," Cho said, "or BESS will pace it for you."

She knew the drill of waking up from deep sleep, but it didn't make it any easier anytime she did it. All of their bodies had been put into a suspended state, their brain functions lowered and their bodily functions maintained by BESS, the Biological Equilibrium Sustainment System. For the duration of their sleep, BESS had been doing the breathing, swallowing, and basic living functions for them. BESS had run the show, and BESS would decide when to hand the power back over. Meg decided she hated BESS.

"Everyone else up?"

Cho grunted. "Would you believe Wagner woke up with a hard-on?"

Meg laughed and then winced at the ache it caused. "Aren't you violating his confidentiality rights by telling me that?"

"Report me." He helped her to her feet, holding his hands out until he was sure she could balance. A few tentative steps and Meg turned her naked back to him, letting him whisper in her ear. "I like this part."

"Shut up." She laughed, tipping her head forward as he removed the thin netting of wires that branched out from her neck, down her back, and out to her limbs. She knew she'd have little red marks where BESS's stimulators had kept her muscles from atrophying during the journey. Cho's hand felt warm where he carefully peeled a glue pad from the back of her knee. "No wonder Wagner had a hard-on, if you were touching him like this."

Cho wrapped the wires into a bundle around his hand. "I should have paid more attention to how he was wired up. Maybe I'm stimulating the wrong muscles."

"Are you saying we're not going to have morning sex?"

He watched her tie her robe around her waist. "Give me a light-year or two."

Meg licked her still dry lips. "Yeah and a toothbrush. Morning breath takes on a whole new meaning out here."

They were on schedule and on course, inasmuch as they had a schedule or a course. The *Damocles* and her crew followed instructions and star charts for a portion of the universe that no one in the fleet had ever ventured into. Launching off of Hyperion, the deepest of the deep-space exploration stations to date, their faster-than-light travel had been guided by directions some heralded as the ultimate leap of faith, others as a suicide mission. They followed directions that had arrived from deep space seven years ago, directions in an unknown language, directions that Meg had been instrumental in translating. If her translations had been correct, and it was too late to doubt them now, they followed directions from The Set, an ancient race that had originally seeded Earth and brought humanity into existence.

All of that was a moot point at the moment, since Meg's biggest obstacle was getting her pants on. Deep sleep turned the cleverest, most agile space traveler into a mushroom-brained bowling pin for the first several hours of reawakening. She knew all she could do was ride it out. Resting on the edge of the cot, she tried once again to get her left foot into the left leg of the pants, all the way through to the opening at the floor. Finally, with one leg on, Meg began to feel confident she wouldn't have to spend the rest of her life naked.

As the ship purred back to life, the sleep sling retracted into its case above her bunk and the systems around her rebooted themselves. The loudspeakers stopped their squawking as workstations came back online throughout the ship. The six crew members deep slept in their own compartments on separate life-support systems, ensuring that should damage befall the ship during their slumber, the odds of at least one crew member surviving would improve. Meg tried not to think about what it would be like to be the only crew member to survive this far out into space, to wake up and find your companions dead and nothing but vast, empty space stretching out in every direction.

She tried not to think of it and failed every time. It really was a wonder she'd qualified for this mission or any deep-space mission at all. She didn't know if it was possible for anyone to hate the vacuum of space as much as she did. Of all the crews she'd manned she was the only member who never, ever went to the observation deck when they weren't in orbit around a mass. She heard others waxing and marveling at the wonders flying past them. All she saw was the void, the black, and all it made her feel was a deep twisting in her gut. They could keep it.

"On your mark, Officer Dupris. Phase Three recon drones at the ready."

She flexed her fingers to limber them up before tapping on the display screen. After fat-fingering a few incorrect commands, she switched to full audio command. "Placement situation," she said and paused, trying to remember what it was she was looking for. This wasn't a standard trip to an outer colony. She searched her sleep-clouded mind to remember why the drones had been sent in phases in the first place.

"First phase, life signs," the machine droned in the softly modulated female tones Meg had set during programming. "Cross-reference bioscan drones as per Officer Cho. Data uploaded to mainframe." Meg nodded as if the machine could see her. The *Damocles* navigation system would have launched the first round of drones to check for life on the planet, environmental conditions, sustainability, and the like. Each planet programmed into the ship's navigational system was supposed to be compatible with human life. Of course, the data they had received was billions of years old. Planets change. Humans change. The journey to make contact with something that might be human was the ultimate crapshoot. If the biodrones returned with no signs of life or an environment that was too hostile to make contact with, this leg of the trip would have been in vain. The crew would remain in deep sleep and they would go on to the next set of coordinates.

Data streamed on several different screens as Meg rolled her shoulders waiting for good news. As her head cleared and BESS released more water into the drinking tube, she knew the biosigns had to have come back positive. Only good news would have kicked off the awakening procedures. Whatever planet this was, there was life, and the environment was not overtly hostile to human life. The signs had been so good, as a matter of fact, that Phase Two drones had been launched.

Phase Two drones collected research for everyone on board—engineering, bioscience, and cultural protocol. The drones assessed the life on a given planet or moon, determining levels of technology and mineral resources. Had this mission been in the corner of their known universe, the drones would also look for signs of colonization, since people had been terraforming moons and planets for decades. Here, however, the drones were working with a blank canvas. Any signs of human life on this planet might have little to no resemblance to human life that had been nurtured and launched from Earth. That meant the drones had been programmed to look for patterns of inorganic organization of material. In other words, the crew of *Damocles*, and Meg in particular, were looking for signs that the humanoid life on this planet would share that Earthly humanoid need to control their environment.

And they did.

When the initial data of the Phase Two drones began to stream past, Meg felt her stomach flipping from more than just hunger. Images and graphs of structures and roadways flashed by. Registered levels of inorganic noises and bursts clouded the airways, and never in her whole life had Meg been happier to read the long and convoluted list of chemicals and by-products being reported in soil, air, and water. Pollution. There was nothing more human than pollution.

Her voice trembled as she gave the command. "Launch Phase Three drones for maximum contact." She knew the *Damocles* nav system was already interfacing with the drones to determine the optimal launch targets for the next round of drones, her drones. The drones were miniscule, inserted into larger capsules that would burn off upon entering the atmosphere. They would drop down in densely populated areas. Smaller than mosquitoes, they would drift on breezes, drawn by magnetism. They would attach themselves to electronic systems or anything resembling communication devices or manufacturing facilities. They were tiny little spies that would record every sound, every digital pulse, looking for patterns that would be fed into the ProLingLang system Meg had designed. And then Meg Dupris would do what she did best, what she had always tried to do—she would unlock the door to the languages around her.

She pushed back from her console as the screen signaled the launch.

"It's a mind fuck, isn't it?"

Meg spun and saw Katie Prader, the engineering officer, leaning in the doorway, her blonde hair pulled back in a greasy, crooked braid. They grinned at each other.

"Have you seen it?" Meg asked.

"Un-fucking-believable." Prader's lips were chapped, and she still had a sticky pad stuck to her elbow. "I was second up, not long after Cho. When those first phase readings came back, I was afraid to hope. When the second phase started pouring in data about transportation systems? I don't even...I can't..." Meg was on her feet, hugging the shorter woman.

"They were right." Meg pulled away and held Prader at arm's length. "The message. They were right. Humans, down there. All this way from home."

Prader wiped a tear from her cheek. "This calls for coffee."

They could hear laughter coming from the dining room. Cho made a show of disengaging BESS from the kitchenette to great applause from the crowd gathered around him.

"Thank you, BESS," Cho intoned as the yellow screen went black. "You've been a wonderful caregiver and life-support system, but as a cook, you suck. We've traveled millions of miles through who knows how many space dangers mindlessly absorbing liquid reengineered protein. It's time for us to do that one thing we've waited to do—chew. So with no further ado, I give you chewy reengineered protein."

Bowls were slung, spoons tapped together, and as one the crew of the *Damocles* dug into their first self-fed meal since leaving Hyperion.

LOUL

Loul watched his desk mate's eyes as they focused on the images passing before them. He knew that if he waited, if he stayed very still for another couple of seconds, she would lose herself in her work and forget to keep checking on him. He saw her blinks slow down, steady out, and heard the even whistle of her breathing. He was now free to slouch down in his chair and relax. He didn't really mind her that much. He didn't even bother to remember her name. The seat across from him at Workstation 14 had become something of a no-man's-land since Jep had been promoted. People came and people went, with the obvious exception of Loul himself.

He risked a glance down the line of workstations to the window at the end of the room. Between him and the glass, seven other workstations hummed with whatever job they were assigned. At least he'd gotten over his paranoia that other people were being given more interesting work than he got. He could tell just from the way her elbow was twitching that the woman three stations down was playing a game of Flange online. He wasn't the only slacker.

If he leaned back in his chair, he could just make out the edge of the second of the Zobos twins shining through the shaded glass. There were only two or three times a year both suns came into view, paralleling each other on the western horizon. They made the sky turn a sticky shade of yellow and generally put Loul in a grumpy mood, mostly because he would rather be out at the Observatory watching their path than stuck at this workstation charting storm patterns over the Ketter Sea. The way the shadows lengthened in the north, however, gave him an idea for a strategy he'd been mulling over for the game tonight.

Loul let his chair fall forward again. His desk mate—he'd taken to calling her Temporary 7 in his mind—looked up with a scowl that he ignored. She thought she was going to get somewhere in this department. She thought if she worked hard and met her deadlines and researched just a little bit beyond what was asked of her she would rise in the ranks and get a bigger desk and a better desk mate, along with more status and a bigger paycheck. And she was probably right. Jep had done it, and so had the other six people who had taken his seat since. Work hard, think hard, and keep your eye on the future. That was the way to the top.

"Don't be afraid to think beyond what you already know," his bosses were fond of saying. Good advice unless what you happened to think of was aliens.

It was so stupid, such an asinine thought that he still ground his teeth when he thought of it. Eight years ago he had graduated with a degree in telemetry with a guaranteed spot in the Cartar Satellite Telemetry Administration. He had shown up for his first day of orientation with a notepad and a head bursting with ideas. When the commanders had told him to think beyond what he already knew, he knew just where his mind was headed. When he'd received clearance to work at the extra-atmosphere satellite observatory, he'd nearly crowed with enthusiasm. When he had taken his first real look at Space (he always capitalized the word in his mind), the vast, velvety blackness of real Space, he had just known that his work was going to change history forever.

It had certainly changed his. He had spent eleven months of his own time putting together the report. Eleven months he could have been dating or bowling or trying to get some girl to lift her shirts for him. Instead he'd spent them wracking his brain, laboring over minute details, charting probabilities, and researching contingency plans to the point where he had almost convinced himself that the event had actually occurred. And after eleven months of uninterrupted and unpaid labor, he'd marched into the office of his superiors, put the report before them, and sealed his doom.

Six and a half years later, here he sat at Workstation 14, charting storm patterns over the Ketter Sea, plotting his strategy in a stupid game of Circle that he and his friends were still playing even though they all knew they were too old for it. Without an official word, his report had been filed away and an invisible mark had been placed on his career file. Well, not completely invisible. He'd had to report to Employment Resources to answer his superiors' concerns that he was "unrealistic, paranoid, and beset with juvenile fantasies not congruent with the objectives of the administration." In other words, he'd had to stand before a panel of generals and administrators and tell them that, despite the assertions of his report, he did not in fact believe alien life did exist, nor did he believe these nonexistent aliens would ever make contact with Didet or its inhabitants.

Loul's best friend, Hark, had shown his support by exploding with outrage when he'd learned of the inquisition and recanting. Of course, it was easy for Hark to take the high road. He had a cushy job at his mother's furniture plant overseeing the installation of heavy-duty casters for office chairs. His career path didn't have a lot of room for improvement, but at least the only people outranking him were his own family. It wasn't so much a glass ceiling as a blood ceiling, and short of outright embezzlement, he wasn't in danger of losing his job. Loul wasn't either. He just had no hopes of ever rising any higher in the ranks than his current midlevel weather-monitoring position.

Hark had gone so far as to suggest that Loul upload the entire report to the Internet, targeting those fringe groups who believed that alien life could and probably did exist, some even going so far as to claim to have made contact with non-Didet life-forms. After the humiliation at the hands of his superiors, he'd been tempted to. His administrators and the generals above them hadn't even tried to suppress their contempt at his report, some even laughing right in his face at his recommendations. Word had spread quickly throughout the department that Loul Pell was "one of those people," those nut jobs who claimed to have implants under their skin, who claimed to have had years taken off their lives, who knew for a fact that aliens had probed their bodies and attempted to mate with them. If that was the group he was going to be lumped into, why shouldn't he share the hard work he'd put into his report?

Because the administration had seized it. Every word of it. Even though he'd done his research and his calculations and his probability studies on his own computer during his own time, the administration had claimed he'd violated their resources and, as such, his intellectual property was now the property of the Cartar Satellite Telemetry Administration. He'd been chastised for irresponsible use of resources, for attempting to incite public fear, for denigrating the intellectual propriety of his position, and, underneath it all, he could feel the unspoken threat of labeling him a terrorist. They were afraid he would make them all look like fools.

So now he charted weather patterns and ignored his desk mate and waited for his workday to end so he could head out the social center and meet up with Hark and the gang and pretend to be wizards and star kings and minions of the Shadow as they worked their way through another round of Circle. And when the game hit a lull or they got a little too deep in their hot beers, Loul would let his mind and sometimes his words wander back to the ridiculous theories that had trapped him in this cycle of mediocrity. Because despite his recanting and his humiliations and his flatline pay scale, or maybe because of them, Loul Pell still believed there had to be life beyond the yellow skies of Didet.

MEG

Meg ignored the bleating of the alarm firing off again from the engine room. In the six weeks since coming up from deep sleep, it seemed the primary malfunction on the ship was the ship's alarm system. Something was always going wrong, and while there was no such thing as a minor emergency in space this far from any type of help, she wouldn't have minded a volume control on the announcement level. After all, she had a lot of listening to do.

She checked again to make sure the door to her cabin was sealed, shutting out as much noise as possible. Of course it was shut. She'd shut it herself. Plus the headphones she wore blocked out all but the most piercing sounds. Meg knew the real reason she kept peeking over her shoulder was to reassure herself that nobody was going to come into the capsule, pull the plug, and inform her that this entire experience was a simulation.

Voices. Meg clamped the headphones down more tightly over her ears, unnecessary for their function, necessary to keep her mind from blowing out the sides of her head. The drones picked up thousands of voices—articulated human vocal sounds—and as the language program separated the threads of sounds into manageable categories, she skimmed through the groupings to hear the sounds for herself.

She knew the look she had in her eyes. She'd seen it in almost every set of eyes on board when she would force herself away from her console to grab a bite to eat or to drywash the oily grime of recycled air off her skin. She'd passed Cho in the toilets and neither one of them could make a complete sentence. They'd finally just given up and grinned at each other. She'd had to step over Jefferson on the way to the kitchenette. After he'd taken in his drones' data on minerals and inorganic resources in the planet's crust, he'd laughed so hard he'd had to lie down to catch his breath. Prader had plenty to say, most of it of the four-letter variety, as she threatened every mechanical system on the ship that didn't come into line with her demands. But when she wasn't swearing and kicking panels into place, she would look up with a big toothy grin for anyone nearby.

Only Samantha Aaronson, the pilot, didn't join in the rejoicing. She didn't grin, she didn't high-five. She climbed and clambered over every inch of the wiring within the ship, consulting with Prader and Cho and Captain Wagner about the health of the propulsion crystal, but otherwise keeping her eyes on the myriad screens she oversaw. And in the middle of those screens, she occasionally let her eyes drift to a photograph of a handsome man in a military uniform. Sometimes she even let her fingers drift there, and when they did, everyone on the crew knew to look elsewhere.

The ship's log revealed that the first four planets on the path of given coordinates had been a bust. One had been devoured by a supernova; two were simply labeled "hostile"; and the fourth had been deemed "inaccessible" due to "solar conditions." Captain Wagner had worked with Aaronson to read the star charts the nav system had created. He signed off on them and launched another relay beacon that would, in theory, transmit the information from the *Damocles* back to one of the gathering satellites they'd scattered through deep space. It was like shooting a spit wad over the ocean, and they all knew it. The crew of the *Damocles* was on an information-gathering mission like no other, farther than any of their kind had ever dreamed of traveling, following coordinates nobody could guarantee led anywhere.

News of an ancient race seeding the species hadn't set well with the species as a whole. Meg and her language program had come under fire for falsifying information or, as the senator from the Galen colony had suggested, "making it all up." World religions and scientific communities reeled at the concept of something extraterrestrial influencing the course of life on the home planet. Creationists and evolutionists teamed up to fight the mind-shattering revelation that the one concept they all agreed on—the uniqueness of humanity—might be in danger. The message had changed the definition of humanity. But to Meg's thinking, the reaction to that fact did more to damage humanity than any message ever could.

The *Damocles*'s mission might never have happened if not for a horrific organized attack throughout the terraforming ring. Furious at what they saw as hubris, fringe groups of Christian and Muslim fundamentalists banded together for a brutal four-day assault. Firebombs, pipe bombs, and plasma bombs tore through universities and grade schools, laboratories, space stations, and medical labs all in the name of a God who supposedly abhorred science. They claimed they were "bringing down Babel," but the news media gave them the label that stuck: Evang-jihad.

Thousands lost their lives, including Aaronson's husband. Earthers and colonials reeled at the horror, but the International Space Commission reacted decisively. Leveraging the worlds-wide outrage, they pressed for and received expedited funding for the controversial mission.

Despite the uncertainty of the coordinates and the overwhelming probability that the mission would be one-way, a staggering number of officers applied to join the *Damocles*. The physical demands of such a trip were easily met by most fliers; it was the psychological profiling that thinned the herd. Wagner knew he needed men and women who weren't looking for glory, who weren't afraid of isolation, who hungered for discovery, and, most importantly, could say good-bye to whomever or whatever they would be leaving behind.

Even before deep sleep, even before launch from Hyperion, the pressure of the mission had bound the crew together. Knowing at least a third of your species was praying for you to fail hardened a lot of rough edges among them. Each member of the *Damocles* crew had his or her own reason for being out here, for shedding light on the truth of their existence. Haters and jeer-ers and doubters were as far from them now as the believers, the optimists, and the supporters.

Out here, the only signs of Earth and Earth-sourced human-ity were the signs they had brought with them. Photographs and recordings, the Gro-Walls, and their own bodies were the only proof Earth had ever existed. Now they orbited another planet with another humanity and another set of beliefs about their own uniqueness. They drifted in silence above the yellowed atmosphere of the multisunned planet, listening and spying, trying to decode the culture and determine the best way to make contact. They all knew it could take months to bridge the gap between their worlds. It could take years to untangle the language and culture and tech-nology, and they all knew that after all that untangling, it might only result in a humanity so violent and xenophobic that contact would result in their deaths. And if that was the verdict, if the col-lective intellect of the *Damocles*'s crew determined from the ton-nage of evidence being gathered that contact couldn't be made, they knew that they would retreat from orbit, shut the ship's extraneous systems down, and go back into deep sleep. They would go on to the next planet and the next and the next until they either contacted another human race or ran out of resources.

This is what all six of them had signed on for, and now, bur-ied in their respective data streams, they all knew in their hearts they'd made the right decision. They welcomed the work, they reveled in the discovery, and they settled in for the months of work they knew awaited them.

Then Prader got on the loudspeaker from the engine room and spoke the first sentence Meg had ever heard her utter with-out profanity. "Listen up, people. We have forty-eight hours to get off this ship."

T W O

LOUL

"Right there." Po pointed a fat finger at the blurry magazine photo. "The Roana Temple. There have been multiple reports of sightings, unexplained tidal changes, dead fish floating up in masses. But the news doesn't report it, and why?"

"Because dead fish are ugly?" Hark nudged Loul in the ribs with a laugh. Hark and Loul might have some out-there ideas about aliens and government conspiracies, but their buddy Po put them both to shame. Po ignored their laughter as he always did and flipped through the wrinkled, glossy pages.

"And here too, look. This guy right here got fired from his job with Search and Rescue because he made an official statement about unearthing the remains of a craft that could not have been manufactured on Didet. He saw the ship himself when they were clearing up a supposed helicopter crash just six miles from another archaeological dig." Po's face flushed with its usual urgency as he slammed the magazine shut and reached for his laptop. "And that's nothing compared to this."

Loul spoke around the last bite of his lunch. "You know you're going to have to listen to the rest of this alone, right?" Hark rolled his eyes as Loul swept crumbs off the table. "I have to get to work in twenty minutes." He tossed his napkin toward the huge garbage nets hanging against the wall of the social center. As always, he missed, and as always, he ignored the sign posted over the net to not leave trash on the ground.

"Not until you see this!" Po spun the screen around to show them a map of the northern hemisphere sprinkled with red and orange dots. "Look at this. Do you know what this is?"

"Yeah, Po," Loul said. "I work in Weather, remember? I recognize our own continent."

"Do you? Do you? Do you?" Po's head nodded at his own question, and Hark had to stifle a laugh. The three of them had been friends since kinderschool, and they knew that once Po started talking in sets of three, he was really working himself up. "Well then, bright boy, guess what those marks are? You don't know, do you? I do. I do. I do."

"I'm on the edge of my seat, buddy."

"Communication interruptions." Po slammed his hands down on the table.

Loul stared at him for a moment, judging just how far he could push his high-strung friend. "I don't mean to burst your bubble, Po, but we have a dozen of those a day all over the continent. It's called obsolescence. Our satellites haven't been updated since before we were born. They break down. A lot."

"Not like this. Not like this. Not like this."

Hark leaned in on his elbow. "I think Po's trying to tell you that they don't break down like this. Not like this. Not like this."

Po shoved him with both fists. "Shut up, you wad, and listen to me. Since the Zobos twins went off the horizon, there has been a systematic level of interference on the multiple broadcast frequencies all over the globe. And not just video. Independent webcasts, terrestrial radio, cable, and vidaphone. And not just in our hemisphere and not just randomly. Look." He brought up another screen. "Here The Searcher has documented levels of interference in electronic broadcasts that aren't random, natural, or solar-based. Documented. Documented—"

"Documented," Loul finished for him. "Gotcha. But you know, The Searcher also swears that the Roana Temple is secretly visited by the superbeings that live under the volcanoes in the Ketter Sea."

A feminine voice broke in over the noise of the social center. "Oh no, you all aren't talking about the volcano creatures again, are you?"

Loul felt his face flush as Reno Dado, Po's cousin, settled in at the table across from him. She smiled at him and Hark and then nudged her cousin with her shoulder. Loul tried not to be too obvious as he watched the light play off the gold necklace that twisted just so across the smooth expanse of skin underneath her jaw or the way the violet of her overblouse set off the slightly rosy tone of that skin. She didn't look up as he tried and failed not to stare. Instead she spun Po's computer around to see the screen.

"What is this?" She squinted at the screen. "Nonsolar textural interspatial...what the hell are you all looking at?"

Loul shook his head, floundering for words the way he usually did in Reno Dado's presence. Po jumped in before he could think of anything to say. "The interference. The communication interference. It's happening all over. Disrupting communication all over the—"

"I've heard." She laughed at Po's shocked face. "Hey, you're not the only one who reads the news, although you're probably the only one who starts with The Searcher for your headlines." She swiped a chip from Hark's plate, and Loul wished he hadn't thrown the rest of his chips away. "We lost three shifts of transactions today at the bank because of some weird interference in the wire system. The tech guys couldn't explain it, but it did let me get out of there early. Anyone want to go to a movie?"

"I'll go," Hark said, and then bit back the groan of pain as Loul's foot drove into his ankle. "Oh no, I can't. Sorry, I forgot I had to get back to the warehouse for inventory." He looked to Loul be sure his excuse was good enough to spare him another painful kick. When he saw the flush on his friend's cheeks, he kept the chatter up. "And of course Loul's got to go back to work too, right?"

"Yeah. Back." Loul resisted the urge to crawl under the table and hide from his own brilliant eloquence. He brightened a little, though, at Reno Dado's disappointed frown.

"Aw shoot. That just leaves me with you, Po, and no, you don't get to pick the movie." She shouted down his protest. "I'm serious. We're not sitting through another alien movie, and I'm not playing Circle with you."

Loul prayed that Po wouldn't bring up the game they were halfway through. Even though he loved meeting his buddies at the social center on their off shifts and even though he threw himself into the role-simulating game with as much enthusiasm as any of the others, he didn't need Reno Dado to see him as any bigger of a geek than she already saw him. Hark especially knew what a crush he had on her, so Loul felt he had to work doubly hard to not make an idiot of himself in front of her. So far, his record wasn't great.

Fortunately, the bell for the fourth shift sounded. "That's my cue," he said, pushing back from the table. He braced himself on his knuckles as he spoke to Reno Dado. "I'm off at tenth shift if you're going to be around. We could get something to eat or something or, you know."

She tilted her head in a way that showed off the rose-tinted skin beneath her jaw that made it hard for him to make out her words. "I'm heading to my parents' place at twelve to help get ready for the holiday. Maybe next round? Loul?"

It was Hark's turn to kick, and he did so with power, snapping Loul from his reverie. "Yeah, yeah. Okay. Next round. See you here. I'll be here. I come here usually for most of my off shifts." He tried in vain to stop talking as he backed away from the table. "Because, you know, we have this booth and we're usually here, so yeah, next round, I'll see you and…"

He didn't know exactly how long it took him to stop babbling as he backed his way through the crowded aisle of the social center, but he was pretty sure he was out of Reno Dado's hearing range before he stopped talking. Someone grumbled at him when he bumped into a booth, and he felt his cheeks burning red as he hurried out to the street. Now that the Zobos twins were off the horizon, the North Sun shone red and warm, no doubt matching his blush as he hurried back to the satellite office. He felt his phone buzzing in his pocket and fumbled it open. It was a text from Hark.

"Could be worse," the message read. "You could have fallen on your ass."

"Thanks, buddy," Loul muttered to himself, shoving the phone back into his pocket. He had two shifts ahead of him monitoring storms over the Attar Mountains. Two shifts to relive in great detail another brilliant example of looking like a dork in front of Reno Dado. He tried to comfort himself that at least she wouldn't be there after his shift, so he couldn't make it any worse. He pushed open the door to his office building and swiped his ID card against the scanner. Some days, he figured, all you could hope for was for things not to get worse. That's when two thickset guards stepped in front of him.

"Loul Pell?" the thicker of the two really thick men said to him. "Come with us."

MEG

Trying to comprehend syntax at five g's was not advisable, Meg knew as she bit down on the mouthpiece and let herself be shoved into the molded chair, but she couldn't stop herself. What might very well have been a four-year job had been shortened to forty-eight hours when it turned out that the last set of alarms from the engine room could not be ignored by any of them. While the rest of the crew had been throwing themselves into the massive amounts of data streaming in from the drones, engineering officer Prader had been unraveling a complicated series of misfires snaking through the life-support system of the *Damocles*.

The first sign had been the Gro-Walls. Only 80 percent of the genetically modified vining plants had sprouted after stasis. That percentage alone wasn't unusual. Everyone knew Gro-Walls always had a dead spot or two in them. Meg hadn't paid a bit of attention to the wilted patch of vines that had spread over her bunk in the weeks they'd orbited the planet. Some sprouts just didn't survive. The rest of the wall had been fine, tiny white flowers opening and quickly turning into the dense purple-pod beans that tasted like boiled peanuts. The Gro-Walls reminded Meg of the hyacinth beans that used to grow along the fencing of her childhood home. Of course, the hyacinth beans hadn't been genetically modified to mature in less than a week in deep space, and the beans themselves had not contained a balanced mix of protein and amino acids to sustain human life. But, Meg assured herself with a petty Earth bias, Gro-Walls weren't as pretty as hyacinth beans.

Pretty or not, the Gro-Walls did more than supply ready living food for emergencies. They also filtered the air, helped recycle water through the root system that was engineered to integrate into the ship's plumbing system, and acted like a deep-space version of a canary in a coal mine. If anything disrupted or tainted the atmosphere in the ship, the Gro-Walls' leaves had been designed to change color according to the chemicals affecting them. When the Gro-Walls near the engine room turned red, Prader had sworn. When they'd turned red in the kitchenette and yellow at the navigation system, Prader had kicked the panel to the central wiring system so hard she'd had to take it down. When the Gro-Walls around the edges of the observation window turned black and fell to the floor, Prader had gotten quiet.

She and Captain Wagner had met in several muffled huddles. Navigation officer Aaronson had joined in, but the rest of the crew had gone about their business. First contact with a human-inhabited planet this far from home, a planet that had not been terraformed by an Earth-based people, took precedence over any event that was not immediately life-threatening. They each had their field of expertise, and for Meg, Cho, and Jefferson, those fields were expanding with a knowledge curve that was blowing all of their minds.

Meg's ears had ached with the press of the headphones. ProLingLang, the language system she had designed and reengineered specifically for this mission, hummed with an efficiency that made her want to pound her chest. The enormity of its undertaking could hardly be grasped. The drones she had deployed were dumping in millions of human vocal sounds, sorted by regions of the planet, sorted again by volume, tone, and situation. Broadcast sounds, and the planet certainly had its share of broadcast technology, were the easiest to capture. The program grouped those sounds into types of broadcast and categories of tone and delivery. It also scanned each vocalization for patterns and repetitions.

Meg knew she was working under enormous assumptions. The name of the program itself reflected some of those assumptions. ProLingLang stood for Protocol, Language, and Linguistics. The fact that she hadn't chosen to call it ProLangLing was her own little salute to her beliefs in the nature of language. Easiest sounds won out: ProLingLang sounded better and flowed more smoothly for Meg than ProLangLing. Plus it was her program, and she had a reputation for being persnickety, a reputation she reinforced by forbidding the crew to call her by her last name. She hated the way they pronounced Dupris.

For any Earth-based language translation, the assumptions were a given. Whether she was translating an ancient text, making first contact with a lost tribe of the Amazon rain forest, or translating a treaty with a long-isolated renegade colony in deep space, Earth-originated human language had several factors in common. There were limitations to the vocal ranges of humans. Even if the language relied heavily on gestures and expressions, humans could move only a finite number of ways, and thus parameters could be set, standards and equivalents understood. The biggest assumption, however—the assumption that had made it possible for Meg to translate the ancient deep-space message, that had gotten Meg this spot on the *Damocles*, that had Meg listening until her ears nearly bled sorting through the cacophony of vocal sounds—was the assumption that humans didn't make noise for nothing. They had something to say.

She knew the Space Administration hadn't fully understood her point, and she'd long since come to terms with the fact that she could never truly explain it. And no, the irony wasn't lost on her. What made Meg Dupris such an outstanding protocol and linguistics specialist was her intuitive understanding of the underlying human urge to communicate that which could never be truly communicated. It was the eternal need to shout "You should have been there!" that compelled humans to tell stories and pass on advice and seek comfort and safety and love among their own kind. The only way that need could be fulfilled was for a community to agree upon a set of sounds and gestures to carry consistent meanings. That agreement became language.

She could be wrong. This far out into the universe, a million variables could have made her language program useless. The inhabitants of this planet could be psychic, communicating on a mental level that required no sound at all. But the vast amount of broadcast technology told her that wasn't the case. They might be isolationists, living like Japanese fighting fish and clashing upon the slightest contact, each person an island. But the first glance at the manufactured topography and population reports told her that wasn't even close to true. These people lived in dense communities across a long ribbon of land that circled the equator.

The data that really put her doubts to rest, however, was a stream of electronic broadcast that had come into the system two weeks earlier. The vocalizations were drawn out, several different tones in a pattern the system had struggled to categorize. She'd only noticed the file by chance as she'd looked up from a dense packet of what might be a recognizable syntax pattern. When she'd clicked on the audio, she'd winced at the vocalizations, the warble in the tones clashing in her ears with a deep, throbbing undertone. And then, behind all the vocalizations, she'd heard a metallic pinging and what sounded like air being forced through wires.

She'd listened to the sound, turning the volume up as much as she could without the deep undertones hurting her eardrums. The sound resonated through her jawbone and some notes even made her eyes water. She'd listened and listened, and when the vocalization and background noises repeated themselves she'd grinned, and her eyes had watered for an entirely different reason. Every fiber of her intuition told her that she was hearing what this planet called music. If they made music, they wanted to talk. Meg listened for over an hour, finally finding a complex rhythm hidden beneath all those sounds. She'd fallen asleep with her headphones on. She couldn't wait to meet them.

But that didn't mean she wanted to go right now. When Captain Wagner had agreed with Prader's assessment, he'd called them into the kitchenette at once. The Gro-Walls had been responding to a malfunction in the Chelyan crystal, the self-regenerating propulsion crystal that made deep-space travel feasible. Maybe *feasible* wasn't the right word since the crystals could be so capricious that they were often thought of as an extra and particularly prickly crew member. Something about the excessive solar radiation in the multisun system had, as Aaronson phrased it, "put her off her feed," *her* being the crystal. Getting her back on her feed involved shutting down the systems and venting the *Damocles* for a full space freeze.

The isolation pods did not have enough room, power, or resources needed to shelter all six crew members. The fewer requiring life support, the quicker the crystal could be reset. It was decided, therefore, that Aaronson would isolate herself in a pod tethered to the outside of the *Damocles* while the rest of the crew loaded into the shuttle and headed for the planet's surface. Once the ship had been thoroughly vented and frozen, Aaronson would reboard, reboot, and run diagnostics to repair and reactivate the propulsion crystal.

Jefferson, the resources officer, abandoned his data research and began implementing the emergency ship-to-land protocol. All around Meg the crew exploded into action, barking packing lists into the computer and prioritizing inventory for decontamination before loading into the shuttle. Nobody panicked, but five crew members seemed to arrive at the same panic-worthy conclusion quite a few moments after Meg. Wagner spoke the realization she could hear pounding in her chest, and Meg thought he sounded much more optimistic about it than she felt.

"Listen up, everyone." Wagner had the chiseled good looks of a movie star and the deep voice to match. His dark-brown skin seemed always to catch the light just so, and as he stood there, every inch the captain and commander of the *Damocles*, Meg felt a sense of unreality washing over her. Part of her mind tried to tell her that this was a training video. This was that simulation she'd been so afraid of learning about just weeks ago. This simply couldn't be real. Wagner must have seen the look in her eye because he kept his gaze level, his voice calm. He knew his crew; he'd picked them himself. He hadn't hit his rank by misjudging the men and women who relied on him at moments like this. One by one, everyone settled down to listen to him.

"In less than thirty hours, we will be on planet. We will be making our first contact with a non-Earth-originated species of human." One by one, he looked into each person's face. "Officer Jefferson, Officer Cho, Officer Prader, Officer Dupris, Officer Aaronson, there is no finer crew with whom I would like to make history. To preserve the integrity of orbit, the *Damocles* will burn on slow thrust for the reset, which means she will be on the dark side of the planet for the majority of the diagnostics. Assuming everything goes according to plan, Aaronson will be light side again within ten days. We've set the countdown on your screens."

Aaronson gave her usual stony nod, her face unreadable as always. If there was anyone who could stand the isolation of space all on her own, it was Samantha Aaronson. Wagner cleared his throat. "Obviously we are preempting our schedule." Prader muttered a string of profanities and Cho rubbed his hands over his face. They all knew how grossly unprepared for contact they were, but none of them knew it better than Meg.

"We don't know what to expect upon arrival. We may be landing very hot. The possibility of attack is high since Jefferson's research has revealed warfare technology. We have no way of knowing if these people have had interplanetary contact or if they are even open to the possibility." He leveled his gaze at Meg, who could feel sweat dampening the hair around her face. "Officer Dupris, it is asking too much to expect you to have a language and cultural protocol in place, but that is exactly what I'm asking you to do in T-minus thirty hours."

Thirty-three hours later, the *Damocles Sub 2* cooled and groaned on its landing legs on an enormous limestone pad Aaronson had spotted during recon. The nav system had calculated which landing spots were most advantageous for the situation and Meg had insisted the choice be narrowed down as quickly as possible. The shuttle had the capability to circle the large planet several times to scout out landing sites close up, but every minute within the atmosphere was another minute they were exposed to the military intelligence of the planet. Plus, the sooner they knew where they were landing the sooner Meg could eliminate language data gathered from other parts of the world.

She knew she had to pinpoint the regional language as quickly as possible. Dumping 85 percent of the data tore at her heart in ways she would deal with later, but for now she focused the program's attention solely on data gathered from a two-thousand-kilometer region stretching out from their landing site. It helped that the site was coastal, the strange platform resting on an otherwise abandoned stretch of land not far from a saltwater sea. Both Wagner and Jefferson had remarked on the distinct lack of population along the saltwater ways, raising questions about contamination or other natural risks in the seas, but Cho's research showed nothing overtly dangerous about the waters themselves.

"This site might be religious. It could be sacred." Meg chewed her lip as she voiced just a few of the millions of thoughts she struggled to get in order. "Our first act on this planet may very well be the act that damns us forever."

Prader squinted into the eyepiece that opened to the camera scanning the quiet horizon around them. "Well fuck them if they can't take a joke."

Cho unlatched a biokit. "Thank God you're not our protocol liaison."

"Hey," Prader snapped. "Which would they prefer? We leave skid marks on their church parking lot or set fire to their kids' schools with our plasma burners?"

"Focus, people." Wagner shuffled packs along the narrow shuttle, pushing a heavy bundle before each of their seats. "It won't be long until we have company. If they have any air-monitoring systems, they're sure to have seen our afterburn."

"Hold that thought," Prader said, spinning the viewfinder. "The welcome wagon is here. And I don't see any muffins. Oh shit."

The four of them continued to unpack and repack their supplies as Prader gave them a play-by-play of the arriving vehicles. Most came over land, while several flew in. Although she could not make out anyone inside the vehicles, she felt confident that the open-ended cylinders pointed their way from every direction were weapons.

Cho tapped Meg's leg, giving her the sign that he would pack her kit for her. They knew she had better things to do at the moment. Her data pack hung in a pouch on her belt, and she used the screen on the shuttle's wall to work. She'd save her drag screen until necessary. The wall screen was easier to read and Meg needed every bit of her focus on the work before her.

With most of the data removed from the calculations, ProLingLang had recognized syntax patterns more quickly, grouping them into sets and subsets. But for all the program's efficiency, for all the tags and triggers Meg had programmed into its workings, she knew actual translation was going to require intuition and luck. Lots of luck. All the way down from the ship, even at maximum gravity pull, she'd been listening to vocals that most closely matched what they needed.

Data still streamed into the system from the drones she had kept contact with, but when a rash of profanities broke out around the ship, first from Prader, then from Cho and Jefferson, and finally from the captain himself, Meg didn't need to look to see the data stream had stopped. Whoever was parked outside their shuttle had set up some sort of jamming technology. All any of them had to work with was the data they had brought with them. They all knew it wasn't enough and they all knew there was only one solution. They had to go out there.

LOUL

"Am I in trouble?" Loul held his hands up to the two men blocking his way. Now that he looked at them he saw they weren't wearing uniforms. They had on the same suit jackets as most of the men around him, but that didn't change his perception of them as guards. Just the size of them, the solidity of their broad chests, told him these men were soldiers of some sort. When the one on the left held out his arms to block Loul's way, the butt of a gun came into view. Not that he knew much about guns, but something told Loul that was a big one.

Loul stood almost a head taller than the taller of the two men, but side by side they were more than double his width. There was no question they could stop him if he chose to flee, which he quickly ruled out as an option. The men stepped even closer and slightly to his side, flanking him. It felt like an incredibly mismatched game of Pummel, a game in which even one-on-one he was usually mismatched for.

"If you'll come with us, Mr. Pell. There's a car waiting for you out front."

"What is this about? Am I in trouble?"

"No sir." The shorter of the men guided him by the elbow, and Loul tried not to wince at the pressure of his grip. "Everything will be explained on the way."

"On the way where?"

"Please, sir, just come with us."

They moved Loul through the lobby of the satellite building with speed and precision, and before he had the presence of mind to shout out for help, he found himself bundled into the back of a black-paneled transit bus, the kind used to shuttle high-end travelers to and from hotels and airports. The door slammed behind him, neither of his escorts joining him, and Loul fell into his seat as the vehicle sped away from the curb. A wall of shaded glass blocked him from seeing the driver as anything more than a shadow, and a tinting on the windshield made seeing the road ahead even more difficult. The windows on the short bus had been blacked out entirely. Only the ceiling remained clear. Loul had no idea where he was.

He fumbled in his pocket for his phone. It was gone. One of the goons who grabbed him must have lifted it from his pocket during their kidnapping. He'd been kidnapped. Loul felt all the air go out of his gut as the realization hit him. Kidnapped. Why? He leaned forward and pounded on the glass but his only reward was to fall onto the floor of the bus when it made a sharp right turn. If the driver could hear him, he made no sign of it. The doors were locked. His pockets were empty. Loul climbed back into his seat, put his hands on his knees, and tried to pull himself together.

Why in the world would anyone kidnap him? He had no money to speak of. His family was comfortable but by no means people of notice. As for his access to satellite information, he'd heard about people being bribed and coerced to perform as spies, but he hardly had the clearance for the sort of information anyone would pay for. Someone had to have mistaken him for someone else, someone with higher clearance or more authority.

"Great," he said aloud, hoping his voice would help calm him. "I can't even get kidnapped right. Another Loul Pell success story."

But the men who grabbed him had called him by name, right? He had swiped his identification card, which was also missing, he noticed, and when he'd been cleared to enter the secure area, they'd grabbed him. They had singled him out. But why? All he could do was wait for something or someone to come along and give him more information.

He didn't have to wait long. Less than hour later, he could hear the sounds of traffic abate, and it sounded like the bus had pulled into a garage or warehouse of some sort. Loul could hear heavy machinery and the rumble of engines. He squinted through the glass to see what the driver would do but turned when the side door slid open.

"Mr. Pell? I'm General Dar. Will you come this way please?"

A general? Loul could only stare at the broad, black-haired man waiting for him beside the van. He didn't know much about military rankings but there was an awful lot of shiny stuff on the front of his tunic. Loul knew enough to know that this was a man others obeyed. "Yes sir. Where am I?"

"You're not there yet, son, but you will be soon. You get motion sick?"

"Motion sick?"

The general turned and smirked. "Not a lot of ventilation." He waved his arm ahead and Loul found the presence of mind to take in his surroundings. They were in a trucking depot. Rows of long, over-the-road cargo trucks idled at open bay doors. Heavy industrial fans blew the exhaust outside, but even with their heavy blasts, the air stank and stung his eyes. As they walked toward the row of rumbling vehicles, Loul saw smaller trucks and tanks and weapon carousels being loaded into the backs of the big rigs.

He stopped and read the signage. Not one of the trucks had any military or government markings. One truck had the logo of a produce company, another of an office supply company. Loul craned his neck and saw the truck at the last door had the markings of Hark's family furniture business. Before he could put it all together, the general handed him over to a team of six soldiers, all dressed in black, who lined up on either side of him and handed him into the back of a truck marked with a grocery store logo. Everything happened so quickly, and it was all so surreal, Loul found himself strapped into a seat bolted to the floor beside two women and across from three men who all wore the same bewildered expression he did. The only light within the cargo hold came through the strips of glass in the ceiling.

"What the hell is this?" He didn't ask any of them in particular, and none of them answered. Apparently he was what the company was waiting for, and as he buckled his seat belt, a small woman in a combat uniform climbed in, slammed the door shut, and banged on it. In minutes, the truck rumbled to life and Loul was once again traveling with no idea of where he was, who he was with, or where he was headed.

After twenty minutes of silence, the soldier smiled around at the group, none of whom smiled back. "I know this is sudden, and I know you have a lot of questions, and I promise we will answer as many of them as we can. For now, though, I'm going to ask you all to sit back, relax, and get some rest. We have a long drive ahead of us and we're going to need you rested when we get there. If you need anything, food or drink, just let me know. Until then, I have to ask you not to speak to each other." She shook her head with a bemused expression. "Trust me when I tell you, you'll have plenty to say when we get there."

What felt like a full shift later, they got there. The truck slowed. They could hear other trucks and other people over the sounds of heavy machinery. Finally the door to the cargo hold opened, and Loul had to squint as the glare of the Red Sun hit him directly in the eyes. The soldier stood silhouetted in the light as she waved her arm before her.

"Ladies and gentlemen, if you'll follow me."

Once he stepped down from the truck, Loul's first thought was, "Po is going to shit."

They stood within a circle of military vehicles that were contained by a privacy-webbing wall that stretched around an enormous perimeter. The smell of saltwater was heavy in the wind, and Loul didn't have to wonder what he was smelling. It was the Ketter Sea. He was on the coast of the Ketter Sea staring at a spaceship. An honest-to-goodness spaceship. And if that weren't enough, if that didn't completely blow his mind, the spaceship was parked exactly where Po had always said it would be—on the ruins of the Roana Temple.

THREE

MEG

"Let's go over it one more time."

They stood in a circle at the shuttle door. Each of them wore a suit although all of their helmets were pushed back. Meg fidgeted with Wagner's wrist monitor one more time, checking for volume and brightness and that the data was moving as it should. She rechecked the thin speaker patch sewn into the front of his suit, a patch each of them wore on both their suits and undershirts, although only Wagner's would be active until Meg gave the command. Wagner stood still as her hands flitted over his equipment.

"I've narrowed the vocals down to what appear to be three of most likely greeting phrases based on repetition, tonality, and call-and-response patterns." Uttering the jargon relaxed her enough to take her hands off the captain and speak candidly. "Of course, it's important to remember that we don't know exactly what we're saying. I mean, literally, we do not know what these words mean, so let's all rub our lucky charms that we're not repeating some popular piece of profanity or this planet's equivalent of *sieg heil* or, you know, like, a popular order at Taco Bell or something. It could be gibberish, and since we're using the recordings, it could be cut off wrong, edited wrong. I could have cut out the wrong undertones. I might have ruined whatever the message was to begin with. I might have—"

Wagner grabbed her shoulders, silencing her. "You might also have correctly identified a common greeting. Because that's what you do and that's what you're good at." Cho reached out and squeezed her shoulder. Jefferson and Prader followed suit, each assuring her with their touch that they had faith in her ability. When she had calmed down, Wagner nodded at her. "Give us one more rundown on protocol."

"Right, protocol." Meg looked to each of them. "Best option in any foreign situation is mirroring without aggression. We've seen how they've grouped. The soldiers are behind shields but it's safe to say they stand in formalized group formations so we'll do the same. I recommend a chevron. Captain, you in the front, Jefferson and Cho flanking you on either side, and Prader and I on the far ends. We won't touch each other but we will stay in easy hand's reach."

"Our biopacks?" Cho asked. Each of them had a pack containing food, water, and water purifiers, as well as rudimentary first aid and a compressed-film sleep sack.

"Keep them on you," Meg said, "hooked to your suit. We haven't gotten a clear visual of the physiology of these people, and they sure haven't seen us, so they don't know that we don't have big humps on our backs. It's better to be safe than sorry since it could be a while until we can request food or water."

She checked the captain's patch speaker one more time. "When we disembark, we'll take formation and stand perfectly still. Let's see what they do, who approaches. Helmets and gloves on until we see faces."

"I'm going to follow your lead on protocol," Prader said, shifting her biopack, "but there's no way in hell I'm going out there without my sidearm."

"You're damn right you're not." Meg patted her own leg where her gun rested hidden in a holster. "Every one of us is going to be armed and ready. We don't know what to expect. Prader, stay close to the door. Leave it open. The first sign of violence, we're in and up."

Wagner nodded at that. "If worse comes to worst, we can hop around this planet until Aaronson's got the all-clear. It won't be easy and it won't be comfortable. That's also where our survival odds are the lowest so that is a last resort."

Meg put her hand against the door of the shuttle, a little ritual she liked to perform at the doorway of every translation, negotiation, or first encounter she'd ever experienced. It almost seemed like she could feel the conversations she was getting ready to have. The coolness of the surface smoothed over her nerves, and when she spoke again, her voice was level.

"These are people. These are humans." She looked at each of them in turn. "They may not look like us or talk like us but they are human and so we can reach them. We're scared. We're outnumbered by, like, a billion to one, and we're definitely out-armed, but there is no sign that these people have had any space travel. Except for the unmanned communication satellites, there's no sign they've ever been up where we were, so it's probably safe to say that we've got the element of surprise on our side. That's our advantage. Let's use it."

She checked her earpiece and waited while the rest of the crew checked theirs. "The vocals indicate a lot of guttural sounds and hard consonants. Also, unless the drones were wonked, speech volume is really high with these people. The sounds are loud. That means we should be able to talk under our breaths through the coms. Try to keep your mouth movements limited and they may not even know we're talking."

Jefferson spoke up. "Why don't we want them to see us talking?"

"Psychology," Meg said. "The only advantage we have is that they have no idea who or what we are. They may be able to communicate psychically or nonverbally, but judging from the audio volume of the sounds, I'm guessing not. If it seems like we move as a unit by signals they can't pick up, they may hesitate to act aggressively."

"Our coms are on." Wagner reached for the door handle. "Everyone keep your eyes open, your sidearms ready, your movements slow and controlled. Meg, we'll follow your lead via the coms. What do you say?" He gave them his best movie-star wink. "Let's go make history."

The rumble of machinery doubled as they stepped out of the shuttle, down the metal steps off the slab. Wagner went first, his head held high, his shoulders back. Cho and Jefferson stepped off next, followed by Meg and Prader. As they cleared the steps, the tone of the machinery changed, getting higher and more intense. Jefferson whispered through the coms. "A lot of directional equipment being pointed our way."

"Could be cameras," Meg said, her eyes moving across the assembly before her.

"Could be weapons," Prader said.

"Let's assume it's all of the above." Wagner's voice was level. "Stopping in three steps. Three, two, one." With that, they stopped as a group in the chevron position. Meg could see the side of Cho's face through the slant of his helmet, and just those few smooth inches of tan skin calmed her nerves. "We move on your signal, Meg."

Meg struggled to keep her breathing steady. All around them, shields rose. Some looked like plastic, some seemed to be made of a glass-like substance. No faces showed anywhere in the patchwork of black and gray that reflected the lowering rays of a red sun. It felt like they stood that way for an eternity even though Meg doubted it was more than a few minutes. She listened to the sounds around her, going so far as to close her eyes briefly to maximize her attention. Humming, rumbling sounds came from every direction, machinery sounds, but underneath that she could just catch the tinny sounds the drones had caught. People were speaking over radios to each other behind the shields.

The center wall of blockades parted. Whoever held the tall barricades stepped to either side of the center, and three figures stepped forward, dressed alike in rough fabric tunics that wrapped around squat, broad forms. Over her heartbeat, Meg could hear Cho cataloging the physical features into his data pack under his breath, comments about humanoid features and stunted bone structure, approximating the height at one and half meters. She also heard Prader swear to herself and Jefferson's breath catch. Wagner was silent.

"Now, Captain. Play the audio."

LOUL

The first question posed to him by the ranking trio of generals left Loul speechless.

"Is it safe to assume by now you know the reason you're here?" It was so hard to wrap his mind around the fact that he was here and that there was a spaceship right outside the door that it hadn't occurred to him to question *why* he'd been brought to the site. They seemed to be waiting for an answer.

"Not really." It was a better answer than the first one that popped into his head, which was something like "Because it's freaking awesome and everyone should see this!"

"I'm surprised by that, Mr. Pell." The general on the left, General Ada, one of the two male generals of the trio, pushed his hands together on the table at which the trio sat across from Loul. "From what I've been led to believe, you saw this coming several years ago. As a matter of fact, your report even mentioned the likelihood of this event occurring in this hemisphere after the setting of the Zobos twins."

"My report?" Loul forgot he was already sitting down and tried to drop lower in his chair. "My report for the Telemetry Administration? Six years ago? That was destroyed."

The generals shared a look and Ada spoke again. "No, Mr. Pell. It was classified."

"I had to recant the whole thing. I got called by administrators and told to drop my research immediately." The memory of that humiliation, of all the wasted years regretting his work, kicked Loul's mouth into gear. "I was threatened with psychological evaluation if I didn't take back everything I'd said. My career went into the pipes after that report and I've been trying to live it down ever since. They told me I was irresponsible and delusional and—"

"You were right." Ada pulled out a folder. "I'll be perfectly candid with you, Pell. Your report became classified the minute you turned it in. It is required reading for an entire department of Telemetry and Defense."

"And you just let me founder there in Weather? You didn't tell me? Let me be part of the research? The extra-atmosphere satellite closed down before I even got a chance to—"

"The EAS is not closed." The central general spoke, his name tag obscured by a thick burlap strip signifying something military Loul didn't know. "As per yours and other recommendations of like-minded scientists, the satellite was recommissioned for outer space listening and tracking. Many people in the administration fought the redesign but your report was one of the more convincing arguments."

"And you just left me in Weather?" Loul couldn't seem to get past that fact. "You just let me sit there and think you thought I was crazy? You didn't think I could help further the research? You didn't think I would have some input in developing more effective procedures?"

The third general, General Famma, the only woman in the trio, held up her hand to silence him. "The question is now, Mr. Pell, which would you rather have? An apology or the chance to be on the team to assess the threat level of this extraterrestrial invasion?"

That snapped him back to reality. The humiliation, the recanting, the dismal pay all disappeared in light of the chance to be on the team with first contact to a non-Didet life-form. "I'm in. What do you need from me?"

"We'll keep you informed."

And just like that, he was out again. Military escorts lifted him from the chair and moved him out of the staging area, behind the barricades where he could only glimpse the edges of the strange shuttle that had been perched on the ruins of the Roana Temple for almost an entire day. He'd already missed two shifts of work and at least one hand of Circle at the social center. He could only imagine what theories Po was coming up with to explain his absence. He'd give almost anything to get a message to his friends, anything but the chance to be here in person.

He busied himself for the next several hours moving along the barricade, trying to peer over the shoulders of the military archivists who filmed the uneventful scene before them. Cameras and audio recorders cranked along at full speed, capturing the ship from every quiet angle, no sign of any activity within the strangely shaped vessel. Finally, one of the archivist teams took pity on him and let him take a seat beside them on a pop-up bench holding the monitor for a high-perch camera.

His report had been immediately classified. The idea rang through Loul's head like a bell. It had been so long since he'd read the report but he still remembered many of the details. He'd come up with variations of approach and containment, possibilities of attack from the alien visitors, military tactics to subdue weaponry the likes of which Didet had never seen. Sitting here now, however, listening to the pops and clicks of cameras and weapons carousels wheeling about the silent ship, he wondered if he had overlooked the possibility that maybe the real aggressors were actually on the ground, surrounding him. And while part of his report had touched on the possibility of benign contact, he doubted the military would focus their attention on that scenario.

With no work partner of his own, the archivists let Loul help out monitoring the screen and readings. The atmosphere within the barrier screens was one of hurry-up-and-wait, everyone on high alert to watch nothing happening. Still, none of them wanted to close their eyes for even a moment, each work partner afraid they would be on break when whatever was going to happen happened. When Loul did settle back to drop out for a moment, his eyelids flickered with tension, his mind unwilling to shut off for the three or four minutes necessary to refresh. He popped back up with a start, his imagination using the few quiet moments to create all sorts of scenarios that weren't happening. He could see people starting up from their own rests with the same surprised then disappointed expressions.

He overheard snippets of discussions around him. Maybe the occupants of the ship hadn't survived the landing? Maybe the ship was only a probe or maybe even a decoy distracting them from an invasion set to occur elsewhere? Maybe the occupants of the ship had already exited and had slipped through their security barriers with their stealth technology. Mamu, the archivist sitting next to him, passed around another of his seemingly endless supply of candy rings.

"So you're some kind of expert?"

Loul took a green ring and popped it in his mouth. "Hardly." The archivists had been nice enough to let him join them on the bench but had been slow to warm up to him, eyeing him with suspicious detachment. "I work in Weather. I wrote a paper on the ramifications of alien contact six years ago. I didn't think anyone had actually read it, much less acted on it."

"Yeah?" Mamu relaxed a bit at that. "So you're not one of those wads waving their badges around, telling everyone how to behave? Hiding behind the artillery lines and recording their deathless wisdom for the archives?"

Loul laughed. He'd seen the men and women Mamu was talking about, presumably from the Science Administration. Badge waving seemed to be their number one activity. As for their contributions to the audio record of the event, Loul hadn't heard anything worth listening to. "I'm no expert. I just had some ideas, you know?"

"And is this what you imagined it to be?"

He stared at the shuttle, the black streaks scarring the hull, probably from atmospheric burn. "I guess, yeah. There are all kinds of arguments about shapes and mechanics the ships would use, whether they would use some sort of propulsion engine or actually be able to teleport themselves without a vessel." He heard Mamu laugh at that. "Hey, it's all been theory up to this point. When you're dealing with an advanced race, you can't make assumptions."

"What makes you think they're advanced?"

"Well, they just landed from outer space. I think that's a clue."

Before Mamu could comment, a flurry of activity rippled back from the barricade. The door of the shuttle cracked open, the seal breaking with a hiss quiet enough that only the most sensitive recording equipment tipped off the crowd. The soldiers holding the barrier bars tightened their stance as cameras and pom-guns wheeled into position to cover every inch of whatever was emerging from the vessel.

Loul pressed in tight against Mamu and his work partner to watch the video display of the high-mounted camera. The Red Sun fell low on the horizon, warm light pouring between the barricades and the ship. He wondered if the occupants had waited until the harshest of the lights would not be shining directly into their eyes. If they had eyes. The ship's door swung out and metal steps lowered to the ground. This was really happening. Contact with extraterrestrial life was happening right now.

Loul's first thought was "shit, they're tall." Then, "shit, they're real." Then, "shit, they're really tall." Again he felt a deep and juvenile longing to have Po and Hark here with him so they could celebrate this unbelievable sight. Also so he could throw it in Po's face that Loul's belief of what space travelers would look like was more accurate than Po's. Po had always held out the belief that alien life would be reptilian and very small due to the demands of space travel. Loul had held that gravitational and environmental conditions would be different on different worlds and space travelers could well be twice the size of an average Dideto. Squinting at the forms in the monitors, he wouldn't say they were twice the size, but they were certainly a head or two taller than even himself.

They wore space suits, again something Loul silently applauded himself for predicting, and he wondered how much of their size was suit and how much body. Or was it possible that the bodies and the suits were interrelated, a sort of biomechanical composition that made space travel possible? He could hear his own pulse pounding beneath his jawbone as he resisted the urge to push the barricades out of the way and see these creatures with his own eyes.

They moved silently, slowly. Their impossibly long legs bent with the gracefulness of the waterbirds that staked out the lake behind his parents' house. That's what they put Loul in mind of—tall, silver waterbirds. They even moved in the same chevron formation. Gray shaded visors covered their faces, and Loul's mind nearly melted running through the possible facial formations hidden beneath them. Were they birdlike? Reptilian? Despite the elongation of their bodies, they had a human appearance. Maybe they could take on any shape they encountered?

Several steps away from the ship the team of five stopped, standing perfectly still. With no view of their faces, it was impossible to tell if their stance was aggressive or passive. With every inch of their bodies encased in the gray suits, Loul couldn't even be certain they were alive and not some sort of humanoid machine. They stood still for several long moments, the crowd behind the barricade rippling with excitement and activity, radios squawking as archivists and consultants jockeyed for the best position. Finally Loul saw the three ranking generals lining up behind the central barricade and felt a pulse of pride shoot through his gut. They were following the protocol he himself had recommended all those years ago—that if alien contact occurred, to face it with ranking officials unarmed, surrounded by military in a nonaggressive stance. He had explained that by showing the invaders weaponless leaders, they would be silently giving a message of fearlessness.

It had made sense at the time, but at the time there hadn't been a chevron of aliens—aliens!—standing on the slab of the Roana Temple encased in what might be impenetrable space suits. What if he was wrong? What if the barricades parted and the aliens unleashed some sort of weapon? What if this was just a ploy to lower the barricades and begin an assault that couldn't be stopped? What if he, Loul Pell, went down in the last days of Didet history as the man who suggested the very actions that enslaved the human race?

Then the strangest thing happened. Considering he was standing in the midst of a makeshift military compound at the edge of the Ketter Sea hidden behind media-blocking webbing and staring at aliens who had just disembarked from a space-ship parked on the ruins of the Roana Temple, his parameters for strange had broadened greatly in the past day. And this was still strange. The leader of the alien band, the tallest of the tall creatures before them, slowly lifted its long arms, twisting them so that one hand wrapped around the other wrist. Then, with no other motion, voices could be heard. Three distinct sentences:

"What can I do to assist you?"

"Hi! Welcome back!"

"What did I tell you about that pie?"

That third one made barriers drop and radios fall silent. All around the barricade, people rose up, leaning over each other for a better look, an unfiltered and unprotected look at the assembly before them. Then the voices repeated themselves.

"What can I do to assist you?"

"Hi! Welcome back!"

"What did I tell you about that pie?"

Loul heard someone behind him mutter something about killing someone if this turned out to be a prank. A cluster of people whispered behind the ranking trio who, Loul had to give them credit, kept up a solid noncommittal front. All around him, he could hear the name "Baga" being whispered, followed quickly by "stunt" and "gone too far."

Everyone on the continent recognized that stupid pie phrase from Baga Baga, the trickster radio host who was always pranking people into admitting cheating on their wives or stealing from their bosses. He had two catch phrases: "Dig a hole" and "What did I tell you about that pie?" His show played everywhere, and every kid above the age of six hung on his every move. His last stunt, spray-painting the dome of the Eastern Bank to look like a nipple, had gotten him house arrest and an enormous fine. It had also boosted his ratings and made him an even bigger star among his fans. But this? Staging a stunt this big? Did Baga have that much clout?

A weapons carousel wheeled closer to the right of the generals, and a line of military police stepped together in tight formation waiting for orders. The generals conferred, talking over their shoulders with their counselors behind them, but Loul didn't try to hear what they said. Instead, he ran over and over the words he'd heard. That stupid pie comment—that had been Baga's voice, no doubt about it. But that first phrase—"What can I do to assist you?"—wasn't Baga, but it was just as familiar. That was the voice of the automated service of Eastern Bank. Loul knew that voice as well as his own from the dozens of times he'd started to call Reno Dado to ask her out, only to chicken out, hang up, and try again.

Three different voices. Three different sentences. The first one a recorded voice, the second female, the third a famous broadcaster. All of them in perfect Cartar dialect. The second one even had a lower-county accent.

"This is General Ada of the Cartar Military Assembly." The voice boomed out from a bullhorn pressed to the general's lips. Loul could see a heavy flush of rage on the man's throat as he barked out his orders. "You are under arrest for violating a protected archaeological site and for inciting public panic. Stand down immediately."

The group of five didn't move, and Loul found himself drifting closer to the front of the lowered barricade, transfixed on their strange, silent stance. Ada repeated his order, and after a few more silent moments, Loul caught the slightest turn of a head of the second figure from the end closest to him. He waved a hand back toward Mamu. "Give me a microphone."

"What?" Mamu whispered. "Why?"

"Give me a microphone. A long one." He kept his eyes on the two figures closest to him. "I think they're talking to each other."

Mamu handed him a wand mic with a slip-on padded windscreen. The wind from the Ketter Sea pounded across the plain and the padded cover helped block out the sound of it. Trying to be inconspicuous, Loul leaned forward, holding the wand mic out. All eyes were either on the generals or the five strangers and Loul was several feet clear of the barricade before anyone noticed him. When they did, several things happened all at once.

Someone shouted, an MP probably, as well as a few catcalls of "moron" and "what the hell." Loul couldn't hear them over the pounding of his pulse when the five strange beings before him also noticed him and turned their heads in perfect unison to face him with those strange gray shaded visors. And vying for even more terrifying, at that moment the wind shifted, catching the slip-on windscreen of the microphone, popping it off the end of the long wand, and sending it sailing like a bouncy ball directly to the feet of the figure closest to Loul, the alien at the end of the chevron. Loul could hear nothing then but his pulse and the sucked-in breath of the stunned group behind him.

He couldn't have moved at that moment if he'd been shot in the gut by a pom-cannon. The wind made the only sound for several long moments. The figure closest to him, the figure he had just shot the windscreen at, just barely moved its head. As one, the five figures shifted slightly, and another surprised gasp rose from the barricade as the gray shaded visors lifted, folding into themselves faster than his eye could follow. The helmets of the strange gray suits seemed to evaporate from the suits, revealing long, narrow but human-looking faces staring back at them. Each figure moved its arms and detached the gloves on each side, revealing even skinnier hands with long, flexible fingers that looked impossibly fragile. In perfect synchronization, the five figures slipped the gloves into unseen pockets and brought their hands to rest at their sides.

Loul didn't know where to look. His eyes moved from face to face, taking in the thin cheeks, the large wet eyes, the strange pelt-like texture of what could be hair. All Loul could hear was his pulse, his rasping breath, and the pounding of the sea wind over the open plain. All he could see was the collection of alien life in front of him, and all he could think was "This isn't Baga Baga."

The figure at the end of the chevron moved slowly, bending its long legs in that waterbird-like way, lowering itself with an odd grace. Thin, pale fingers wrapped around the windscreen, their fragile grip delicate enough that it made no indentation on the soft foam. It brought the screen up closer to its face, and the wide wet eyes watched as the deft fingers turned the foam over and over. As slowly as they had bent, the legs straightened, bringing the creature up to its full height. It stared straight into Loul's face, and he found he couldn't blink, couldn't turn his face away. He wondered if it was hypnotizing him or reading his mind or taking over his body, but he couldn't seem to find it in himself to be afraid.

It made a sound, a soft whispering sound that blew away in the Ketter wind, and Loul sensed a ripple of movement through the five tall beings. He felt his pulse quicken and knew his mouth hung open as the creature stepped forward. They moved so slowly, he thought. It took one step, then another, its spindly hands cradling the windscreen, its eyes locked on Loul's, until it stood less than two feet from him. Now Loul could hear weapons cocking and cameras clicking but he didn't move. He stared up into the eyes staring down at him, noticing details, noticing everything.

Its skin seemed almost translucent, smooth like the inside of a river shell. The eyes were amazing, a brown circle with flecks of color surrounded by white shot through with red filaments. They blinked like Dideto eyes although he couldn't see any sign of the third inner lid. The mouth moved with small rippling motions, generating smaller movements in the narrow throat that would have been difficult to see if he hadn't been standing so close. He was so close. He was so close he could reach out and touch the thing if he wanted to.

It turned out he didn't have to. The creature broke eye contact with him, dropping its gaze to the windscreen in its hands and then moving to the wand microphone Loul forgot he was holding. Slowly, slowly, like something from a movie, the arms moved, lifting the thin hands toward him. One hand touched the tip of the microphone, tilting it forward. The other raised the windscreen and with no more than a simple flick, slipped the screen back onto the microphone. Loul had seen the machine the archivists had needed to get the windscreens on their equipment and yet these long, spindly fingers managed to do it effortlessly.

The fingers brushed softly across the end of the microphone and then drifted across his knuckles with no more pressure than a breeze. Loul didn't flinch. He didn't move a muscle, until he realized the slender hands rested once more at the creature's side. He lifted his gaze to find the brown, shiny eyes meeting his once more. The creature lowered its head just a fraction, tilting forward and then straightening. The mouth broadened but remained closed, and with the same slow grace, the creature reversed its steps, somehow walking backward until it took up its original position in the chevron.

Loul kept his eyes on the creature but turned his head enough to be heard by the generals.

"This isn't a prank."

FOUR

MEG

It took all of Meg's self-control to resist drawing her weapon. She'd been so caught up in the reactions to the recorded audio and then the vocals coming back she hadn't even seen the man sneaking toward her. Sneaking was hardly the right word—the lumbering gait had little stealth—and she couldn't be sure if the figure was male or female, but with that much facial hair she sure hoped it wasn't a woman. Regardless, while she and the captain hurried through an assessment of the crowd's reaction, the man moved within feet of her, pointing some sort of wand in her direction, and only Prader's warning had snapped her to attention.

Wagner's voice sounded steady and unpanicked in her com. "Any closer and we move. On my mark. Sidearms active. Watch the weapon. Watch the weapon."

"Wait," Meg said, trying to take in the entire tableau. Something was wrong. Something was off in the scene before her. The three portly figures stood at the center of the barricade. When the audio loop had been repeated, the shields lowered and all attention turned to the trio. Meg had heard her data pack recording and processing the vocals around her, hearing the beautiful pinging sound anytime a vocal matched a recognized pattern. Whatever the central figure had shouted at them had mobilized a line of guards and captured the group's attention. Everything before her spoke of group movement. So why was one lone figure out of formation?

"Captain," she said when the figure stopped moving closer, "I think this might be a good time to lower our helmets and deglove."

"What?" Wagner tilted his head just an inch in her direction. "Now? With that thing so close to you? I don't like it."

"I get the feeling he's not supposed to be here. Look how nobody's following him."

Jefferson made a scoffing sound. "Great. So we've got a lone assassin. Let's definitely drop visors and make ourselves vulnerable."

"It might be a gift." Meg stared at the broad rough face in front of her. "It might be a...hell, I don't what it might be, but he's alone and he's close. He might just be curious. If he's brave enough to break ranks, let's give him something to see."

Wagner gave the go-ahead, and in unison they activated the helmet retractors. Once the visors collapsed into the ringed collars, he gave the sign to detach their gloves, talking them through the movements with a one-two-three prompting. Meg knew they could all hear and feel the shocked response from the crowd assembled before them, a thrumming sound that underscored every sound rising in pitch as faces were revealed. She could hear it clearly in the figure before her, her keen ear working to separate the rumble of machinery from the deep throat-humming sound. She desperately wanted to enter a programming note into her data kit but the proximity of the figure and the angle of whatever it was he held prompted her to stay still.

The wind shifted, blowing hot and dry across her damp forehead, and she nearly jumped from her boots when the round tip of the stick flew off and bobbled in her direction. She heard Prader swear in her ear and knew that if their positions had been reversed, weapons would already be drawn. And protocol be damned, she probably should have drawn her weapon. An unknown figure approached her with an unknown object in its hand, pointed at her, hurling projectiles at her. But one thing Meg had learned in her diplomatic dealings was to trust her gut, and her gut told her this person, this guy, meant her no intentional harm.

"Stay with me," she spoke low into the coms. "I'm making contact." Ignoring Wagner's warnings and Prader's cursing, Meg slowly bent to pick up the round object. It looked like a windscreen, similar to the foam pads over a standard microphone, only the foam felt harder, more like Styrofoam than soundproof padding. It would make sense in the heavy wind. Maybe her visitor was a reporter of some sort. The planet had shown plenty of signs of broadcast.

Keeping her arms close to her body and her movements small and slow, Meg stepped toward the man. At five foot eight, she stood a head taller than him, but he had the same broad, solid build of everyone around him. She took in the coarse skin and small narrow eyes, knowing her suit camera downloaded visuals to Cho's bio-file. As she got closer, she could see a pulsing beneath the man's jawbone and heard a rapid humming hammering out a matching beat. Despite his lesser height, the man easily outweighed her by fifty pounds. If she frightened him, she had no doubt he could overpower her. And if that stick was a weapon, Meg knew she was screwed.

Putting this all out of her mind, she reached forward and tilted the sticklike object toward her. The foam ball had an obvious opening and she'd seen where it had launched from. It took only seconds to slip the cover over the end of the stick. When no bullets or any sign of aggression came forth, she wanted so badly to let her fingertips brush over the man's skin. It was stupid and Cho would probably rip her apart when he had a minute. There could be lesions, infections, bacteria. Her own training told her that uninvited physical contact could lead to disastrous breakdowns in social order. The possibility of taboo was astronomical.

But she was millions of miles from Earth. She stood face-to-face with a fellow human like none she had ever seen before, and he was just looking up at her, his gray eyes hooded but wide, a thick line of hair ringing the lids from nose to temple. He didn't yell. He didn't flinch. He just stared, meeting her gaze with what looked very much like wonder. And for just a moment, Meg didn't hear the heavy rumbling machinery around her. She didn't hear her crewmates breathing in her coms. She forgot the bewildering reality of multiple suns on the horizon. For several heartbeats, she just stood face-to-face with another human being. And she touched him.

Bowing slightly and coming somewhat to her senses, Meg carefully stepped back in line with Cho. Her friend, and that was how she saw him now, stayed still as she retreated, watching her with his mouth slightly open. Once she regained her spot, he shouted something to the three figures standing before the barricade. Two seconds later Meg bit back a smile. ProLingLang had put together another set of syntax.

"Captain, bring up the screen."

LOUL

Over the machinery, over the shouted orders and crash of barricade shields being repositioned, Loul heard the voice. It rang out high and soft, and again he thought of the waterbirds calling across the lake in the cool season when the Green Sun sat fat and far on the horizon. It had touched him. It had traced its feather-like fingers over his hands so quickly he hadn't had time to react. He wished he'd turned his hand over, opened his pads so he could have really felt the skin. He wanted it to come back to him, to look at him again, but Loul saw its attention was on the leader.

Once again the leader maneuvered its hands around its wrists, only this time, the fingers didn't wrap around the wrist. Instead they pinched the long, tapered ends together and pulled away, dragging a translucent film into the air from the band on its wrist. Loul squinted, the light striking the film at an oblique angle, and he saw that the film wasn't a film at all. It was merely light, a prism-like effect that distorted the red sunlight, creating a three-dimensional panel of light. Without thinking, he stepped closer to the leader, within an arm span of the second figure in the chevron, but oblivious to all but the flat panel of light.

They spoke again, the tones quick and clipped, the leader's deeper and easier to hear than the one who had touched him. Loul glanced over his shoulder at that one, who he started to think of as his contact. He saw it too was focusing and touch-ing a band on its wrist. Loul turned back to the leader and saw from the corner of his eye General Ada raising the bullhorn once more. Loul held up his hand to silence him, and surprisingly, the general put the horn down.

The leader moved the light plane before him so the generals could plainly see its surface. Almost faster than his eyes could follow, Loul watched the long fingers flit over the back of the translucent plane as if tickling it or scratching it. From where he stood, red sunlight obscured what the generals must have seen because another collective gasp sounded around the barricade. As Loul stepped around to see what they saw, the leader tapped his wrist again and another series of recorded sounds issued forth.

"This isn't."

"Doing for."

"There are."

Again, Loul thought, three different voices. Three separate recordings. Before he could think of what that might mean, he saw the image on the front of the light plane. Didet. A brilliant, full-color, three-dimensional image of their planet, clearer than any image ever captured by the extra-atmosphere satellite. Oblivious to the hubbub behind him and deaf to the hissed warnings to step away, Loul stepped closer to the screen. The voices sounded out again.

"This isn't."

"Doing for."

"There are."

The rough voice of an MP broke into his consciousness. "Pell! What the hell are you doing out there? Get back here!"

Loul turned to the generals, who were conferring with flushed and stern-looking soldiers. He recognized the charts the soldiers held—the military weapons sites. To effectively monitor satellite information, everyone in the Telemetry Administration had to know the general location of weapons sites to account for any interference their security systems might produce. That the talk had turned to weapons made all the hair on his body stand on end.

"Why are you pulling weapons charts?" He knew he didn't have the clearance or the authority to ask such a question and certainly not with such a demanding tone, but Loul had seen enough sci-fi movies to know where this scenario was headed.

"Step away, Pell." General Ada didn't look up as he spoke. "They have intel on our planet. We have to assume—"

"Of course they have intel on our planet. They just landed here." When nobody looked up, Loul pressed on. "They're making contact."

"They're making a threat," General Famma said, her voice tight with determination. "They said 'this isn't' and then produced a satellite image of Didet. I suggest you step away, Mr. Pell, or we cannot be responsible for your safety."

Loul turned back toward the chevron of aliens. He saw the leader and his contact exchange rapid glances and heard the bell-like sounds of their voices ringing softly between them. "This isn't doing for there are." That's what the recorded voices had said. And repeated them twice just like before. He said the words aloud but under his breath. "This isn't doing for there are." How was it possible that a race advanced enough to travel through space and create images like that one of Didet on a screen of light would sound like Loul himself when he was fumbling through one of his many mortifying attempts at asking Reno Dado out on a date?

Fumbling.

"They don't know our language."

It was so obvious. No longer concerned with the group behind the barricade, Loul stepped closer to the leader, his eyes moving from the brilliant image of Didet to the leader's smooth brown face. The leader was even taller than the one who had touched him, and its skin was darker although just as smooth. The eyes were the same wet, wide brown, and for the first time Loul could begin to distinguish between the figures before him. This close, he could see distinct differences in their shading and shapes, although every one of them towered over him.

The leader fixed its eyes on him, and a glance to his left told him his contact watched as well. The other three kept their gazes on the assembly behind him, and Loul noticed that those who watched the generals kept their long fingers near the sides of their legs. Where the fingers brushed against their space suits, he could see hard shapes underneath. Weapons. They may not know the language but they understood danger. Loul figured he had nothing to lose.

He stepped even closer to the leader and pointed at the image of Didet. The leader glanced to the contact, who tipped its head in a quick, birdlike nod. The leader tapped its wrist once more. "This isn't. Doing for. There are."

Loul pointed to the image of his planet. "This is Didet."

His contact made a breathy sound and the leader tapped its wrist again. Loul heard his own voice coming from the leader's chest. "This is Didet." A few quick scrabbles of the long brown fingers and another image appeared on the screen beside Didet. Another planet, smaller and colored in shades of blue and green.

"This is…" Loul heard his own voice again then a pause in the sound. He glanced up at the leader's face as the mouth moved, the sound soft but deep. He looked back at the screen.

The image of Didet lit up, and Loul heard his recorded voice say, "This is Didet." The image of the blue planet lit up, and he heard his recorded voice say, "This is." Then he heard the sound the leader had made amplified by the machinery they were using.

"Urf."

Loul smiled. "That is Urf."

MEG

Meg broke ranks. She didn't think. She didn't weigh the decision. She let out a high cry of joy and sprinted to the captain's side. Cho nearly shot her as she passed him, surprised by her sudden movement, but Meg only had eyes for the squat man speaking into the drag screen. Part of her was vaguely aware of the ever-increasing rumbling and shouting from the group at the barricade and she was pretty sure Prader had her weapon drawn. Wagner tried to maintain a semblance of calm, keeping his movements small as he gripped her by the elbow, asking her what the hell she thought she was doing.

The only person who didn't seem surprised by her leap to the front was her new friend. He turned to her and his narrow mouth widened as she grinned at him. She knew she could be projecting. She knew she might not only be jumping the gun but using that gun to shoot the entire mission in the foot, but for a linguist, a translator, a diplomat, that first "aha" moment felt like falling in love and bungee jumping and being set on fire all at the same time. And to have that moment in the situation they currently faced, with no context, no background, no shared culture of any type, reduced Meg to a wiggling, squealing mess of breathy grins.

People thought languages were just substitution puzzles, like the old pony texts she'd used in grade school to learn Latin. One side of the book had been written in Latin, the opposing page had the translation in English, and the students were supposed to break down the language visually, word for word, phrase for phrase. It worked with a parent language, a root language. It worked for most Earth languages as a whole, but it didn't work because languages were easy. It worked because the people who had written the languages in the first place had already struggled through the growth pains of transcribing thoughts to words to writing. Everyone accepted, without it being explained, that enormous amounts of cultural communication and accord had already been achieved before the first scribble had been made.

But now here she stood face-to-face, well, chest-to-face with someone who got it. Or seemed to get it, she reminded herself. Someone who seemed willing to try to get it, to go with his gut and make the sounds that might bridge the gap between their two worlds. Someone who might instinctively understand how enormous that gap was but still be willing to reach across. Despite all the mission preparation, despite the hours of bored conversation during the days and weeks of travel before their final launch, she knew the rest of the *Damocles* crew didn't really understand what her job was, any more than she really understood what Cho faced in classifying an entirely new range of life-forms. She knew that they were waiting for the chance to say to her, "Tell them we need electricity. Ask them about their transportation. Put me in touch with their presidents and scientists and engineers."

She knew they would get impatient with her and be bewildered by her transportation into ecstasy at the simple point-and-speak statement she had just heard. If they knew, if they truly understood how rudimentary the starting point was in bridging this language gap, they would probably collapse under the staggering amount of work that lay ahead. Well, she figured, dropping to her knees at the feet of the squat smiling figure before her, they had better get ready to stagger, because she was starting with the most basic of basics.

She activated the drag screen from her data pack, drawing the flat plane of light out parallel to the ground. She hadn't liked the way the sunlight tampered with the image when Wagner had dragged his screen out before him, and with all the work she was preparing to do, she wanted a nice, crisp visual. Screen open, text boxes open and ready to be activated, she looked up at the Didet man before her. She didn't have to bother motioning or pantomiming to him to join her. He dropped into a deep squat beside her before she had fully raised her head. Meg really hoped showing her teeth wasn't a social taboo because she couldn't have stopped grinning at that moment if she'd been hit with a board.

A text box opened with the same images Wagner had shown, only now the image took up a much smaller part of the ProLingLang program screen. Beneath the pictures of the two planets were touch buttons to replay the assigned audio. Meg touched the button beneath the larger, yellow planet, and her companion's voice came through the speakers.

"This is Didet."

The man shifted in his crouch, the knuckles of his thick fists bumping together. Meg pushed the button beneath the picture of Earth, activating the combined audio of the crouching man and Captain Wagner.

"This is…Earth."

His knuckles knocked once more and Meg relaxed about the showing-the-teeth thing. He looked up at her and revealed a smile that seemed to be made up of nothing but brownish molars. It was the most beautiful smile she had ever seen. Taking a deep breath, she brought up a few prompts and prepared for the next step.

She lifted her hand, making sure he saw her movement, and tapped the ground beside her. She let her fingers dig a bit into the dirt and then pounded the ground more firmly with her palm. His eyes moved from her hand back to her face and she touched the screen once more.

"This is Didet." She pounded the ground again and then pointed to the image of the yellow planet. "Didet."

"Didet." He spoke the word, his knuckles shaking where he had them pressed together, as if they were doing the heavy lifting of his struggle to understand. Meg watched him for any and all body signals and she prepared to make the next leap. She pointed to the yellow planet again and pushed a different command.

"This is…Earth."

The smile faltered and she could feel the hooded gray eyes staring into her with a silent plea to understand. He didn't move any more, so she repeated herself, pointing to Didet and playing the "This is...Earth."

His fists fell away from each other. "Didet." Meg bit her lip and pointed to the yellow planet. She pushed the audio button.

"Didet."

His knuckles bumped together once more and Meg felt all the breath rush from her lungs. If she was right, if they could make this connection, the first and biggest wall would come down.

She pointed to the yellow planet and held her hands up before her face. She made fists and turned them toward each other, pushing the knuckles together. Dropping one hand quickly, she pressed the audio button and drew her fists back together.

"Didet." She bumped her knuckles together. "Yes," she said loud enough for the program to record her. She bumped her hands together again. "Yes."

Willing him to stay focused on her, she dropped her hand again and pointed to the yellow planet. Then she pushed the alternate audio button. As the words "This is...Earth" played, she pulled her knuckles apart.

"No," she said, pulling her knuckles apart again.

With the patience that only came from the deepest need for knowledge, she repeated the process again. Point to Didet, play the Earth audio, pull her knuckles apart, and say "No." And then she waited.

His eyes flitted over her face, over her hands, down to the screen, down to the marks she had left on the ground, and back again. His eyes were so different from hers, so deeply set in thick folds of coarse skin, that skin ringed in coarser hair, his blinks punctuated by a milky film that rose like a cat's inner lid from the bottom. They looked so different from hers, so alien, but she knew the moment he understood. She saw it in his eyes.

He pounded the ground beside her. "Didet," he said and brought his knuckles together. She brought hers together too. He pounded the ground once more and said "Urf" and pulled his knuckles apart. She pulled hers apart and laughed as all his teeth came back into view. He rocked in his stance as her laughter made her shift on her knees, bringing them closer to each other. She could smell his breath and hear the low thrumming coming from his throat. Without a prompt, they raised their pressed fists together and very gently he bumped the outside of his hands against the outside of hers. Meg thought she might float away on the sensation.

"Yes."

"This is fascinating." Prader's voice shook Meg from her celebration. "Seriously, Didet/Earth, Didet/Earth, got it, but could we speed things up? I'm getting a fucking sunburn and I'm pretty sure those are guns rolling up to us."

"I have to agree, Meg," Wagner said. "I'm no expert in body language but I don't think our welcoming committee is thrilled about our guest breaking ranks."

Meg looked around and stood up, seeing the encroaching line of soldiers. Her new friend looked back as well and rose from his crouch. Whatever he shouted back to the soldiers stopped them although the business ends of what looked to be rolling cannons still pointed in their direction. The man with the megaphone shouted something that the man before her waved off.

"On my mark," Wagner spoke softly into the coms, "we move back to the ship."

"No," Meg said. "I'm sorry, Captain, but I think that's the wrong move. Move back, form a line. I'll stay in front with our boy here. Jefferson, when I give you the signal, very slowly and very carefully withdraw the shelter tent from the Captain's pack." She heard Jefferson's huffed reaction but cut him off. "Listen to me. Do not point the end of the tent toward the soldiers. Keep it from popping into shape too quickly. When I tell you—"

"Dupris." The captain's voice had dropped and she knew he used her last name to remind her of his authority. "Unless you can give me some hard evidence that we are not about to be fired upon, we are boarding the ship on my mark."

"Captain, with all due respect, if we fire the ship up they are going to see it as aggression." As she spoke, she could see the Didet man before her straining to listen, his eyes never moving from her face. "Or they'll think we're fleeing."

"We are fleeing. We can reassess contact from the air and—"

"And what? Land somewhere else? Do this again? Do you have any idea how far we've gotten since we've landed?"

"No I don't, Meg, and that's exactly the problem. So far we think we know the name of the planet and we are a lot more certain we have a large weapons array trained on us. I'm sorry that circumstances forced us to make contact before we were prepared, but I'm not going to risk the lives of this crew on your guesswork."

"Then what am I here for?" She turned toward him, forgetting to keep her voice down, forgetting to keep her movements small. Her hands flew out to punctuate her anger. "What do you think this is? Algebra? Did you think we could just slide these people under a microscope and break them down like rock samples? This is what I do. This is why you chose me for this mission. And I'm telling you that if we get back onboard, we might as well go back to *Damocles* and take turns in the isolation pod because we're not going to get another chance on Didet."

Cho cleared his throat. "Uh, Meg, is your boy translating for you?"

Meg spun and saw the short man mirroring her gestures almost exactly to the crowd assembled behind him. His shorter arms and broad stunted fingers made the movement look more like punching than gesticulating, but when he finished talking, the Didet crowd stood as still as the Earth crew for several long moments. Then the openings of what looked to be weapons trained on them lowered. The line of soldiers seemed to relax and a general sense of standing down passed through the group behind the barricade.

Meg arched an eyebrow toward the captain. "Well?"

Wagner sighed. "If we die out here, I'm coming back to haunt your ass. Okay, everyone, on my mark. We move back toward the ship. Jefferson, prepare to retrieve my shelter tent."

Meg turned back toward her new comrade, getting ready to invite him to join her once again on the ground. Instead, he stepped closer to her, his eyes on her face, his smile wide. He tapped his chest with his flat palm, the way he had pounded the ground.

"Loul."

Her stomach did that flipping thing she loved so much. "Loul," she repeated, trying to get the sound correct. He watched her mouth move and leaned in closer. It occurred to her that her voice might not easily be within his hearing range. Lowering her register, she repeated herself as loudly as possible.

"Loul." She pointed to him and he smiled, knocking his knuckles together. Needing to clarify, she waved her hand toward the crowd behind him. "Loul?"

He looked over his shoulder and back at her and she could see him working the thought through in his mind. He pulled his knuckles apart and gestured to the crowd. "Dideto." He touched his chest again. "Loul."

"Ah," Meg said as much to herself as to the coms. "They call themselves Dideto." She waved her hand over the crowd and he brought his knuckles together. She pointed at him. "And this is Loul. This is my friend Loul." He tapped knuckles again, smiling.

She waved to the crew that now stood in a line several feet behind her, near the shuttle. "Earthers." She spoke loudly, both so he could hear her more easily and to drown out Jefferson's protests. Jefferson had been raised in the Galen colonies and had never set foot on Earth. At home, the distinction often proved to be a sore spot. This far out, Meg thought the issue moot. She watched Loul work his mouth around the new word, and when he got it mostly right, she brought her fists together. Then she tapped her own chest.

"Meg."

Loul's first several attempts to say her name came nowhere near a recognizable version. Meg kept repeating it until finally he stared her straight in the eye and said, "Beg."

She tapped her knuckles together. "Close enough."

She heard the muffled laughter from the crew as Cho muttered under his breath. "That's not the reaction I get when I say that to you."

Speaking through clenched teeth with her voice very low, she whispered, "That's 'cause you don't smile at me like this."

"Sucker."

FIVE

LOUL

Loul wasn't sure which surprised him more—the fact that he had just screamed at the ranking trio of generals or that they had listened to him. Right before Meg had turned her back on him, he had decided it was a she. He told himself he based the decision more on the paleness of her skin compared to her companions, not the swell of flesh under her suit where there might be breasts. And the thought of her having breasts in no way triggered his memories of the pornographic Magagan comics that he, Po, and Hark had spent way too much of their youth poring over, memorizing every tale of the lustful female aliens seeking sexual satisfaction on their many invasions of Didet. Okay, maybe it triggered them a little, because he now felt the same thrilling, pleasurable terror in front of these Urfers as he had in front of real girls at that age.

Adolescent triggers aside, he sensed a graceful beauty in this Meg that he figured would probably transcend any species line. Her teeth unnerved him. Their translucent paleness seemed even more fragile than the long, tapered fingers and her incredibly flexible neck. The way her head snapped around to ring out a warning to her people made his stomach clench in imagined pain. When those long arms unfolded themselves and the fingers fluttered so quickly he could hardly follow, he just knew she had noticed the weapons carousels moving into place.

He didn't know why she had singled him out to try to make contact. Maybe his accidental flinging of the microphone cover had acted as some sort of greeting on their planet. Maybe they could read minds and sensed he meant them no harm. Whatever the reason, Loul felt they had forged a bond, and he would be damned if he'd let even a ranking trio of generals rob him of this moment. So he'd shouted at them to stand down. And they did. And when everything had gotten quiet, Loul had taken the chance of introducing himself to the first alien race to ever step foot on Didet.

The Urfers were definitely reacting even with the lowering of the pom-cannons. All but Meg stepped backward in that bizarre slow high step that he'd thought was their only means of locomotion. Meg had sure proven that wrong by leaping like a flickerbug when he'd addressed the leader. He wondered for a moment if maybe he'd offended her by stepping up to speak to the leader of the chevron instead of staying by her, but when she'd dropped to the ground—and she sure could move quickly—he just knew she wanted to show him something. Maybe they really were mind-reading. Or maybe the sight of another of those cool light screens appearing out of nowhere and lighting up on the ground with strange symbols and images was more than he could possibly hope to resist.

The way she had stared into his eyes, her strange wide mouth and glass-like teeth shining when he stared back at her, made him hope she could read his mind. Every fiber in his being wanted to scream, "We're friends! We're friends! Take me into Space!" He couldn't shake the stupid kinderschool thrill of being in the coolest place in the world and for once being the center of attention. And she had stared and stared, her liquid eyes so expressive even while bewildering him. Then all that pointing, all those stabbing gestures to that amazing screen, and it had dawned on him like the Red Sun. Yes and no. She wanted to learn how to say *yes* and *no* in Dideto. Well, Cartara, technically, since there were plenty of languages on Didet that said it differently. For the millionth time since he'd seen the ship on the Roana slab, Loul said a silent thanks that he'd found himself at this very spot.

Now the generals waited for a cue from him. The Urfers lined up in front of their ship, the crew member on the other side of the leader withdrawing some strange cylindrical package. It could be a weapon. He knew the generals were certainly thinking that, and if it turned out they were right, Loul hoped the aliens would have the decency to shoot him first and spare him the disgrace of his misplaced trust. Instead, the cylinder opened up into a large bubble made of what looked like a slippery, reflective film. At first glance, Loul thought it was made of liquid, but the bubble form held its shape as the Urfer secured it to the ground with small white pegs.

"Pell!" Ada shouted at him, but his tone sounded more cautious than angry. "What is that? Can you see it? Can you see what that is?"

Loul glanced at Meg, although he knew she couldn't give him any explanation. Then another bubble popped up and got attached to the ground. One of the Urfers, the smallest of the team, who was as pale as Meg so he decided it was a female too, kept its eyes on the soldiers while the others scrabbled their fingers over the front of each bubble, creating a gap in the reflective film. Moving slowly and occasionally turning their heads in that bizarre bendy way to see over their shoulders, they reached into the bubbles and laid something out on the ground inside.

He looked to Meg, who watched him watch them. How could he ask her what they were doing? *Yes* and *no* had felt like an incredible breakthrough, but now these Urfers, these aliens, were getting busy doing something that made the enormous battalion of armed guards behind him nervous. Everyone, himself included, counted on him to figure out the explanation. He was going to have to get down to basics.

He pointed to the strange bubbles and pushed his chin down into his neck. He knew the gesture made him look like an infant, but everyone knew the universal gesture for confusion, right? Meg watched him as he repeated the sequence, her own head tilting strangely to the side as if the slender neck could no longer hold the weight of her long skull. Then she straightened, and he thought he recognized in the widening of her eyes the same expression he'd seen when they'd solved the yes-no confusion.

She pointed at the horizon over the Ketter Sea, where the wind whipped sand and dust into a frenzy in the lowering light of the Red Sun. He followed where she pointed, and when he looked back at her, she flattened her long hands out, palms facing out and slightly overlapping, and held them to the side of her face, her eyes tightly closed. She stayed that way a moment then opened her eyes once more, the question clear in her expression. She repeated the gesture again. Loul thought she could probably repeat it a thousand times and he wouldn't get it.

Were the bubbles somehow related to the Ketter Sea? What would that have to do with their faces? Was the gesture some sort of warning? A greeting? It could mean anything and Loul knew the generals wouldn't wait forever. Meg's head shivered in a strange back-and-forth way that made him marvel again at the willowy structure of her body. Her eyes glanced around him, and when she looked back at him, he saw a settling in her stance that he understood. She was going to try to explain again.

She pointed to his right, to the Ketter Sea, where the Red Sun nearly touched the roiling water. When his gaze returned to her, she then pointed behind him and up to his left where the archive cameras gathered high on metal poles, their shade screens blocking out most of the pale light of the Fa Sun behind them. Then she pointed behind her right shoulder to the media webbing that rose high enough to block out terrestrial media and scramble most satellite receivers. The rising Ellaban Sun had just started to color the white webbing a rich shade of orange. When she turned back to Loul, Meg bent her slender neck, her head dropping forward as her long, thin arms came up and wrapped around her skull. She sat that way a long moment, her head almost totally hidden within her arms, before looking up at him again.

The Ketter Sea, the archive cameras, and the media webbing had something to do with the reflective bubbles and the strange arm-head gesture. His first thought when she'd brought her arms up was that she was hiding, coiling up the way a sand snake did when a predator came near. Was she afraid? Was she injured? He brought his hands up and pulled his knuckles apart, saying the word with the gesture. "No."

She flattened her hands once more, the way she had the first time, and faced her overlapping palms again toward the Ketter Sea. Then she pointed them toward the archive cameras and then, twisting around, toward the media webbing. Each time she made a point to keep her face behind the thin, splayed fingers. When he dropped his knuckles once more, she turned to the Urfers and chimed out a soft, high sound. One of her crew—Loul thought it might be the Urfer who had stood beside her—chirped something back and made a strange lifting motion with its shoulders. Then, turning its back on the crowd, it dropped into a crouch and clambered inside the bubble. A moment later, it stuck its head out of the opening and showed its palm to Meg and Loul with a back-and-forth motion. Once more Meg pointed to the sea, the cameras, and the webbing and waited for Loul to put it together.

Was he just dense? Did anyone else on the other side of the barricade see what she was doing and understand it? He ground his teeth together in frustration and looked again in the directions she had pointed to. The Ketter Sea. The archive cameras on their posts. The high media webbing. Why not to the sky behind the shuttle where the scrub brush still smoked from whatever sort of fuel the ship had burned landing? Why not directly behind the generals where another wall of media webbing rose high and white?

Color? He looked again. The Red Sun made everything in that direction red, and the webbing behind her glowed more orange by the minute as Ellaban rose. But the archive cameras didn't match. The shadows grew around them as the light changed, but for the most part the screens stayed the same dull gray as always. They were hardly even needed since the cameras had been positioned in such a way that all they had to block out was the faint light of the Fa Sun.

And then he got it. He banged his knuckles together, grinning as he saw Meg's teeth come back into view. He knew she knew he got it, and once more they bumped the outsides of their hands together.

Loul turned as much as he could to speak to the generals without losing sight of Meg. Not that he feared turning his back on her. He just didn't think he'd ever get enough of watching those wet eyes widen for him. "General Ada? I think those are shelters. I think they're some sort of protective film. It's the suns. They don't like the suns."

"What do you mean they don't like the suns? What are they doing here then? What's inside those bubbles?"

"I think they will be." Loul watched the Urfers set up two more bubbles. "I think they stay inside them."

"Why?" The voice sounded gravelly and feminine so he assumed General Famma spoke.

"I don't know. Their skin is...different. It's really smooth and shiny. And their eyes are wet. I wonder if the suns are too hot on them or maybe interfere with their body chemistry." He'd run these and other possible scenarios years ago in his ill-fated report on an alien invasion.

"Well, tell them they can get in their bubbles back at the military research station just as soon as we get them loaded into the trucks."

Loul huffed in frustration. It had taken him forever to figure out how to say *yes* and *no* and he was still only guessing about the bubbles. Now Ada thought he could casually explain that the military planned on moving them?

"I'm not sure I'll be able to explain that, General."

"You'd better start trying, Pell. We can't keep this webbing up forever. The reporters are already getting nosy about why the site is shut down. We've got to get these...these things into lockdown before we start a worldwide panic."

Loul ground his teeth. How was he supposed to pull this off? "Keep it simple," he muttered to himself and saw Meg's head tilt again at the sound. Her eyes fixed on his mouth and he knew she'd heard him. Sharp hearing, he thought. Good to keep in mind.

He brought his hands together between them, trying to mimic the settling stance he'd seen her take before, what he was coming to think of as the start-over position. Meg seemed to recognize it because she mirrored him immediately.

"Urfers." He waved his hands over her crew. She tapped her knuckles together.

"Trucks." He waved his hands over the line of cargo trucks lined up to the left of the archive cameras. Feeling a little bit stupid, he swung his hands like a monkey from the alien crew to the trucks. "Urfers. Trucks. Go."

Meg tilted her head again, narrowing her eyes. Something told him that was her equivalent of the chin dip confusion pose. So much for universal gestures. He repeated the motions again. "Urfers. Trucks. Go." He didn't know how she'd react to his grip, so he let his arm sort of hover in the area near her side, rocking on his feet toward the trucks. "Urfers. Trucks. Go."

He saw the moment she understood. She made a wide sweeping gesture that held a thousand times more grace than his had, her sweep encompassing her crew before whipping like a palm frond toward the trucks. She even turned her body toward the trucks and took a small step in that direction.

He grinned, knocking his knuckles together. "Yes!"

She held her hands before his face and let the knuckles drop. No.

Maybe she had misunderstood, so he repeated himself, rocking toward the trucks as he had before, starting a small step as she had. "Urfers. Trucks. Go. Yes."

Again her knuckles fell away. No. "Urfers." He could just make out the high, breathy tone of her voice, but he clearly understood the strong stabbing motion she made with both hands toward the ground. He looked up into her eyes, noticing that in her refusal she had pulled her body up to its full, narrow height. He sighed, feeling tension building in his throat as he turned.

"General Ada? I don't think they're going to go." He ignored the rumble of disapproval as a familiar feeling washed over him. "Oh, and General? You're gonna want to send someone out here. I've got to drop."

MEG

"Get ready for some more synchronized swimming, everyone." Meg backed away from Loul while he shouted to the officers at the barricade. "They want to move us into those trucks."

"Why?" Jefferson asked, standing up from where he'd been fastening a shelter tent. "Are they planning to take us to some top-secret medical lab and dissect us?"

Cho didn't pretend to see any humor in that. "That's what we would do."

"Yeah," Meg said, backing up several steps, keeping her eyes on Loul. "I think it's safe to say that leaving the ship is a very bad idea until we have a much stronger language bond."

"What do you recommend, Meg?" Wagner asked.

"Go back to standing absolutely still. Look how they fidget." She scanned the crowd before her. "They never really stop moving, adjusting."

"I'd wager it's their musculature," Cho said. "Their build is incredibly dense. The muscles on their legs alone could probably take a bullet. I don't think they're fast but my money's on them being strong."

"I'm with you." Meg stopped retreating and now stood halfway between Loul and Cho. She wished she'd thought to get out of her suit at some point before now. The heat pouring in from the direction of the sea baked her skin, even with the steady salty wind pounding against her. She noticed with envy that Cho had shed his suit while inside his tent.

She heard his low laugh in the coms. "You're wishing you had that suit off, aren't you?"

"Stop reading my mind."

"Get over here." When Meg didn't move he sighed. "I'm the chief bioscience officer and I'm telling you to get your ass over here and get out of that suit."

Prader snickered. "That's a new one. Why don't you two get a room?"

"Well, unless any of you packed IV fluid bags in your packs, I suggest you all get out of your suits." Cho knelt at the edge of his tent. "This sunlight is going to drain us. Keep your sleeves rolled down and put on a hat, but these suits are going to overheat us all. Meg, keep your eyes on your boy and back up toward me. I'll get you out of yours."

She did as he told her, backing up until she felt his hands on her shoulder. The suit had two release clips, one beside her left ribs and one just inside the rigid rim of the collar ring. Either one would release the magnetic zippers that ensured the suit remained sealed. She felt Cho's warm, dry fingers against her sweaty neck as he deactivated the fastener. A puff of stale air blew out from the suit as the fabric separated down the length of her spine.

"I bet I smell good," she laughed, knowing how sweaty she was.

His hands slid around her waist, doing more than was strictly necessary to help her step from the suit. "You smell okay." When her right leg and arm were free, he helped her pull the rigid collar over her head, shucking the rest of the suit. As Cho slipped her gun from the suit pocket to her pants, she pulled down the sleeves of her lightweight regulation shirt, feeling the specially designed fabric wicking moisture from her damp skin. When she sighed at the relief, she heard Prader and Jefferson laugh and speak in unison.

"Get a room."

"Look at me." Cho ignored them and turned her to face him. She tilted her head, lifting the back of her thick brown ponytail to get a breeze on the damp curls beneath. Cho leaned in close and shocked her by kissing her right on the mouth. "Did you feel that?"

She stepped back, staring at him. It wasn't that he'd kissed her—he'd done plenty of that and more—but this hardly seemed the time.

"Did you feel that?" His voice was soft and low.

"Uh, I…this is…Cho?"

He smirked. "My mouth tastes like glue. So does yours. We're all getting dehydrated and we don't have a lot of water. Why don't you make your next conversation with your new boyfriend about finding us some supplies?"

She rolled her eyes as she turned around. "You could've just asked, you know."

"Uh-oh." She and Cho spoke in unison. A section of the barricade had separated, and two Dideto approached, pushing a squat wheeled cart between them. The cart came to their shoulders and the uneven terrain didn't make the movement any easier. They moved steadily, their eyes fixed on Meg and Cho, dropping only to navigate a bump or divot.

Loul called her name. She pointed to the trucks and pulled her knuckles apart. No. Loul did the same. "What do you suppose this is?" she said to Cho as much as to herself.

"They're opening it." Cho stepped in closer to her, pressing up behind her shoulder. They watched as the two newcomers punched into the top corners of the carton, releasing some sort of catch. The sides of the carton dropped slowly on pulleys, revealing racks filled with metal containers. The figures—women presumably, judging by what looked like heavy breasts riding low on their torsos—crouched down beside the carton and began selecting containers. Beside them, Loul crouched, watching them and talking to them in low, rumbling tones. Meg heard Cho's breath catch. "Let's go closer."

"Cho," she said, but he stepped ahead of her and she hurried to keep step. "Slow down, Cho. We don't want to seem aggressive. What are you doing?"

"I'm thinking what we would do if the situations were reversed."

They heard Prader snort in the coms. "If the situation was reversed, we'd have blown these fuckers out of the sky before they hit atmosphere."

"Thanks for the encouragement, Prader, you psychopath." Cho stopped a yard away from the open carton and its handlers. He crouched down for a better look and Meg could hear the pitch of the Dideto thrumming rise. "We're a new life-form to them. We haven't hurt anyone. We don't have laser beams coming out of our eyes, so now they're trying to figure out who or what we are. And how do you do that?" He smiled to himself. "You send in scientists."

One of the women took a damp cloth from a jar and handed it to Loul. After a brief exchange, Loul began wiping his hands with the cloth thoroughly, getting in between fingers and scrubbing especially hard on the outsides of his palms. Another word from the woman and he dropped the cloth into another container, which the woman promptly sealed.

"They're testing him for contamination," Cho said softly. "They saw you two touch and they're assessing any threat level. Maybe they're going to run a DNA sequence."

"Are we a threat?" Meg asked. "Didn't you test for microbes and contaminants before we opened the hatch? Isn't that part of the initial probe?"

"Shit," Jefferson hissed in her ear. "It's a little late to be worrying about that, isn't it?"

"I found nothing that would contaminate us. It doesn't mean I found everything or that we won't contaminate them."

"Oh my God," Meg said. "Did we just bring smallpox to the new world?"

"Hey, have a little faith in your science officer, okay? In the first place, BESS expunged our systems of most lingering parasites and viruses. Second, why do think our protein tasted especially bad the past few days? Purifiers. We're as clean as we're going to get and we have no choice but to take our chances." He huffed out a breath. "We're agents of change and evolution just by being alive. Deal with it."

The scientists turned to face Meg and Cho as Loul held out his hands for them to see. "He's showing us he's fine," Meg said. "He wants us to come to them."

"Hang on," Cho whispered, rising from his crouch and shuffling backward toward his tent. All Dideto eyes followed him and he returned a moment later with a small metal case.

Jefferson snickered. "Hers is bigger than yours."

Prader laughed too. "He's used to hearing that."

Captain Wagner's voice was all business. "I'm glad to see this momentous occasion in human history isn't interfering with your need to be ass clowns. Let's cut the chatter."

A round of "yes sirs" came through, although Meg could hear Prader swallowing the words "ass clowns" and a laugh. Cho seemed to hear none of it, focusing on opening his testing case and pulling out a drag screen of his own. Once things were set up to his liking, he pulled on latex gloves.

"Are those supposed to make me feel confident?" Meg's eyes had widened along with Loul's but the scientists seemed to take the action in stride. One did lean in closer to watch as Cho slipped the stretchy material over his hands.

"Our hands must look strange to them," he said, holding up a gloved palm for the woman on the left to see more clearly. "Their hands are so blunt compared to ours. I'd guess they didn't evolve from an arboreal species. I'm running a scan of the known wildlife to see if I can narrow down what their ancestry might be."

Meg recognized that breathy monotone he spoke in. She could almost hear the wheels spinning in his head as he took in the reality of standing so close to these people. She leaned into him enough to brush his shoulder. "Not thinking about water now, are you?"

"Shut up." He didn't look at her but she could see the corner of his mouth resisting a smile. "Here we go."

One of the scientists held out a wet blue cloth. Cho reached out and took it from her with one gloved hand while reaching into his kit with another. He drew out a small tool that looked like a combination clamp and flashlight. He held the cloth between the prongs of the tool and waited as light shone over the fabric. A ding sounded from his drag screen and Cho nodded as he read the scrolling data. He handed the cloth to Meg.

"Me? I have to touch it? Do I need gloves?"

"Gloves would sort of defeat the purpose. You touched him. They want to know what you're made of. They can compare the samples off of his hands."

She saw Loul tap his knuckles together, rocking a bit in his crouch as if encouraging her. She took a deep breath and rubbed the damp cloth over her hands. "Ooh, it's cool. Feels kind of good. I wouldn't mind swabbing down my neck with this."

"It's a neutral mineral-based fluid. Seems nonreactive. Probably a testing solution."

"Probably?" Meg asked, holding the cloth out with two fingers.

Cho shrugged. "Of course it could be a unique solution that reacts with your skin chemistry to transform into liquid nitrogen and freeze your fingers off. How cold is it?"

Meg saw that smirk again. "Bioscience humor. Hilarious. Do you need this cloth or can I give it back to her?"

Cho snipped off a corner of the fabric and caught it in a plastic vial. Again the scientists didn't react. The one on the right just held out a jar and Meg dropped the cloth inside. Cho held up the lighted tool for the women to see. He placed his finger between the glowing prongs and held it there for several seconds. Then he held up the scanned finger for them to see. A few grumbled words exchanged and the scientist on the left held out her finger.

"Huh," Meg said. "Maybe you don't need a translator."

She saw the smug arch of his brow as he shifted to reach the outstretched finger. "Science. The universal language. Shit." The woman's thick finger didn't fit between the prongs and Cho hurried to find a different scanner. Meg laughed under her breath.

"Hers really is bigger than yours."

Cho scanned the back of the Dideto scientist's hand with a wand-like scanner. "I believe the words 'ass clown' have already been used today, if I'm not…" His words trailed off as the woman turned her hand over and extended her fingers. "Would you look at that?"

The woman held her open palm up for them to see. Fully extended, the fingers were shorter than any of the Earthers' hands, and the same rough sand-colored skin on the back of the hands covered most of the palms. But where they expected to see the same folds and creases they knew in the bends of their own hands, the Dideto's skin separated, revealing tender swaths of smooth pink skin. Across the palms, in the crooks of the knuckles, and tapering up into the pads of the fingertips, the pale-pink skin flexed and pulsed where the darker skin pulled away.

"Is it a scar?" Meg asked.

"I don't think so." Cho spoke softly, his voice filled with awe. "I think it's, I don't know, maybe how they feel." He peeled off his latex glove and held his palm out toward the women. In unison they dipped their chins, leaning forward for a closer look at Cho's unbroken skin. "I should really use the scanner first, check for…surface…tissue…" Meg held her breath as his words faded and his hand moved forward until his longer, narrower hand touched the broad pink-and-brown palm before him. She knew the moment they touched. She could hear it in Cho's breathing and in the dropping pitch of the woman's throat.

They held their pose for several shallow breaths and Meg could see the effort it took Cho to withdraw his hand. Even just as a bystander, she felt that same everything-falling-away sensation she'd felt when she'd looked into Loul's eyes up close. They were scientists, explorers, billions of miles from home on a controversial one-way mission to rewrite human history. They had mind-melting amounts of data to gather and process, tests to perform, and analyses to make, but all of that seemed to fall away when they could see and hear and smell the presence of these wondrous creatures in front of them.

Cho took a deep breath and focused on scanning the woman's hand. Meg had seen him use these before. The wand was a simple bio-identifier used for everything from security to wildlife tagging. She knew he had a much more complex scanner he wanted to use, but even with the rapport they all seemed to feel, the full-body scanner would probably require a little explanation, and that would require some language. She doubted even a scientist would willingly step into a glowing square of light that popped up out of nowhere.

As Cho set his data programming in motion, the scientists picked through the jars in their cart. They spoke in low, guttural tones to each other, and their motions suggested they worked together often. Meg had to laugh. Even with the marked differences between the Dideto and the Earthers, something in their expressions reminded her of the serious distracted scowl Cho wore whenever he lost himself in his work.

She glanced at Loul, assuming he'd been as enrapt in the encounter as she'd been, but he sat deep in his crouch, his eyes closed and his head settled down low into his neck in a strange turtle-like way. No humming sounded from his throat.

"Loul?" She moved to him quickly. He sat too still, no muscles fidgeting at all. "Loul?" She reached out to touch him, fear souring her mouth when he still didn't move. Before she could reach him, the scientist closer to him barked out a sharp sound, making her stop. The scientist pulled her knuckles apart. No.

"But Loul?" Meg pointed, knowing they couldn't understand her. "Is he okay?"

The women grunted to each other in rapid exchange, and while Meg felt confident she could move faster than either of them, she sensed they would do what they could to keep her from reaching Loul. Cho put his hand on her arm to pull her back.

"Cho, what's happening? What's wrong with Loul? He's not moving."

"Well, they don't seem very worried about it so that's in our favor." His voice didn't match the optimism of his words. "Can you...how do ask them a question?"

Meg settled back into a neutral stance and could see the women relax. She pointed to Loul and mimicked his position as best she could, closing her eyes for just a moment before looking back to them and holding out her hands in surrender. The women shared a few more grumbling words. The one on the right, closest to Loul, pointed to the still man and then scrunched her head down between her shoulders in the same strange way as Loul's. She closed her eyes for a moment and then opened them, tapping her knuckles together. Yes.

She repeated the sequence—scrunch, close, open, yes—and looked at Meg and Cho, waiting for them to understand. Cho shifted beside her. "Is he...asleep?"

Meg made a sound of disbelief. "Here? In two minutes in the middle of a field? In a catcher's crouch with all this noise and these people? With us here?"

Before Cho could answer, Loul's eyes popped open and he blinked several times. When he saw Meg so close, he smiled. Then he yawned.

S I X

MEG

"Huh." She and Cho spoke in unison as Loul shook off his strange stillness. His eyes widened as he smiled at Meg and said something to the scientists. Everything in his body language suggested that nothing out of the ordinary had taken place. Judging from the punchy gestures the scientists were peppering their words with, they had a different story to tell. The scientist in the middle kept jabbing a stubby finger in Meg's direction.

"I don't think they're happy with you," Cho said, following the guttural exchange.

"Well, I'm sorry if I think that turning to stone in the middle of first contact is a little unusual." She watched Loul as he shifted in his crouch, inching closer to her.

"Meg." He pressed his knuckles together, barking out her name loud enough to make her wince. "Loul." He tapped his own chest and made the yes gesture two more times, alternating hand bumps with quick dips into the odd still position that had so unsettled her. Each time he reopened his eyes he made the yes gesture again, repeating a low popping sound. The third time he started the series, Meg activated the recording program and opened a text screen. Loul hesitated, watching her fingers scrabble over the lighted screen, and then resumed the sequence.

Cho watched her arrange the data on her screen. "Did you just get something?"

"Okay."

"Okay what?"

"Let's see if this is right." She tapped the screen before her, activating the audio command function. Looking up at the Dideto before her, she spoke in clear, clipped tones. "Loul is okay." After a pause, her speaker patch emitted the recorded sounds of Loul's voice. She could hear the gaps where the computer had pieced together the sounds but it created the desired effect. Loul and the scientists' eyes widened enough that Meg could see white around their gray irises, and all three mouths fell open. The women remained frozen, but Loul dropped forward on his fists, his mouth opened in a wide grin as he leaned in close. As he spoke, she heard her own voice in her translation com pieced together by the program.

"Yes. Okay is Loul. Yes."

She didn't realize she was leaning forward too, their faces less than a foot from each other. She grinned at his grin. "How about that?" she whispered to herself and then quieted, listening for the familiar ping of the program organizing the next set of sounds he made.

"Meg is yes okay is yes."

Cho frowned at the screen. "What does that mean? Did you just say that?"

"Shh." She didn't want to interrupt the audio capture to explain the process to Cho. In time, the program would change the translation voice to a gender-neutral generated voice, but for now she had it programmed to translate into her own voice, making it easier for her to add vocabulary as she came across it. In the coms, she knew it must sound strange to the rest of the crew, like she was babbling to herself, but she couldn't worry about that now. Instead, she dipped forward slightly, urging Loul to repeat himself.

"Meg is yes okay is yes."

She grinned again as comprehension dawned. "Oh there you are, oh you beautiful, beautiful thing." A few swipes on the screen and Cho saw the text boxes double. Her speaker patch emitted more guttural sounds as she spoke into the translation com. "Yes. Meg is okay."

Cho watched as she and Loul bumped hands again, she giggling, he rumbling low in his throat. "Do I even want to ask what just happened?"

Meg laughed louder. "Funny you say that. I just found the interrogative structure."

Cho snorted. "Is that like porn for language nerds?"

"As a matter of fact it is." Meg arranged the text boxes on the screen, moving her hands so that Loul could watch. It would be a while before he'd be able to operate a screen of his own, but she could tell he was putting together the function of the program. All the Earthers would have a similar screen to Meg's, each customized to their particular programs and all with access to the full databank. Meg arranged the screens intuitively, organizing text-vocal patterns in what she felt was an organic pattern.

The layout wasn't dissimilar to the old Ouija board she and her sister, Maddie, used to play with when they were kids. *Yes* and *no* held prominent spots at the top corners of the screen. Now that the program had recognized *okay* as similar to *yes*, she grouped the sounds nearby. It had worked for the translations of the last isolated tribe she'd been called in to work with. It had worked with the seemingly impenetrable pidgin language of the outer Werthery Colonies. Affirmatives and negatives could usually be grouped together: *yes/okay/good* versus *no/not okay/ bad*. To be able to signify the interrogative, whether by tone, word, or symbol, meant actual conversation could take place. It would be rudimentary at first. Hold something up. Interrogative. *Yes* or *no, good* or *bad*. From there, the general question base could grow quickly. *Who/what, where, how,* and the hardest of them all, *when.*

Objects were the easiest to classify. The main database already held hundreds of thousands of images that could be labeled in Dideto by any member of the crew. With a little luck Wagner might even find a way to interface with whatever passed for a computer system on this planet. He had even asked her about that long before the mission parameters had been set. He and Prader had argued that if a civilization used any type of mathematics and/or a binary system for their communication devices, the language gap could be bridged. To them, numbers were a universal constant exceeding the limitations of language. After all, a great deal of the ancient message that had incited this entire expedition had been mathematically based. But after the numbers had stopped rolling in and the coordinates and engineering aspects had been calculated, there had remained within the transmission a message that would not compute as numerical language. That was when Meg had been called in. That's when the argument for language and protocol had begun, and that was when Meg had truly believed she would finally be leaving Earth for good.

She'd had to fight hard for respect from Wagner and others on the mission committee who still didn't completely understand what purpose she served. Like so many people, the word *protocol* evoked thoughts of properly folded napkins, diplomatic niceties, and the fine-tuned formalities of political maneuvering. Cho had backed her authority and not, as some had suggested, simply because they had become lovers on the last mission to the Werthery Colonies. He had seen her in action. Plague had broken out on an isolated moon and all attempts at contact had been met with aggression. As a bioscientist, Cho wanted to be on the ground, to see firsthand what had gone wrong in the terraforming chain to create such a deadly pestilence. He and more than two dozen other aid workers had hovered in the atmosphere listening as Meg, accompanied by only one armed guard, shuttled to the planet's surface, met with the military leader, and created a language and protocol bond that finally allowed her to reassure the president that the aid workers' intentions were honorable. Thousands of lives had been saved on that mission and research into the genetic malfunction had broken new ground. The rescue workers and medical staff had been hailed as heroes, but every one of them had attested before the International Space Commission on the finesse of her diplomacy. They had all seen and heard the delicate give-and-take, the patience and instinct Meg had brought to the incendiary situation.

During a break in the aid campaign, after the worst of the crisis had abated, she and Cho had lain together in a shuttle bunk too small for two people. Both exhausted, they had been able to do little more than rest against each other in pale-blue nightshift lights. Cho had been working around the clock stabilizing inoculations; Meg had spent six tense hours smoothing over an unintentional affront to the president's mother that had led to a lot of guns being pointed at a lot of people all at once, she in the middle trying to remember the symbolic hand gestures of mediation she'd been absorbing like oxygen since arriving. Her nerves were frayed to the point of physical pain, and when Cho slid a warm, calloused hand up her spine, she nearly wept.

"How do you know?" He whispered into her hair. "How do you know how to give them what they want? How to talk them down?"

She pressed her face into the privacy of his neck, breathing in the smell of him. "How did you know to rub your hand like that up my back? How did you know how much I needed to feel that, to feel you close like this?" She pressed her lips into his throat. "You know because you care. And you care enough to take the chance of being wrong."

"Am I wrong? Do you want me to stop?"

She shifted her body, throwing a thigh across his hips. "You can't be that bad at reading body language."

And so Cho had testified on her behalf to the selection committee. Their relationship had come under scrutiny during the psychological profiling sessions, and through it all Meg had stood her ground. She refused repeatedly to rise to the bait of justifying her skills or bragging about her achievements. She knew, just as she had known when she and her team had cracked the internal deep-space message, that if this mission involved putting human beings in an unprecedented situation, it would involve more than math. It would involve language and protocol. New situations almost invariably invoked fear in human beings, and the only remedy to fear was communication. Without language, without communication, all the numbers in the world would be useless. Without language, fear became deadly. Meg knew this all too well.

It didn't surprise her in the least, therefore, that now that the mission had hit a critical snag, now that they were on the ground months if not years before they were prepared to make contact, it was Cho who stepped forward to stand beside her. She had already broken at least a dozen of her own rules of interaction, had contradicted the orders she had set in place, and yet she could feel Cho's confidence in her. She could sense the way he followed her lead and she could see the way he checked her movements from the corner of his eye even as he bonded with the scientists in front of him. And with a crew as varied and hardened as that of the *Damocles*, the tacit approval of a hard-ass like Elliot Cho carried a lot of weight. That and the fact that without Meg, they would all be standing with their proverbial dicks in their hands, a fact she was more than prepared to point out if necessary.

LOUL

"The generals aren't going to let them stay out here forever." The scientist beside him kept her eye on the aliens while she reached for a sample jar. "They're talking about moving them by force if necessary."

"We can't do that." Loul watched as Meg's fingers whipped around the light screen. "We don't know how they'll react. We've got to tell the generals that."

"That's exactly what we've been doing." The other scientist spoke up. "We're trying to convince them that maybe this terrain is unique for them, that they need this exact location to be able to breathe. We're saying it's the combination of the sand, limestone, and salt air."

"Really?" Loul looked around. The uniqueness of the locale hadn't occurred to him.

"Do you mean 'really that's what we're telling them' or 'really that's what we think'?"

Loul looked up at the two women, who were biting back smiles. "Uh…"

The one closest to him laughed first. "We've got them mostly convinced that there's something unique about the Roana Temple, some way their ship is interacting with the minerals that's either keeping them alive or keeping them calm. We're sort of playing both stories at the same time."

"Do you believe that?"

"No." The second woman lowered her voice even though it would be impossible for anyone behind the barricade to hear them. "But if they believe it, they'll keep the soldiers back. For a while, at least. That gives us time to study them. If the military gets them back to the base, who knows what science team they'll bring in."

"They'll bring you in, though, won't they?" The woman next to him looked at him with a shy smile. "You're Loul Pell, aren't you? I've read your report a thousand times. It's really brilliant work. I couldn't believe you weren't in the science academy. Especially now. I mean, look at them. Your anatomy predictions were really close."

Loul could only blink at the two wide-eyed scientists staring at him. According to the badges clipped to their overshirts, they were part of one of the highest-ranking science teams in Cartar, and they thought he was someone to be admired. Him. A midlevel weather watcher. Loul worried that maybe the unreality of this day would eventually melt his brain.

The woman next to him bumped him with her shoulder. "I'm Effan. This is my work partner, Effan."

"You're both named Effan?"

"Yeah." Effan Two shrugged. "You get used to it. It's really an honor to meet you, Mr. Pell. Do you, uh, do you think you could introduce us to…" She rocked on her heels in Meg's direction.

The shock of being admired by the high-ranking scientists had momentarily eclipsed the presence of Meg and her companion, of the aliens and their ship and their strange and beautiful sounds and light screens and filmy shelters. He felt thankful he had gotten his drop in, but his rest had done little to wrap his mind around the situation. If anything, it all felt more surreal. But when he turned back to Meg, he knew she and her partner were discussing him. Effan One had told him his dropping out had agitated her for some reason. All that pride, all that sense of being special dimmed in light of the enormity of the gap between them and the aliens.

Meg and her partner stopped talking for a moment when he looked at them and then resumed their discussion. At least he thought they were speaking. He could see their thin throats working and their wide mouths moving but any sounds they made disappeared on the Ketter wind. Finally, they turned back to him and Meg's partner tapped his chest.

"Cho." His voice was deeper than Meg's and thus easier to hear, but Loul could still see the effort he took in projecting the sound. He tapped his chest again. "Cho." Then he tapped Meg. "Meg." Meg fiddled with the light screen, and the sound of a combined recording came from her speaker.

"This is…Cho."

The scientists laughed and tapped knuckles. The one closest to him giggled. "Their voices sound like wind whistles."

"What should we do?" The other Effan looked from Loul to the aliens.

"Do what he did." Even as he said this, Loul knew the confusion that would arise. Effan was a very common name in Cartar. He had two cousins with the name but he didn't know if names worked the same way with the Urfers. Effan Two tapped her chest.

"Effan."

Meg and her partner, Cho, showed their glassine teeth, tapping knuckles as they worked to make the sound. Cho got it first to a great round of knuckle bumping and a breathy bell-like sound from Meg. "Effan," they said together, bumping their hands against the woman's. With a nod from Loul, Effan One tapped her chest.

"Effan." She smiled large when she spoke but Loul saw Meg's already wide eyes widen farther. Her glance moved from Effan Two to Effan One to Loul and back, and her head tilted in the way he recognized as meaning confusion. Her partner tilted his head toward her, his mouth moving with small tremors, only the faintest hint of sound escaping. Effan Two's smile faded. "What's wrong? Did I do something wrong?"

Meg held up her hands and, like Loul, the Effans were helpless to look away from the long, flexible digits. She swept her hand over the women and tapped the screen. A recorded sound issued forth. "Yes is this Effan." She pointed to a symbol on the screen, a slender curl that looked like a hook. "Yes is this Effan," the recording repeated.

Beside him the women peppered him with worried questions. "Is there something wrong? Have we offended them? What's the matter?" He ignored them, instead watching Meg's eyes watching him, seeing again that longing to understand something he couldn't explain. As the women talked, Loul noticed small flashes of light appearing and disappearing around the edges of the screen. Meg's eyes occasionally flitted to them, seeming to make a note of them, but always returning to Loul.

He had to stick with the basics. Moving his hand from one woman to the next, he said. "Effan. Effan."

Meg and her partner watched him, speaking to each other too quietly to be heard. She pointed to each of the women. "Effan. Effan." Loul tapped his knuckles. She then pointed to the portable science lab opened between them. "Effan. Yes is this Effan." Her long finger rested on the curved symbol on the screen.

He could feel comprehension circling his mind, nipping and teasing but not showing itself. He thought he knew what she was asking. It was the same as when he'd told her his name and she'd waved her hands over the crowd behind him, wanting to know if

Loul was a group name or his alone. Did the Urfers name themselves after the equipment they worked with? Maybe Meg was
not just her name but also a term to refer to the light panel she
worked on. So then would the leader also be Meg? And what was
the symbol she pointed to?

He ground his teeth in frustration at the question in her
eyes. This was impossible. Surely there was somebody behind
the barricade with more experience in translating foreign languages than him. He checked himself. Not foreign. Alien. This
wasn't some exchange student from Ton struggling to read off
the menu. These were aliens, extraterrestrials, the very creatures
he had incorrectly assumed he'd thrown his whole career away
over. They were right in front of him, she was right in front of
him, and she was looking to him for answers.

He could do this. He had done this already. He was the only one
so far the Urfers had spoken to in any sort of conversational way.
Waving a hand toward the two women beside him, he spoke clearly.
"Effan. Effan." Then he pointed to the opened testing kit between
them, debating on the simplest way to explain it. "Lab." It seemed
the shortest word to use. Meg and Cho communicated in that silent
way of theirs, Meg's eyes occasionally flitting down to the screen,
where lights and symbols continued to light up and disappear. The
one symbol she had pointed to earlier remained illuminated.

The little hook symbol pulled at him like a real hook, tugging
at a recalcitrant corner of his mind that simply would not make
the connection. He had no idea how this screen thing worked.
For all he knew it could launch codes for missiles or turn on the
ship's engine. Hell, it could be tied in with the Urfers' life-support
systems, but since what he was doing now—nothing—was getting him exactly nowhere, Loul decided to take a chance.

He pointed the tip of his blunt finger at the hooked symbol, slowly lowering his hand closer to the screen, giving Meg

plenty of time to react if he was committing a no-no. She watched his hand, her eyes widening, and just as his finger broke the light plane, it occurred to Loul that this could be a really stupid idea. The light plane could burn him or cut the tip of his finger off or capture him. It could explode or shatter or send a jolt through his nervous system that would leave him paralyzed and drooling for the rest of his life. A million increasingly miserable possibilities raced through his mind as his finger slipped into the space of the little illuminated hook; but all that happened was a flashing red light and the faintest pinging sound.

Meg watched him, leaning in closer, her head tipped to the side. She wondered what he was doing. So did he. He could barely follow his own wispy logic in this proceeding, so he figured he'd just let momentum carry him along. Meg had touched this symbol when he thought she'd asked if he was okay. Maybe this was some sort of permission symbol, an information symbol, a status checker of sorts. When she did nothing more than stare at him, expectation and confusion on her slender face, he amended his plan. Knowing he might just be adding to the confusion, he kept his finger on the symbol and said "Cho."

Cho shifted at the word, nudging Meg, who flitted her fingers over the screen.

"This is Cho," the recorded voices said.

Loul put his finger through the symbol once more and pointed to the small silver box beside Cho. "Is that Cho?" His mind worked so hard trying to mentally bridge the gap between his stare and Meg's he could feel heat radiating up from beneath his lower teeth. He heard the Effans muttering about what the hell he was talking about but he kept his eyes on Meg. He really hoped she could read minds, although at the moment all she would probably see in his was bewilderment and bedlam.

Meg brought her hands up and let her knuckles fall away. She fiddled with the screen, ghosting her hands around Loul's unmoving finger, and the word issued forth. "No."

Loul pressed into the symbol space again. "What is this?"

Meg smiled, once again leaning in even closer while her fingers flitted and his voice emanated from the gray patch on her shirt. "This is lab." The Effans tittered in excitement, whispering about wanting to see the alien's small lab, already thinking about bridging their own gaps in extraterrestrial science. From the corner of his eye, he could see Cho peering into the larger lab kit across from him, but he knew, or at least he felt, that he and Meg wrestled with a different gap, a gap that felt like it was about to close.

Meg's finger brushed against his at the hooked symbol. "What is this?" Her face hovered near enough that he could hear her breathy voice half a second before his own voice rumbled forth. She pointed to the Effans' kit. "What is this?"

"Lab." Loul answered.

Loul settled back into his crouch, thoughts falling into place. He didn't even realize Meg mirrored him, settling back onto her heels, both of their eyes narrowing in thought, both waiting to see if they had reached the same conclusion. Loul wondered if maybe he was going a little crazy because it sure felt like he and Meg were communicating, not just through words and gestures, but really connecting. For the first time in his adult life, he felt no awkwardness at the possibility of making a mistake. Even though the fate of the planet might literally rest on him getting this conversation correct, all the pressure melted away in light of the improbability of the entire situation. What did he have to lose?

He jabbed his finger at the symbol then jabbed his finger where he had seen Meg press when the words *yes* and *no* had issued forth. Symbol, *yes*. Symbol, *no*. Symbol. No sounds emerged but the *yes/no* words. Meg rocked forward, her narrow shoulders hitching in that way he understood to mean she wanted him to repeat himself, so he did. Symbol, *yes*. Symbol, *no*. Symbol. A rash of heat burned beneath his jaw where he held his teeth tightly together, and he held his breath.

Then all of Meg's teeth came into view. Her head tipped back at an impossible angle and he could see the fine bones and tendons that made up her pale, slender neck, and he heard that staccato bell sound coming from her lips. Cho stared at her. The Effans stared at her, but Loul stared at her so hard he thought he might set her on fire with his mind until she bumped her knuckles together with enthusiasm. If that wasn't joy on her face, Loul didn't know his ass from a hole in the ground. He grinned along with her.

She jabbed at the *yes* button again and again. "Yes. Yes. Yes."

Without thinking, Loul rocked forward as she did, their hands bumping hard between them, this time not separating. They continued to lean in closer and closer, close enough that he could see the tender pink skin that held her fragile white teeth, could see small dark spots scattered over her narrow nose, and could see that her wide, wet eyes were fringed with fine black hair. He knew he grinned too as their foreheads touched and he smelled her strange warm breath.

One of the Effans, or maybe both, demanded to know, "What? What's happening? What did you do? What did you push?"

"I think," he lowered his voice so as not to shout into Meg's mouth, "that the symbol is a question mark."

"It doesn't look like a question mark," Effan Two said. "It looks like a hook."

"Doesn't matter what it looks like." Loul drifted back so his eyes could focus more clearly on Meg's smooth face. "I think that's how we ask questions."

The Effans seemed unimpressed but Loul continued to grin. A question mark. How appropriate. He knew he'd use that button a million times.

SEVEN

LOUL

It really was no surprise that the media found out about the arrival. The arrival—that's what the Cartar Federal Administration called it when it finally held its press conference. The media webbing could only block out visuals for so long before the world became curious, especially at a popular tourist site like the Roana Temple. Normally, once the Zobos twins set, the Roana Temple drew hundreds of visitors a day, with the warmth of the Red Sun and the low-hanging Ellaban Sun making the temperature and light perfect for picnicking during high light and any manner of mystical conjuring and hard partying during the low.

What did surprise Loul was how ordinary this had all become, inasmuch as spending all of his shifts communicating with extraterrestrials could be. The invasion of the news helicopters and the scuffles and skirmishes going on behind the military barricades occurred in a distant world from his. For Loul, the rounds he had spent since being abducted from the telemetry building had become a lifetime unto themselves, a world inhabited by him, Meg, and some other people who came and went.

Not that there hadn't been plenty of surprises to discover with the Urfers; still most shocking was their pattern of falling into stasis every four or five shifts. The first time it had happened, that first bewildering day, Loul and the Effans had talked the generals down from their insistence that the aliens be transported to a private facility. The Urfers had set up their filmy little bubble shelters, drawn water from a reservoir on the side of their ship, and generally set about making a camp in sight of the entire Cartar military and Space Administration. After the Effans had made contact, other teams had come forth and started their own uncertain dance with the visitors.

It took Loul a while to get used to hearing his own voice booming out of the speaker patches each of the Urfers wore those first few days. It seemed the light screen that Meg worked with was patched into the screens each of the others used, and so, one awkward phrase at a time and with much pointing and gesturing and more than a few big misunderstandings, a fragile communication bridge emerged, with Loul's voice being the ipso facto voice of the Urfers. As other members of the military and science teams gained confidence, Loul heard their voices peppering conversations. The Effans' voices rang out quite shrilly as they worked with Cho, and of all the combinations in the restricted space, the scientists seemed to be covering the most ground. Tissue, skin, and hair samples had their own language that both sides felt conversant in.

After several shifts that first day, the Urfers had pulled away, conferring around their shelters. Cho spoke with some animation, gesturing to his screen where Loul had seen his data streaming by. Something he had discovered in the scans of the Effans required a closed circle for the aliens. As they met, Meg kept looking over her shoulder at Loul, the remarkable flexibility of her body not quite as shocking as it had been hours before. Her body language, as alien as it was, reassured him that she would return to him, that they would pick up their new and exhilarating game of building a language.

The other teams within the barricade were not so reassured. The mechanical engineers stomped their feet when the smallest of the Urfers turned its back on them, leaving them with only a jabbing-stabbing hand gesture toward the ship, as it joined its crewmates in the circle. Engineers, soldiers, scientists, archivists—all of them huffed in various stages of frustration as the Urfers withdrew for consultation. When they turned back to the impatient assembly, they stood as a tight group, only Meg stepping forward toward Loul.

She did that settling stance twice, giving him the impression that she was preparing to tackle a difficult concept. Great, he thought, another challenge. So far he knew he'd been skating by on luck and instinct, the bulk of whatever success they might be having resting squarely on Meg's patience and clever machine. For all he knew, he might have already gotten everything wrong. Every friendly sentence and word construct they had might be completely misconstrued by him. The specter of being the man who opened the gates to the evil aliens that destroyed Dideto reared its hideous head for the millionth time that day.

But when she started to gesture, her eyes fixed on him, the doubt dissipated for millionth time. She watched him so carefully, her strange smooth face so expressive, even if he couldn't exactly read those expressions. She put her hand on his chest (and he was getting fixated on the sensation of her light touch) and said, "Loul." Easy enough. Then she did this strange thing with her shoulders and her neck. The thin yoke of bones that made up her shoulder carriage rose high up on her long neck and her narrow chin dropped, folding the pale skin in ripples beneath her face. She closed her eyes for several seconds and then opened them. With shoulders back down and her long line of posture restored, she touched Loul again. "Loul."

Effan One whispered behind him. "I think she's talking about dropping."

"Oh," Loul said as he watched Meg repeat the strange sequence. "Dropping," he said, pointing to her screen where he knew she captured the words. He closed his own eyes, feigning the dropping position. When he looked again, she was tapping her knuckles and smiling. His voice sounded from her speakers: "Dropping."

"That really agitated her when you dropped earlier," Effan Two said. "Like it scared her or something."

Meg ignored the scientists, watching only Loul. "Urfers," she said, gesturing behind her to the waiting crew, "dropping."

That was it? That required a team meeting and a halt to all activity? Sure it seemed odd that they'd all drop at once but maybe that's what happened when they worked as a team. Maybe that's what space travel did to them. Of course, the opposite was true on Didet. The more time you spent around someone, the farther apart your drops became. There were old couples in the family who had been together so long, their drops alternated exactly every eight shifts apart, equally breaking up the time of a full round. It made sense that Urfer biology might be a little different, all things considered.

"Urfers dropping," he said, tapping his knuckles. "Okay."

"No." Meg shook her head in that dizzying way, more like a goalpost trembling from a hit than a human body in motion. "Urfers dropping..." Her long fingers bent into the air, grasping at nothing. He'd seen this gesture. Whatever she was trying to say, she seemed to need to claw it from the air.

"Urfers dropping," she started again and then brought her fingertips together, holding them up between them at his eye level. He could see her through the oval loops her long hands created with the gesture. As he watched, she pulled her hands away from each other, but not like the knuckle-drop gesture of *no*. This looked more like the move the Urfers used when they drew their light screens from their wristbands. Loul expected to see another screen emerge between her fingertips but saw only Meg's expectant face.

As he knew she would, she repeated the sequence: "Urfers dropping," with fingers drawn apart. He knew she could see in his face that he didn't get it. She resettled and tried a new approach. "Loul dropping." She jerked her shoulders up in that uncomfortable way she had earlier. "Yes?" She jabbed the question mark.

"Yes," he answered, not entirely sure what he meant by that.

"Urfers dropping?" She hunched her shoulders again. "No." She pointed back to the bubble shelters where the aliens watched the exchange. She held her hand out toward the group, palm down, and made a fluid and utterly bewildering gesture, letting her long fingers dip and ripple toward the ground. "Yes?"

"No." What else could he say? They really needed to find the word for *Huh?*

Meg covered her face with her hands, breathing loudly enough between her fingers for Loul to hear it whistling. With a quick glance at him, she turned and walked back toward her crew. They conferred a moment longer, pointing at one another and bobbing their heads in matching rhythm. The leader pointed at the two Urfers who had stood to the far side of the chevron, the smaller one who had been meeting with the engineers and the larger one with a reddish tint to its skin. Loul couldn't tell if they were happy to be pointed to, but the group bobbed their heads once more and the two selected Urfers dropped to their knees and crawled into a bubble shelter.

"That's weird," Effan One said. "Where are they going?"

That seemed to be the question the engineering team asked too, especially when several minutes passed without the Urfers returning. The three remaining aliens turned back to the crowd as if ready to resume work as usual. Meg walked toward Loul, her long strides a little less certain than before. She pointed behind her toward the occupied shelters. "Urfers dropping."

MEG

What did it say about the unpredictability of the universe, Meg wondered, when sleep was an oddity but press conferences were universal? There was no mistaking the abrupt intrusion, the shouted words, and the demanding tones she could hear on the far side of the barricade. Prader had first seen the oddly shaped orbs hovering over the scene. They looked like volleyballs with tiny sails that rode the breezes over the landing site. Someone had followed her pointing finger and the soldiers had erupted into action.

Captain Wagner withdrew his sidearm as one of the hovering spheres drifted closer to him. "Looks like someone's upstaging us for attention. Whatever these are, our hosts don't look very happy to see them."

"We'll get to see one up close," Prader had said, her gun at the ready, "if this little son of a bitch gets any closer."

"Put your guns down." An orb bobbed in fat waves over Meg's head, the little sails adjusting themselves for steering. "Whatever they are, we let the Dideto handle them."

"Unless they shoot ray-gun laser beams and melt us."

"Okay, that's the plan." Wagner kept his voice level. "We let the Dideto handle it unless they shoot laser beams and melt Prader."

Jefferson snorted. "How badly melted does she have to be before we start firing? Like, completely liquefied or can we start when she starts to smoke and bubble?"

"Keep it up, laughing boys, and when it turns out we're being groomed to be household pets for these hairy bastards, you can all—"

Meg tuned out the chatter, turning instead to Loul, who pounded his fists against the front of his hips, his eyes watching the hovering orbs. He bent forward in a half-crouch that made the muscles in his arms and legs strain. Whatever these things were, they were making Loul tense.

"Loul?"

He jumped when she spoke, springing from his rigid posture as the orb dropped lower, almost close enough for Meg to jump up and touch. She stared up at the intruder, noticing small, transparent panels in the sphere's surface. Loul stepped in close, close enough to break into the light screen, and held his thick fists up at the thing but came nowhere near high enough to block Meg's line of sight. The orb wheeled about, circling her, and Meg could hear the low vibration in Loul's throat rising, picking up an erratic hitching rhythm. That sound, more than the proximity of the strange object, put her nerves on alert.

"Loul?" She asked again, and this time he met her gaze, his eyes narrowed and a dark flush blossoming around the edges of his face. She pointed to the hovering orb. "Yes? Okay?"

He growled a low sound in his throat, his fists pumping once again at his hips. "No."

"No." A cold spot formed in her gut. "Loul," she said, tipping her head toward the hand that held her sidearm. "Okay no?"

She really didn't want to have to start firing at these things. She knew that decision would take this encounter down a new, dark, and probably explosive road, but if Loul was in danger, if any of them were in danger, she wasn't going down without a fight. An unfunny thought crossed her mind, that this is probably how Prader felt all the time.

Loul followed her gaze to her hand, and she tipped her body forward enough to block anyone but Loul from seeing the handle of the weapon. She had to assume he knew what this was, at least in theory. Apparently he did because as soon as the trigger of the gun came into view, his breath caught, a high yelp escaped his throat, and he dropped his voice to a rough tone. "No. No. No." He even reached out and pressed his hand against her arm. "Meg. No."

She saw that he no longer looked up at the orb, his gaze boring into hers with more intensity than she'd seen so far. "No." She let the gun slip back into her pocket, keeping her gestures small, and she saw him relax. "Guns down, everyone." She heard mumbling through the coms. "Whatever these are, shooting them is a bad idea."

"Unless these are their way of taking us down once and for all."

"Hey, Prader," Cho said, "dial it back a notch. You don't have to be Meg to see that these people didn't send these things in. Whatever they are, they're making them as nervous as us and for all we know they could be flying nuclear warheads. Put your freaking gun down."

"You know what they look like?" Jefferson asked. "They look like the hovercams they used to use at the football stadium. You know the kind with the parabolic microphones that hover over midfield? When I played for the Belters, we used to try to nail one each game."

"But they've got cameras on posts," Meg said, glancing over Loul's shoulder at the high-mounted slender cylinders pointed their way. "Isn't that what those are over there?"

Wagner squinted up at an orb that hovered just out of his reach. "They have a lot of broadcast on this planet, don't they? Maybe somebody else is trying to get in on the show. That would explain why the authorities are so nervous about it. Second rule of an unknown situation is to control information."

"What's the first rule?" Jefferson asked.

Prader snorted. "Don't get killed."

Meg saw Loul watching her, watching her crewmates, leaning in trying to hear their words. He also kept an eye out on the hovering orbs. "Let me see what Loul wants us to do." He heard his name. Meg kept her hand low, close to her body, and pointed up at the orb.

"Yes? Okay?" She didn't know what else to do, so she slipped a finger to the light screen and pushed the question mark button repeatedly. Loul watched her, grinding his teeth, and she could see he wanted to tell her something but didn't yet have the words. He tilted his body as the orb swooped down closer, and Meg could see him trying to put himself between it and the light screen. Jefferson was right—these were cameras or spy objects of some sort.

Loul ground his teeth a moment longer, pointedly not looking at the orb. When Meg pulled the screen down closer to the ground, bending over Loul's shoulder and effectively blocking any overhead view, the orb spun and swooped and Loul smiled. If Loul didn't want those things to see the screen, she'd do all she could to keep it from happening. That it felt like a secret pinkie swear between grade-school kids just made it that much nicer.

"Okay?" Meg asked again.

He flicked his gaze to where the orb hovered and then spoke in a low tone. "Yes. No."

Prader's voice hissed through the coms. "That's helpful."

"It is helpful," Meg said. "It means it's not good but it's not too bad. If those are cameras, I think it means the military here has got an uncomfortable situation on their hands. Someone else has found out we're here, someone they probably wanted to keep this a secret from. Maybe another government? Maybe the population as a whole? It's what we would do."

"Which begs the question," Wagner said, "what are they going to do about it now?"

They didn't need to wait long for an answer. The trio in charge at the barricade reemerged from the huddle they'd slipped into once the orbs had appeared. From behind the barricade, a team of men unpacked a squat metal box, pulling out an equally squat metal dish, like a small satellite dish. All around them, people shouted gruff words, and down the line of the barricade the sound of machinery stuttered to silence. When all the machinery was quiet, Meg couldn't help but notice just how loud the human-made thrumming sound really was. At first it registered on several notes, like cocktail party chatter. As the machinery went silent, however, the sounds came together, an audible harmony that was nearly palpable.

"What is that?" Cho asked. Meg didn't know if he meant the machine or the sound. Before she could venture a guess, a piercing squeal emanated from the squat metal dish, a sound pulse loud enough to be felt like a wind. Before she could react, Loul yanked her arm hard, sending her sprawling toward him, the crash of her body not moving him an inch. He held her tight enough against him that she knew she would have bruises on her back, but that wasn't what took her breath away. Seconds after the dish's loud squawk, the hovering orbs stilled and their sails collapsed. As one they crashed to the ground.

E I G H T

LOUL

Blacking out the news cameras had done nothing to stop the tide of reporters on the site. He knew the orbs had captured perfect visuals of the Urfers and might even have captured the sounds of their voices. Images of the ship parked right there on the Roana Temple would shoot around the web, and for just a second he wondered if Po and Hark had seen him there in the middle of the action. If his face had been captured on video, even for half a frame, he knew Po would see it, doubtless scanning frame by frame over each second of video to find the truth.

The generals had conferred with him about the press conference, making it clear he would not be a part of it. Their main concerns, understandably, were to keep the population at large from panicking. That's what always happened in the movies. Aliens landed. People died. Terror burned through the streets. He'd even recommended measures against such events in his report— that bunkers be stocked in the lowest tunnels, crucial personnel prepared for evacuation, and international communication set up for a team resistance effort. It seemed so strange now, all that work, all those eventualities he'd spent months considering. And the administration had believed him. They'd probably implemented a lot of his plans.

But this? He had never anticipated this. The immediacy of it, the...well, there was no other word for it, the intimacy of it. The generals had their press conference and the archivists had broadcast it within the barrier. Images of the Urfers were posted to the web and reporters were given carefully constructed answers to their raging questions. Details were kept to an absolute minimum due in large part to the fact that details were at a premium. Even with the language building, even with the bond he could feel between him and Meg as surely as he could feel the ground beneath his feet, they still had surprisingly few hard facts about the Urfers.

The stasis events drove the frontline team to distraction. The engineers who had been trying to communicate with the palest and smallest Urfer had huffed and stomped and thrown down their equipment when the two aliens did not reemerge from their shelter. The Urfers stayed hidden away for nearly a shift and a half before climbing back out. Loul had urged Meg to follow him to that side of the field to help convince the engineers to remain calm. When two engineers had decided to approach the shelter, Meg and the leader had stood in front of them blocking the way.

It was Cho and the Effans who managed to smooth things over. Cho had invited the scientists to see the shelter he had climbed into earlier. They had both squatted down, peering into the low dome, and Cho had climbed in between them. Several moments later, the women returned to their portable lab and began writing out a long list of notes.

"They call it 'leep' or something like that." Effan Two didn't look up from where her knuckles furiously pounded in the input box. "I can barely hear him but it seems like a necessary biological function to them. Like dropping but it looks like they have to be on the ground."

"Do you think the domes have an effect?" Effan One rechecked the data her partner entered. "I didn't pick up any trace minerals or chemical interactions. It didn't seem like the dome emits any type of chemical or pheromone."

Loul, with Meg peering over his shoulder, listened in. "What do they do once they get inside the shelters?"

Effan One shrugged. "All he did was lie there, eyes closed. Maybe they extract something from the soil beneath them, some sort of nutrient."

"Holy crap," her partner laughed, "maybe we were right about them needing to land on this site. Wouldn't that be a hammer to the head?"

Loul watched them work, fascinated and happy that they were making connections with Cho. The more people able to communicate, the faster communication would develop. If the Effans could explain this "leep" thing to the engineers, maybe they would cool down and work with the two reemerged Urfers to gain some real technological headway. The Urfers were clearly scientifically advanced, and the chance to learn from their knowledge could change the history of Didet forever.

He occupied himself with these and similar lofty thoughts until he realized Meg had grown very quiet. She watched the Effans working at their lab with eyes that were only half opened. The white surrounding the remarkable brown circle had grown redder by the moments, and once Loul had thought she was going to tell him something, snapping him to attention, only to watch her open her mouth impossibly wide showing every single one of her white teeth. She squeezed her eyes shut as her mouth kept opening and opening and he could hear a sound as breath rushed from her mouth.

He jabbed the question mark button but she only blinked at him. "Okay?" He asked.

"Yes." She pressed the tips of her fingers into the skin over her eyes and then blinked hard several times. The leader called out something behind her and she bobbed her head. Putting a hand on his shoulder, she smiled. "Meg dropping."

"What?" He asked even though he knew she couldn't understand him. "No."

"Yes." She turned away from him and headed toward the shelter where Cho also squatted. Loul followed her.

"No, Meg. Are you going to drop like those other two? For a shift? Two shifts?" He felt stupid. He knew she didn't know what he was saying and he could tell nothing he did get through would stop her, but the thought of her disappearing from his sight, even for just a shift, made him want to stomp his foot and throw a tantrum. It terrified him.

Cho crawled into the tent and Meg folded her long legs down to follow him. Loul dropped into a deep crouch, hearing the Effans hurrying up behind him. The realization must have hit them too. Meg and Cho were their only links to the world of the Urfers. The other three crew members remained aloof, less adept or maybe less inclined to communicate. It might only be a shift or two but Loul and the Effans burned with need to interact with these beings. How could they just interrupt the encounter like this?

Meg disappeared within the dome, the filmy flap falling into place behind her. Loul couldn't help himself. He grabbed the film and pulled it back. In the milky light filtering through the dome, he saw Cho unfold himself on his back on a dark, puffy pad. When he saw Loul's intrusion, he made a low sound to Meg, who turned and smiled at Loul. Sitting on the ground beside Cho's supine body, she pulled out the light screen.

"Meg dropping," she said and pointed to the screen. Her finger hovered over the yes button. "Yes." She pressed the button several times, much as she had pressed the question mark button earlier. Another voice came from the speaker patch, lower but not Dideto. Cho's probably, amplified in the recording. "Leep." That's what the Effans had said Cho had called it, although he thought he could hear more sound in the word, more like *fleep* or *gleep*.

Loul pressed the question mark button several times.

Meg smiled and touched his hand. "Meg is okay. Meg dropping. Yes." And with that, she lay back on the ground beside Cho, dragging up a thin sheet of fabric to cover their bodies. Cho had one of his long arms draped over his face, covering his eyes, and Loul could tell he and Meg were speaking softly to each other. Whatever they said made Meg smile, her breath coming out in short puffs that moved the fabric over her body. Loul and the Effans waited, watching, but within minutes both Urfers grew unnaturally still, the only movement the rising and falling of their thin chests beneath the fabric.

MEG

"Landing on a planet of people who don't sleep—proof there is no God." Cho groaned, throwing his arm over his eyes. Meg laughed and settled in beside him.

"Looks like we may have an audience while we sleep."

"Nothing creepy about that."

She pulled the blanket up over them both. Every inch of her wanted to roll onto her side, throw her leg over Cho, and fall asleep, but she knew the Dideto were puzzled by sleep. She didn't need to complicate information. Of course, if Loul and the other two watched them the entire time, who knew what they would see? Cho snored, and she knew she talked in her sleep, to say nothing of the ordinary shifting and thrashing through dream sequences. There was nothing to be done about it now, however. They'd been awake for nearly twenty-four hours. They all needed at least five hours of sleep to continue to function. Prader and Jefferson had gone first. As captain, Wagner volunteered to go last. All Meg knew for sure was that she had to sleep right now, and despite the hard ground, she felt herself drifting off.

"What the hell is that noise?" Cho blew out a loud breath, pulling her out of sleep. "Are they talking? Humming? What is it?"

It took her a minute to understand what he meant. Then she heard the low throat sounds of Loul and the Effans where they sat perched at the door of the dome. "It's their sound. It's like a vocal body language, I think."

"Can they tone it down?"

"I doubt it. Think of it as white noise, like the sound of cicadas." She murmured a happy sound as he rolled onto his side and pulled her toward him. She rolled too, pressing her back into his chest, relaxing under the weight of his arm on her waist.

"I hate cicadas."

"Grumpy." She yawned, settling in. "I like the sound. I like these people."

Cho's only response was a soft breath against the back of her neck.

When the alarm went off on Cho's armband, Meg lay on her stomach, the small pillow damp beneath her cheek. Cho sprawled off the pad, the sound making him jump.

"Oh my God." His voice was thick with sleep. "What did we sleep? Five minutes?"

Meg rolled over and stretched long, feeling her body complain at the movement. Before her eyes were fully focused, the flaps to the dome opened and three Dideto faces appeared. She covered her face with her hands to smother a giggle as Cho sighed.

"You know, I used to have a dog that did that every morning. Just stand there and breathe on me until I woke up." He sat up and raked his hands through his rumpled hair. "I didn't keep that dog long."

"Yeah." Meg pulled herself up too, smiling at Loul. "You didn't land on your dog's planet. Their world, their ways. Their smiling faces everywhere we go."

Cho sighed as the Effans started talking to him, his name the only word he could understand. "Well I'm going first and then you can let your boy there follow you into the port-toilet. That should make for some interesting syntax building."

"You're the bioscience officer."

"I'm also bigger, faster, and meaner than you."

"Yeah?" She shook her hair out from the loosened ponytail. "But I have breasts."

He shot her a side eye, trying not to smile. "Cheater."

"Yep." She kissed him on the cheek before crawling toward the door. "Breasts always win. Remember that."

Loul was already talking to her as she climbed from the dome, squinting in hot sunlight. She nodded at him and let him follow her as far as to the door of the small port-toilet dome. When he made motions to follow her, she put her hands on his chest. "No."

"Dropping? Meg dropping?"

"Meg is okay." She nodded again, trying not to giggle at the accidental toilet humor. She put her hands on his chest and could feel the powerful muscles beneath her hands. If he forced himself, she wouldn't be able to stop him. Not that there was anything to hide really. It was just that there were so many things they needed to learn to say to each other. Explaining why she was pulling down her pants and squatting over a bowl of genetically modified algae and underneath a solar panel was not how she wanted to start her day. Besides, Cho was the bio-science officer. That would be a fun part of his information sharing.

Cho waited outside the door for his turn, Loul and the Effans talking over each other. She had to laugh at the still-grumpy expression on his face. "You know, you're going to have to turn your translation com on today. There's no avoiding it."

He scowled as he passed by. "Science in the morning is never a good thing. If it's even morning. Tell Wagner to get some sleep. And tell Chatty Cathy and company that we're going to talk about food when I get out."

"I'll get your kit."

Meg held out her arms wide, gesturing to Loul and the Effans to move away from the dome and back to the center of the field. She grabbed Cho's small biokit from outside their shelter and needed only to nod at Wagner to give him the signal to take his much-needed sleep. Prader and a cluster of Dideto in green suits were crouched by one of the landing boosters of the *Damocles* sub, the sounds of metallic clanging and shouting bursting out now and again. Jefferson worked alone, scanning through his light screen, still gathering geological data from his probes that had come back online.

Meg settled Loul and the Effans in a semicircle, motioning for them to be still while she got some food and water. She'd need Cho to help her explain what they needed nutrient-wise and to analyze whatever the Dideto ate to see if their food was compatible with Earther biology. Grabbing a couple of protein blocks and a bag of water, she settled across from her Dideto friends. Cho joined them a moment later.

"I suppose it's too much to ask," he said, crossing his legs beneath him, "to hope that coffee is a required nutrient on this planet."

Meg took a deep drink of water. "Why? Do you think they have trouble staying awake?"

Cho finally laughed, the restorative effects of even their brief sleep brightening up this mood. He took the water from Meg, toasted the wide-eyed and fidgeting Effans, and drank.

"Good morning, ladies. Let's get started, shall we?" He activated his translation com.

The days sped by, Cho warning them to set their alarms. Although the levels of daylight shifted as the various suns rose and fell, true nightfall never came and their bodies adjusted with some difficulty. Eating, sleeping, and even bathroom breaks had to be scheduled to keep their bodies working smoothly. There were only five Earthers on the planet and a never-ending stream of new teams of Dideto to work with. The Dideto didn't sleep in the sense that the Earthers did, their regularly spaced dropping sessions adequate to refresh them. Meg laughed and teased Cho when she saw that he had become as obsessed with understanding the dropping as the Effans were with examining his sleep.

The food and water discussions made headway at a pretty decent pace. Fortunately the Dideto also required water, although not as much as the Earthers, and Cho had little trouble explaining to the Effans that the crew would need a large vat of water on hand. Cho set up a solar-powered purification system, at which Jefferson had smirked: "Do you think we'll have enough daylight to run it?"

As the bioscience officer, Cho had volunteered to be the guinea pig for the first sip of the purified liquid. He'd swirled the water around in a beaker, eyeing the clear liquid and then taking it all down in one gulp. He'd smacked his lips, nodded his approval, and promptly dropped to the ground, gripping his stomach and collapsing in a twisted, writhing mess. The other four were just overworked, underfed, and sleep-deprived enough to shatter into giggling huddles. "The first sip'll kill ya" routine was about as corny as deep-space humor got, but even Wagner laughed until he snorted at Cho's little show. For their part, the Dideto had become accustomed to these short outbursts of strange behavior from the normally calm aliens.

They rationed out their dwindling supply of protein blocks and the carefully contained Gro-Wall within the shuttle. Both Cho and Jefferson had strenuously urged caution with the food source. As a plant genetically modified to grow quickly and in harsh conditions, they stressed the danger of releasing the plant into the flora of Didet. If it took root or even managed to cross-pollinate, it could easily overwhelm the ecosystem, so Prader rigged up an isolation barrier, keeping the plant contained in the now-empty loading bay of the shuttle, and Meg made it clear the Dideto were to stay far from the door. The pods of the beans were counted out and recounted when collected to be sure not a trace of the plant remained unaccounted for.

The Effans and their fellow scientists brought forward all manner of food for Cho to analyze. Most of it, while compatible in the strictest nutritional sense, was inedible. The Dideto teeth were as dense as the rest of their bodies, further strengthening Cho's theory that they had evolved from a burrowing race of primates. The grinding strength of their teeth suggested they had the capacity, if not the digestive need, to consume a certain amount of grit in their food. While nothing in his research suggested they still actually sifted their food through the dirt before eating it, most of the foods presented to him were far too grainy, fibrous, or pitted for any of the Earthers to chew.

"Does this mean we're going to run out of food?" Wagner asked, showing the closest thing to anxiety he had ever shown. The captain had a fast metabolism and a big appetite, paired with a badly disguised dislike of the Gro-Wall beans.

Cho shrugged. "My guess is we'll be eating something they don't consider food."

"That sounds appetizing," Prader muttered.

"You're welcome to try to chew on this...gravel bread."

It was Loul who brought in the first Earther-edible foodstuff even though he did so accidentally. He and Meg were seated in their favorite spot, underneath an awning the soldiers had constructed on the edge of the military barricade. Cho had managed to explain to the Effans that the Earthers needed a break from the endless sunlight. The military had certainly been pleased to block out the occasional media spy cam that slipped through the barrier. The awnings served both purposes, and Meg and Loul had staked out a spot at one of the portable booth-table setups the soldiers had installed. It felt cozy in the booth, the sides of the chairs curling around them, creating a sense of privacy.

They worked together on sorting through the vocabulary the other teams were building. As she had expected, Loul took to the light screen and the program itself with a natural intuition that couldn't be taught. She had given him his own earpiece, rigging it up with some bandage wiring to help it fit more snugly against his flatter ear, and he had gasped when he'd first heard her voice clearly. She hadn't realized how much he hadn't been hearing until he responded to her laughter and voice with renewed enthusiasm.

Meg was trying once again to find a way to express the concept of time, starting with before and after. It was difficult in a culture whose concept of time she didn't understand. Day and night—even in deep space, even in the most remote space colonies—Earth-originated humans clung to a day-night basis for time. Some colonies lengthened their day-night periods, but even those who lived in regions where daylight lasted for weeks on end clung to a cyclical diurnal-nocturnal schedule of timekeeping. Cho had explained that Earth biology demanded it. Until landing on this multisunned planet it had never occurred to Meg to consider another way of expressing time.

Loul tried. She could see he wanted badly to understand the nature of the question she tried to ask, but whenever she thought she was expressing a sequence of events, and thus the passage of time, he responded with an answer of location. *Here* and *there*, not *now* and *then*. They did stumble upon a general understanding of the concept of *more* and *less*, which easily adapted to *bigger* and *smaller*, *older* and *younger*, *better* and *worse*, with varying degrees, all with the activation of a simple wedge symbol. For some reason, that had made both of them giggle for almost a quarter of an hour. Language was such a strange thing.

Taking a break to just enjoy the laughter, Loul had pulled out the lunch he'd packed. Meg called it lunch, since it fell lunchtime-ish on her clock. She'd yet to discover any sort of pattern to the Dideto and their meals. Maybe it was just the pressure of working nonstop within the barrier; maybe they didn't schedule their world around meals. The very thought of the latter and Meg could feel her mother roll over in her grave.

Loul unwrapped what looked like a dark-green ear of corn. Meg had seen them before and knew peeling back the fibrous leaves revealed only more leaves, denser and damper than the dried outer sheaths. Cho had declared the plant edible or at least not poisonous, but further analysis showed that the nutritional content was hardly worth the hours of chewing the Earthers would need to do just to bite off a piece. A truck had recently delivered cartons of these plants—*mogi*, Loul called them—and left them in stacks near the water vats. These plants seemed to be fuller and rougher, less trimmed than the other *mogi* she had seen. At the tip of the plant, where Loul peeled back the leaves, he picked off a dry, brownish pod that he dropped beside his bowl.

Meg had rolled the little pod between her fingers, knowing Loul watched her. He seemed fascinated by her fascination with the everyday objects he brought to her. While he ate, she picked at the pod. "Loul eat?" She asked him, holding it up.

"No. No good." They had worked on clarifying the difference between bad and not good, an important difference when trying to determine if completely alien items were simply useless or incredibly dangerous.

Meg had let Loul eat, picking at the useless pod and thinking about a new way to approach the time problem, when her fingers broke through the husk and dipped into a mushy white center. At the same time, an idea occurred to her and she turned back to the light screen. Without thinking, she stuck her fingers in her mouth to clear off the white mush and froze.

She tried not to swallow, knowing Cho had not tested the dried pods on the ends of the *mogi* to see if they were safe. "Cho!" The bioscience officer held up a hand toward her, not turning away from the test he was running, and she yelled again, her voice muffled by the spit pooling up in the bottom of her mouth. He turned to look at her and she pointed to her face.

"I ay suh-hing." She held her tongue out, hoping the white mush had just stayed there.

"Really, Meg?" Cho didn't panic but hurried to her, pulling a disinfectant pad out of his kit. "You just decided to snack on something? After all this time?" She rolled her eyes in exasperation as he wiped all the residue he could off of her tongue.

"Ick." She licked the antiseptic taste out of her mouth.

"Yeah, because you wouldn't want to taste anything gross like an alien life-form." Cho dropped the pad into a testing vial and grabbed the broken pod. "This?"

"Yeah, it's the dried end of the *mogi* so it's probably not poisonous, right?"

"Right," Cho said, smashing the white pulp against the scanner over it. "And we have absolutely no plants on Earth that are edible in some parts and poisonous in others."

"Just scan it." She looked over at Loul, who watched their interaction with wide eyes. Since being fitted with the earpiece, he couldn't get enough of listening to conversations among the Earthers. She saw him focusing when tones changed and knew he was starting to piece together the different tempos and temperaments different crew members used. Meg had yet to learn if the Dideto engaged in sarcasm. If not, Cho would be difficult to translate.

"Good news and bad news," Cho said, shutting off the scanner. "Good news? These little pods are packed with nutrients— potassium, vitamins, even some calcium. They're practically a superfood."

"Is the bad news that they're poisonous?"

"No. The bad news is they probably taste like plantains and I hate plantains."

Meg giggled at Cho's deadpan revelation of the best news they'd received resource-wise since landing. "Dammit. Another failure, huh? Maybe they come in strawberry too."

Cho swiped a finger's worth of the pulpy mess off the scanner and held it up to his face. "The things I do for science." He swallowed it down, his expression unchanging.

"Well?"

"It ain't strawberry." He smacked his lips. "But it is better than the protein blocks."

Meg grinned and turned to Loul. "Talk this?"

Loul swallowed hard, staring at the pod husk. "*Tut.*"

"*Tut.*" Meg repeated. "Earthers eat *tut.*"

"Okay." His expression could best be described as unenthusiastic.

Meg whispered to Cho. "I think maybe this grosses him out."

"Have you heard the sounds they make when they eat that gravel bread?" Cho asked. "Let's just say this makes us even."

And so the cartons of *mogi* were stripped of their *tut* and the Earthers finally had a Dideto source of food. The fact that the scientists and engineers and archivists and generals turned away whenever the white pulp emerged from the brown husks didn't deter the crew from enjoying the new foodstuff. Of all the things the two civilizations were anxious to share with each other, it became clear rather quickly that mealtime was not one of them.

NINE

LOUL

Loul used to think it would have been cool to be a news reporter. He used to think they dashed into dangerous situations, uncovered deeply hidden secrets, and were obsessed with reporting life-shattering news to the masses. Then he had to deal with them. Sure, he had missed the first ripple of shock around the world as news of the Urfers broke, watching the press conference on the portable screens in the barrier area without really paying attention. Instead, he'd paid attention to the way Meg and her team watched it. He wondered if they pitied the Dideto for the dull, grainy pictures.

The press blew the story up in every way possible and yet, from what he had seen, they never really touched upon the truly amazing reality that there were aliens sitting, breathing, talking, and walking around on Didet. The news crews speculated on the presence of a mother ship in the sky and the probability of invasion, using clips of the latest blockbuster films to animate their theories. The generals made quick work of nipping those stories in the bud, assuring the world media that there was no invasion imminent. They played their roles convincingly, especially since they hammered at Loul incessantly to find out if indeed there were more Urfers coming. Loul had tried to ask, but either Meg didn't understand the question or she didn't want to answer.

He surprised himself at how little he cared about the answer. All those years he and Po and Hark had talked about alien invasions; all the time he had spent calculating the eventualities of such an event for his telemetry report; all the unimaginable possibilities and questions their presence raised—but all he could really think about was what made Meg laugh. He'd put together the high breathy sounds as laughter. He wanted to know what she thought of Didet and of him and why she had traveled so far from her home and what it was like. Dangers and threats and warnings just sort of evaporated every time he sat down with her over her screen.

And what did the media worry about? The fact that Urfers ate *tut*. The media went insane over the information. Some sides proclaimed the aliens as the solution to the world's garbage problem, *tut* heaps being a heated debate topic in urban management. Others declared this would upset the entire farming ecosystem, since the Briggen livestock subsisted mainly on discarded *tut*. Dire predictions were made of future famines, vying with rhapsodic visions of utopia, all because five rather tall beings ate a dozen or so *tut* every round. Loul decided to stop watching the news.

But the news crews were far from done with the Urfers. The generals had assembled a media handling team consisting mostly of those science members who had spent their time pontificating to anyone behind the barrier who would listen. Loul recognized several of the faces from their appearances on news shows and press conferences over the years. He had yet to see any of them making one-on-one contact with the Urfers so far. Instead, the barrier zone broke into three distinct groups. There were the contact teams—he and the Effans, the mechanics and engineers, a dozen or so geoscientists, and a handful of roving archivists who hovered around the edges recording unobtrusively. These were the groups who made the majority of contact with the Urfers, who worked up close with them, struggling through language and technology barriers.

Behind this group, the bulk of the barrier zone was filled with the clerks, soldiers, and science teams processing the enormous amounts of information being relayed back to them. Dozens of teams worked nonstop coordinating information, bringing in supplies, and making plan after failed plan to move the Urfers to another location. And finally, on the outer ring of the barrier, were the faces of the event, the talking heads of the Cartar Administration, the polished professionals who picked through the mountains of information and selected the most appropriate and manageable factoids to deliver to the media.

Every now and again Loul would get an urgent missive from the outer ring needing clarification on some point or another. He usually dismissed them with a perfunctory answer, knowing they would spin it how they liked it, regardless of the facts. When the missive came in carried by none other than Ba Mo and Addo Lat, the two most famous spokespeople for the Cartar Administration, Loul paid attention. The team, popularly referred to as "Baddo" for their uncanny ability to finish each other's sentences and seemingly read each other's minds, swooped into the inner ring of the barrier accompanied by a security team and a camera team. Loul noticed these cameras weren't the run-of-the-mill archiving kind. These were the eyes of big media, and they were trained on Baddo.

Meg looked up with interest at the well-dressed man and woman as they approached the booth amid their entourage. Loul knew she had seen nothing of Cartar fashions except the work clothes everyone wore inside the barrier, and he wondered what she thought of the dark, rough overshirts both reporters wore. All Loul could think was how expensive they looked.

"The Red Sun agrees with you, Mr. Pell." Ba Mo's smile perfectly matched her overblown greeting. Obviously the cameras were rolling.

"And you, Ba Mo." He saw Meg's fingers flashing over the light screen, capturing the exchange in her program. He smiled when he noticed how she kept her long fingers over the bulk of the screen, shielding it from the camera. "Is there something I can help you with?"

Addo Lat nudged a security guard at his side, and two men rushed off to grab another booth, dragging it over to where Loul and Meg sat. "We're hoping to share an up-close look at our guests with our audience. We understand that you, Mr. Loul Pell, are the first contact." He spoke smoothly, never missing a beat as the guards put the booth beside their own and he and Ba sat down with perfect synchronization.

Ba Mo laughed with that self-deprecating squint that had made her famous. "You may not know this, Loul—may I call you Loul?—but I was a language major back at West Face College. Go Ellers!" She winked into the camera, knocking her knuckles together. The camera panned back, moving behind Loul, but Meg's attention was over her right shoulder. She stared at the back of the booth as if she could see through it, her eyes tracking something Loul couldn't see. She leaned away from the reporter, putting her weight on her thin arm, and craned her long neck toward the far edge of the seat. Just a moment later, another cameraman slowly slid into sight, obviously trying to be stealthy. He jumped back, dropping his camera when he saw how close Meg had come. In his earpiece, Loul could hear Meg laugh.

"Cut." Addo's voice dropped its buoyant charm. With the cameras off, Baddo became a serious pair of unsmiling professionals. Professional what, Loul couldn't be sure, but the high-spirited bantering disappeared. "How did it know our guy was coming up behind it?"

Loul shrugged. "First of all, it is a she. This is Meg. Meg, this is Ba Mo and Addo Lat." Meg bobbed her head, her smile not showing her teeth. "And I don't know how she knew he was sneaking around behind her but she knew it. They have very keen senses and we're not sure we even know what all of them are. But we do know that you can't sneak up on them."

"We weren't sneaking up on them," Ba said with a sharp rap on the table. "We were hoping to get a candid shot, one that wasn't prepared and staged."

Loul couldn't help but snort at that. "It's pretty candid in here. We don't have the time or language for staging things."

Addo eyed the light screen hovering over the table. "You have the technology, though. What can you tell me about that?"

"Not much," Loul said. "It's a language program of some kind. She records what we say and somehow sorts it out to translate. That's what we've been doing, finding common ground in the languages so we can communicate."

"And it's working?"

"Obviously." Loul waved his hands at the teams working around the field. "The engineers have been going nuts over whatever compound that ship is made of and the bio teams have already gotten full-body scans, blood tests, and neurological readings."

Addo Lat, who sat on the same side of the tables as Meg with the booth's dividing wall separating them, leaned forward and smiled a toothy smile at the Urfer. Keeping all his teeth in sight, he spoke loudly and slowly. "Can you show me how to work your screen?"

If Loul hadn't spent so much time with Meg and hadn't been wearing the earpiece, he probably would have missed the fluttering of her stomach and throat muscles and missed the breathy sound of her muffled laughter. Instead, she turned to Loul, knowing he had heard her, and flickered her eyes toward the screen. Her expression stayed still as her finger trailed down along a notched symbol on the edge of the light. He barely saw her lips move but heard her voice soft in his ear.

"Loul hear Meg?"

His eyes widened. She must have turned the volume of her speakers down because he only heard her in his earpiece. Trying to make it look casual, he brushed his finger over *yes*.

"This—this okay?" She didn't move her head, but her wide eyes darted to the two reporters. "Loul is okay?"

How could he answer that? They hadn't yet come across the words for *trust* and *mistrust*. He didn't think Baddo were a danger in any real sense. He didn't need to describe them as bad but he couldn't comfortably tell Meg their presence was good either. The fact that she had arranged to ask this question in private told him she probably sensed something like this.

MEG

Meg didn't know who these two were, but their entourage, their big smiles, and their ugly black shawl shirts weren't doing much to win her over. More than that, the sharpening of the pitch of Loul's thrum alerted her more than any warning could have. He didn't like these two and thus neither did she. Of course, she didn't have to answer to them, whereas they might be Loul's superior officers. She liked the way Loul didn't give away their private conversation. Unbridled openness was not necessarily a virtue on Didet, a quality she could work with.

She sat quietly as the three conversed, watching out of the corner of her eye as the ProLingLang program pieced together phrases. She only half-listened to the soft translations playing in her ear. Instead she focused on the throat sounds of the people around her, developing a keener ear for the varying pitches. Loul sounded agitated, even a touch angry, his pitch rising and hitching. The two in black, Ba and Addo by name although she didn't know which one was which, had an unnervingly similar pitch. If she closed her eyes, she would have been hard-pressed to identify them as two people. The undertones beneath their voices rolled in a low wave that felt almost hypnotic. Around them, the security forces and camera people made what she would describe as a skittering tone. That's all she could think, that their throats worked in an almost sympathetic reaction to the conflict unfolding before them.

When she heard the growling sound coming from behind her booth, she knew someone was trying to sneak up on her. Something about the low pitch, to say nothing of the low and slow approach, compelled her to catch whoever was doing the sneaking. So far in the landing field, all approaches and contacts had been up-front, face-to-face, with plenty of visual cues and approach warnings. It only took a few times of watching an engineer throw a wrench or hearing the Effans scream to learn that the Dideto did not have a strong sense of hearing. They were easy to sneak up on, and, knowing that, the Earthers had adjusted their behavior accordingly. This was not a place you wanted folks to be nervous.

That a Dideto thought he or she could sneak up on her? Well, that just lowered her already dropping opinion of the group that had insinuated itself into her and Loul's discussion. She reminded herself that as a protocol liaison, she was supposed to remain as neutral as possible, but that hitching from Loul's throat felt like fingers jabbing her ribs, shortening her temper. When the man beside her (Ba? Addo?) yelled at her with that big fake smile, it was all she could do to not roll her eyes.

In truth, all she should do was let Loul handle it. She didn't know the power structure of the assembly amassed before them. She didn't know the fallout of defying authority, and she knew they had to be prepared to comply with Dideto policy—to a point. When Loul slammed his hands down on the table, Meg began to pay more attention to the translations whispering in her ear. She heard a lot of "no" from Loul and "yes" from the woman and a general tone of condescension from the man. Whatever they were saying, it was irritating Loul. When the man gestured over the barricade and she heard the word *move* she spoke up.

"No."

The newcomers and their entourage jumped at the sound of the voice magnified through the speakers. It was the first time any of them had been face-to-face with the Earthers, having only heard their voices on the news clips.

"Earthers no move."

The woman gave a squinty-eyed smile that looked like it should be accompanied by a hiss and started talking loudly and quickly. Loul held up his hand, making a downward motion, hopefully telling them they didn't need to shout.

"Earthers no move." The woman leaned forward unnecessarily to shout into the microphone on the table. "Earthers move..." A few words were lost in translation, then, "...little less talk... move...yes camera...Dideto. Yes?"

Loul barked out a few hard words and turned fully toward Meg. He made the settling stance and she wondered if he was fighting back the urge to make an obscene gesture. She wished he wouldn't fight it. Call her an adolescent, but she was dying to know what passed for profanity in this language. If he had the urge, he resisted it because she could see his knuckles hovering over the table the way they did when he was getting ready to approach a new concept.

"Meg move." He lifted his fists quickly before she could protest to let her know he wasn't finished. "Earthers no move. Meg no move…all. Meg move…a little."

He clasped his fists together on the table, making sure she watched. "Earthers no move." He separated his hands a bit, as if he were holding a small bowl. "Meg move a little." Hands farther apart, holding a larger bowl. "Meg move Earthers." Hands even wider. "Earthers no move. Yes?"

She buried her chin in her hands, staring down at the table as if the explanation would suddenly materialize between his spread hands. She nodded, their sign to repeat the sequence, and he did. Ba and Addo started to shout over him but he shushed them.

The widening circle of his hands niggled at her mind. If she could understand the gesture, she could untangle the strange phrases. He said the Earthers wouldn't be moving but he moved his hand outward when he did. Meg would move and move the Earthers and not move? All the while his hands spread farther and farther apart, creating a widening ring. Did he mean he wanted her to change her mind? Like the center of the ring was her original idea but he would broaden the idea and make her see it differently? Kind of a complicated thought process but not impossible. She let her own hands act out the sequence on the table, Loul watching her, willing her to understand. It was harder to think with that low, rolling thrum coming from the two newcomers, to say nothing of the high, jittery twinges from their entourage.

Her hand slid across the table and she felt something wet clinging to her hand. Pulling up she saw a strand of *mogi* fiber clinging to the underside of her pinkie. She peeled the wet string off, preparing to flick it away, and thought about the *mogi*, the way it unwrapped. She could see Loul's thick fingers peeling back the dried husks to get to the fresh green leaves within. Several of the foods she'd seen him eat were handled that way, the old on the outside, the new within.

Time. She didn't know how she knew it, but she knew it, and she knew Loul could see it in her face. He wasn't telling her options; he was telling her a sequence. First, in the middle, the Earthers didn't move. Then Meg would move. Then Meg would move the Earthers, and then the Earthers didn't move again? She knew she was right up on it but couldn't quite grab it.

"Meg move Earthers?"

"Meg move a little." He widened his hands. "Meg move... Earthers."

She heard his teeth grind in frustration, trying to find the words. When the woman beside him interrupted, Loul did shout, slamming his fists on either side of the light screen, making the woman squeak, the man jump, and the soldiers shift their batons. One of the cameras purred.

Meg gave Loul a chance to compose himself, keeping her eyes on him and ignoring the staring duo on one side of her and the encroaching camera on the other. This was between her and Loul and she made sure every inch of her body language said so. Loul stared into her eyes and she heard the pitch of his throat hum level out. They sat that way for several minutes, just looking at each other. Meg had to fight back a smile. The low, rolling hum of the two newcomers grew higher, less in sync with each other the longer she and Loul kept up their silent bond. Whoever they were, Ba and Addo did not like being left out.

Finally the woman couldn't sit still any longer. She reached into her pocket and slammed down a handful of small, thick, round discs. She and her partner talked in tandem to Loul, sliding the discs around on the tabletop until a cluster of five sat in the center. She swept the other discs off the table and back into her pocket, then jabbed at the air over the screen saying "yes." Loul reached for the discs but she pushed his hand away, her voice getting sharper until Loul surrendered. The woman looked up at Meg and smiled that very big smile again.

"Meg!" Her voice boomed out so loudly Meg couldn't help but flinch.

"No." Meg held her hand over the microphone, then put them over her own ears. Whatever this woman had to say, she was going to have to learn to say it more quietly. Loul spoke up again, again making the down gesture with his hands. Just as the woman took a breath to start again, Loul cut her off with another short comment and the too-broad smile disappeared. Meg could see what looked a lot like a smirk on Loul's face as he sat back.

"Meg." She started again, her voice softer, her face in a more natural expression. "Ba."

"Ba. Yes." Now at least she knew which one was which.

She spoke some more, the translation program humming into action trying to capture her words, and once more Loul spoke in low tones to her. Now Ba's teeth ground in frustration as she struggled to figure out this broken way of speech. She pointed to the five discs.

"Earthers." She waved her hand over the discs. "Earthers."

A quick glance at a silent Loul and Meg shrugged. "Okay."

Ba pulled one disc away. "Meg."

"Okay. Yes." Meg tapped the disc. "Meg."

"Earthers no move. Meg move." Ba slid the disc a few inches away. "Meg move little. Talk cameras. Meg move Earthers." She slid the lone disc back to the cluster.

"Oh." Meg could have smacked her head against the table. It was so simple and yet she and Loul had become so accustomed to talking things out, going on their guts and sheer will, that it hadn't even occurred to her to make a simple visual association. They wanted to her to go talk to the press and then she would return to the camp. Duh.

She reached out and grabbed the disc, speaking directly to Loul. "Meg moves *away to* talk to cameras *and then* Meg moves *back to* Earthers. Earthers no move. Talk this." She needed Loul to say this in Dideto so the translation program could fill in the vocabulary gaps. It seemed like it was always the little words that hung up translations—pronouns and conjunctions that seemed so small and yet did so much heavy lifting in conversation. Loul spoke, and the program lit up and repeated his words back to him. He tapped his knuckles together.

"Yes."

"Yes." Meg wanted to smile at the breakthrough, but she hated that it had come from Ba and not from her or Loul. Especially since the solution to the misunderstanding was so simple.

"Yes." Ba and Addo spoke together too loudly, their teeth showing brown and thick. "Meg move...talk cameras." They rose in perfect unison, gesturing for her follow them.

"Okay," Meg said rising. "Meg Loul talk cameras."

"No." Loul didn't move and Meg sat back down. "Meg Baddo talk cameras."

"No. Meg Loul."

"No." Addo's tone was sharp. "Baddo. Baddo. No Loul."

Loul wouldn't look up at her, so Meg dropped down beneath the table, scrabbled around in the dirt, and sat back up with a rock that she held up before her. "Loul." He dipped his chin, not understanding what she meant. She pointed to the discs. "Earthers." Then held up the rock. "Loul." He huffed a sound that told her he was following her now. She set the rock next to the discs and pulled one disc away. "Meg move and then move back. Loul no move."

"No." He looked down at the table. "Loul move. Baddo no move."

Baddo and their entourage started chattering again and Meg ignored them. Instead she jabbed the question mark repeatedly. Ba's hand clamped down hard on Loul's shoulder and he spoke in low tones to her, obviously explaining the confusion. Addo smiled at Meg, holding his hands over the discs. "Baddo no move. Loul move." He took the rock from her and threw it over the back of the booth. "Baddo Meg. Baddo Earthers."

Meg rose slowly from her seat, leaning across the table to come very close to Addo's wide, hairy face. She leaned over far enough that she could smell his breath. His smile stayed very wide but his eyes twitched as she drew close. When she could hear the hitch in his hum, she spoke loudly enough for him to hear.

"Bite me."

She knew he couldn't understand her. At least he couldn't understand the words, but she thought his instincts would have to be pretty dull to not glean her meaning. He ground his teeth.

"Meg talk cameras. Loul move."

"No." Meg felt a stream of profanity ready to leave her mouth when she heard Prader shouting those very words to the far left of the field. The team of engineers she'd been working with at one of the ship's landing legs crouched and shifted as another dark-clad team pushed its way through. It seemed Loul wasn't the only one being replaced.

"What the hell is this?" Prader waved a wrench at a thick Dideto woman who was unlatching a metal box in the middle of Prader's work area. "Get out of here."

Meg switched on her coms. "Are they pushing your team out?"

Jefferson switched his com on midargument. "—isn't going to work. Put it down. Meg! How do I say put it down?"

All around the field, the number of work teams had more than doubled, the usual Dideto personnel being pushed aside by well-orchestrated teams in heavier, darker work clothes. She heard Cho protesting over the rising tones of the Effans as another bulkier testing lab was rolled into his area. Wagner rose from the table where he had been working with a computer team, closing his light screen when the dark-clad group crowded in.

"Good idea," Meg spoke low in the coms. "Everyone, screens closed. Shut them down." A grumble of surprise and protest rose from the work site as all five light screens disappeared. "Tools down. Stand up and back away." She moved her mouth as little as possible, knowing the only Dideto that could hear her was Loul with his earpiece. To the rest of the group assembled, especially the newcomers, the sudden synchronicity would be unnerving.

Baddo and crew barked rough words at Loul, at each other, and at the crews on-site. The original teams stood around uncertain, clearly getting orders to move and yet sensing tension. Meg activated the audio command for the translator.

"Loul need/want move?" *Need/want* had been an important breakthrough concept, especially when the discussion of food and water had arisen. "Loul," she jabbed her finger at him where he sat sunk low in his seat. "No Ba, no Addo, Loul need/want move?" Ba and Addo, Baddo presumably, shouted loud and convoluted phrases the translator caught, picking out "yes" and "need/want," but Meg didn't care what Baddo needed or wanted. She leaned in close to his face and whispered, "No Baddo. Loul. Loul need/want move?"

Loul's voice was gravelly and low. "No. Baddo need/want Loul move."

She leaned down farther so he had to look in her eyes. "Fuck Baddo." The word itself didn't translate but the meaning certainly did. Loul sighed and Meg straightened up, turning off the translator com, leaving only the crew coms active. "Everyone, on three, step away from your work site and meet in the middle at the captain's shelter. Small, slow, controlled movements. You know the drill. One, two, three."

Meg stepped out of the confines of the booth, not deigning to look left or right, and moved with small, precise steps toward the center of the field. One of Baddo's security guards made a move to step in front of her but she froze him with an imperious glare. Eyes front once more, she made her way to join her crew, who matched her calm, steady strides.

Wagner put his hands on his hips, a furrow of frustration between his brows. "Anyone want to guess what the hell is going on here?"

"They want me to talk to the press."

"And so what?" Jefferson rolled a sample case around in his palm. "You talk to the news and the goon squad rolls in? Who are these people?"

"Maybe whoever is in charge wants their team in place when the cameras are rolling. Maybe they've just decided to replace our crews." Meg struggled to keep her hands from flailing. She knew all eyes were on the five of them, and she wanted to create the illusion of calm. That grew harder and harder as she thought of Loul being forced out. "I don't know about you guys. Maybe you want new teams. Maybe it's the-more-the-merrier, but I for one do not want Loul replaced, especially with the gravel-tooth duo they're throwing at me. And Loul doesn't want to go either."

Wagner sighed, shaking his head. "Do we have a choice? Could this be some sort of conscription thing? Their work laws? Maybe they're legally only allowed to work so many days without a break."

"Come on," Jefferson said, "they don't sleep. Have you gotten the impression from anyone you've been working with that they want a break? They practically fall apart every time we have to stop to sleep."

"So what do we do?" Cho asked, looking around the group.

"I'll tell you what we do," Jefferson said with a grin. "My daddy was a titanium miner on Galen and I was a pro football player. Trust me when I say I know the power of a strike."

Prader's eyes grew wide. "You mean just stop working? Stop everything?"

"I'm with Jefferson," Meg said. "We stop interacting in every way until we're sure our work crews are allowed to stay."

"Do we really want to create an incident?" Wagner asked.

"It's more than just personal preferences," Cho said, although Meg knew how fond of the Effans he'd become. "Meg's been breaking her back building the language, but each one of us has made our own sort of, I don't know, pidgin language with our crews, haven't we? Haven't we all found a rhythm, even without words, to make ourselves understood? We get all new teams and we're right back to square one. We're right back to making the same mistakes and committing the same offenses as we did in the beginning. Oh, and for the record," he shrugged, shoving his hands deep in his pockets, "you know that dark spot of skin underneath their jaws? Where the sound comes from? Don't touch that. It's sort of the equivalent of sliding your hand between their legs. Found that out the hard way."

Prader laughed. "That would explain why Kik/Kek, whatever his name is, has become so fond of me." She kicked at the dirt with her toe. "He drives me crazy. He's stripped five valves in two days and he's like a wrecking ball, but he's my wrecking ball, you know?"

They looked from one to the other, each shrugging and nodding. Meg knew then she wasn't alone in the bond she'd formed with Loul. This far from home, this much pressure on a mission, this type of isolation couldn't help but make each of them struggle to reach out. Even a grinder like Prader who claimed to be so callous had clearly been affected by her team. After several minutes of silence, the captain nodded.

"It's decided, then. We keep our original crews or we shut them out. If we have to, we leave. There's no avoiding the fact that if we cave on this, if we start giving ground to their authority, we're going to lose our control over the camp, our safety, and our privacy. Meg, any ideas how to handle this?"

"I do, sir. I get the feeling the two at my booth are kind of important." She tipped her head toward Baddo. "They have the biggest entourage. Let's move as a group toward them." They turned on her cue and walked slowly toward the pair of booths where Baddo, Loul, and the crew stood waiting. Loul pressed his fists into the front of his hips, a sign Meg recognized as anxiety. Ba and Addo straightened up as the Earthers approached, smiles wide, their thrums rolling low and in sync.

The Earthers stopped in a straight line three feet from the crew. The cameras purred, catching the encounter from several angles, and Baddo stepped forward together, Addo holding out his hand to block Loul from stepping forward as well. Meg took a deep breath to control her temper before taking another step out in front of the Earthers.

She pointed at Addo, looking at the Earthers. "Addo." She spoke loudly so the Dideto could hear her. Her four crewmates repeated the word, nodding at the man. Then she pointed at the woman. "Ba." Again, they repeated the name and the Dideto duo smiled large.

Then Meg turned to Addo and tapped her own chest. "Meg."

"Yes," Addo shouted through a smile aimed at the cameras.

Then she pointed at Cho and said nothing. Addo blinked at her, not understanding. She tapped Cho's chest and tilted her head. She tapped her own chest. "Meg." Then tapped Cho.

Addo looked to his partner first and then to Loul. Neither said anything. Meg moved down to Wagner, tapping his chest and arching an eyebrow at Addo. When still nothing came, she moved to Jefferson and then Prader, all to silence. "No?" She asked Addo.

She turned to Ba, whose smile dimmed. Meg got the feeling Ba was the smarter of the duo. Meg started from the top, pointing as she went. "Addo. Ba. Meg." When she pointed to Cho, she tipped her head and waited. Ba's hum hitched as she barked out what sounded like a command to Loul, who remained silent. One after another, she pointed to the Earthers, who stood as still as stones, waiting to hear their names.

"No?" Meg asked again. She made a little huff of disapproval and walked slowly until she stood directly in front of Loul. She had to struggle not to grin as he raised his eyes to her.

"Loul," she said, loving the way the flush rose around the edges of his face. She repeated the list of names. But this time, when she pointed to Cho, she didn't have to wait.

"Cho," Loul said, his voice steady as she moved on. "Agnar, Cheffson, Prader."

Meg turned toward her fellow Earthers, who made a point of glancing up and down the line at each other. After a moment, Wagner shrugged. "Close enough."

"Indeed." Meg smiled and turned back to the Dideto. "Loul no move." When Ba and Addo started shouting protests, she held up her hand directly in Addo's face, silencing them both. "Baddo move. Meg Loul talk. Loul no move."

She stepped back in line with the Earthers. "Loul no move."

Cho spoke next. "Effan Effan no move."

Wagner: "Olum no move."

Jefferson: "Ben Na no move."

Prader: "Kik no move."

Nobody moved. Meg could hear teeth grinding and pitches rising and falling as the simple statements sank in. Addo broke the silence, stomping up to Meg and letting loose a torrent of words loudly enough to blow the hair away from her face. Meg didn't flinch. She let him talk and yell, never looking away from his eyes. When he finished, she said simply, "No."

On her whispered cue, the five Earthers turned on their heels and, as one, sank cross-legged to the ground, their backs to the stunned Dideto.

TEN

LOUL

"You want to tell us what the hell is going on here, Pell?" Ba squeezed his arm, her breath unpleasantly sweet as it blew across his face. She was the first to break the long, stunned silence after the Urfers' remarkable standoff. Nobody moved; even the camera operators froze when the five aliens turned and folded down onto their legs in that bizarre way of theirs. Of course, to the contact crews, the teams who had been working face-to-face with the Urfers since their landing, the flexibility and agility weren't so shocking anymore. And once he'd been fitted for the earpiece, Loul now understood how they pulled off that eerie synchronized movement. But even with that, the effect of the movement and the sight of those slender backs sitting perfectly still amazed him. He could only imagine the effect it had on the newcomers.

True to what he'd learned of the reporters, however, Baddo reacted with a distinct lack of wonder and huge dose of umbrage. It didn't seem to matter that a team of space-traveling aliens had confronted them; all that seemed to matter was that someone had dared to defy them, block them, and turn them away. And that those someones had chosen lower-level work crews over the vaunted presence of the world-famous Baddo, well, that was beyond science fiction, wasn't it?

"I don't know what to tell you, Ba," Loul shrugged, keeping his voice low in the habit he'd assumed since working with Meg. He didn't really need to. With their backs to the crowd, he knew the sound wouldn't be as loud to the Urfers. But he sort of hoped the altered tone would remind Baddo that he was the one who knew how to talk with the aliens. He was the one who knew how to express and explain concepts to them, and, most importantly, he was the one Meg had insisted on working with.

Meg had more than insisted. The look on her face and the way her voice had dropped into a low, hard tone sent a thrill through Loul he could barely contain. These Urfers seemed so frail in so many ways, their limbs fragile and their voices high and breathy, but when she'd leaned into Addo and held that bony palm in his face, there had been no mistaking the power radiating from her. It was almost ferocity. And after the weeks roaming freely though the work field, Loul had gotten used to the loose expressiveness of the Urfers, their reedlike body movements and wide liquid eyes. To see them lock up like they had and stand as one rigid, unmovable force before Baddo and the administration's work teams, that they had come together like that because of the lower-ranking work crews, Loul really wasn't lying to Ba. He didn't have the words.

"You tell them to stop doing…that." She waved a thick hand at the backs of the Urfers. Loul saw the black bands tattooed on her fingers, another pretentious status symbol, like the black overshirts. "You tell them they're not running this show and if we want them to move or stay or serve us up a *mogi-ketcha* pizza, they're going to get their bony legs moving, do you hear me?" She grabbed his arm tighter. "You tell them that."

Loul looked her in the eye. "You tell them."

And so after much posturing and bluffing and rationalizing the standoff as a win-win for everyone (Loul still couldn't follow that logic, but that was hardly the issue); the original work crews were allowed to remain on-site. It had taken almost a full shift to come to the final terms, throughout which the Urfers remained perfectly still. Loul could see sweat trickling down the sides of their faces and he knew they had to be wanting water, but when he stepped into Meg's line of sight, she had only looked at him and smiled. Note for the archives, Loul thought: the Urfers were stubborn.

The work crews had assembled around the argument site. The generals had stepped in, insisting that the original crews and the official black-clad crews stand on opposite sides of the Urfers. Not surprising, the original crews chose to stand in front of the unmoving Urfers, crouching low and probably sharing similar glances with their respective Urfer. The final arrangement declared that the original crews would continue to perform the bulk of the duties and the official crews would "stand by and oversee in an official capacity." A badly hidden ripple of laughter had moved through the crews at that piece of bureaucratic candy-speak. General Ada clapped his hand on Loul's shoulder and told him to break the news to the Urfers.

Crouching in front of Meg, Loul knocked his knuckles together, resisting the urge to grin. "Loul no move." Down the line, the crews responded in kind, each Urfer face loosening into a smile. When each team had reported their status, Loul leaned in closer. "Okay?"

Meg's little pink tongue slipped across her lips. "Okay." With muffled sounds of discomfort the Urfers rose to their feet, unfolding their legs and twisting their backs. Long fingers brushed dirt off of flat backsides, and slender shoulder carriages rose and fell as they swung their arms back and forth. They did all of this with their backs still to the official crews, who couldn't see the wide smiles each Urfer shared with their Dideto crew.

The stiffness of the long standoff worked out of their muscles, Meg slammed her flat palms together, making that sharp snapping sound that always startled Loul when she did it.

"Okay, Loul." She bobbed her head and turned to face the generals, Baddo, and the cameras. "Meg Loul move. Talk cameras. Loul? Effan Effan Cho talk camera?"

It shouldn't have surprised him but Meg and Cho seemed the most relaxed at the press conference. They probably didn't know that over a billion people were watching them all over the planet, their every utterance being translated into dozens of languages. Or maybe they did and that fact paled in comparison to the fact that they'd flown billions of miles through space in a spaceship. All things considered, that fact made a press conference a pretty small affair. Only Loul hadn't flown anywhere. Sure, he'd bonded with an alien and stood up to the Cartar Administration, but the crowd, the purr of the cameras, and the mountain of microphones pointed at him conspired to entirely unnerve him as the five of them took their places at the press table.

A special platform had been constructed at the edge of the barrier zone, a long deep awning set up with industrial filters to correct the shifting colors of sunlight for maximum clarity. The microphones clung to the edge of the long table, and Loul noticed that at the front of the table, where an official banner would usually hang, the area was open. The press wanted to see as much of the Urfers as they could, including the way their long legs had to bend and fold to get comfortable on the portable chairs. Meg and Cho seemed perfectly at ease as the event started, looking calmly into the cameras that passed before them, even laughing under their breath as Baddo took center stage and held forth at some length. He didn't know how much they could understand of their speech, but he thought they could read their self-aggrandizing posture. Everyone once in a while Meg would shift in her seat, her thin elbow brushing against his arm.

He pretty much relied on those touches to keep himself from bolting off the platform. This wasn't just some local news story on a turbine failure or missing livestock. This was the world media—the entire world. Every single person who had access to television was probably watching this live wherever they were. He tried to tell himself that all eyes would be on Meg and Cho. His certainly were, but when she turned to smile at him, her eyes crinkling around the edges, he realized that at that particular moment, all eyes were on him, including the dozens of cameras pointed his way. Baddo had just introduced him and now they expected him to speak.

"Mr. Pell?" Ba and Addo smiled at him and he couldn't be sure who spoke. Then he heard Meg's voice soft in his earpiece.

"Loul is okay." And he felt the tension drain from his neck.

"Hello, everyone." The technicians had told him not to lean too far forward into the microphones, an unnecessary warning since he felt like he was going to fall backward in his chair trying to escape their puffy points. "Thank you for being here today. Um, my name is Loul Pell and…and"—Meg's elbow brushed against him and he took a deep breath—"I'd like to introduce you to my friends Meg and Cho."

Meg smiled at him, those glassy white teeth picking up the light to maximum effect. He wondered what they must look like on the television screens, if people could see just how fragile they looked up close. The Urfers gave the cameras plenty of opportunity to capture the image, turning to face the crowd with the same broad smiles.

"I don't know how much exactly you've been told," Loul said, feeling less nervous seeing Meg so relaxed in the focus of attention. "I assume you've seen pictures of their planet, Urf, and seen at least some of the footage the archivists have taken. To be honest, I'm not really sure what I'm doing up here." Warm laughter rippled through the crowd. These were seasoned media pros who were all too familiar with official runaround and media speak. They must have been waiting for dozens of shifts, if not several rounds, for this press conference and probably sympathized.

"Can we get a close-up?" an older man with a shield of press badges shouted.

"I assume you mean of them. I'm not that photogenic." More laughter and he found himself smiling along with Meg.

"How are you communicating?" a woman he couldn't see shouted. "We were told they don't speak our language and that this is the one with the tool that's supposed to learn it. They said it has some kind of light screen?"

Loul leaned his forearms on the table. "First of all, Meg is a she. Cho is a he. Neither is an it." He wondered just how little information had been shared and how much of that small amount was accurate. This press conference could deeply affect the world's view of these visitors. He shuddered to think how much damage Baddo could have done already.

Effan Two, who was seated at the far end of the table next to her work partner, leaned in close enough to the microphone to make it hum. Effan One pulled her back as she spoke. "Our biology scans have already determined that genetically we and the Urfers are more similar than different. They are gender specific, male and female, mammalian, of a primate species."

Effan One picked up her spiel. "Of course, there are distinctive differences and we're still running a number of tests to determine nutritional requirements, evolutionary developments, neurological variances. Our work is just beginning."

"But how do you communicate?" the reporter asked again. "We've gotten the bulletins and the data reports. We know at least some of what you're learning but we don't know how. If they don't speak Cartar and you don't speak...whatever it is they speak, how are you learning this?"

Loul cleared his throat. "That is what Meg and I have been doing. That seems to be her specialty. She has a translation program. We work together, trying to express ideas and words and concepts, and when we realize we're talking about the same thing, she puts it in the program and we're able to talk." Trying to explain this made Loul realize just how little he understood the process.

"Why you?" someone else shouted.

"Excuse me?"

"Why you?" The crowd peppered him with questions. "Why is she working with you? Aren't you in telemetry? Why isn't she working with one of the administration's interpreters? Can she understand what we're saying?"

Meg squeezed his arm and looked at him, her smile gone. "Loul is okay?" she asked quietly enough to be heard only in the earpiece. Questions kept raining down on him from the reporters assembled, but Loul held up his fist to block them. "Screen okay?"

"Yes," he said softly. Then he turned back to the crowd. "Give me just a second. I'll show you the program we're talking about." He bumped his knuckles as Meg pulled the light screen from her wristband, tilting it up so it stood like a translucent shield between them and the press. The crowd surged, trying to get a better look at the wondrous sight, and Meg ducked her head closer to his.

"Loul is okay? Camera talk is okay? What is this talk?" She pointed to the question mark, letting the cameras capture the image lighting up. Loul could see that Cho had opened his screen for the Effans, keeping it flat against the table and thus out of sight of the reporters. Meg had fitted the Effans with earpieces as well, and he could see the flashes of surprise on their faces every time Cho or Meg whispered.

"Camera talk is…" He struggled to find a way to explain it. There hadn't been time to teach the word *reporters*. For Meg and Cho, the men and women who held the cameras were the cameras. Meg must have picked up on the aggressive tone of the questions. It never failed to amaze him how tuned in she was to temperaments and intentions. "Cameras ask why Loul talk Meg."

"Why?" Meg tilted her head. "Meg Loul talk. Need/want talk."

"Yes." Loul touched the space between the *yes* and *no* buttons, a gesture they'd both come to understand as a kind of *maybe* or *but*, a gesture of indecision or lack of clarity. "Cameras ask why Loul. Cameras no ask why Meg. Ask why Loul."

Meg's face made a strange change, one of the fine lines of hair over her wide eyes lifting in a way he hadn't seen before. He could hear Cho laugh a short laugh, and the two Urfers conferred in tones soft enough he couldn't make out the words even with the earpiece. When she looked back at him, her expression was very similar to that she had worn after facing down Baddo. Before he could say anything, a reporter banged on his chair for attention.

"Is it saying something? Can we hear it?"

"She!" The Effans yelled in unison.

Loul smiled, happy that distinction irritated the Effans as much as him. It was crucial that the world understand these were people just like them. Okay, maybe not just like them. They were taller and thinner and paler and had odd smooth skin and weirdly long fingers and arms and legs and necks and really wide, wet eyes and glass-like teeth, but he and the Effans had to prove that the more time they spent with these aliens, the less alien they became.

"Can she talk? Is that a she beside her? Can either of them talk to us?"

"Meg talk?" She still spoke only for the earpiece. "Meg talk cameras?"

Loul grinned at her. "Okay." He saw her finger slide up the screen, activating the volume on her speaker patch. He addressed the reporters. "Meg is going to speak, using the program. You're probably going to hear mostly my voice since I'm the one she's been recording, but other words have been added from other members of the crew. It might sound weird at first, but trust me, you get used to it. Oh, and the concepts are still really rough so don't expect complete sentences or anything."

Loul wouldn't have thought it was possible for this many people to become this quiet but every person in the crowd grew still. Only the cameras purred as Meg sat up straighter.

"Hello. I am Meg. This is Cho." A ripple of excitement moved through the crowd followed quickly by shushing sounds. Cameras closed in, trying to capture the lack of synchronization between how her mouth moved and the sounds emanating from her patch. "Thank you, Didet, Urfers thank you. Urfers..." She paused, scanning the screen for the correct words. "Urfers like/ happy Didet."

A reporter stood to ask a question but Meg continued. "Cameras ask Loul why Meg talk Loul. Yes? This is question?"

Loul tapped his knuckles and explained to the crowd. "Cameras are you guys. She heard your question about why me. To tell the truth, I don't know what her answer is going to be." Another sympathetic wave of laughter poured out.

Meg laughed too, the microphones picking up the faintest sound of it, and Loul saw the crowd lean forward even more.

"Meg talk Loul because Loul talk Meg." She bit her lip, a sign that she was thinking. "Loul talk good/okay." Her finger hovered between the *yes* and *no* buttons. This wasn't exactly what she meant. "Loul talk Meg this is good/okay." She looked only at Loul, waving her hands out over the crowd. "Loul talk Didet is good/okay. Meg talk Loul. Urfers talk Dideto because Loul talk Didet is good/okay. Loul is Didet is good/okay."

Someone shouted for clarification but Loul ignored them, watching Meg's soft brown eyes staring at him, her smile not as wide but just for him.

"Mr. Pell, please!" Ba stomped on the stage, demanding his attention. "Can you interpret that? Does that even mean anything?"

"Yeah," Loul said, bumping his knuckles against the table softly, turning back to the crowd. "She said that she talked to me because I talked to her first. It was sort of an accident. I was just supposed to be holding a microphone for one of the archiving teams and I sort of forgot myself and stepped forward too far. I came right up on Meg and the cap of the microphone blew off and hit her." The crowd made a collective gasp. "I guess it could have been a disaster but instead she just handed me the cap back and smiled. And she touched me. That's what she means that I told her that we were okay. That she could talk to us, that they all could."

"How do you know that?" Addo asked, using his hard-hitting reporter voice. "I didn't hear any of that. How do we know that you're translating accurately?"

"Trust, I guess." He answered without thinking, putting his finger on the *record* button. "Loul trust Meg. Meg trust Loul." Meg's eyes widened at the new word, her fingers ghosting over the screen. The cameras zoomed in even tighter on the image. "Loul talk good/okay. Meg good/okay. This is trust. Trust."

Meg sped her fingers through a series of commands and then smiled at him. "Meg trust Loul. Yes."

"Loul trust Meg. Yes."

Effan Two spoke up. "The Urfers have been nothing but accommodating and open, making every move to bridge the gap between us. It may not seem like it from where you're sitting, but we have a different perspective, those of us who have been there since the first day they landed." She smiled a flat smile at Baddo.

Addo diverted the conversation back to the press. "We have a lot of questions to get through today. You there, in the red, what is your question?"

For the next half shift, Loul and the Effans answered whatever questions they could about the Urfers. The Effans did most of the talking, especially once someone raised the topic of the aliens' strange stasis patterns. He and the scientists occasionally shared loaded glances when it became apparent that the status reports fed to the media were not 100 percent accurate.

For example, the press kept referring to the Urfers' "research mission" as if it had already been determined as the purpose of their visit. The fact was nobody knew for certain exactly why the Urfers had arrived at all. While all the contact crews felt certain the purpose was benign, nobody knew if the aliens had plans to stay, what those plans might be, or if Didet served only as a stopping point on a longer journey. Olum, the programmer working with their leader, had said they were closing in on linking up the two different computer systems, hopefully unlocking the bewildering array of navigational data the leader had been trying to share. No matter how many different ways Loul tried to ask Meg direct questions about their mission or anything beyond general information of the five visitors, she didn't or wouldn't get the gist of the inquiry and answered off the point.

One of the reporters interrupted the Effans while they dis-cussed the Urfer blood clotting. "Are there more Urfers coming?"

Loul leaned forward to try to explain that they hadn't been able to get that concept across yet when he saw Baddo rise as one, their posture tense. A security guard stepped from the ranks, closer to the reporter. "I believe we have made the answer to that question very clear, sir. Please refer to the data printouts you've been given and keep your questions within the necessary guidelines."

"But how do we know they're telling the truth about being the only ones?" The reporter saw the security guard approaching but didn't back down. "Why would they come this far and send only five people? Doesn't it make more sense that there would be a mother ship or a fleet following them?" The guard grabbed him under the arm and rocked him off his feet. Two other guards stepped in to help but the man kept shouting, even as he was dragged out of the press area. "Don't believe the hype! Think for yourselves! The Searcher knows the truth!"

A ripple of disbelief and laughter rolled through the crowd. Whatever credibility the reporter might have had among his peers vanished when he revealed he worked with the cult quack The Searcher. Loul sat back quietly, trying to hide the twist of tension in his gut. As usual, Meg found him out, her eyes search-ing his as he stared out at the screaming man.

"Loul okay? This is okay?"

He looked at her, trying to see her with some detachment. She always tuned in so quickly to what he was feeling, when the mood of the room changed. She communicated so many com-plex ideas and concepts and picked up on so many questions and explanations he put forth. How was it she couldn't grasp the question of other Urfers arriving on Didet?

Baddo used the reporter's removal as a cue to wrap up the press conference. Meg and Cho rose and stood before the table, giving the reporters the opportunity to take close-up photos. Then the security detail moved in, blocking the steps off the platform from the press, allowing the Urfers, the Effans, and Loul to make their way through the barricade zone back to the landing site. He could hear Meg and Cho talking softly to each other, too softly to be picked up by the translation program. They walked together in that loose, limb-mingling way he'd seen them use before, their long arms and fingers brushing up against each other with no apparent intention other than the comfort of contact. Their conversation seemed light and casual, but when Loul stepped in closer, his shoulder brushing Meg's arm, they both fell silent.

Maybe he was being paranoid but something niggled at him. He kept seeing the impassioned face of The Searcher's reporter being dragged from the scene, and with that he couldn't help but think of his friend Po urgently insisting the administration hid the truth from the people. Someone had told the press that it was a fact no more Urfers were coming, something he knew they could not prove because if Meg couldn't answer the question he had no doubt the rest of the aliens couldn't. Or wouldn't.

"Meg." He stopped her as they reached the edge of the landing site, Cho and the Effans moving back to their lab layouts. The wind had picked up in their absence and all around the site people were hurrying to tie down tarps and cover tools. A bank of clouds rolled in, filtering the Red Sun to a dusky rose that brought out a pretty pink shine to Meg's face.

"Loul is not okay?" She tilted her head down at him, a line of skin folding along her usually smooth brow. "Cameras talk. Camera talk not okay. Loul is not okay. Why?"

He stopped her before she could pull the screen from her wrist. He wanted to look at her face, watch her eyes, as they talked. "Camera talk is not okay. The man, the Dideto who…" He gestured throwing something over his shoulder. Meg tapped her knuckles. She knew who he meant. "That camera asked a question Meg won't answer."

A powerful gust of wind blew sand and rocks through the air and Meg shut her eyes, twisting her face away from the blast. Loul simply squinted, the sand not bothering him as it seemed to bother her. She wiped dust from the side of her face and blinked back wetness from her eyes as she looked back at him. "Meg talk. Meg answer questions."

"Yes?" Loul tried to keep his hands from making fists, not wanting to seem threatening but not willing to be evaded again. "Meg talk to Loul. Answer this question. More Urfers?"

She tilted her head, that sign of confusion, but this time Loul had been watching carefully, differently. He noticed the smallest delay in her reaction. She waved her hands behind her toward the crew. "Urfers."

"No Meg. Meg not answering Loul. More Urfers?" He leaned in closer. "You know the word *more* and you know what I mean. Tell me. Are there more Urfers coming?" When she only stared, he pointed to the sky. "More Urfers coming?"

She followed his finger, looking up into the sky as if she would find the answer there. A fat raindrop splashed onto her forehead and when she looked back down at him she was grinning. She made a breathy sound, not a laugh but more like a sound of wonder as another drop splashed against her cheek. She tilted her head back so far Loul thought her neck might break. Was there no limit to their flexibility? Holding her long arms straight out from her sides, she turned her palms up as if to catch each raindrop as it struck her. She stepped back from him, turning her body so her arms spun like a strange turbine, laughing as the rain peppered down on her face. All around the work site he saw the other Urfers reacting to the rain, stepping away from their tools and out from under awnings, turning their faces up to the rain, laughing and calling to each other.

The storm moved in quickly, the rain falling in sheets, drops hitting hard enough to rattle the gravel. Soon the site was pocked with puddles. The Dideto crews hurried to the shelters, covering their equipment and huddling together under the awnings, but the Urfers raced into the rain. One by one they peeled the thin fabric off their bodies, tossing the damp garments into heaps around them, their laughter ringing out and disappearing in the bang of the rain on the awnings and cartons.

E L E V E N

MEG

She'd never been happier to feel raindrops in her entire life. When that first wet splat dripped onto her forehead, she closed her eyes, relief pulsing in her chest. She didn't want to see Loul's face, not the way it looked at her at that moment. And the rain? Oh the rain.

The Dideto had been more than generous with water, keeping two enormous vats filled every day for their drinking and washing. But between the rapid evaporation from the never-ending sunlight and the ingrained sense of rationing all deep-space travelers carried with them, none of the Earthers splurged when it came to water. Bathing consisted of sponge baths and dry shampoo; clothes were rinsed in shallow bowls and air dried. Even on the ship, especially on the ship, dry showers were the norm, so when the fat, warm raindrops began to drop, harder and faster by the minute, Meg acted without thinking. She saw the same visceral reaction in her crewmates, a skin hunger for water that had them peeling off their shirts and bending backward to feel the rain on their faces.

Jefferson had the presence of mind to collect their discarded shirts and throw them in the washing bowl, letting the rain fill it up and soak them. Everyone else wandered blindly, blissfully, opening their mouths to catch the drops until the rain fell hard enough to choke them. Meg saw Cho glance at his kit and she knew he had to be thinking of checking the falling rain for dangerous contaminants or irritants. She also saw the moment the sensation of wetness washed his worry away. He tipped his face up to the storm, his black hair, grown longer and shaggy after all this time in space, turning glossy and sleek as the water ran through it, pouring down the muscles in his back. The hammering of the rain drowned out all other sounds and for several minutes Meg just let herself watch the water move over Cho's body. Before she could act on her body's suggestions for follow-up, a thick clot of mud splattered against her bare stomach.

"Sucker!" Prader laughed, covered in mud from her hands to her shoulders, long ribbons of it streaking down the pale skin shining behind her black sports bra and gray pants. She scooped up another handful of mud, but before she could launch it, Wagner slipped in behind her and dumped an armload over her head. She screamed and laughed, sucking in mouthfuls of the runny clay and spitting them back out in every direction. The wind shifted, bringing the rain down in hot, blinding sheets into Meg's face, and she just barely had time to jump to avoid Jefferson, who had thrown himself chest forward into a long mud stream sluicing through the work site. He arched his back, arms thrown out behind him, laughing as he bodysurfed the little river, mud spraying out in a wake around him.

Cho followed suit, outdoing Jefferson by spinning midslide and somehow managing a backward somersault at the end of the long puddle. He came close to sticking the landing but slipped in the mud and wound up on his butt in the next deep puddle, every inch of him slathered in mud except for a toothy grin. Before she knew it, the five of them were throwing their bodies across the work site, sometimes surfing on carton panels, sometimes sliding on their butts or their chests, sometimes sliding on each other. The rain poured and poured, flooding the work site, and after checking to be sure the shelters had maintained their water-proofing, the crew lost themselves in the much-missed sensation of water.

Meg couldn't be sure, but it felt as if at least an hour had passed and still the rain pounded down. Her knees and elbows were bleeding from banging against gravel and she knew she'd have a killer bruise from Prader's last leap onto her back for a piggyback through the long mud channel. Her sides ached from laughing, and every time she bit down she tasted mud and grit. The light had changed, though, the reddish light from the sun over the sea burning through the thick clouds just enough to tinge the rain orange and pink. Pulling her mostly useless ponytail band from her hair, she ran her fingers through the mud-matted curls, letting the water wash away rocks and sticks, feeling the runny clay drip off her skin and puddle in her soaked shoes.

Prader did the same, her blonde hair slowly coming back into sight as she let the rain shower wash over her. Cho came near to Meg, watching her watch him as the thick mud slid down off his bare shoulders and chest, scrubbing at his hair to loosen the packed-in dirt. Soon the five of them fell quiet once more, moving their hands over their skin to clear it of Dideto soil. All of them were scraped and bruised. Jefferson's pants were torn at the knee and Wagner looked like he might have sprained his wrist judging by how he held it gingerly. But all of them smiled to each other and to themselves. Slowly the rain let up, the pound-ing dropping down to a pattering that gave way to a slowing drip from awnings and work sites.

Without realizing it, they had formed a loose circle once again, facing each other. Prader spit out a muddy wad into a puddle at her feet and all of them laughed. With the rain gone, the rumble of machinery could be heard once more, as well as the mumbling and hum of the Dideto work crews watching them from under the awnings. Jefferson pulled a twig from his matted hair. "Good luck explaining this to them, Meg."

Meg unbuckled her wrist screen, wiping away the muddy grit that had collected beneath it. The screen was undamaged—they were designed to go through a lot worse than mud wrestling—but she hesitated to activate the coms. She knew Loul couldn't hear them. None of the Dideto could, and for just a moment longer, she savored the privacy. It wouldn't last, she knew. She had to face Loul. Their little mud show wouldn't be enough to distract him from what he'd been trying to say to her earlier. He knew she was lying. She knew she would continue.

LOUL

The Effans sounded like they would break their knuckles, they typed so fast taking notes on the bizarre behavior of the Urfers. Mamu, the archivist, found a tarp to cover his camera sufficiently to get some footage that would probably never see the light of day since there was nobody who could think of a way to describe to the public what they were seeing. Seeing it themselves, the crews still couldn't believe it. Kik and his crew thought at first they were trying to kill each other and then trying to kill themselves, but when they kept getting back up, all those white teeth the only thing showing though the masks of mud, the crews had no choice but to accept that for some reason the Urfers were enjoying this.

For the first time since arriving on the site, Loul didn't care. He saw Meg laughing even though he couldn't hear her over the pounding of rain on the awning. He saw her grinning and happy, inexplicably throwing herself again and again into the mud in that bizarre flying-on-the-ground way they did. He saw the cuts and tears in her skin and the red blood weeping to the surface and washing away in the downpour, but he didn't feel the urge to rush out and comfort her or bandage her the way the Effans so wanted to do for Cho. And when they all stopped one at a time and turned their faces up to let the waning rain wash the mud from their skins, when they turned their backs on the work crews sheltered beneath the awnings to stand in a circle together, Loul felt farther from Meg than he had since first laying eyes on her.

It figured it would rain. Loul hated the rain, always had. He hated it more than the average city dweller, more than even his parents who lived close to the river and always feared the rain's flood. He hated the sound of it and the smell of it and the way it made the light milky and dim. Most of all he hated the way it drowned out all the sounds around him, making him hear only the sounds in his head. It never failed. It always rained when things went wrong.

The administration was lying to the media. The media was lying to the public. By not saying anything when that reporter from The Searcher had been dragged from the press conference, he had lied to the world. He had lied to his friends, Po and Hark and Reno Dado; he had lied to his family. He had lied to himself. The worst part of all of that was that he could live with it. He could live with the fact that people lied and fudged the truth and omitted facts for whatever expediency they could rationalize. He didn't expect any better. What hurt the most, what made the rain feel like it was crashing down like gravel on his skull, was that Meg had lied. Meg was still lying and maybe it was adolescent of him, but he wanted, no, he needed to believe these Urfers, these aliens who had made it all the way across the stars had reached a point in evolution where they didn't need to lie. He wanted them to be better than him, better than the Dideto. He wanted them to have their own version of those old oaths in the Magagan comics he'd read as a boy.

The rain tapered off, the drips and pings still splattering mud under the awnings. Crews began uncovering work kits and tools, considering ways to keep the equipment out of the mud, discussing the fear that the Urfers wouldn't help since they clearly had an affection for the gunk. Loul stayed where he sat, at his and Meg's booth. Mamu had piled some lenses and cables on the table and Loul made no move to clear them. He didn't know how he was going to get through these next few minutes, much less these next days, weeks, and months until whatever the Urfers had planned, whatever secret they were keeping, came to light.

He wanted to go home. Security had given the crews permission to access their cell phones, all of them retrieving dozens of panicked messages from loved ones. The administration had sent messages to their families assuring everyone that the work crews were safe and well, working on a classified mission. When the news of the aliens had broken, the majority of Loul's messages were from Po and Hark, well, Hark with Po yelling in the background. He knew they were excited for him. They thought the way he had thought—that he was on the cutting edge of the greatest event in Didet history. They would have seen him on the press conference. They would have seen him lie.

Meg scraped her boot on a board outside the awning, clearing a thick wedge of mud from each sole before wiping her feet on the sheltered grass. She had a towel draped across her shoulders, her skin pale and spotted against the brief black harness-like shirt that covered her small breasts. He'd never seen her stomach before. The movement of the dripping water caught the light, making the soft, flat plane of muscle look like glass. Her hair, normally floating around her face in fuzzy tendrils, lay flat against her skull, shining and damp, tamed in the elastic band at the back of her neck. When she slid into the booth across from him he saw she still had mud beneath her transparent fingernails and a smudge of dirt beneath her chin.

Around them, the Urfers were laughing, slapping their crews' backs and chattering words the Dideto couldn't understand, but they laughed along anyway. The spirit under the awning was light if slightly bewildered. Crews hauled boards and tarps out onto the work site to cover the worst of the mud pits, marveling at the grace with which the long-legged aliens navigated the slippery terrain. The black-clad official crews hung back, not quite willing to soil their expensive uniforms, but the original work crews made do as best they could. Soon everyone was getting back into the routine of their work except Meg and Loul.

She pushed aside a ring of cable and carefully packed the heavy lenses within the ring. Loul stared at her, not helping, not moving, watching her face and catching the guarded glances she threw his way now and then. She took longer than necessary to clear the spot in front of them, her face still and lowered. Then she folded her hands in front of her, her long fingers interlacing with that ease that still sent a thrill through him.

"Loul." She spoke loudly enough to hear her without the earpiece. She used her own voice, not activating the translation com. The word sounded like wind through the water reeds when she said it and he wished she'd turn on the coms. He even pointed to her wrist screen. He didn't want to fall under her spell again. He wondered if she really could use some kind of magic to enthrall him. Right now, after the rain, after the lie, he wanted to see her with some sort of detachment, some sort of prejudice that he hadn't seen her with yet. He didn't want to lean in to catch the bell-like sound of her voice or watch the way the light played pink and orange on her skin, picking up the small brown flecks that broke up the smooth surface, visible only when he sat very close to her. He wanted to see her with different eyes. He wanted to see her the other way she was— tall and pale and flimsy and weird. Alien. If it turned out the secret she kept from him was dangerous, he wanted to have the thoughts in place to protect himself.

She pulled the screen out, laying it flat against the table. A few jabs at the symbols and he could hear her in his ear once again. She didn't say anything but he could hear her breath when she sighed and the brush of the towel as she squeezed water from the rope of hair that hung down her neck. "Loul," she said, still in her own voice. It was the only word she could say in his language. His own voice took over her words. "Meg need/want..." She didn't finish the sentence even though he saw her mouth moving. Before the earpiece he would have thought she was talking in that silent way. Instead it looked like she was trying on words but couldn't find one to come out. He knew how she felt.

"Meg." He looked at the screen, wishing he could read it, wishing she had designed it so he too could pick out words amid the red blocks of symbols. "Loul need/want talk. Loul give word to Meg—trust. Yes?"

He heard her swallow and saw the muscles in her thin neck move. "Yes."

"Trust is ask question and talk answer. Answer is good/ okay, not bad/no good. This is trust. Yes?" He finally lifted his gaze to meet hers. Maybe it was the light filtering through the post-rain haze but her eyes seemed shinier than usual, almost brilliant. "Trust is Loul need/want answer, Meg has answer, Meg talks. Yes."

"Yes."

"Loul need/want answer. Meg talk?" He stared at her, waiting. "No?"

When she still said nothing, he looked back at the screen. "Meg show Loul word *trust* here. Where is *trust*?" Meg pointed to a slim red box near the bottom right corner. Loul made the settling stance, making sure she saw him. He placed his hand on the box for trust. Being sure she followed his hands, he pressed it again and then slowly and deliberately moved his hand to a button he knew and pressed. "No."

MEG

Meg covered her face with her hands, blinking hard to keep the tears from spilling out over her lashes. She didn't need the language screen to know what Loul was saying. She could see it on his face, in his eyes, the way his third lid kept creeping into sight as if it could protect him from the pain she knew she was causing him. She didn't know exactly what happened at that press conference but the translator had picked up enough to give her a pretty good idea.

The Dideto wanted to know if there were more Earthers coming. It seemed like the reporter who'd been dragged out of the press conference had been demanding an answer to that. Baddo had given a reply that the translator was still working on but the gist of it seemed to be that the people in charge had come to their own conclusions about the answer. Whatever that conclusion was, it made Loul unhappy and tense. She could hear it in the thrum of his throat. Even worse, she could hear the change in that pitch when he looked at her, when he had asked her directly, more directly than he had asked her anything up to this point, and she had pretended to not understand.

Now her newest word, *trust*, was being used to let her know that he was on to her. He knew she was lying and she could only imagine the nightmares he was dreaming up to explain the lie. Of course, she couldn't use those words, could she? Did they dream? They didn't sleep, but when they dropped, did they dream? Would they even know what nightmares were? For one stupid moment she actually considered resettling and starting to broach that topic. Stupid, she knew, because if they didn't get across this hurdle, they might as well bring in Baddo to do the translating. The bond was straining between them and it was her fault.

But how could she tell him? How do you explain to people who have never seen the blackness of space, who have never left the gravity of their own world and thrown themselves into the upside-down reality of interstellar travel that some things were just not spoken of? If it had taken this long to learn the word for trust, how long would it take to teach the word for superstition? Because that's what it was, a superstition, and they all knew it. But when you stake your life on the stability of an improbable and unstable propulsion system to catapult yourself beyond the known edges of your universe because you're following the ancient message of strangers who might be your ancestors, you didn't have to be a psychologist to see why people clung to small comforts and less than logical assurances.

It was one of the oddest reasons Meg felt at home among deep-space travelers. In the beginning of her career, she had stuck to the inner colonies, those stops within the terraforming ring that were reached with traditional transport ships. The voyages took weeks or even months, but the ships were well appointed and safety records so unbroken nobody even bothered to consider the dangers. But as her career had progressed and her reputation had grown, she'd been compelled to strike out farther, to the outer colonies and the experimental stations where international and cultural tensions ran high.

Her first trip to what was then the deepest of the deep-space stations, Excelsior, had made her so nervous that she'd been tranquilized to the point of stupidity by the ship's med team. She remembered trying to sneak in a lucky nickel her grandmother had given her as a child, terrified the security team would find it and strip it from her. As carefully as they had scanned her bags and body for unnecessary and dangerous metals and weights before departure, she'd been stunned when she'd gotten to her cubby and found the nickel in the pocket where she'd left it. Of course she couldn't hold it during deep sleep, but when she'd come out of stasis, the first thing she did was pull that nickel out and squeeze it, thanking it for her safe arrival.

That first trip was where she saw how deep-space travelers really worked. The men and women on these crews were the bravest of the sailors, the biggest risk takers, the most prepared for any type of emergency. They were the innovators, the pioneers, the Magellans of space travel. These pilots made enormous amounts of money they never spent on anything except more travel, their timeline so out of sync with their planet-bound families and friends that they tended to seek out only each other for company. As her job took her farther and farther into the reaches of human space, she came to feel at home among the deep spacers. Not because she had even a fraction of their knowledge of physics or engineering or navigational computation but because when all the computations had been completed and the limitations of physics were under control, she saw these men and women pull out their pendants and their fetishes and their touchstones and keepsakes and prayer cards.

Jefferson carried the three stone fetishes that the Galen miners carried as protection against danger. Prader, she knew, always wore a piece of red silk somewhere on her body, going so far as to weave it around the edge of her sleep sack during stasis. Wagner had a small ebony box, the contents of which were unknown to anyone else on board. Cho had a series of tattooed symbols scattered across his body, adding to them with every deep-space trip he made. He never told her the meanings of them but she would catch him touching one or the other as different problems arose on voyages. He would even place her hands on some of them when they made love, the sight of her hand on his markings moving him in ways she never asked him to explain. And she, of course, wore the dented brass locket she told anyone who asked was broken and could not be opened. All the deep-space crews she'd worked with knew that was a lie, and to date none had called her on it.

How could she tell this to Loul? How could she reconcile the technology the Dideto found so intriguing, so revolutionary, with the inexplicable need to cling to talismans and charms? They had propelled themselves through billions of miles of empty space using a recombinant crystal that in all probability should have blown them to stardust months before. They had Earther medical advances that clearly outstripped the Dideto by decades if not centuries, so how could it be that not one of the five crew members could bring themselves to answer the simple question of whether or not more of their kind were coming?

That answer was that no Earther who had ever ventured past the first ring of terraforming would ever, even under pain of death, break the immutable law of the dark side. When the first voyagers had gone out, before the terraforming ring had even been imagined, it was common practice for shuttles—really just primitive ejection pods at the time—to be dropped onto surfaces while the main ship remained in orbit around the body. Communication with those on the surface was often broken up by radiation and the distance from surface to ship. The main ship would go "dark side," go to the other side of the space body, leaving those on the surface cut off, alone.

In those early years, more people didn't survive the missions than did, and those that did let it be known that while the main ship was on the dark side, it was never to be mentioned. Psychologically, it proved too easy for the isolation and possibility of being stranded to break even the most vetted astronauts, and more than one surface walker had cracked the helmet, taking his or her own life rather than face the terror of the main ship not returning. And so, decades later and billions of miles deeper into space, that psychological safeguard had taken on the profundity of scripture. When you were on the surface and your ship was dark side, nobody uttered a word of its absence. The names of the absent crewmembers were as good as forgotten, and no deep-space traveler would ever consider breaking this code for any reason.

Meg hadn't realized how deeply ingrained this understanding was in her and the rest of the crew. It had never been tested. People in the deep-space colonies knew the law as well any traveler to their port and thus nobody ever demanded the rule be broken. Now, all the understood rules of Earthers and the colonies and the terraforming rings were gone. Nothing could be assumed anymore, and the five of them were facing a breakdown in communication that could jeopardize all of their lives because Meg couldn't be certain that even thinking the name of the woman remaining in the ship outside the Didet atmosphere wouldn't bring catastrophe upon all of them.

Part of her screamed that it was stupid. It was a superstition. Nothing she could say or do could in any way affect the fate of the *Damocles*. The capricious crystal worked on its own logic, and it certainly wouldn't be words that made it malfunction, especially words spoken thousands of miles away on the surface of a planet. But staring into the gray, three-lidded eyes of this stranger from another life stream so different from her own and yet so similar, logic didn't hold much sway. She couldn't even ask Cho or the other crew members what she should do. It was That Thing That Would Not Be Spoken Of. Period. Until That Person Who Could Not Be Named made contact, the terror of the dark side held them all in its grip.

She wondered if she should try to teach Loul the word for *crazy* because that's how she felt. Crazy and helpless to fight it. Unwilling to fight it. But that didn't mean she had to let it tear apart her bond with Loul. She took his hand in both of hers. He started to pull it away but she wrapped her fingers around his thick wrist. They both knew he was more than strong enough to break her grasp and she felt heartened that he didn't. He didn't cling to her hand, though; he just let her hold it.

"Loul." Pulling one hand free she moved over the screen. "Trust Meg." He moved his free hand over the screen but she pushed it away, pushing one button repeatedly. "Need/want. Need/want. Need/want." She spoke again. "Trust Meg."

"Meg talk Loul. Questions. Questions Meg talk Loul."

Biting her lip in frustration, Meg pressed Loul's hands down through the light screen, holding them against the table, and stared at the language prompts illuminating their intermingled hands. She flicked off the screen and brought her hands together between his. Maybe she could tell him without telling him. Cupping her hands as he had earlier, she looked at him as she spoke. "Meg no talk. Meg no questions."

She heard his teeth grind together and then stop as she put her hands outside of his, still curved as if cupping a much larger bowl. "Later Meg talk. Loul ask. Meg answer."

He stared at her hands, the pitch of his thrum dropping in intensity. When he spoke she could see he didn't use the broken half-language they'd been using. He spoke in his real language, not bothering or maybe not able to think in the half-speak they'd built. Meg activated the screen once more and saw the program filtering through his words, recognizing several that had come up in their discussions of food and water. When she saw the translator put together the meaning of his question, she leaned forward, pressing her forehead to his clenched fists.

"Yes, Loul, yes. Didet is safe. Didet is safe. Earthers are no danger."

He pulled back his hands, and she sat up, her shoulders slumped. She suddenly felt exhausted, the cuts and scrapes and bruises of their mud fights making themselves known all over her body. She wanted to sleep and not dream for about a month or two. Mostly she wanted Loul to believe her and free her of this burden of secrecy.

He gripped the sides of the table, staring at the light screen then glancing up at her. He looked at the ship and the crews and the archiving cameras. He looked at Mamu's lenses and the line of wet clothes Jefferson had hung out to dry. His thrum went silent for several long seconds and Meg thought she might scream if he didn't give her his answer soon. Finally his thrum returned, low and steady. His hand hovered over the light screen but he put it back down, choosing instead to look up at her, his inner eyelid back out of sight. He considered her a moment and then spoke.

"Yes. Loul trust Meg. Okay."

T W E L V E

LOUL

What could he do? It was like in the game Circle when you drew that duel block and you had no arsenal. All you could do was go all in, put all your magic in the pot and in the hold of the Great Sail and hope you made it across. Hark hated it when Loul used that strategy; he told him it was the same as cheating, that it wasn't a strategy at all but the kind of stupid blundering that ruined the game for everyone. He usually said these things because he was angry that nine out of ten times the strategy worked for Loul and he wound up on the Mountain of Power before anyone else. What could he do? He was the kind of guy who, when face-to-face with an alien species that he knew was lying to him, thought about a kid's game he was too old to still be playing.

Meg's face took on yet another new expression. It seemed the long bony planes of their faces had no end to the permutations they could bend into. She folded up her body too, bringing her skinny knees up to her chest, somehow wedging them in between her chest and the table, wrapping her arms around them and resting her chin where her forearms piled up. She looked small enough to shoot through a pom-cannon, and he noticed that the thickness of both of her forearms pressed together still didn't match the thickness of one of his. Her fingers draped like a fringe over the bend of her arms.

He just looked at her and let her watch him. Everything was different now. The official crews, those black-clad work teams the Urfers had refused to acknowledge, Loul knew the truth about them now. All his life he'd watched the official crews working at accident sites, fires, science labs—anywhere the news crews were, the black-clad crews worked with that quick, crisp efficiency he and everyone around him so admired. Videos of those professionals had been shown in schools to encourage all of them to work harder, study harder, strive to be better. He'd even dreamed, way back in the day when he'd written his special alien-invasion preparation report for the Telemetry Administration, of being a member of one of those crews, of donning an expensive black overshirt and manning the extra-atmosphere satellite control.

Now? Now he saw how they really worked. Maybe this site was an exception but Loul doubted it. Loul doubted everything now. What happened here probably happened everywhere, every day, every time the news crews reported from a site. There were probably hundreds of work teams all over the world just doing their job every day, showing up, getting it done until, for whatever reason, what they were doing became newsworthy and just like that the official crews moved into place. Cameras got footage of handsome, well-dressed men and women with shiny equipment and determined, serious faces.

And why? Because people like him and Kik and Olum didn't come across as handsome on television? Because Effan Two had a tendency to spit when she got excited? Would it so traumatize the people of Cartar to see that the geologist working with the Urfer Cheffson was missing two side teeth and had a tendency to huff his solvents before he dropped? Loul knew he was working himself into a solid sulk and that he'd been sitting there far longer than was normal or proper not saying a word to Meg. It didn't seem to faze her. She just watched him, curled up into herself in that impossibly flimsy way that he knew he was helpless to not be fascinated by. He knew he'd always give in to the fascination, he'd always let his mouth drop open in wonder, and he'd always choose the course of stupid curiosity over practical safety. That was probably one of the reasons the official crews replaced people like him.

Okay, he was definitely in a sulk now. He didn't know how to get himself out of it. In time, he figured he and Meg would get back to talking, muddle through the awkwardness until something resembling the old rhythm would fall into place. He wanted to get to that place now. He wanted to skip this part and get to the part where it would be easy again. He wanted to go home and he wanted to talk to Hark and Po. He wanted a hot meal. He wanted to be back in that place where he didn't have to think so hard about how things worked. He wanted…he just wanted. And he wanted to be able to say this to Meg but he had no idea how to start.

"Loul." Her eyes were wide and strange looking, stranger looking than usual. They bent down in the far corners in a way he hadn't seen before and the fine line of hair over them bent in a graceful upward curve. "Loul." She didn't say his name as a question and she didn't say anything else. She just untangled her arms and legs from their tight knot, putting her feet down and resting her hands lightly as always on the table for just a moment. Then he couldn't see exactly how she did it but she seemed to somehow ripple her spine, bending in a fluid curve until she flowed like oil beneath the table. He could only stare, watching the empty space where her head had been and jumping in surprise when her head popped up at his side of the table. She reversed her weird ripple, lifting and bending herself until she folded into the seat beside him.

He didn't say anything, couldn't say anything, surprise robbing him of words. It was harder to see her without turning his body all the way around since she tucked herself in slightly behind him in the booth. She slid closer until the thin line of her legs pressed against his, her pale bare shoulder nudging the thin cloth of his work shirt. He thought at first she was pushing him to move but the pressure was so light he hardly had to resist it. Even folded up as she was, her body was still longer than his and the ridge of her shoulder carriage rested above his. She bent forward, folding one leg sideways, draping the other over it, her hands puddling up in the space between her thin thighs, and she brought her face close to his.

"This is okay? Loul okay Meg here?"

He didn't know if he was okay or not. He'd been close to Meg before. They'd touched and walked together, brushing up against each other as the Urfers did when they walked but this was different. Meg was different. Hell, he was different. Her skin looked bumpy when her arm brushed against his shirtsleeve, the fine hairs standing on end across her pale skin. He could feel her vibrate as she leaned into him.

"Cold," she said. Of course, she had stripped off her shirt in the storm.

"Shirt?" he asked, looking toward her shelter where he knew she kept another.

"No. Loul." She leaned forward enough that he could turn and look into her face. She slid one thin hand around the inside of his arm, pushing until she was fully entwined with his. She rested her chin on his shoulder and pressed her forehead into the thin hair at his temple. He could feel and hear her breath in his ear.

"Loul is okay. Loul is..." With her free hand she flicked at the corner of the light screen, spinning it around to adjust to her new position. Her hand hovered over the buttons until she found what she wanted, looking to make sure Loul could see too. "Loul is safe. Meg is safe."

MEG

She was freezing but that wasn't why she climbed over to Loul's side of the table. She slithered out and under the table because she couldn't take another minute of listening to the low pitch and roll of his thrum, rising and dropping like a hummed sob in his throat. She'd never heard him make that sound, had never heard any of them make it, and it pushed into her heart like a nail until she had to move, had to do something to soothe it, to silence it. She didn't know if touching Loul would help or make him more uncomfortable. He was already unhappy with her, that she knew, but she was sorry and scared she would lose him. Her skin felt chafed and sore from the mud slides. She was hungry and cold but most of all she felt as if she had brutalized her new friend with her silence. If she couldn't explain with words, she'd explain with warmth, with sheer proximity.

The rough cloth of his shirt scratched her skin, but she wrapped her arm around his anyway, resting her chin on his shoulder. She could see the dark skin beneath his ear flush darker when she breathed on it and was thankful for Cho's warning. At the moment, she very much wanted to brush her lips against that dark, pulsing skin. It wasn't a sexual compulsion, it just seemed intimate. Instead she leaned her head against his and assured him that he was safe. They were both safe. When Loul didn't pull away, she decided to try a new concept.

LOUL

Meg turned her head on his shoulder, her cheek near his, and looked down at the screen. The hand that didn't grip his arm swept away the red boxes in the middle of the screen, opening up a new empty box. She had a new word or concept she wanted to teach him. He waved his knuckles toward each other with a faint movement, a half-hearted yes. He also didn't want to accidentally yank her arm where it was wrapped around his. He could feel her fingers settle into his bicep, not squeezing but just taking their place, and he had to admit, he liked the sensation.

Meg's fingers flitted along the side of the screen, lines and symbols flying by in a blur. She flicked and pushed, shifting boxes within boxes, looking for something in what he understood to be the Urfers' database. It seemed to him to hold an enormous amount of data, and her fingers flew through the labels. She found what she wanted, drawing a data box onto the middle of the screen. A few more flicks and the box filled with other boxes; photographs, Loul knew. The pictures were tiny, impossible to make out, but Meg seemed able to sort through them. They'd used photos before for simple vocabulary words and Loul had always hoped she would show him more pictures of Urf.

The picture she opened wasn't a photograph but a graphic. Her language program had a lot of those, simplified images of basic objects. It made sense although they'd both had a few laughs when what was a basic object to Meg had completely confounded Loul. This time, he knew what the picture was supposed to be—a man and a woman. It was funny to see the Urfer rendition of male and female, skinny and long like the Urfers themselves. A few more flicks of her finger and two smaller people appeared between the man and woman. Meg kept shifting through the data and pulled out what he recognized as audio commands, lining them up beneath the figures and pressing the buttons.

"Mother. Father." It was Effan One's voice. "Child. Children. Family." She must have recorded these words with Cho when discussing gender and reproduction. When Meg and Cho went into stasis, he spent most of his time with the Effans, listening to them gush about the information they were learning. This vocabulary had already been established. Why was Meg bringing it up now?

She waved her hand over the image of the family. "Loul family?"

Loul jerked away from her, not caring if he jerked her arm clean off her body. He pushed away, fear punching into his stomach as he scrabbled from the booth, putting the table between them. Meg's eyes were wide, her hands held palms up in what he knew meant no danger. He'd seen the Urfers use that posture before, usually when they'd startled someone on the work site sneaking up behind them with that silent glide of theirs.

His voice poured from her speaker patch in broken phrases, just pieces of "Loul no. Meg no good. No Meg. What this? No Loul move." He swung his fists through the air, the sign to be quiet. He needed her to be quiet. He needed to not hear her words in his voice.

She said nothing for several moments, letting him stand there and pound his fists into his hips, thinking. When she moved, it was with that very slow movement he knew they only used when they needed to make a point or when the work crews had been startled. He used to think the slow movement was soothing, a way to give the Dideto a chance to follow along. Now there seemed to be something dangerous in slow grace. Her hands floated over the light screen.

"Loul? What? Meg need/want ask. Family is no good?"

He couldn't believe how still she could sit. He watched her, staring at her, not blinking and trying to wait her out but he knew he couldn't. It was like they could turn to stone if they wanted. Loul unclenched his fists, trying to relax. He had a question he had to ask and it scared him. The possibility scared him breathless but the thought of not knowing scared him more.

"How did you know?"

This wasn't in their vocabulary; he knew that but he had to ask the question anyway. Meg's head tilted just a fraction, an involuntary sign of confusion. She kept her eyes on him, even her blinks slow and controlled. She bobbed her head slightly, asking him to repeat.

He leaned in toward the table. It was stupid, he knew, to have jerked away like that. If it was true, if she could read his mind, she'd have seen it coming. She would know what he was doing right now. She wouldn't have been confused by the question. The more he thought about it, the more absurd the idea became but he had to ask anyway. He had to find a way to make her understand.

He crouched beside the table. He wanted to sit back down but he didn't really want to be sitting beside Meg when he asked the question because, for one thing, it hurt his neck trying to turn to see and, for another, if the answer turned out to be yes he couldn't trust himself not to leap out of the booth again and look like an idiot. At the same time, he didn't want to sit on the other side of the booth because, well, Meg had climbed over to his side to be close to him. To purposefully move away from her, even after he'd just jumped away, seemed rude. Loul ground his teeth at his own absurdity.

"Meg." He gripped the table tight and saw her draw into herself, her shoulder carriage stiff in that way that meant she was not relaxed. She stared hard into his eyes and he could just make out the edge of sharp white teeth biting her lower lip. "Loul need/want know. Meg, um, Loul talks, yes?" She tapped the *yes* button, her lip whitening where her teeth pressed against it. "Loul talks and Meg, um"—he tapped his ear—"Meg hears, yes?"

"Yes." She spoke, her head tipping and bobbing forward, her neck looser now, telling Loul that she was really listening to him. When Meg listened, she listened with her whole body, which was part of the point of his question.

He hit the question mark and tried to phrase the next part right. "Does Meg hear, uh, Loul no talk?" She bobbed her head and he repeated the nonsensical question. No sign that she got it. He crouched down closer to the table, getting more engrossed in communicating the concept than in his fear of the concept itself. "Let's try this," he muttered. He looked at Meg. He pointed to his mouth. "Loul talks words, yes?"

She tapped her knuckles.

"There are words here." He pointed to his mouth. "Yes? Words here?"

She tapped her knuckles again. Somewhere during his questions they had come to lean in closer to each other. Loul watched her pupils widen as he tapped the side of his head.

"And words here." He tapped his skull. "Loul talks here. Yes?"

Her fingers slid near the *yes* button. She wanted him to continue to explain. He couldn't have stopped if he'd tried.

His voice was thin and tense as he whispered his question to Meg. "Does Meg hear Loul talk words here?" He tapped his skull. "Does Meg hear words Loul talks here?"

Her shoulders dropped and a soft breath blew from her open mouth. Meg's whole body collapsed into a relaxed slouch. Loul knew this meant she had understood him. What he didn't know was what her answer was going to be. He didn't know how she would react to it.

She laughed. She laughed a breathy laugh that turned into a choppy laugh. Her head fell back, showing all her teeth, and her flat palms smacked together in a loud slap. Of all the reactions he'd expected, this wasn't one of them. She covered her wide-open mouth with her fingers and kept laughing long enough for him to wonder if she was laughing at him rather than in relief at understanding him. No sooner had the thought crossed his mind than she reached for him, wrapping her fingers around his hands where they clutched the table and leaning in close.

"No," she said through a smile. "Meg no hear words here." Her fingers brushed the side of his head. "Loul hear Meg talk here?"

"No," he said. "Of course not. But how do you know? How..." He pressed the question mark again then touched his head. "Loul talked here about family and Meg asks family. Loul is not okay and Meg asks why Loul is not okay. How? Meg hears words, yes?"

"No. Meg hears..." She bit her lip again, her hand hovering near his face. Her fingers trembled, hesitating. "Meg hears this." And very softly she slid her fingers across his rose spot.

MEG

She remembers a dance at Queen of Heaven School. She and her sister, Maddie, were in C School so they couldn't have been more than twelve or thirteen years old. It was their first "real" dance, with boys and shadows and slow dancing. Clayton Harvey had asked her to dance just like Maddie said he would. Maddie said Clayton had a crush on her, and while it had been almost impossible to believe, Clayton Harvey being Clayton Harvey, Meg had believed her. Meg always believed Maddie because even though they were twins and did almost everything together, Maddie always seemed to know so much more than Meg. She made it through the first dance without throwing up on herself or tripping, and then, unbelievably, Clayton Harvey asked her to keep on dancing with him. And it was a slow song, a really slow song, "Cries in the Dark," which everyone knew was a super sexy song, although Meg didn't really know what was so sexy about it. But when she wrapped her arms around Clayton Harvey's neck and he wrapped his arms around her waist, his hand coming really close to her butt, she started to get the appeal of the song. They danced the whole song like that, getting closer and closer even though they were touching almost everywhere from shoulder to knee. And then she'd heard Clayton's breath catch and felt him go tense where he stood and when she pulled her head back, she saw a look on Clayton Harvey's face that she would never forget. Especially since he dropped his arms and ran off the dance floor, leaving her standing there like a dork.

Maddie had laughed and laughed, explaining to Meg in the bathroom what had happened, and for the countless time Meg had wondered how her twin knew these kinds of things. She wondered why if it had felt so good to him would he look so terrified. Of course, that was a lot of years ago and Meg had eventually caught up to her sister in such matters, but she still keenly remembered that white-eyed look on Clayton Harvey's face during that first slow dance.

All these years later, she was seeing it again. Loul didn't have Clayton Harvey's apple cheeks or baby-blue eyes, and he probably wasn't about to go off in his pants, but Meg knew that look. She was still able to draw that look from Cho on the rare occasions they had the opportunity to get a little adventurous. She knew, or at least she hoped, Loul wouldn't act on the gesture since from what Cho had told her the logistics would be awkward at best. But Loul had asked where she heard his thoughts. He wanted to know how she gauged his feelings. She had lied to him enough. For this, she would tell him the truth.

She drew her hand away from the pulse point, hearing his thrum stutter in surprise, then settle into a steady yet higher pitch. She sat back down in her seat, tucking her hands under the table in hopes that if they were out of sight it would somehow lessen whatever embarrassment Loul might be feeling. She didn't know what embarrassment looked like on him; she wasn't sure if she'd seen it yet. She'd seen surprise and bewilderment and anger, but if he'd ever been embarrassed around her, he'd hidden it. He was hiding it now unless it looked a lot like happy wonder.

Loul climbed back into the booth beside her, turning his body so his back was to the small dividing wall and he could face her more easily. He put his finger against the dark pulse point and for one awkward second Meg didn't know if it was her turn to be embarrassed.

"Meg hears words here?"

Apparently they were going forward. Good. "No words. Meg hears...Meg hears."

"What hears?"

How could she describe it? She couldn't make that sound in her own throat. The closest she could come was a hum, a deep vibrating hum, like the kind the therapist had taught her to make for meditation. She knew Loul could hear the sound in his earpiece, and she raised the tone, humming a tune she thought might be Mozart. She hummed until her throat started to itch, then she opened her mouth and la-la-la'd a few notes. She was way off the real sound of the thrums but something in the music came closer to explaining it.

"This Meg hears? This Loul Meg hears?"

"Yes. Loul is okay." She hummed low and even. "Loul is not okay." She raised the pitch, letting her throat choke the sounds to a stutter.

Loul's mouth hung slightly open, his thrum soft and even. He brought his hands up between them. "Meg...is okay...Loul..." His hands hung in the air like he'd forgotten how to use them. He shifted, rocking on his thick legs until he leaned toward the table, still facing her.

"Loul? Yes?"

His right hand reached out slowly toward her face and his teeth ground together. "Is okay...Loul...here?" His hand came close to her jaw.

Meg smiled, tilting her head to the side, exposing the soft skin beneath her ear to him. She turned a bit, showing the pale expanse of her neck. "Touch?" She drew his hand and put it to her own pulse point, wondering if he could feel the faint movement there. She felt the tender pads of his fingers open against her skin, could feel the warmth where the rougher skin parted. A small part of her worried they were crossing some line of propriety, but as always she went with her gut, not her rule book.

"Yes? Talk this." She put her hand over his on her throat. ProLingLang captured his word for the pulse point, which she labeled the thrum spot since the Dideto had other pulse points that didn't make any noise and weren't darker in tone. Cho had declared the spot sexual in nature, an erogenous zone, but sitting here with Loul, his tender fingertips on her throat, having been forgiven for lying and scaring him near to death, she thought maybe there was more to it.

LOUL

Under the sensitive skin of his finger pads, Loul could feel the blood rushing beneath Meg's skin. He could feel how soft the tissue was there, and he thought her slender neck might be even more fragile than it looked. But she didn't flinch or tense as his thick fingers rested against the warm skin. He felt the muscles flex as she breathed and swallowed, her eyes closing slightly at his touch. The Effans had discussed the absence of the rose spot, speculating that perhaps it was simply a pigmentation issue. The range of colors of the Urfers varied so much, from the very pale Prader to the very dark Agnar. Cho's midtone skin bore darker-than-black symbols; Meg and Cheffson both had spots of color sprinkled across their skin, although none of the colored patches were large enough or showed any sensitivity to serve as a rose spot.

Meg relaxed into his touch but somehow it felt different from the Dideto way. Maybe she didn't know enough to really relax into the touch. And maybe Urfers only really responded when they were in their stasis mode. The Effans had let Loul watch Meg and Cho when they were in stasis, their bodies alternating between limp and active, responding to stimuli the scientists couldn't explain. Maybe their rose spot rested somewhere else on their bodies. Maybe they didn't have one at all.

Grandma Bo used to tell him stories about the old sea gods who didn't have rose spots. She would gather all the kids around the shucking pit, keeping them captivated with her stories so they would keep shucking the *mogi* and *ketso* and stay out of their parents' hair. In her stories, the sea gods rose out of the water and left enormous footprints all across Didet, needing to keep their feet from getting muddy. She said the sea gods had come from the center of the planet, and because they could breathe underwater, where sound travels faster than on land, they could speak in the slightest whispers. According to Grandma Bo, the people on the land couldn't hear them when they spoke, so the sea gods put magical shells just below the peoples' ears. The shells dissolved, leaving the rose spot. And after the sea gods went back to the center of the planet, the people forgot how to hear with the rose spot but they never forgot what it felt like to hear the gods.

"That's why only the most important people, only the people you truly love," she would say, brushing her fingers across each of their young necks, "can make your rose spot blush."

Loul pulled his finger away from Meg's neck, smiling when he saw the flush of color where his fingertips had been.

THIRTEEN

MEG

Meg and Loul were still smiling at each other when Wagner started to shout. He and Olum, the leader of the Dideto work team, both fell back from their table where wires and screens and plugs and clamps teetered in a mess nobody dared approach. Olum and his crew shimmied and jumped, bumping into each other as Wagner held his hands high in the air, bellowing a wordless cry. Everyone spun toward the scene, not knowing if the news was good or bad. Jefferson swore, then Cho, and when Meg looked down she saw her light screen had gone black, her wristband flashing in warning.

"Hey!" she shouted at Wagner, who ignored her. "What did you do?"

Loul rose from the booth, trying to see what the ruckus was over the heaps of equipment. On the far side of the site, Prader threw down a wrench, nearly taking Kik out at the knee, and she stalked toward the captain. Before anyone could reach them, Wagner, Olum, and two others in the crew body slammed into each other, chests first. Unfortunately for Wagner, his chest was a great deal higher than the crew's and he took the brunt of the thrust in the gut. They also outweighed him and in seconds the captain disappeared under a huddle of muscular, grunting bodies. Jefferson and Prader were first to reach the pile, stopping just sort of throwing fists when they heard Wagner laughing.

"We did it!" His breath caught as another shoulder hit his gut, but he wheezed out another laugh. "We did it!" Olum and crew pounded the ground around them, rolling off of the captain when they realized the damage they were doing. Olum's second, a gray-haired woman with faded black bands across her fingers, started a two-two-one beat on the ground that the rest of the team quickly picked up. Wagner laughed, catching his breath, and then joined them in hammering his fists against the ground.

Cho, with the Effans in tow, sidled up to the edge of Meg's booth. "He crashed our computer system? Yippee. Maybe Prader can blow a hole in the fuel cell and we can make a party out of it."

Meg laughed, craning her neck to watch the captain and Olum pounding the ground, grinning at each other. When the captain threw back his head and let out another one of his unmistakable bellowing laughs, Olum reached forward and cupped his hand around the captain's neck, just under his ear. The captain responded in kind, bringing his hand up and clutching the man at the neck, his long dark fingers covering Olum's flushed thrumming spot. She heard Cho make a little sound of warning but put her hand out to stop him.

"I don't think it means what you think it means. I think there's more to it."

Unless Olum and Wagner had secretly become lovers at some point, Meg seemed to be right. The two men grinned at each other, pulling each other in until their foreheads bumped. Around them the work crew continued their rhythmic pounding of the ground, crouching and rocking. It might have gone on for hours if an empty cable wheel hadn't sailed through the air and hit Wagner on the back.

Prader saw her missile hit home. "You two want to take your make-out session somewhere else? I just lost my propulsion diagnostic!"

Meg heard Cho mutter something about a psychopath as Wagner and Olum rose to their feet, their grins not diminished a whit. "For your information, Officer Prader, you have lost exactly shit. Not only have you not lost your precious propulsion diagnostic, you have now gained the ability to run your data in two languages."

"I can already run it in Mandarin," Prader said.

Wagner looked heavenward, shaking his head. "Reboot your screens. All of you."

Meg reset her wristband, and when the light flashed, she pulled the light screen across the table. It flickered, taking longer than usual to reset, but when it did, she heard Loul's thrum rise. The text boxes came to life across the screen, the words and questions and syntax grouping where she had left them. Only now, beneath each text box, another blue box appeared with groupings of dots and lines she couldn't decipher. She couldn't decipher them but Loul could. He leaned over the table, pushing back into the booth to sit beside her, his hands hovering over the screen as he hummed to himself.

"Loul talk to Meg."

It took her a second to realize that he hadn't spoken. Instead he had pressed the correct buttons on the light screen to activate the recorded audio.

"Loul has words for Meg. Loul has words...here."

He grinned at her.

"Here." His finger jabbed the word button for *here* as he laughed.

"You can read this?" Meg asked, knowing they didn't have the word for *read* yet but Loul knew what she was saying. Wagner and Olum had found a way to interface the two disparate computer systems. Loul and the rest of the work crews would be able to read the data the Earthers worked with. They would be able to share the information both sides so desperately wanted to share. This changed everything.

It didn't change everything perfectly. Glitches and miscommunications still riddled the interface. Dideto expression of chemical compounds differed significantly from Earther science, and Cho and Jefferson teamed up to work with their respective teams. Whether a biologist or a geologist, chemicals were chemicals, and together the teams made more headway than alone. The breakthrough in the sharing of navigational charts caused what could only be called a ruckus among Wagner's team, dozens of officials being called in to handle the flood of data the Space Administration officials had never dreamed of seeing in their lifetimes. Prader and Kik and company didn't see too much of a difference, Prader concentrating more on teaching Kik to weld the polymer compound around the thrusters than teaching him the physics of propulsion.

It was Meg and Loul who hit the biggest stumbling blocks. The Dideto database contained a large number of words that the Earther computer stalled on, churned over, and inexplicably translated consistently as *turkey*. Meg suspected this was a deeply hidden joke put in place by the original programmers back when the idea of an interface this unusual was inconceivable. Like most of the technology, the language, and the sense of time, the computer programming used throughout the terraforming ring and in deep space had all originated from Earth. It had all been designed to interface relatively easily with other systems. Like language itself, it all hailed from the same sensibility. Apparently Dideto data storage didn't fall along those same lines, and more than once Meg had snorted at the computer's bizarre translation.

"Government based upon equal distribution of life resources, population safety, and social turkey," Meg read, laughing. Loul didn't know why this important line from the Cartar Charter made her laugh until she explained the snafu. She brought up a picture of a turkey, one of the old huge-breasted white tom turkeys that had gone extinct in the late twenty-second century, because the absurdity of the bird perfectly captured the essence of the translation. Loul laughed too and they kept the bird in the center of the light screen. Every time it came up, Meg tapped it, activating the audio command so the "gobble gobble gobble" sound did the talking for her.

LOUL

The interface changed everything. When Loul saw the script filling in the boxes beneath the Urfer symbols, he almost flipped the table in his joy. He drummed his hands, watching as words populated the screen, filling in the audio prompts Meg and the Urfers had recorded. Olum kept shouting something about a sound mirror, and Loul could only assume that he and Agnar had found a way to let the computers listen to each other. It was all beyond him. He'd never been much of a computer guy even though he spent the majority of his workday tethered to one. At least, he used to.

With the screen labeled in Cartar, Loul was able to phrase questions differently and flesh out the broken phrases he and Meg had been using. Vocabulary lists tripled and then tripled again and again as images met their equivalents in the communicating databases. Loul had no idea what that fat, white monstrosity was in the center of the screen—some sort of comic book animal?—but for some reason it kept popping up, making Meg laugh.

They had been way off in some of the assumptions. Those strings the Urfers sometimes ran through their mouths weren't any type of feeding or relaxation method. It seemed the *tut* sometimes left fragments of fiber between their glassy teeth and those teeth were sensitive enough that the sensation drove the Urfers to distraction. And the small packets of gel they rubbed on their skin weren't to protect against the sun or wind, as the Effans first suspected, but to heal the small breaks in their skin where even small rocks thrown by the wind would cut them. It seemed the skin all over their bodies was as sensitive as the tenderest skin in Loul's finger pads.

They also had a complicated sense of humor, the tempo of which changed depending on who was teasing whom. As the vocabulary screen filled itself in with Loul's language, he started making sense of the low phrases Cho often muttered to himself or to Meg, usually when the smallest Urfer, Prader, was making one of her large gestures. The computer didn't translate all the words, but Loul began to get a sense that the further from the truth Cho spoke and the flatter he kept his tone, the more Meg laughed. In a way, Cho's soft-spoken commentary reminded Loul of Hark and his knifelike friendly teasing.

Numbers self-populated in the database as well. Meg and Loul didn't deal much with numbers in their conversations although it was nice to have the means to discuss sequences and preferences. *First* and *last* and *next* and *later* followed naturally from the language of numbers, and soon both of them ignored the number bar scrolling along the bottom of the screen. Meg let the ever-emerging text boxes move over them, sliding them into bundles that now made sense to Loul. But there was one box of numbers she never covered. She never referred or pointed to it but very casually made a point of always keeping it mostly uncovered. Before he'd known the number system, he'd assumed the flashing symbols were some sort of data counter like the kind used in telemetry, a marker of sort for tracking research. Once the small box of Cartar writing appeared under it, however, he saw the box was indeed a counter, only these numbers were going down, steadily decreasing and heading toward zero. A countdown.

MEG

She wound up sleeping with Prader after Kik swung the welding arc and burned Prader's hand too badly to be ignored. All the excitement of the communication and data breakthrough had made the engineer jittery, and Prader had sworn like it was her job when the blue arc whipped across the back of her wrist. The injury wasn't too serious; she didn't need surgery, and she wasn't in any grave danger. However, the Ply-Patch needed to cover the area and regrow the skin, which required her to keep her hand immobile for at least six hours. Cho declared that the only way Prader could remain immobile for six hours was to either tie her down or tranquilize her. With as straight a face as she could muster, Meg suggested that the tying-down option was too difficult to explain culturally. And so Prader and Cho had swapped sleeping shifts.

Cho wanted to keep an eye on the Ply-Patch while Prader slept, not trusting the restless engineer to be still enough even while unconscious, and Meg had bitten back her laugh watching Cho wrestle with the logistics. Meg needed sleep. She was two hours behind her sleep time and could feel her brain getting foggy. Cho and the Effans worked close by the tent she and Cho shared. It made sense that Prader would swap out and sleep in the tent with her. The problem was she knew Cho was more than a little particular about things like tent sharing.

"Have you seen their sleep pad?" he'd asked her one day after Jefferson and Prader had climbed out. "It's like a gravel driveway. Do they even brush their hair? I mean, I don't want to fall back on any Galen Colony stereotypes, but does Jefferson even own a brush? And when's the last time Prader washed that halter?" Meg had laughed, letting Cho gripe. They all had their peculiarities. Now, however, that peculiarity was being tested as Prader climbed into the shelter beside her, flopping back on Cho's sleep pad without even kicking off her shoes. Her arm was splinted, the Ply-Patch was securely taped down, and Cho tried not to look as a clatter of small pebbles poured from her pockets when she settled back. He gave her the sedative and crawled from the tent without a word.

"He's always such a crab," Prader said, shifting against the small pillow. "How can you stand him? Does he ever smile?"

"He smiles plenty."

"Yeah, I bet," she snorted. "Especially when you're in here, right? Well, just remember I'm not him. Don't be rolling over into me copping a feel tonight."

"I don't know, Prader," Meg said around a yawn. "You smell pretty manly."

"I do, don't I?" She laughed, not sounding at all affected by the sedative. She draped her arm over her eye the same way Cho often did. "I wish it would get dark. I miss it being dark."

Meg closed her eyes. "Me too. I can't understand how it is we have the technology to travel across space and yet nobody has been able to design a pair of eyeshades that actually stay on while you sleep."

"Tell me about it. Ow, shit. My hand hurts. That freaking Kik."

"Keep it still. If you bend the patch it won't bond."

"I know, I know, I know."

Prader sighed, fidgeting and kicking her feet against the edge of the sleep pad. Meg almost told her to knock it off, but there was something nice about her restlessness. The high pitch of her sighs and impatient sounds reminded Meg of sharing a bed all those years ago with Maddie. Her twin had never been able to just let go like Meg could, and instead fought sleep with the boundless energy that always gripped her. Prader flipped the sheet off of her legs, pointing her feet toward the ceiling of the low tent and softly tapping along the brace there.

"You know what I wonder about?"

Meg laughed. "Why tranquilizers don't work on you?"

Prader ignored her. "Where do they live?"

"What do you mean? They have houses and stuff. We saw it on the recon."

"Yeah but, I mean, what do they do there?" Prader dropped her legs and rolled onto her side, carefully keeping her injured hand on her hip. "They don't sleep so why do they have houses? What do they do there?"

Meg squinted at her in the red filtered light. "We do more than sleep in our houses."

"But think about it. Why do we have houses in the first place? Every creature on Earth sleeps, right? Everything sleeps. And everything, on land at least, is vulnerable while it sleeps. It digs a hole or builds a burrow or climbs a tree so that it can sleep. It makes a safe place so it can sleep and its kids can sleep, right? That's the whole reason humans banded together in the first place, to light the fire and circle the wagons and be safe in the dark while we slept."

"True."

"So why do they have houses? How big are they? Are they just like 'Here's my kitchen and my closet and, uh, here's where I stay awake all the time'? See what I mean? What the hell do they do all day? When there aren't aliens invading their planet, I mean."

Meg thought about that. "Well, they have families. They have entertainment—movies and TV and stuff. I guess they just have a lot more time for it."

"Man," Prader kicked her toes together, her voice thickening with sleep. "Can you imagine if you never had to sleep? How much you could get done? That'd be awesome."

"It would be awful. I love sleep." She pulled the sheet up to her chin even though she wasn't cold. Heat came off Prader's body in waves. "I love dreams. Even bad ones."

Prader snickered. "You like sleep because you get to get busy with Dr. Cho, Evil Eye. You like to get your hands on all those mojo signs he's got on his body."

"You're one to talk. I've heard more than one bump-'n'-grind groan coming from your tent. Gettin' a little orange slice, are ya?" They both giggled at the slur. After a few generations, the minerals in the Galen Colonies soil had added a copper tinge to the residents' skin. The Galens wore it with pride but were not above throwing a fist if someone cast aspersions upon their skin tone. Prader made it her mission to bring it up to Jefferson at every opportunity. He took it in stride, referring to himself as her "personal vitamin C."

Prader yawned large, her breath sour from her steady diet of Gro-Wall beans. "Well just between you and me, I think Jeff and the captain are trading more than data packets, if you know what I mean." She rolled onto her back, her injured hand cradled to her stomach.

"What?" Meg asked, sitting up. "You've got to be kidding me?" Prader said nothing, her breathing soft and even. "Now you fall asleep? After that little nugget of gossip?" She flopped back down, shaking her head. A rough rasping started beside her. Of course Prader would snore.

LOUL

Loul tried not to show his relief when he saw that Cho wasn't going into stasis with Meg. That meant the Effans would be busy and he would have time to think. He wanted so badly to talk with Po and Reno Dado, especially Reno Dado. Of all the crazy alien stuff she had laughed at over the years, she had always believed that psychics could hear vibrations from people. She had even taken meditation courses trying to "align her vibrations with her true vocation." Po had ridiculed her for it but Loul had managed to keep a straight face. He couldn't wait to tell her she'd been right. Sort of.

Meg had been more preoccupied with her injured crewmate and the treatment Cho provided than with Loul's disappointment at her need for stasis. After all these rounds, he still felt that ache when he knew she would disappear for at least a shift. He was getting better at sensing when her stasis was due. The Urfers followed a time schedule that worked independently of the shifting colors of the suns. According to Cho, via the Effans, their bodies functioned on an Urf rhythm that couldn't be altered. The more strictly these rhythms were observed, the better the Urfers functioned. Even with the schedule, each Urfer spent several moments after stasis unprepared to return to work. Meg called those periods *morning*.

Cho warned the Effans that because he was missing his normal stasis shift he might become less energetic as they worked. Meg had laughed at that, recording the word *grumpy* into the language program. When Loul went to repeat it, she touched *no* and laughed. More Urfer humor. Whatever *grumpy* meant, if Cho didn't go down with Meg, that meant the Effans would be occupied while Meg was gone. Before she climbed into her shelter, Loul tapped her arm, resting his knuckles on her wristband.

She'd stared at him and then grinned. "Yes." She unbuckled the thin band and handed it to him. "Loul read words. Loul open screen?" He tried to replicate the pinching movement she used to draw the screen from the red light but nothing happened. Meg drew the screen out for him, showing him how to balance it on his fingertips so it wouldn't close when he moved. He watched the screen fill with text boxes, pictures, and symbols, all filling in with the ever-improving Cartar vocabulary interface.

He balanced the incorporeal thing on his fingertips, afraid to move. She smiled, patting his arm. "Screen no good then ask Cho. Cho make screen good. Okay?"

He wanted to tap his knuckles but didn't want to disturb the screen. "Okay," he said, rising up with the light above his hands. "Loul read." Meg smiled and he stepped away to make room for Prader and Cho to climb in after her.

She hadn't given him any warning about the screen. She hadn't made any sign to hide anything or change the program in any way that he could tell. Surely she understood that he was going to look through the files, and, as his language filled in the gaps, he would understand what he saw there. That meant she wasn't hiding anything, right? He didn't kid himself about the very real probability that anything secret wouldn't be on this database to begin with. Even he, a lowly weather watcher, had access and passwords for classified files. Information could be hidden. As he made his way across the work site, moving as carefully as possible so nothing would happen to the screen, he kept his eye on the numbers ticking down in the upper-right corner of the screen. He had a theory, and he had at least a shift alone to work on it.

He had 08:42:33 to work on it. Whatever that meant. The thirty-three counted down so quickly he could hardly follow it, and by the time he made it to his booth, he had 08:39:57.

He didn't just watch the numbers ticking off. That made him too nervous. Maybe it was nothing, maybe it was part of the clock that kept their rigid sleeping and eating schedule. Maybe it was nothing more than the battery life of whatever was powering this computer. He poked around on the screen, listening to the strange pastiche of recordings putting together phrases. Maybe those numbers didn't mean anything important, but Meg never covered them up. She never explained them, but she never let them disappear. Meg was many things—mysterious, expressive, and enthralling—but she wasn't careless. She kept her eye on those numbers.

He realized the screen didn't respond as well to the rough skin of his fingers, often skipping commands and falling silent. When he opened his pads, however, the boxes lit up easily, the screen scrolling through prompts as it did for Meg. He pulled up photographs of Urf and lost himself in images of rolling seas and grassy plains, huge buildings and crowded squares. It some ways it didn't seem that different from Didet. The people obviously looked a lot different and their clothes were nothing like the Urfers on-site wore. The clothes in photographs were full of color and pressed into strange shapes and designs. Sometimes everyone in a picture wore the same outfit; sometimes everyone dressed differently, but so many of the pictures could have passed for badly developed Didet photos. If the film got overexposed and somehow the images lengthened so that the people were longer and paler, he could almost see the pictures of his own family gathered around at different events. People smiled, crowded in close. Babies were held up to cameras, and there were even pictures of mothers and fathers pressing their lips into the spot where the babies' rose spots should have been.

He could spend all day looking at the pictures. He scrolled through, looking for the photos Meg had spoken of when Urf was in darkness. *Night* she called it, but since there was no word equivalent in Cartar, he couldn't scan for it that way. He couldn't even find the button for it on the language screen, the nontranslated words having fallen behind the opened translated boxes. He took care as he searched, however, to keep the rolling numbers visible.

04:22:13 and counting.

Meg had gone into stasis halfway through full red. Now the Ellaban Sun rose over the peaks, and they were in the thick of Eller-orange. By his calculation, Meg should be coming out of the shelter just as the Eller shift ended, early in high orange. He did some simple math. The countdown should be right around 02:40:40. He could remember that. Two-four-four.

At 03:05:05 he shifted in the booth so he could keep an eye on Meg's shelter. He had found the pictures of *night* and hadn't even noticed how far into Eller-orange they'd gotten. The photographs were incredible, somehow capturing light against the velvet blackness of the Urf sky. He'd seen Space, he knew that blackness, and he longed to see it again. He never imagined he would be seeing it captured on film over an alien planet. One sun. Urf had one sun. He had stumbled upon photographs of huge sections of the planet that were too cold to live in. They were white with ice—ice on the planet. He'd only ever seen ice on the satellite lenses when they went above the atmosphere. He couldn't imagine these long, thin creatures, the Urfers whose skin was so delicate that wind rocks could cut them, being able to exist, to thrive on a planet extreme enough to have ice on its surface.

02:50:52. Cho moved to the door of Meg's shelter, sticking his head inside the flap. He climbed inside, medical kit in hand. Moments later Meg emerged, rubbing her eyes against the sea wind and high orange light. She yawned and stretched her body into an almost comically long pose, her arms jutting from her body in a crooked line. Loul watched, applauding himself for being so close on his calculations, and saw Meg jump, clutching her wrist where the wristband usually rested. Her gaze flew to their booth and Loul held up his hand in greeting. She blinked with that look she and the Urfers always seemed to wear when experiencing *morning*. As he knew she would, she waved back and headed for the Urfer waste station. Then she would get a water bag and either some *tut* or those strange green blocks and join him.

The Urfers stuck to their schedules. They had routines and rhythms. According to his calculations, Loul had only to wait until high orange began to fade into Fa-pale for the countdown to zero out. He'd know if his gut was right. He tried to prepare himself as he had all his life to be disappointed, to have overestimated the importance of what his imagination rendered, but the longer he spent on-site with the Urfers, the more faith he put in his gut. He knew that after Meg arose, Agnar would go down for his period of stasis. Agnar always waited for the signal from Meg and Cho that they were back on-site before heading into his shelter. This time, however, Meg and Prader finished in the waste station and signaled to the leader. He signaled back, and Loul watched the leader, Cheffson, and Cho all check their screens. Only two units of Urfer time remained on the clock. Nobody went down into stasis.

FOURTEEN

LOUL

Meg was acting differently. It wasn't just *morning*, and although he only understood part of what she said about Prader and stasis, he didn't think that was what made her seem different. Maybe he was just reading into it; maybe staring at that countdown getting closer to zero had him imagining things. Meg's long fingers fluttered more than usual and she didn't so much sit in the booth as fidget lower and lower until she settled in place. Her thumb flicked at the refill valve of her water bag, and she kept squeezing the clear plastic, forcing the bubbles up and down. She smiled and made a happy sound when she saw the pictures of Urf on screen.

"Good, very good," she said, pointing to a picture of rough sea underneath a multicolored sky, one lone sun sinking beneath the horizon. "Meg likes sea very much." She waved her hand in the direction of the Ketter Sea, invisible but very much present behind the site. Normally Loul would have asked a question or picked another photograph or maybe even invited her to walk with him again to the edge of the work site where they could see the water beating against the rocks, but he couldn't find it in himself to do any of those things. He couldn't think about anything but that countdown, and he wanted to see if Meg had noticed that he had noticed the numbers. If she had, she didn't make any sign of it.

She also didn't seem to notice the change in their conversation tempo. Her fingers flitted through commands and prompts, topics and directions changing in no discernible order. Loul kept up with her, keeping his answers simple, keeping questions to a minimum. He felt calm, which surprised him, since that ever-decreasing number seemed to tick off faster and faster the lower it got. A sense of inevitability misted down over him, a helplessness to whatever was going to happen as he watched Meg's gaze flit around the work site, meeting the eyes of her crewmates. One to another, their gazes passed over the Dideto crews, never holding one spot too long but always flickering back to their work screens. Back, Loul just knew, to that countdown.

He saw the moment she knew she'd been found out. He'd asked an uninterested question about a large, leaping sea creature when Meg's gaze had shifted to Cho. Cho had been staring in Meg's direction, his long fingers pushing his lips back and forth. The Effans bustled around him and he didn't seem to be listening. He didn't seem to be looking at anything either until Meg turned her face to him. Nothing remarkable happened. There was no big change of expression, and if Loul hadn't made a point of noticing how subtle the Urfers could be, he might not have noticed the gesture at all.

Cho had kept his fingers over his mouth, his elbow braced on the Effans' high medical lab. When he and Meg locked gazes, he stopped rubbing his face. He stood very still, and Loul hardly even noticed when the longest finger on the Urfer's hand, the middle one, slipped ever so slightly over the first finger. Just the tips crossed and only for a second, as if he were scratching an itch. It probably wouldn't have registered at all if Loul hadn't chosen that moment to glance back at Meg, whose hand rested on the edge of the table. Her fluttering fingers stilled when she looked at Cho. As Loul watched her, the first two fingers of her right hand twisted, second over first. It didn't look like a casual gesture when she did it. It didn't look like scratching an itch, and when Cho saw her do it, he dropped his hand from his face and went back to work.

Loul didn't move when Meg looked back at him. He didn't scowl. He wasn't angry. It was too late to be angry. He'd told Meg he trusted her; he had let the media think everything was fine. The Urfer time units were flying by too quickly for anything to be done to stop whatever was going to happen. Whatever those looks meant, whatever those twisted fingers signified, whatever the Urfers (the aliens, he reminded himself) were waiting for was going to be here in just a matter of heartbeats, and Loul felt oddly free of concern. Whatever it was, he told himself, at least he'd be the first to see it.

Meg sighed and brought her hand up between them. She twisted the fingers. "Yes?"

She knew he'd seen them. There was no point in pretending now. He pointed to the numbers ticking down in the corner of the screen. 00:12:04.

Meg bobbed her head. "Yes." When Loul said nothing, that strange sense of peace and surrender stilling him, Meg rested her chin in her hands, staring at him. Loul thought back to the first time he'd seen her do that, just a few rounds ago, although it seemed like a lifetime, and he'd wondered at the time if their heads were too heavy for their thin necks to hold them up. He knew better now, of course. He knew those thin limbs and long muscles were deceptively strong. Deceptively.

Meg swept the light screen of the photographs, opening up a large blank box in the center. A big box usually meant a difficult concept. Well, they had 00:09:54 time units to get there. Her fingers hovered over the screen, digging at the air the way they did when she looked for a way to start a concept. A thousand howling inevitabilities pounded in the back of his mind trying to predict the revelation she was about to share. Invasion, explosion, conquest, uprising, escape—all the things any comic-reading kid knew followed the end of a countdown, and yet Loul found himself drifting in a peaceful absence of concern. Probably denial, something whispered in his head, but at least he felt ready for anything.

Except that big white thing. Shaking her head and making a sound of impatience, Meg pulled the picture of the fat, white animal that had shown up on the screen when the computers had interfaced. "Turkey," she said, jabbing at the image. "Turkey. Okay?"

He didn't know what to say. So much for being ready for anything. Meg scrubbed her face with her hands the way Cho had been doing just moments before. Anxiety. That was the only thing the gesture brought to mind for Loul. Like they thought they could scrub unhappy thoughts out of their mind by scrubbing them off of their skin. After a few noisy breaths, Meg dropped her hands to the side of the screen, her fingers dancing lightly on the edges as she faced him. Her shoulders dropped, her head leaning forward in that full-body attention way she did. Loul felt himself responding automatically, her attention triggering his. 07:38:22.

"Loul need/wants turkey, okay?" She let one hand hover between the *yes* and *no* buttons, a sign that this wasn't exactly what she meant, their unspoken way of saying "sort of" or "maybe" or even "hang on." He tapped his knuckles.

"Okay." He put his hand beside hers between the buttons. "Loul need/want turkey." He had no idea why he would need or want that hideous thing, but he would give it a chance.

"Okay." Meg took a deep breath, her fingers splayed over the screen. "Meg need/want Loul has turkey. Meg need/want to Loul need/want." She shook her hands, her fingers fidgeting over the screen in that way that told Loul she was frustrated. Muttering to herself, she pulled up the audio/text combo boxes she had just pushed aside. Now that Cartar had filled in the boxes beneath them, Loul could read the boxes as she assembled them. She pointed to each box as she read it:

"Meg—need/want—Loul—need/want—turkey."

"Why would you want me to want a turkey?" Loul asked, knowing it was the wrong question and that she couldn't understand it anyway. Or maybe she did because she pushed down her palms in a gesture he'd come to know as "wait."

"Turkey to Loul is okay/good." She flipped the boxes in place, pointing as she spoke. "Loul need/want turkey."

"Okay." 05:15:48.

"Meg—need/want—okay/good—to Loul." She touched Loul's hand and then pressed her palms together in front of him. "Meg Loul." She pressed her hands harder together. "Meg Loul okay/good, yes? Meg trust Loul. Loul trust Meg. Okay/good, yes?"

He felt a warmth rising around his face. He knew what she was saying, or he thought he did. She was assuring him that they were friends. Considering how fast the numbers were counting down, the assurance didn't comfort him. But Meg continued, her focus drawing him in as always. "Yes. Meg Loul okay/good."

She ran her finger along the string of text boxes. At the *need/want* box between Loul and the turkey, she pressed the audio. "Loul need/want." Drawing her finger back to the text box between her name and his, she spoke again: "This need/want is..." and she made a sound he could barely hear. It sounded like a sigh or the rush of wind. He watched her mouth as the machine recorded her word but could only hear air pushed out between her pursed lips. The program filled in the new text box with Urfer symbols, but because he couldn't understand it and thus couldn't translate it, the Cartar box remained empty. He let his knuckles fall away.

Meg bit her lip, seeing the gap in the program translation. She scrambled some more text boxes onto the screen. "Loul need/want turkey. Then Loul has turkey. This is good…" A few jabs at the screen and she recorded another word. She held up both hands, the second fingers twisted around the first in that gesture she and Cho had shared.

Loul stared at the text boxes. If he wanted a turkey and he got a turkey, it was this new word, this new gesture. He turned up the volume to hear more clearly and hit the buttons to play back the words.

"Loul get turkey. This is good luck."

Meg held up her twisted fingers and glanced at the numbers as they sped toward zero. "Meg need/want good luck. Urfers need/want good luck."

Loul didn't think this had anything to do with turkeys.

MEG

00:00:00.

She could only imagine what he was thinking. He'd seen the numbers. Nothing good ever happened when a clock hit zero, at least not on Earth. He hadn't pressed her, and for that she would be eternally grateful, but the blind, helpless trust he put in her was almost worse than an angry confrontation. His thrum had softened. She'd heard it changing, lessening, as if he were drawing away from her. It hadn't been her imagination either. Nothing had changed with the Effans. Meg could hear them chattering away as always, and Kik and his crew seemed as determined as ever to do their damage despite Prader's distraction. Meg had heard Olum pound the table more than once trying to get a point across to Wagner. Jefferson dug and scraped his samples, but all of their minds were elsewhere.

Only Loul seemed to pick up on the distraction. Only Loul seemed to want to call Meg out on her evasion. She tried to tell herself she was just projecting, but one look in his hooded gray eyes and she knew he knew. She tried to teach him the word *wish*, but like the concept itself, the word was too soft, too ethereal for him to pick up. So she'd gone with *luck*. She didn't know if he understood the concept or if the Dideto even had an equivalent word. It didn't matter now. The timer hit zero. She and the rest of the crew were going to learn if they had any luck at all.

Loul didn't stop her when she rose. He didn't even seem surprised. She held her hands out, palm down, in an unnecessary gesture encouraging him to wait for her. He always waited for her. He'd never let his attention flicker from hers since their first encounter. As she slipped out of the booth she was grateful they hadn't tackled the concept of loyalty.

Nobody needed to call out or signal. The five Earthers just moved as one to the clearing at the center of the site. Funny, Meg thought as they gathered in their usual circle, the whole site was packed with equipment and cables and work crews and yet this ring, this little five-foot circle, repelled clutter. She wasn't even sure the Dideto even walked through it. Some patches of dirt just seemed to create their own energy.

Cho stood nearer to her than he usually did, not touching but just an elbow bend from it. Prader gripped and flipped a wrench in her hands, holding on to it like the handle of a roller coaster. Jefferson rubbed his thumbs over his forefingers, loosening the grit from the creases there, grit that had long since become permanent. Wagner looked to each of them before opening his screen and raising a volume control that the rest of the crew had kept on mute. They all knew he'd kept the volume of this channel just at the edge of hearing range, his captain's ear incapable of not listening for it.

They stood silently, waiting, the hot orange of the sun fading. Meg was thankful for that. After this period, the air would cool just a little, the light become a little less flame-like. She thought it was the time they called Fa-something because the light came mostly from the paler sun that always hung over the archiving station. Wagner would know. He'd made a point of knowing the suns and their schedules. She and the rest of the crew had just moved through the shifting light trying not to get sunburned or light-blinded. Wagner paid attention to the suns. He was a navigator. The solar patterns directly affected this mission. He had to pay attention to them, just like he had to keep a certain audio channel open.

They waited, hearing the unmistakable white noise of an inactive audio channel. Around them, the Dideto crews thrummed and muttered, curious about the withdrawal of their Earther teammates. From the corner of her eye, Meg saw crews heading toward Loul to ask him. Loul was the unofficial authority on all the strange behavior the Earthers exhibited. She wondered what he was telling them.

"Contact, *Damocles Sub Two*, this is the *Damocles*, contact come in."

As one, the five Earthers blew out a sigh of relief loud enough to be heard over the sea wind. Prader slumped forward, hands on her knees still clinging to the wrench. Jefferson bent backward, eyes closed, mouth open. Cho bumped against Meg, who had to cover her face with her hands. Wagner stayed still as he spoke.

211

"*Damocles*, this is *Sub Two*. We have contact." His voice broke on the last word and he dropped to one knee. "It sure is good to hear your voice, Aaronson."

The tremor in the usually unshakeable voice brought the rest of the crew to the ground as well. They settled cross-legged, listening. "It sure is good to be heard, Captain. It was, um…" Static crackled and Cho grabbed Meg's hand. "It was a little more exciting than I cared for. Especially since I had to worry about your candy asses getting Roswelled down there. Can I assume Prader hasn't shot anyone yet?"

They laughed and Meg felt tension she hadn't even realized she'd been carrying running out her spine. Prader spun her wrench on the ground before her. "Don't assume anything, Aaronson. And don't think you can help yourself to my stuff. My underwear had better all be in place when we get back."

"Trust me when I tell you this, Prader"—Aaronson's voice regained its stony tone—"there is nothing in this universe safer than your underwear. Jefferson's underwear, on the other hand…"

"Okay, okay, let's knock off the chatter." Wagner tried to sound stern but his grin gave him away. "We still have a mission and we've got a lot of confused Dideto around us wondering what the hell we're doing right now."

"Oh shit." Meg spun from the circle and found Loul's wide-eyed, flushed face staring back at her. She'd forgotten to turn off his com. The other Dideto had earpieces but Meg had restricted the channels they could access. Only Loul's had full access to anything she could hear. She'd wanted him to hear the interplay among the crew. He was fascinated by the tones and tempos even when he couldn't understand the words. Now he heard a new voice, a voice he believed she'd lied about.

"What's it like down there?" Aaronson asked as Meg opened her screen. She didn't want to do this. She knew the message it would send to Loul but what they were discussing here would be too difficult to explain. She didn't know what the verdict was going to be and she couldn't let Loul stumble upon information he might misunderstand. There were limits to anyone's loyalty. She shut off his com.

His hand flew to his ear, tapping the piece as if he thought it had malfunctioned. When he realized the truth, he pulled the piece from his head, dropping it on the table. Meg held out her hands in that gesture that begged patience but he turned away from her. For the first time since their landing, Loul turned his back on her.

"Shit." She turned back to the circle, shutting off her screen. Wagner raised an eyebrow at her but she waved him off. One thing at a time.

Prader, Jefferson, and Cho continued talking over each other, answering Aaronson's questions about the planet, the people, the discoveries they'd made. They bragged about Meg's language breakthroughs and Wagner's computer interface miracle and teased Cho about his new girlfriends. Aaronson laughed, an unusual sound from the serious woman, and kept peppering them with questions. At first, they lost themselves in the happy conversation, but as the questions kept coming, Meg saw Prader raise a worried glance to Wagner. Cho took Meg's hand again, and while they kept up the chatter, the tension in the circle rose.

Wagner, as captain, took the lead. "So now that you're light side again, we're going to relay this information back to the ship's database. We've got a megaton of information that's going to take three lifetimes to process, so we'll have plenty of work on our hands. But the pictures don't really do it justice. Officer Aaronson"—he cleared his throat, the muscles in his jaw working to spit out the question—"will you be joining us on the surface?"

Static ripped through the coms and the five of them leaned forward, unconsciously urging the answer from their crewmate. She took a moment before answering. "That's a negative, Captain. The Chelyan crystal is not recovering. I repeat, the crystal is not recovering. I cannot put the system in automatic." Even through the static, Meg could hear Aaronson swallow hard around the words. The five on the ground grew very still.

"Prognosis?"

"I believe the crystal is still viable. It hasn't shown signs of terminal damage but as yet I cannot reactivate the growth cycle." Aaronson kept her tone level, her words technical, her speech familiar to all of them as that of a pilot in crisis. Aaronson had been a combat pilot before becoming one of the most decorated deep-space navigators alive. She knew more about Chelyan crystals than anyone in the crew, and Meg knew her greatest asset was her ability to remain calm and realistic. If Aaronson said the crystal was still viable, it was. That she wouldn't leave the system to automatically tend to the situation spoke volumes on the seriousness of their situation.

Wagner's lips were pale around the edges where he held his mouth so tight. "Recommendations?"

"A direct injection. The space debris I've picked up in orbit hasn't had sufficient amounts of the silicates needed to reactivate the recombination. To be honest, I think all this damned solar radiation is burning off the elements we need." They all heard the sound of something banging. Meg could picture Aaronson in her navigation cubby hurling her coffee cup across the panel. That action was the equivalent of any of the other crew members having a complete histrionic meltdown.

"What are you looking for?" Jefferson dug his nails into the dry soil. "We've got an abundance of Class I and II silicates within easy reach."

Aaronson sighed, a whispering sound through the static. "I don't think we can do it without Class IV. Maybe, maybe we can hump 'n' jump with Class III, but, I'm not going lie, I haven't been feeling especially lucky lately." They could hear her breath through the com. "It's really good to hear your voices. These suns, that star pair we rode in behind, they do weird things with the light up here."

Meg shivered despite herself.

"How are we with hard fuel?" The captain's voice was all business.

"Uh, we've been better but we're okay." The sound of keys clicking came through beneath her voice. "Someone had the decency to smash up a pretty large moon a couple hundred years ago and there's enough hard metal to keep the magnets busy. I've shut down all systems on the ship except mine so the cells can recharge. I hope nobody minds but I broke into the whiskey to toast the innovator who decided to equip the *Damocles* with solar rechargers. We're going to have enough to break orbit and give her a good running start if...you know."

"Yeah." Wagner gnawed on the edge of his lip. "Jefferson?"

The geologist pried a small stone loose from the ground. "We've got traces of Class IV but so far I haven't found a solid source. Hopefully now that the captain's started the interface I can research the Didetos' files for the silicates. So far I can't really figure out how they classify their minerals. Seems they don't break them down quite the same way we do. Plus the surface is pretty uniform, at least where the drones have touched down."

Aaronson cut him off. "It's not an accident that Class IVs tend to cluster in the black. Solar radiation and higher-class silicates—not exactly a love story. We didn't have them on Earth for that very reason. A planet with seven suns? Well..."

Meg only understood a fraction of the discussion. She knew the crystal needed certain elements combined at varying temperatures to reactivate. The crystal had been designed to operate in the cold void of space.

"This hump 'n' jump you're talking about." Prader tapped the wrench against her open palm. "How much humping and jumping are we talking about? Can I retrofit the fuel cells for a little more jumping and save the humping for the deep-space burn?"

The sound of keys clicking came through the coms once more as Cho squeezed Meg's hand. She looked up at him and he gave her a shrug. So much of this propulsion talk was beyond him as well. He and Meg were the least qualified to make an engineering decision.

"If we can get a large enough dose of some clean Class IVs and you can boost our burn out of orbit, I think we can probably limp up enough speed to hump the crystal. I won't know until injection but it's worth a look-see. Can you run a diagnostic down there?"

"Hell, yes." Prader threw down the wrench and pulled out her screen.

Wagner looked to Jefferson, who worried smooth pebbles from the ground. "How about it, Jefferson? Can you find some clean Class IVs? A sufficient amount?"

His words rolled out with a heavy Galen drawl. "Well, it's a slightly larger needle in a slightly smaller haystack, so yeah, I think I can trace the traces, so to speak. Send me down some specs, Aaronson, and I'll start digging."

"Let me do some figuring," the pilot said, typing as she spoke. "I'm going to try a few more things up, you know, since I have all this time on my hands. Also, since the deep freeze isn't the answer, we'd save a lot of juice if I can drop down into closer orbit. I don't suppose you could clear that with your new friends?

Keep them from shooting me out of the sky? I've been playing hide-and-seek with a couple of bad-looking satellites up here."

Wagner nodded. "They're decades away from having anything to reach you, Aaronson, but we'll wait to see if they spot you. We don't want to start a panic."

Cho squeezed Meg's hand and she realized she had drifted from the conversation after Wagner's remark about creating a panic. It seemed that everyone else's teams had enough hard data to distract themselves from the question of another Earth ship. The Dideto were nothing if not focused on their jobs. Only Loul had pressed the issue and it had hardly been a press at all. Maybe it was a natural lack of curiosity, although she doubted that. Maybe it was politeness. Maybe the Dideto simply didn't evade questions, choosing to be honest at all times. That seemed impossible to imagine as a human being. Whatever the case, Meg had to face Loul now and try to explain what she had hidden and why. Before she could even begin to formulate how she would approach this, Aaronson's voice caught her attention.

"Here's the thing, Captain. If this works, if you find adequate silicates and if Prader can pull off a hump 'n' jump on the thrusters, it's going to change our parameters. Significantly."

"How so?"

"Sir, I know these crystals. I know this crystal, this kind of crystal. I've seen this kind of affliction before." They could hear static crackle as she cleared her throat. "After the injection, we've got to let her digest it. If it takes, if she lets it in, she's going to be a shark. She's a shark."

"A shark?" Meg asked.

"Yeah. If the injection feeds her then she's got to move. She's got to move fast and she's got to keep on moving for at least a year. If we can fix her, we have to leave."

LOUL

The generals had their backs to him, talking into the heavy radio set as they always did just before Fa-pale, when the signal was clearest. They were filling in the presidents on the day's activities and discoveries. Loul knew they didn't know the biggest discovery of all.

He had to tell them. He had to let them know that he'd been wrong, that there were more Urfers and that they were close, close enough to contact their ground crew. There was another ship and there were more Urfers and he had lied about knowing otherwise. He hadn't known, of course. None of them had, but by not admitting such in front of the world media, he'd let it be implied that he knew differently.

He kept seeing Meg's face when she'd turned off his earpiece. She knew he had heard the voice. The expression on her face was yet another one he hadn't seen before. If he had to guess—and really wasn't that all he'd been doing this whole time?—he'd have said it was a look of fear. Like she was afraid the secret was out. Like she was afraid he would tell the generals and foil their plan.

Was she afraid? Did she have a plan? Was it all a lie? The specter of being the man who had vouched for these Urfers, these aliens, these invaders to his planet, swooped down and pushed all the air out of his lungs. It was very similar to the feeling he'd known when he'd stood in front of the panel of officials and heard them laughing at his alien-contact preparation report. The long-term repercussions weren't what hurt. He hadn't thought about the death wound he had just inflicted on his career. He'd felt only the humiliation. And now, crouching down watching the generals file their daily report, he felt the same immediacy of shame. Death, destruction, enslavement of his planet—stupidly they paled in light of going down in history as the man who didn't have sense enough to keep his guard up, the dork who'd treated the entire encounter like a ridiculous child's role-playing game.

He had to tell them. Rising from his crouch, he banged his fists against his hips, trying to fortify his resolve. Then he felt the unmistakably delicate touch on his shoulder. Meg.

He felt helpless to resist turning to her. Part of him hoped, as he'd hoped the very first time they'd shown their faces, that she'd have the courtesy to kill him first and spare him the shame. In the Fa-pale, her skin looked colder, paler, like the skin of water snakes. Small patches of redness scattered across her brow where wind pebbles had struck her. Such a strange fragility.

"Loul." She held out her hand, unfolding the long fingers to reveal his earpiece. He hesitated and then took it from her palm. He didn't put it on.

"More Urfers are coming, aren't they?" He knew she wore her translator.

"No."

He ground his teeth at the lie. He wanted to crush the earpiece and shout to the generals but then he realized what he had heard. She hadn't spoken through the earpiece. She hadn't spoken through the speaker patch. She hadn't even spoken in Cartar. She had said "no" in her language, a small puff of a word, and he had understood it. It still didn't make it true.

He jabbed his fist toward the sky. "More Urfers are coming, yes?"

"No." She put her hand on his, pulling the earpiece toward his head, but he jerked his hand away.

"Yes, Meg. Loul hears. Loul hears more Urfers. Urfers coming."

"No, Loul." His name in her voice sounded so soft, and he had to fight losing himself in the fascination of her expressions. She dropped her head forward, letting it sway like a reed. Her wet eyes looked from his hand and the unused earpiece then back to his face.

"Loul. No Urfers…" He couldn't hear her voice over the wind and rumble of the machinery but he understood her gesture. She lifted her hand to the sky and pulled it down, as if drawing down a string. She was telling him no Urfers were coming down. She swept her hand behind her, encompassing the work site. "Urfers," she said once more and made another gesture that froze him to the spot. Without thinking, he tipped his head, falling back into their conversational habit of requesting a repeat. She made the gesture again, her eyes shining in the Fa-pale light. He scrambled to put on his earpiece.

"More Urfers coming, Meg? Yes?" His tone was softer now, almost pleading. The bad news he'd feared suddenly preferable to what he thought she was telling him.

"No, Loul." The translator left no room for misunderstanding. "More Urfers not coming. This, Urfers here," she swept her hand in a graceful arc toward her team. "Urfers move. Urfers move from Didet. Urfers go." The water that puddled up along the rim of her eyes overflowed, leaving tracks along the pale skin of her narrow face. She didn't wipe them away, and Loul thought that just maybe he could hear the sound of the drops hitting the ground at his feet.

FIFTEEN

MEG

None of the other conversations mattered now. The syntaxes, the subtleties, the yawning gaps in data—Meg couldn't make herself care about any of that now. She had less than seventy-two hours now to tell Loul all the things she'd wanted to tell him, to listen to him tell her everything she needed to know about him. She knew it was sentimentality but even the now-pale light seemed a little rosier, a little softer than usual. Seventy-two hours left and she didn't give a crap about Dideto's political structure or cultural inclinations. She didn't want to upload their historical records or study the impact of the ancient message on their collective unconscious. She didn't want to do all of the things she had thrown herself across space for because now that she had less than seventy-two hours, all she wanted to do was know Loul.

This was assuming, of course, that the crystal injection worked. If it didn't, seventy-two hours would just be the warm-up for the rest of their lives spent on this sun-warmed world. Meg couldn't even begin to approach her feelings about that.

The way Loul stared at her made it difficult to swallow. She knew her tears confused him, but she couldn't and wouldn't make them stop. She didn't really cry, at least not with any force, but the tears kept puddling up and spilling over her cheeks, and she just couldn't think of a reason to stop them. This whole mission had been such a fuckup, and if there had been anyone she could put the blame on, she'd have beaten them within an inch of their life. They hadn't had time to prepare for contact, and now they didn't have time to wrap up the contact that they'd made. It made her think of those stories of people who went into the light after they died only to get jerked back into their bodies upon resuscitation. It felt like hell.

And this kind of woolgathering and teeth-gnashing was exactly what the situation didn't need, but everything she could think of to start talking about seemed so trivial, so pointless in light of their impending departure, that all she could do was stare at Loul and let the tears fall. They had at least made it to their booth. All around them, the crews worked with a new urgency, although the Earthers had decided to keep the news of their departure a secret until they could be certain Jefferson could find a source of the proper minerals.

"I'm going to tell Loul," Meg had said in a tone that accepted no discussion, and none had followed. "He won't tell." Cho had let go of her hand, and the five Earthers had gone back to work. Four Earthers. Meg had rendered herself pretty much useless.

LOUL

He was a young man. He kept himself in pretty good shape. So how did he know his heart didn't have the strength to keep up with the shocks he kept putting it through? Just minutes before he'd been ready to denounce Meg and her company to the generals as a threat to the safety of his home, and now that he knew they were leaving it was all he could do to not arm cuff himself to Meg's leg and demand she take him with her. Or at least lock down the ship somehow so they couldn't take off and fly away with the only interesting, worthwhile, and notable thing Loul Pell had ever been party to in the course of his entire life.

He did none of those things, of course. He couldn't do anything but sit across from Meg and watch the drops of water slide down the long, pale cheeks. They didn't need the translator to explain those drops. Of all the conceptual leaps Loul had made since the Urfers' wondrous arrival, he knew he correctly read the emotion on Meg's face, and although he hated to see her upset, he had to admit to himself he was glad she was sorry to leave.

Meg was leaving. The Urfers were leaving. Like a sticky message that has lost its glue, the truth of those words just wouldn't sink in. Funny how it had been so easy for him to accept the fact that the Urfers had arrived, that aliens existed and wore pants and wanted to talk with him. That he'd gotten on board with right away. Throw a wrench into those plans and his brain shut down like a social kitchen at cleaning time.

He knew just what he wanted to do, what he needed to do. Meg would go along with him. There wasn't any more time to argue about it. Climbing from the booth, Loul held out his hand to Meg. He'd seen her intertwine her hands with Cho, had seen them walk the site together in the quiet moments before and after stasis. Clasping hands was something Urfers did when they trusted one another, just like the Dideto. Her hand didn't fit into his the way a Dideto woman's would, her long fingers wrapping almost all the way around his thick fist yet barely wide enough to cover the tender pads of his palms, but Meg slipped her hand into his without a question. Her elbow knocked lightly against his shoulder as she loped along beside him, their intertwined hands bumping between them. It was a strange and awkward way to walk and Loul loved it.

Two of the generals looked up at their approach, and the third was dropped out on a low bench away from the table. General Ada watched Meg as if he expected her to draw a weapon and leap upon him.

"Something on your mind, Pell?"

"Yes sir. I've come to requisition an airvan."

Ada dropped the papers he'd been reading. "Are they moving? Have they agreed to be moved off-site? Well done, Pell. Good work. We're going to use the cargo trucks for—"

"No sir, you misunderstand me. The Urfers aren't moving." Loul felt Meg's fingers shift and tighten in his hand. He explained his plan to the generals, who now stood shoulder to shoulder, faces darkening in surprise.

"Impossible, Pell. Have you lost your mind? We don't have the security in place."

"That's exactly why it will work, sirs. Nobody knows about it. Not Baddo, not any of the media. Nobody knows we're coming so nobody can plan any trouble. We bring some soldiers with us just in case, but nobody else will know. Make it happen." He couldn't believe he dared demand so casually from the ranking generals on-site, but something about the dwindling time made him bold. "Oh, and General Ada? I'm going to need my phone back. Now. We'll be at the airvan." Without another word, he led Meg from the general's setup to the small airvans parked at the edge of the barrier.

As they moved farther from the work site, Loul saw Meg checking over her shoulder, her eyes moving back where she could see her crewmates. When she saw the line of vehicles, she froze in place, her grip on Loul's hand tight enough to jerk him backward when he didn't stop with her. "Move? Urfers no move. Meg no move."

"Yes." He stood in front of her, looking up at her and not breaking eye contact as his other hand reached for hers. They looked like a badly matched dance pair, he too short, she too nervous. Loul gently squeezed her fingers, careful of the shift of thin bones between his pads. "Meg go with Loul. One go. Meg see Cartar. Meg see Loul Didet."

Her eyes were wide, the brown centers surrounded by white all the way around. "Meg Loul come back, yes? Meg need/want come back here."

"Yes. Meg Loul come back soon. Much soon. Now Meg Loul move. Good/okay."

Her smile took a moment to fully arrive but when it did, it was brilliant.

"Okay/good. Meg Loul go. Talk this to Cho." She touched her earpiece and Loul heard the soft, bell-like sounds of her words punctuated by the lower sounds of Cho. Something in the scientist's voice sounded harsher than usual but Meg smoothed it over. Touching her earpiece again, she looked to the airvans. "Talk this?"

MEG

Wind truck. That was the closest she could get to the translation of the ingenious contraption she and Loul bundled into. On the ground, it had looked like a giant pill, oblong and smooth, all glass except for the top and bottom panels. Bench seats, low like all Dideto seats, ran the length of the truck, and Meg, Loul, and the eight soldiers accompanying them barely left enough room to clamp down the clear door. The soldiers and Loul straddled the benches back to front, but Meg couldn't contain her curiosity. She clambered forward to look out over the driver's shoulder, watching his thick fists punching into the console, activating the mechanism. She expected to hear a loud motor, like a combustion engine. Instead she heard gears whirring and a metallic clicking on the overhead panel. Seconds later, the capsule lifted off the ground with a jump.

She spun around to Loul for an explanation. Whatever he saw on her face made him laugh and he reached out a hand for her. Maybe he thought she'd fall, but unlike the Dideto riding with her, she could easily brace herself on the ceiling of the truck. She saw more than one soldier's eyes go wide at how far her reach really was. Loul just kept smiling that smile she loved and tapped his knuckles against the bend of the glass beside him.

Sails. Above and below the capsule, sails had unfurled, and then she understood why they called it a wind truck. "Amazing," she said to nobody, high-stepping over the bench between Loul and a soldier, pressing her face to the glass for a better view. So mesmerized was she by the broad, billowing canvas sheets, it took her several moments to even realize what they flew over. Didet. The planet rolled along beneath them; smooth, rounded structures with shaded glass ceilings, shaped and positioned such that she could see pale dust blowing like ribbons up, over, and around them. In the fading light of the palest sun, the glass ceilings seemed to shift and lighten, and if she squinted, Meg could make out walls and tables and moving figures within.

LOUL

He didn't know how Meg kept from tipping over in the unsteady airvan. She didn't even need to keep her hand on the ceiling—and wasn't that a sight, that long arm shooting up, the fragile fingers splaying wide to grip an ungrippable surface. Where he and the soldiers had to press the low benches between their thighs to keep from being pitched around, Meg's reedy legs and whip-thin body somehow managed to ride the drafts, bending and balancing itself with a shift of her hips and a lift of her shoulders. Loul hadn't had many rides in an airvan, but he found Meg far more interesting to watch than the windows of the city below him.

Her heard her voice in his earpiece and knew she spoke into the small microphone as she so often did, describing things for her database, taking note of details her camera couldn't pick up. She spoke too quickly for the translator to decipher, using words the computer hadn't converted, but the sounds she made sounded like delight. They had the long, lilting sounds she'd made when Loul had brought her fresh *tut* or shown her a comic book. They were the sounds that were often accompanied by the quick slaps of her palms together, although she didn't do that on board. Instead, she lifted one leg impossibly high, easily stepping over Loul's thighs and nearly shocking the soldier in front of him to death as she slotted in between them to press against the glass and watch the city fly by beneath them.

Loul slipped his phone from his pocket, hating to tear his eyes away from Meg for even a second, but he had to send this message. He thumb moved quickly, rolling the letters out.

"Get to the booth RIGHT NOW. Leave work. Leave everything. Booth. Now." He sent it to Hark and Po and, after less than a second of hesitation, to Reno Dado.

MEG

She never thought she'd see a day when she ran out of words, but watching the world flying by beneath her feet in this strange, silent wind truck, Meg thought she might be wrong. She commented on details as quickly as she could—buildings disappearing behind her, she tipping the camera on her shirt forward to be sure it captured as much as possible. The first three rounds of drones launched from the *Damocles* had brought back grainy images, unfocused but for the largest details. The video drones were to have been launched much later, once the crew had some idea where to focus. All they had seen of Didet was what had flown toward them upon descent and the images the newly interfaced computers revealed. This? Nothing had prepared Meg for this.

No building was more than a story high and all were rounded, topped with clear ceilings and dotted with large windows. It had never occurred to Meg that on a planet with seven suns nobody would feel compelled to invent a lightbulb. Now the thought made her laugh out loud. Or continue to laugh out loud. Every turn revealed some new sight, colors shifting in the changing light, tinting the landscape with pastels. The pilot shouted something and the soldiers braced themselves more rigidly on the benches. By now Meg had thrown propriety to the wind and perched on Loul's thigh, her face pressed to the glass.

He grabbed at her hip when the wind truck dipped in a descending spiral. She yelped in surprise and then laughed at herself, balancing herself between the glass and Loul's solid leg. Loul's thrum stuttered a little, and she wondered if he was nervous about flying or just about flying with a crazy alien jumping around the ship. That made her laugh even harder and she could feel an edge of hysteria washing over her. She was sailing in the air in a glass pill over an alien planet surrounded by soldiers watching mounded sand-colored buildings tinted pink and orange by multiple suns, sitting on the lap of her short, new best friend. She gave herself permission to feel a little unhinged.

"Meg okay?" Loul smiled up at her as she continued to laugh. He seemed wholly entertained by her reaction. She turned and put her hands on either side of his face, her pinkies just brushing the edges of his thrum spots. She leaned in closer, the tip of her nose brushing his as the ship dipped again.

"Meg okay. Very okay. This wind truck—Loul has wind truck?"

Loul huffed out a choppy sound she knew was laughter. "No. No. Wind truck is for Dideto..." He said something the program didn't pick up, and when he saw she didn't understand, he tugged at the front of his tunic. She'd seen him do that when they spoke of the generals at the work site.

"Generals?" she asked. Maybe these were military-only vehicles.

"Generals and cameras and Baddo and..." He said a few more lost words and then one word came through. "Black."

"Black?"

Loul waved his knuckles, a one-handed *yes* gesture, and pulled at his shirt again. "Black."

"Oh, the people who wear black? Like the crews who tried to push you out." She knew he couldn't understand her but there was no room to pull out the light screen. Plus the way the ship tilted and dipped she could hardly imagine being able to focus on it. She gripped Loul's shoulder as they tipped hard to the side and she nearly tumbled from his lap. His breath caught but Meg could only laugh.

A long, fat building came into view before them, the rough stone exterior blushing red in the changing light. The ceiling shone back their reflection until the ship hovered directly above it and Meg could see the space below filled with people moving through snaking corridors and around high partitions. Whatever this place was, it was busy. Before she could ask Loul to explain what it was, the ship dropped quickly enough to make Meg bounce on his leg. Another little cry of surprise and she couldn't help but laugh again. Loul looked down into the building as if searching for something.

"This? Loul talk this? Meg Loul go here? What is this?"

She felt him shift beneath her. He seemed to have spotted something that made him grin even harder. "This is Loul...site."

They hadn't refined the word *live* well enough to distinguish anything clearer than residing on the planet, Meg assuming she would have enough time later on to clarify social-structure issues. She'd been surprised by Prader's insight. If the Dideto didn't sleep, what sort of home life did they have? The building they were landing on was enormous and seemed to be very full of people.

"Loul go to this site much?"

Loul grinned. "Loul go to this site very much." As the wind truck maneuvered through its bumpy landing on the roof, Loul started to laugh. By the time the clear door opened and the soldiers climbed out ahead of them, they were wrapped arm in arm, laughing to each other.

LOUL

The arrival of an airvan at the social center brought more than a few curious stares up through the glass. The team of soldiers surrounding them would spark some more excitement. But Loul knew nothing would prepare the crowd below for the arrival of Meg. He knew they couldn't see her yet, or at least see what she was staring up at, just their feet, but once they stepped out of the elevator he knew word would spread quickly. Meg stood more than a head taller than him, and he was tall. She'd be easily visible over the crowd. That's why he instructed the soldiers to take them down through the E elevator, the one closest to his booth.

How many rounds had he been gone? Eleven? Twelve? Loul had lost count, but the instant the elevator doors opened, the noises and smells and sounds of the social center blew in at him, filling him with longing. He'd missed it. For all the unbelievable events he'd experienced, he missed his friends and his center. All around them people froze, conversations dead in midsentence, as the soldiers cleared a path for Loul and Meg through the narrow E Corridor. This section of the center contained mostly service quarters—laundry, dishwashing, recycling pickup. That's why he and his friends had been able to afford the booth for as long as they had. You didn't see a lot of people in black in this part of the social center.

Meg's eyes were wide, her fingers holding tight to his upper arm, and he could feel her tremble against him. He knew it wasn't fear. He could tell she struggled to keep her movements small and contained the way the Urfers had when they'd first arrived. He'd become so accustomed to Meg's quick, willowy gestures and broad range of expressions he'd almost forgotten how strange they'd seemed at first. From the stunned looks on the faces of the people they passed, however, he doubted she could have shocked them any more if she'd flown in on flaming wings.

He heard her make a long, whistling sound as they passed a row of vendor stalls. Cheap overshirts, tacky movie toys, fake finger tattoos—the vendors on this side sold to their market, the underemployed or overly cheap. Loul could see Meg draw her fingers through the air and curl them up to her side, knowing the temptation she felt to trace every surface with her hands. He wanted to let her. He wanted to show her everything but he had something to show her first. They turned the corner he found without looking, watching instead the open-mouthed stares that followed them. Before they could get halfway down the corridor, Meg squeezed his arm with force, drawing in a loud sudden breath and pointing her long arm toward the ceiling.

He turned to see what she pointed at as she dropped all pretense of keeping her gestures small. Her head fell backward, her spine dipping over as well, and her mouth opened wide. The hand that didn't clutch at Loul pressed into her stretched stomach and she let out the loudest laugh Loul had heard any of the Urfers make.

MEG

It was official: her mind was blown. This building, this rabbit warren of walls and shelves and cans and cabinets, teeming with Dideto pushing shoulder to shoulder through the throngs to the hammering pulse of machinery and music and voices and thrumming—it pushed up against her senses, clamoring for attention, and making her cling to Loul. After the ride in that amazing machine she thought she'd be ready for anything, but this was beyond her comprehension. Had she been shorter, Loul's height or smaller, she probably would have balked with claustrophobia, but standing an easy ten inches above the throng it felt like standing waist-deep in a bizarre, colorful tropical aquarium—if that aquarium smelled like cinnamon, pepper, motor oil, and dryer lint.

She saw mouths drop open as she passed, ripples of stalled conversation washing through the crowds. But even as their voices dropped, the powerful pulse of the thrums built, pulsing loudly enough to be palpable. She thought if she untied her ponytail, the pulsing of these throat noises would blow the hair off her face like a breeze. She wanted to run her fingers across their faces, between their bodies, to feel the surge of shock and friction as they pushed against each other jostling to either see her better or to move away.

Her first thought was chaos. In every direction with no discernible pattern, corridors opened and branched and turned and forked, divided by stalls and carts and freestanding drapery frames.

Booths like the kind she and Loul worked in clustered together in circles and arcs and train-like chains. Some booths contained wide circular tables with enough room for a dozen Dideto; some were narrow and low. There were booths with built-in closets and shelves; booths with video screens; booths piled high with piles of fabric. Fabric panels and folding screens cut some booths off from sight, but as they moved through the corridors, the soldiers clearing a path for them, Meg saw hundreds of faces poking around edges and popping up from under tables. Nobody shouted. Nobody approached them, but nobody missed their arrival.

Loul let her hang on his arm, and she used every ounce of restraint to resist clapping her hands and pointing and jumping up and down in delight. Rhythms rose and fell, banging against each other in an almost harmony as people reacted to her presence. She prayed the recorders were getting the nuances of the sounds. When Loul guided her down yet another ribbon of a corridor filled with shoulder-to-shoulder Dideto, Meg looked up, trying to maintain her bearings. Hanging from the low ceiling, draped over a long rod, were banners of fabric or paper; she couldn't tell which. She didn't look that hard at the material. Instead, all she saw were the enormous photographs, drawings, cartoons, and multicolor renderings of her face, Cho's face, and planet Earth. It was too much. They were famous. Meg threw back her head and howled with laughter.

LOUL

He saw the soldiers tense at Meg's strange reaction and he gave them a reassuring nod. The comic vendors at the edge of D Corridor were selling posters of the Urfers. Of course they were. If Loul hadn't been on-site with the aliens, he'd have been first in line to buy one of every picture. He'd bet his last paycheck that Po already had. He took a deep breath, hoping with every fiber of his being that his friends had gotten his text. With a look to Meg and the softest squeeze of her thin arm against his body, he urged her forward. She straightened up, the wetness in her eyes a strange contrast to her wide grin, and let herself be led again. He could feel her breaths soft and fast, her laughter quiet now as they moved.

One more turn, two booths in, and Meg squeezed his arm once more. She craned her head forward to look into his eyes, the fingers of her free hand moving as if to touch his rose spot. She didn't. Instead she bit her glass-like teeth into her lip before speaking.

"Loul okay, yes? Loul very okay, yes?"

He laughed. Whatever it was she said she could hear, she could obviously hear it now. He pressed his knuckles together tight. "Yes. Loul very okay. Yes very okay. Here."

He led her another dozen steps to where he saw the wide staring eyes and wider grins of his best friend, Hark, and Reno Dado. Po was there too but he wasn't grinning. He wasn't standing. He sat at the edge of the booth, collapsed over the armrest in a way that must have hurt like hell, staring slack-jawed at Meg. For the first time in all the years they had known each other, Po was struck speechless.

"Everyone"—he smiled at each of them—"this is Meg. Meg, these are"—he pressed his palms together—"my friends."

MEG

They didn't look alike. She'd gotten adept enough at recognizing Dideto features to see there was little resemblance among the four of them. It didn't mean they weren't family, but that wasn't what Loul wanted her to know about them. That gesture, the palms together, was neither an Earther nor Dideto gesture. It was their own sign, their gesture for people together. Thinking she might be leaving forever, Loul had taken her to meet the people that mattered most to him. In the face of it, all Meg could think was "how human."

The man and woman on the left of the booth seemed happy to see her. The little one on the right with the funny wispy strands around his eyes didn't seem pleased at all. She couldn't figure out how he perched on the dividing wall of the booth—she'd never seen any of the Dideto sit like that—and it looked uncomfortable. When Loul made a gesture to invite her to sit down, the little one stuck where he sat, and she wondered if maybe he was disabled in some way.

"Hark," Loul said, pointing to the smiling man and then to the woman. "Reno Dado." Meg thought that even if the Dideto couldn't hear their own thrums there was no way anyone could miss the change in timbre when Loul said the woman's name. She looked different from the women in the work crews somehow. Her thrum spot blushed a deep rose, or maybe it was just from the light catching off the gold strands wrapped across her shoulder. Both she and Hark dressed differently from the work crews, the fabric of their tunics rougher in texture and darker. She'd noticed before the same texture in the generals' clothing. Loul's and the little one's—Po was his name—were both of paler, thinner fabric. For the first time, she wondered if maybe Loul was poor, if such a condition even existed on this world.

After some prodding and not very subtle fist-pounding from Hark, the little one stumbled back into the booth, making room for Meg and Loul to sit. The soldiers took up their posts around the booth, holding back anyone trying to get too close. That was fine with Meg. She could hear cameras purring from every direction. Let them film what they wanted. She was here for Loul.

The shock of her presence wore off by inches, and Meg listened as Hark and Reno Dado questioned Loul, their voices uncertain, their thrums pattering. The two friends tried hard not to stare at Meg, unlike the little one, Po, who seemed incapable of anything else. Po had slid to the far end of the booth, climbing onto some sort of added-on bench that closed the booth off into a horseshoe. Po did finally manage to close his mouth, although Meg couldn't be certain he had managed to blink. Giving him plenty of time to get his fill of the visual, she listened to the almost hiccup-like sounds from his throat.

Loul spoke quickly to his friends, his voice low and relaxed and punctuated often with bursts of laughter. Meg could tell by the way he knocked his knuckles against the table that he was excited by the story. She didn't have to be psychic to figure out what the topic was. Hark, sitting across from Loul, leaned over several times to pound his fists on top of Loul's, both men laughing. Reno Dado covered her mouth when she laughed, peeking at Meg only when her fingers were close enough to her eyes to cover them if need be. She didn't know if it was an etiquette that hadn't shown itself at the landing site or just some sort of timidity, but from what Meg could tell, the Dideto around her would stare until she stared back.

Except Po. Hearing his thrum slowing down to a slightly less frantic tattoo, Meg turned to face him, seeing in her peripheral vision that he had managed to climb up onto the bench and now squatted over the table, leaning on his forearms. It seemed Meg was the only one who had noticed his advance, because when she turned to face him, she heard sounds of shock from the other three. Loul started to speak but Meg put her hand on his arm to silence him.

"Po." She didn't turn the translator on. Even over the din of the room, she could tell he heard her. His eyes widened and his mouth slipped open as he leaned in closer and closer. She didn't pull away, letting him get within inches of her face. When she could smell his breath, she smiled and said, "Meg."

"Meg." The word came out in a rush of breath, and Meg was surprised to hear that of all the Dideto who had spoken her name since arrival, his pronunciation was the closest. She activated the translator.

"Meg touch Po?" She held her palm out and lowered it onto his fist. He didn't flinch although the muscles twitched and jumped under her fingers. His gaze followed her hand, and after a few light strokes of her fingers, he turned his fist over, opening up the tender pads of his palm. Loul had done the same thing early on and she knew how sensitive those exposed pads were. Keeping her touch light, she traced swirls over the pink skin until he smiled.

The translator took a moment to capture his words and refine them to their simplest form. "Po touch Meg?" More mutters and sharp breaths from Loul's friends, but she also heard Loul's soft laugh.

"Yes okay." Meg leaned in closer and then went very still, not wanting to spook the wide-eyed man. She expected him to touch her arms—the Dideto at the landing site had been fascinated by the length of the Earthers' arms—but his hand came toward her face. His eyes moved over her face as if he were trying to decide what he wanted to touch. She couldn't fight back the grin that exposed her teeth. Loul always stared at her teeth. His fingers brushed her cheek, and she could feel the hard edges that surrounded the tender pads, but he didn't stop there. Instead, his hands moved to her hair, petting the pulled-back strands the way one would stroke a newborn kitten. A soft, low sound whispered from his lips.

Moving slowly and deliberately, Meg reached up with one hand and pulled off the ponytail elastic. Po jumped when her hair fell forward toward her face, but she smiled and carded her fingers through her curls, loosening them. Her fingers brushed over the back of Po's hand, encouraging him to trail his fingers along the length of her hair. When the curls slipped over the tender pads of his fingers, his face crumpled into a brilliant, brown-toothed grin.

He said something to her that the translator couldn't pick up. He said it again to Loul and his friends. Then he pounded his knuckles on the table and said it even louder. Meg turned to Loul for an explanation, but the three Dideto friends burst into loud, barking laughter. They pounded their knuckles against the table, laughing and grinning at each other, and even Reno Dado didn't cover her mouth. Loul waved his knuckles toward Meg, smiling at her, and repeated the phrase. She still didn't know what it meant but she smiled back.

Whatever had been said had gotten through to all of them. Meg held her breath, leaning in to catch the sound. The four of them, Loul, Hark, Reno Dado, and Po, were thrumming in perfect, rhythmic harmony.

SIXTEEN

LOUL

"They're real." Po leaned in close enough to bite Meg's nose and she didn't even flinch. His fingers ran through her hair, something Loul had only dared to do once and would never forget. Po finally seemed to be shaking off the shock of meeting Meg, his voice and his face regaining their usual comic expressiveness. "They're real. They're real!"

Loul couldn't hold it back any longer. He laughed out loud, Hark and Reno Dado following suit. The utter stupid delight on Po's face, the shock and nerdy jitter in his voice, broke the last of the tension at the table, and just like that the four of them were pounding the table like they were playing a drinking game. It felt so good, so easy to be laughing and talking with his friends, that he almost forgot Meg's inability to understand.

He smiled at her, wanting to include her, and wasn't surprised to see her smiling back. He wondered if he looked like that when he listened to the Urfers chattering among themselves.

"They're real," Loul said.

Hark's voice was rough with excitement. "And you were there. Man, you were there."

Loul told them the story of his report that was now required reading for a secret department of the Space Administration. Technically, he figured it couldn't be secret anymore. Everyone knew the aliens existed, and, as he had expected, Po had followed every second of the coverage. His friends wanted to hear the blow-by-blow recap of his first encounter with Meg including all the heart-stopping dread of pulling what they all knew was a classic Loul Pell social error. He didn't mind their teasing. He was, after all, the one sitting with an alien.

"Can I show her the book?" Po stared at Meg, making no attempt to hide his fascination.

Reno Dado rolled her eyes but Meg smiled. It seemed she could understand snippets of their conversation, or maybe there was no mistaking the eagerness in his buddy's face.

"Yeah, why not?" As Po ducked under the table to search around the shelves there, Loul touched Meg's arm. "Po has thing Meg sees, yes? Meg know Magagan?"

Hark snorted. "You showed her a comic book?"

"It was there. One of the archivists had it. I'm trying to show her our things but there isn't that much out at the site." Loul tapped his knuckles. "Plus it was Shadow Mountain Four, series nineteen, where the Evanestas clone the Shadow."

"Oh, that is a good one."

"Great," Reno Dado said, "now she thinks we're a planet of nerds."

Po climbed back onto the bench, slamming down a hard-edged binder jammed with pages. "That's gotten a lot thicker since I left," Loul said.

"Are you kidding me?" Po flipped through the pages. "Do you have any idea how much data has been uploaded online since their arrival? And not just from The Searcher, although he's had the best stuff. He's got sources you wouldn't believe."

"Anything from the landing site?"

"No, but he's got people on the barrier who have inside sources."

"Hey, Po?" Loul leaned forward and waited for Po to look up from the pages he studied. "You've got sources on the inside too. You're sitting next to the direct source right now." Meg must have been able to sense she was once again the topic because she looked from Loul to Po with a smile. She leaned sideways in the booth, bracing herself on her long arm, to peer at Po's battered pages. Seeing her interest, he scooted over closer to her, once again clambering over the armrest at that end of the booth. Loul could hear Meg's soft laugh in his earpiece as Po pushed in beside her.

He flipped through the pages, talking so quickly even Loul couldn't understand him. When he finally stopped to take a break, Meg put her thin hand on his. "Meg see?"

"What?"

Loul leaned forward. "She wants to look at the book herself."

"Oh my god." Po's hands slipped from the table and Hark bit his own fist trying not to laugh. "Yes. Yes yes yes. Oh my god, yes. Oh my god."

"She's just going to look at it, Po. Not teleport it into space."

"You don't know that."

Meg ran her fingers over the pages in the book in that feathery way she investigated everything. She seemed as interested in the material that held the cut-out articles against the plastic pages as in the photos held there. She hefted the book, turning it over to examine the cover and the central fasteners. Making little noises of surprise and interest, she tilted her head this way and that. Loul could see his friends' eyes growing wider as they saw up close the incredible flexibility of Meg's upper body. He wondered what they would do if they had seen the Urfers throwing themselves through the air when the rains came.

She skipped over long pages of text. Without the translator they probably looked like nothing but scribbles to her, but she stopped and studied many of the photographs and drawings. One set of pages held nothing but a series of grotesque cartoons of vicious-looking aliens. She pointed to one of the pictures, a cartoon from a controversial comic series about the ancient sea gods that depicted an alien invader as a swimming monstrosity with one enormous eye and dozens of snakelike appendages dragging a helpless woman into his cavernous maw.

"In Didet?" She pointed to the creature. "This is in Didet?"

"No," Loul said quickly. "No, no this is…this is…" He put his hand to the side of his head. "This is here, yes?"

Reno Dado leaned in. "What do you mean by that? What's she saying?"

"She wants to know if the monster in this cartoon is real and I'm trying to tell her that it's just imagination. We don't have the word for that yet so I told her it's just a thought." He could tell his friends weren't totally following him. "It's kind of weird how this works. It's a lot of guesswork and trying to get as close as possible."

"Wait a minute," Po said, reaching to stop Meg from turning the page. "She thinks the Gagarel is real?"

"I doubt it. We just interfaced the computers and they've been studying our animal life. They seem really interested in the seas. Their doctor keeps asking the scientists something about going into them or onto them. I don't know. She's probably just looking for new animal life to tell Cho about."

"Cho," Reno Dado said with a smile. "That's the other one, right? I have a banner with him in my office. They sold a bunch of them right after the press conference when—"

"Wait!" Po pounded his fist on the table, making Meg laugh. It seemed the reaction to Po's nervous fidgeting was universal. "She asked if we had Gagarel on our planet, right? Maybe there's a reason. Can I ask her a question?"

"If you stop shouting. Her hearing is really sensitive. She hates shouting."

Po pointed to the illustrated monster and stared at Meg. When he spoke, his voice was much lower. Loul could see Meg's shoulder carriage drop in what he recognized as relief. "Meg? This creature, this is Gagarel."

"Gagarel." Her voice gave the word a light clicking sound. "This is Gagarel."

"Yes. We don't have them on Didet." Po watched her face as he spoke and when she tilted her head, he spoke quickly. "What's she doing? What's she doing? What's she doing?"

"She doesn't understand what you mean. I mean, she probably gets that there are no Gagarel in real life. She knows what drawings are as opposed to photographs."

Po ground his knuckles on the edge of the table as Meg turned her full focus on him. Loul knew how unnerving that focus could be, like being put center stage at a Pummel arena. There was an excellent chance Po would simply blow to pieces at the pressure. He didn't, though. He climbed up farther on the bench, almost standing, and pushed his finger against the cartoon image.

"No Gagarel on Didet. Gagarel on Urf?"

Loul started to protest. Po could drive the people who loved him to madness. He couldn't imagine the impression he was making on Meg. Before he could push the book away, however, Meg put her own hand on the cartoon.

"Yes. Urfers has Gagarel."

MEG

She could hardly breathe. All the hair on her arms stood on end, and it took all her self-control to not stretch out her hands to touch the people around her. Loul talked too quickly for the translator to keep up with, and his friends interrupted him with happy, high-pitched questions and comments. For just a moment, even though she was no doubt the topic of discussion, they forgot about her. And when they did, the four Dideto connected with each other. It was connection, relation, synchronization. Whatever it was, the moment the four thrums came into harmony with each other, a vibration coursed through Meg with enough strength to drown out the bedlam around her. The crowds, the clamor, the sensory overload—all of it fell away on the wave of this more-than-audible rush of thrumming. She could tell by their relaxed faces and easy laughs that either they didn't notice the harmonizing or it was common enough to be unremarkable. For Meg, it was astounding.

She didn't even notice the little one until he climbed out from under the table with a bulky boxlike contraption. The sight of it made the group-thrum ripple in what Meg could only describe as an audible tickle. She felt giddy in the midst of it. When Loul told her Po wanted to show her something, she could hear a throb of affection in his voice for his friend. At that moment she knew she would let Po show her the pointy end of a knife sliding between her ribs if it meant keeping that happy, thrilling sound coming from Loul.

The box was a book, a bigger, bulkier version of the illustrated book Loul had shown her at the work site, what he called Magagan. Meg loved the feel of this one, the thick sheaths of some sort of fibrous material warped in alternating patterns so thick Dideto fingers could easily get between them. She wondered if the manufacturers of the books warped the pages beforehand or just assembled them, and the pages warped with use. Peering at the binding, she saw fat clamps holding the pages in place and leathery-looking blisters on the inside of the cover that connected to the binding with coarse strips. She prodded one of the blisters, seeing the strip twitch. Like so many devices the Dideto used, the book seemed to require more strength than dexterity to open.

It weighed a ton. Turning the book upside down to see the pages swing free, Meg felt the muscles in her arm struggle under the bulk. Unlike the book Loul had shown her at the site, this one's cover was made up of a collage of images glued over each other. She let her fingers slide over the pictures, some glossy, some matte, all of them faded and frayed. The corner of a small drawing curled up on one side and she knew she could slip her fingernail beneath it and peel it back, revealing the cover beneath, but she couldn't imagine any cultural setting in which proper etiquette allowed defacing a book. She giggled to herself, feeling her thoughts getting loopy, and set the book back down in its proper position. The rising and falling of that beautiful four-way thrum made her feel a little drunk.

Po climbed up close to her as she flipped through the pages. Several pages in, Meg understood this was a scrapbook of sorts, a collection of written pieces and clippings from other books. She recognized the illustration style from the Magagan book Loul had shown her. Some photographs she recognized from the Dideto database, geographic regions of the planet Jefferson had pinpointed in his mineral research. A detailed series of drawings of the sea caught her eye and she wondered if it was the same sea they had landed beside.

Po asked her about one of the pictures. Even though it was only a drawing, it was the most similar to an Earth life-form she had seen yet. The question sparked a flurry of discussion that Loul seemed to dismiss, telling her the picture was only a thought. Maybe he meant the story behind the cartoon, assuring her that the grotesque creatures didn't actually come up from the seafloor and drag unsuspecting Dideto to a grisly death, but the little one interrupted him. He wanted to know if Earth had these creatures, these Gagarel.

"Yes," Meg said, noting only Po didn't seem surprised. "Earthers have Gagarel. On Earth this is a giant squid. In the sea."

The group fell silent but for their lovely thrum. Po's throat kept a high note as he leaned across the table, staring from Loul to Hark as if making a silent point. Loul rubbed his knuckles on the table and turned to Meg.

"Gagarel not in Didet. Gagarel is thought; is…" His words died away, urging her to understand him. Meg nodded and tapped her wrist.

"Screen okay? Here?"

Loul spoke low and fast to his friends and the little one made a noise that could not be interpreted as anything but ecstasy. He tapped his knuckles and glanced at her wrist.

Meg drew the light screen from her wristband, laying it flat across the table. Po nearly knocked the breath from her, pressing in close beside her to see. His teeth chattered and his thrum hitched as his breathing picked up through his flat nose. She knew Loul could hear her laughing in his earpiece.

Low sounds of wonder came from the two across the table as she flipped through the files searching for the picture. It didn't take long to find the bio-file on the giant squid, which she enlarged for the group to see. "Gagarel," she said, sliding the picture to the edge of the screen. While the photo was the realistic image of the giant squid, it wasn't the picture she wanted. It took several minutes to search the library, looking for the scans of the old maritime and folklore images. After several wrong clicks, she found the photo she had remembered passing during a bored perusal of the library. It was a photograph of an eighteenth-century woodcarving. In it, a giant squid had been transformed into a sea monster, its tentacles drawing in a multisailed whaling ship and dragging it into the frothing sea. Meg knew this was just one of hundreds of images like this, the old sea monster being the stuff of ancient legends.

"Gagarel, yes?" She pointed from the etching to the photograph of the much more docile-looking giant squid. "Yes, in Didet? In the sea? Gagarel?"

LOUL

"Dude," Po breathed the word, "Gagarel is real. It's a freaking alien. It's real and it's an alien. Who knows how much of Magagan might be real? Do you realize what this means?"

Loul stared at the screen. "It means we're probably misunderstanding what she's saying. It happens. It's happened a lot since they got here."

They all heard the doubt in his voice. Reno Dado spoke first. "Look, I'm the last to board the crazy bus and I don't know her like you do, but unless they are artists beyond comparison"—she pointed to the photo of the blob-like sea creature—"this is a photograph. And it's a photograph of this." She pointed to Gagarel. "And this." Her hand moved over the illustration that hovered on the screen.

"Well, that doesn't mean..." Loul didn't know what it didn't mean but it couldn't mean what Po thought it meant. It couldn't mean that Gagarel and the Shadow and Sea Gods' Footsteps were real. That was crazy. That was as crazy as…aliens. "I just think…"

Po saved him from having to pull a thought together. He slid the book out from under the light screen, careful not to break the plane of the illuminated edges. "Here, Meg, look at this." For all his original shock, Po seemed to have taken to Meg's presence as the most natural thing in the world, talking to her like he talked with any of them. He flipped through the pages of the scrapbook, opening up to a full-color rendering of a multilevel building. He shoved the picture before Meg, who ghosted her long fingers across the lines delineating the stories.

"This is many, yes? Dideto have this have many?" She looked to Loul to understand what she meant, pointing from the picture to the glass ceiling of the social center. "This? This is many of this? In Didet?"

Loul rocked forward on his knuckles. Maybe it was the noise of the center or the distraction of seeing his friends again, but it felt harder to understand Meg's broken concepts here at the table. Maybe he was just self-conscious, but found he couldn't move his hand from the space between *yes* and *no*. He'd brought Meg here on impulse, thinking she was leaving, wanting her to see who he was outside of the landing site. He wanted her to see his friends, see him as a real person, but now that she was here, he felt like there was no real Loul Pell to show her, like the only value he really had was the imagined connection they'd shared in the isolation inside the barricade.

That wasn't really it, though, was it? If he was honest with himself, and Loul found himself staring face-to-face with the truth, there was more than a small part of himself that wanted Meg to be overwhelmed by the social center, wanted her to cling to him. He wanted his friends to be speechless in her presence, relying on him to bridge the unbridgeable gap. Instead the four of them laughed and talked and stared into each other's eyes as if they were the old friends and he was the alien. It was childish and stupid and even as he acknowledged the emotions he felt shame rushing in to fill the cracks.

And as always, heartbeats behind the flood of revelations washing over him, he saw Meg's face change. Her eyes widened, turning down in the corners as that thin line of hair along her brow arched and curved. She turned her torso toward him, the light screen forgotten, and he could hear the surprised sounds from Hark and Reno Dado when they saw the elegant twist of her thin body. Meg's hand fell onto Loul's fist, soft as always, impossibly light and warm where he opened the pads of his top finger to feel her touch. She had said she couldn't read minds and for that he was grateful. He hoped she couldn't hear the worst details of the childish reaction.

"Loul is okay?" He tapped his knuckles together, careful not to pinch her fingertips as he did. "Gagarel? Is not good/bad to see Gagarel? Is this?" Her fingers traced the drawing of the imagined Roana Temple. "This is no good?"

"It's fine. It's okay. Loul is okay. Loul is..." With her narrow shoulders turned toward him, the bony shelf of her neck taut against her strange pale skin, Loul wondered again if it could be possible to become physically addicted to someone's attention. She didn't try to finish his sentence for him. She didn't try to hurry the words from him. She watched and waited like she always did, like she had all the time in the world to listen to anything he chose to say to her, like her entire life depended upon hearing the next words out of his mouth, like she had never heard anything more fascinating than the things he said. Yeah, he was addicted to her attention.

He looked at the cartoon of the Roana Temple. It was only a rendering from imagination, one of the many archaeological theories about what the long-ruined structure might have looked like. Loul had already processed the shock when he'd seen how similar many of the Urf buildings looked to these types of pictures. It was the stacked buildings, the way the ceilings weren't clear but were both ceilings and floors; rooms stacked upon rooms like boxes. The Urfer buildings he'd seen in Meg's database were constructed just so. He hadn't seen any with the ornate decorations this cartoonist had imagined on the mythical temple, but he supposed it wasn't impossible. At this point, what was?

He pointed to the lines that marked the ceiling/floors the artists had drawn on the building. "On Didet, no. Only…" He pointed to the glass ceiling where the Fa-pale light glowed a little rosier than usual. "Only one. Urfers have many. Dideto only one."

Po huffed out a breath, a flurry of questions on the way, but Meg didn't turn away from Loul. She squeezed his hand with her thin fingers, barely denting the skin where his fist was clasped. She leaned in close, close enough that he could feel her breath on his face. "Is good. Loul thoughts this"—she pointed to the picture of the temple—"Urf has this. Loul thoughts Gagarel; Urf has Gagarel. Is maybe Loul thoughts Urf? Is maybe Loul thoughts Meg?"

He could feel his friends staring and could almost hear Po's teeth grinding, wanting to butt in and ask questions and demand an explanation, but he ignored them. Meg's eyes were wet again, large and flecked with color he could see when she sat so close. He didn't care if she could read his mind. She was reading something, something very clear, because she had just spoken to him the very thoughts that had just risen within him.

"It's like I'm dreaming you." He spoke softly. She wouldn't know the words, not exactly, but she knew the meaning. She had just said that very thing. Leaning in closer he lowered his voice so that only she could hear. "There are all these things that connect us, all these stupid cartoon kid-stuff things that turn out to be yours. Temples and sea monsters and spaceships, all this stupid stuff that we entertain ourselves with and they turn out to be Urfer. They're not legend, they're history. Your history. Our history. And now you're going to leave and I'm going to be stuck with comic books and movies and everybody else is going to talk about how much we've learned but all I'm going to think about is how much I didn't get to hear. Some black-shirt team is going to come in and take all the research and present reports and they're going to ask me for my input. I don't want to give any input, Meg. I want to talk to you. I want you to talk to me. You're the best thing that's ever happened to me and when you go, it's just going to be so—"

"Mr. Pell! Mr. Pell!" A camera arm craned over the guards, bobbing over the edge of the booth. "A moment of your time, please!" The guards crouched together in a solid wall of muscle, forcing the curious onlookers farther from the booth, but the camera continued to weave on its expandable arm.

"Oh my god, oh my god, is it...oh my god." Po rocked up on the seat to see over the heads of the guards. "It's him. It's him. It's him."

A balding figure in a faded red tunic pressed his shoulder into the wall of guards, not moving them but also not being moved. He held up a microphone in his fist, the familiar logo wrapped around the bulk of the windscreen. The camera whirled on its arm to take in his image and then, at his signal, turned back to the group in the booth—four wide-eyed Dideto and one Urfer, motionless except for the glassine teeth worrying a soft pink lip.

Hark's hands fell motionless on the table. "Is that..."

Loul blinked several times to be sure. "I think it is."

Reno Dado snorted a laugh of disbelief. "It can't be. Is it? Is that really The Searcher? *The* Searcher? Himself? I thought he never left his lair or secret hideaway or whatever it is."

The man in red smiled a quick smile, tipping his head to Reno Dado. "I do occasionally leave my lair, young lady." Reno Dado blushed at being caught. "I have powerful enemies who would very much like to silence me, and for that reason I keep my whereabouts unknown for the majority of the time. Sources feel safer, information flows more freely, and—"

Po cut him off, delivering The Searcher's tagline for him. "And the Truth rises."

He bowed with a great show of humility and then gestured to the wall of soldiers before him. "May I?"

All eyes turned to Loul. He hesitated from his instinctual desire to yell "Hell, yeah!" This was The Searcher, after all, the man whose underground information and conspiracy theories had entertained, enthralled, and enraged Loul and his friends for more than a decade. He was a living legend, their hero, even when that admiration made them look like fools. Or had made them look like fools. Ever since the arrival of the Urfers, the verdict on who was crazy and who wasn't was being widely and publicly debated.

But the Cartar administration guards had dragged one of The Searcher's reporters out of the press conference. The Searcher himself would no doubt be asking questions the administration did not want asked. Some of those questions Loul alone among the Dideto knew the answers to. If he let him into the booth, if he opened Meg up to the inquisitive clutch of The Searcher, he might endanger his position at the landing site. Coupled with his requisitioning of the airvan, the generals might finally decide they'd had enough of upstart Loul Pell and yank him away from the site.

Screw that. The generals didn't know that Meg and the Urfers were leaving. The generals didn't know there was another ship within contact range of the ground crew. None of the other crews on-site communicated as well as he communicated with Meg; none of them. They needed Loul even more than they realized because Loul knew things no other Dideto knew. If he wanted to give The Searcher an exclusive, he would. If the only cool thing that had ever happened to Loul was getting ready to disappear, he planned on exploiting it while he could. When would The Searcher ever be interested in him again?

Loul gestured to the guard, who let the infamous reporter through the barricade. He was thinner than he looked on his webcasts, smaller, and the hair around his eyes was sparser than it appeared on screen. But as he leaned against the table, knuckles down with all the confidence of a Pummel coach about to win the season, Loul couldn't help but feel a little cowed. His gaze riveted anyone who met it; his body moved with compact surety that made him seem like a man with a mission. Even Reno Dado, who had never been a fan, sat up a little straighter at his glance, her rose spot flushing just a little deeper as his eyes moved over her.

"Loul Pell?" The Searcher straightened up to his full height. "They call me The Searcher. It's an honor to meet you." Loul hooked his fingers with the man's in a hearty fist clamp, with the same masculine grasp that he and Hark and Po had pretended to do for years, laughing and imitating their hero. This was no imitation though. This was The Searcher, and this was his handshake, and as the words left the older man's mouth, Po sighed aloud. The camera whirred, closing in on a tight shot of The Searcher with Loul and Meg in the background.

Before Loul could decide just how much of the information he planned to share with the underground and unconventional newsman, the camera spun in for an even tighter shot of Meg. The Searcher pulled the microphone from the holster on his leg and brought it close to Loul.

"What can you tell us about the massive Urfer ship that just came into orbit?"

SEVENTEEN

MEG

This was no Baddo. He held a microphone and had a camera crew, but this guy was a far cry from the arrogant and badly dressed team that had led the press conference. For one thing he dressed more like the work crews at the landing site, his shirt a light fabric of pale red. It made Meg wonder if it might be an affectation. It seemed the darker the fabric, the higher the status. It made sense from a practical standpoint, she figured. On a planet with nonstop sunlight, fabrics would fade. To be able to keep your clothing dark would probably require care, to say nothing of an indoor job. She looked again at Loul's pale tan shirt. The newcomer's shirt wasn't quite as pale but most definitely wasn't vivid.

He made his impression with more than clothes. When he appeared over the shoulders of the guards, little Po had squeaked a sound she'd never heard from the Dideto. Po seemed an excitable fellow, but there was no mistaking the stutter in the thrums of Loul and his friends. She didn't hear fear in them or anger as she had in the presence of Baddo. Their thrums, their eyes, the fold of their hands—everything changed with the appearance of the man in red.

He looked at Meg as if he knew her. In a sense he probably did. The posters hanging from the ceiling made it obvious that her face was well known on the planet. It wasn't as if she could blend in or be mistaken for anyone else. While he didn't gape at her the way so many of the onlookers did, he didn't avert his eyes from her stare either. He met it with none of the teeth-gritting smugness that the previous reporters had shown. His expression was collected, settled. She wondered if he knew she could hear the jackhammer beat of his throat pulse. Whoever he was, he was good.

He asked Loul's permission before approaching the table. She'd heard the rise in Loul's thrum, wondering if this was a confrontation. She almost wanted to turn off the translator while she sat in the midst of this group. Words only distracted her from the audible body language. Strange too that the presence of so many Dideto in such close quarters only made Loul's thrum and those of his friends easier to hear, as if they floated on a tide of sound that rose closer to her ear the more people were around them. To be honest, the whole experience made her feel a little drunk, dizzy with the unfamiliar sensation.

Then the man in red pointed a microphone and asked a question that shocked Loul breathless. Any goodwill, any benefit of the doubt evaporated at the pant of panic she heard her friend exhale and the shrill spike in his throat noise. Meg squeezed Loul's hand. Loul stuttered, the translator making no sense of the jumbled sounds. When he turned to Meg, she could see the flush rising on the edges of his face.

She held her hand out, palm up toward the man in red. If he didn't know what it meant, that was his problem. He seemed to get the gist of it, pulling the microphone back slightly, his expression settling into almost a smile. Meg had seen that same expression, that same reaction on dozens of Earther reporters ever since the deep-space message had been translated. The look said, "It's your move." He must have sprung something upon Loul, and the camera swung in closer toward them.

With a quick snap, she flipped the light screen off of the table and up before her face. A short drag and it covered Loul's as well, a transparent wall of light symbols and text boxes. The camera slid in closer and Meg could see the man in red lean in to peer at the images. Before his eyes could settle on any one image, Meg slid her finger along a control bar and the screen went opaque, visible only to her and Loul, impossible to see through on the other side. Another flick and the volume went down on the speaker patches. It would only give them a few moments of privacy but she thought Loul could use it.

"Dideto not see this. Dideto not see Loul and Meg. Not hear Loul and Meg."

It took Loul less than a handful of seconds to react, hunkering down lower behind the screen and dropping his voice to a near whisper. The translator missed his first few words but she caught "see ship...see Urfer ship...not good."

"Oh shit," Meg said. Loul may not have understood the word but he seemed to be feeling the sentiment. "This man, this Dideto, Loul trust this man?" His knuckle bump lacked a certain enthusiasm but he stuck with it. She could hear the red-shirted man raising his voice and could see the camera trying to crane its way over the edge of the screen. She leaned in close to Loul, her nose brushing his. "Loul trust Meg? Yes? Meg trust Loul. Meg trust Loul..." She turned to the screen and dragged up the image of the quantifying wedge. She ran her finger to the widest part of the wedge, the maximum point. "Meg trust Loul this."

He ground his teeth, eyes moving from the wedge to her eyes before bumping his knuckle toward the wedge. "Yes. Loul trust Meg this. Most. All. Loul Meg." He held his hand up, palm

out, fingers stretched straight to reveal the tender pink pads. She smiled and pressed her longer, thinner hand against his. "Okay."
He smiled.

"Okay." Pulling their hands apart they turned back toward the table just as the lens of the camera came into view over the screen. With one hand, Meg flicked the light screen back down against the table. With the other, she reached up and smacked at the camera orb, sending it swinging on its retractable arm.

LOUL

Even he jumped when she hit the camera. Loul had seen how quickly the Urfers could move and he knew how remarkable their reach was, but this was the first time he'd seen the strength they could put into their movements. Meg's hand was a blur, smacking the camera ball like a whip. It sounded like the camera operator might have fallen down behind the wall of the booth. She hadn't hit it hard enough to damage it—orb cameras were designed to take rough landings—but he was pretty sure the operators weren't equipped for an attack like this.

The Searcher crouched, as if preparing for Meg to leap across the table. Loul almost warned him that unless he had invented rocket packs in the last hour and a half, he probably wouldn't be fast enough to catch Meg if she did decide to bolt. The Searcher looked a little disappointed when Meg settled down beside Loul, adjusted the light screen to normal visibility, and folded into herself as if nothing unusual had happened. Loul liked that approach and settled himself accordingly. He did trust Meg. Face-to-face with The Searcher, surrounded by friends and strangers alike, not having any idea how he was going to answer the question posed to him, Loul realized just how much he trusted her. Beside her, aligned with her, he felt safe. He felt strong. And maybe it was vain and shallow, but he felt important.

"Would you care to explain what just happened, Mr. Pell?" The Searcher leaned into the camera's view again. Loul knew what the shot would look like—the bristly brows of The Searcher just visible on the edge of the screen, larger and slightly out of focus, giving the man an almost supernatural appearance. That was fine. Loul had watched enough broadcasts of the show to know how to handle this.

"Allow me to explain." Loul heard Hark snicker. How many hundreds of segments had they watched that began with those very words? He couldn't help but slip into the serious, academic tone he'd heard dozens of experts use on the program. He saw the crease in Meg's brow line, a subtle sign of curiosity at this new tone.

"You see, Meg and the rest of the Urfers have a complex and nuanced system of communication. I assure you, they are very attuned to the social dynamics going on around them, with or without a full Cartar vocabulary." His eyes flitted to the screen where he saw text boxes filling as her program recorded his words. "They are also a very private people who prefer a chance to compose their responses rather than blurting. Under the circumstances, you can appreciate their desire to be understood as much as possible."

"So you're saying their responses to date have been carefully rehearsed? They don't engage in spontaneity?"

Loul laughed in spite of himself. "You might want to ask your cameraman that question. Bet he didn't see that slap coming. And you should see them in the rain. They love the rain."

"Tell me."

Loul considered the man before him, this legend of underground broadcasting. With two softly spoken words he transformed from a polished, mythical Internet icon and infamous threat to the classified secrets of the Cartar Space Administration into just another curious nerd, with the same open-mouthed wonder of Po and needling curiosity of Hark. He didn't frame himself in front of the camera and his microphone hung forgotten in his fist. Loul saw he had made eye contact with Meg, who stared back at him with a soft, closed-mouth smile, her body turned toward him. Loul knew well the effect of that posture.

"They're beautiful. They throw themselves into the water, fly across it like waterbirds. The rocks break their skin but they don't seem to care."

The Searcher's voice was a whisper. "Their skin looks like silk."

"It feels even better. And it heals really fast. But the suns bother it if they stay out too long. Their skin turns red and looks sore and they're careful to keep covered."

The Searcher's lips moved but no sound came out for several seconds, like he was having a silent conversation with himself. He nodded and then spoke a little louder. "That's why they came during the Purpling."

"What?"

Whatever trance Meg's attention had cast over the reporter evaporated, and he pushed his knuckles down into the table. The camera moved into position, needing to adjust as Meg pulled back. With her keen attention to communication, Loul didn't doubt that she saw the shift.

"The Purpling. Surely you haven't forgotten. Come, come Mr. Pell. You can't expect the people of Didet to believe that even at this momentous occasion you could forget the event."

"Oh shit." Loul automatically looked up through the ceiling, really noticing for the first time the rosy tone of the late Fa-pale. "Oh shit."

"Dude." Hark and Po spoke as one. Even Reno Dado looked shocked.

"I…I didn't even…with all the excitement, I've totally lost track of time."

"Time, Mr. Pell?" The Searcher leaned toward him, making room for the camera arm to follow his path. "We're not talking about working through lunch break. We're talking about the end of the Fa Decade, about a planetary event that happens once every generation."

Hark leaned in and hissed. "We're talking about the barbecue. Your parents are having like a hundred people over. We're all packed to head out there. You forgot?"

Loul could only look around him, open-mouthed and speechless. He had forgotten. Not only had he forgotten, but judging from the conversations at the landing site, he'd bet most of the ground crews had forgotten as well. He could feel that flicker of terror flame up in his chest once again that somehow the Urfers had hypnotized them all, that they had a master plan. How else could an entire work site of people forget that within just a few shifts all the suns of Didet would drop below the horizon? Even Fa, the Ever Present Sun. It only happened once every eleven or twelve Red Years, maybe half a dozen times in anyone's lifetime. Everything came to a stop at the Purpling. Everyone went home, everyone. As the Purpling moved over the planet, every family, every city, every country had their traditions and festivals and celebrations. Nobody forgot the Purpling. Nobody. Ever. Until now.

The Searcher's tone sounded sharp and predatory, a tone that used to thrill Loul when he watched the man on his program. Now it made Loul's teeth itch to clamp shut and grind. "Let's talk about that ship. It can't be a coincidence that they've come to us at our most vulnerable."

Without him noticing it, Meg had slid her hand beneath the table. She now gripped his thigh, her long fingers nearly spanning the width of his leg, her fingers pressing into his flesh. Her free hand moved over the screen but her eyes never left The Searcher.

"Meg talk." Her fingers flew among the text boxes. "This is who?"

"I am The Searcher." He tilted the microphone toward her and Loul saw the corners of her mouth twist up. It was a look he'd seen before, a look she'd worn when approached by Baddo. "I'd like to ask you some questions, Meg."

Loul started to translate but Meg interrupted him. "Yes. Okay. Meg talk…" She turned to Loul. "Loul talk this. This. This is who? Talk this."

"You can talk to me." The Searcher jabbed the microphone in closer and Meg held her slender wrist up to stop it from coming too close. She raised her gaze to the standing reporter and Loul thought you didn't have to be psychic—or Urfer—to understand her meaning. If he kept poking that microphone at her face, she was going to give it the same treatment she had given the camera.

Loul tapped his knuckles. "She just wants your name. Names are important when you don't have a lot of vocabulary. It's standard practice at the landing site to make sure both sides can pronounce the names. It's just…polite." He turned as much as he could to face Meg, purposely giving his shoulder to the camera, and carefully enunciated the words.

"The Searcher. The. Search. Er."

Meg mouthed along with him several times before attempting the sounds herself. The syllables came out breathy, the harder sounds impossible for her slender throat to make. Finally she came out with something sounding more like *Hatador*, and Loul gave her a yes.

"Close enough."

"Okay," Meg looked back to The Searcher. "Meg talk Hatador. Meg need/want Hatador talk…" She pumped her hand palm down over the table.

"She'd like you to lower your voice. Her hearing is very sensitive."

The Searcher spared the crowded social center a skeptical glance and then nodded. "All right, Mr. Pell. Meg. I'll keep my voice low but the questions remain the same. Meg, why are you here?"

Meg cocked her head as the translation played out in her ear. "Meg here. Loul take Meg to see Didet. To see Dideto, Loul Dideto." She smiled at Loul's friends. "Is good/okay, very good/okay in Didet. Very…" She raised her hands above and before her, the long fingers waving like river reeds from her slender palms as she smiled up at them. "Very good/okay."

"This is very different from the landing site," Loul said. "Obviously there we're outside; it's not very crowded. The music, the people, the vendors—she seems to be really enjoying—"

"You're kidding me, right?" The Searcher scowled at Loul. "That evasion crap may work with the morons at the Space Administration but we both know that's not an answer. Meg, I know you know what I am asking you. Why are the Urfers here on Didet?"

Loul hoped she wouldn't try to play coy. Meg could be incredibly charming but The Searcher wasn't going to give himself over to her thrall. Loul didn't doubt that his agenda was exactly the opposite of Loul's. The Searcher wanted the news to be bad. He wanted to be known as the man who discovered the Urfers had malicious intent. Even if it meant the enslavement of the entire planet, Loul knew The Searcher would revel in being the man who uncovered the truth. He was probably already prerecording messages for the rebellion he no doubt planned on heading up.

Loul felt his stomach twist as he realized just how well he knew the agenda of the man before him.

Meg remained still for a long moment, her eyes on the reporter. The camera whirled in closer and it seemed to Loul she was allowing it to set up the shot before she answered.

"Urfers here to see."

"To see what?"

"To see all. To see this. To learn."

"Why?"

Meg's head snapped up at the question like she'd been surprised. "Why?"

"Yes," The Searcher asked, his voice hard and low. "Why? Why do you want to see?"

She turned to Loul as if he could explain this to her. Loul said nothing, just urged her to answer with his eyes. Her eyes narrowed briefly before facing her interrogator again.

"Urfers need/want to see. Need/want to learn. Very need/want."

The Searcher growled low in his throat. "What do the Urfers need/want to learn?"

She held her hands out wide. "Much. All. Very all. Meg talk Hatador question." She leaned forward on her elbows, her thin arms breaking into the light screen, her bony shoulder carriage riding up as she craned her long neck up at The Searcher. "Dideto not need/want to see? Hatador not need/want? Why Hatador has this?" She flicked the microphone with a fingertip so quickly The Searcher jumped back from the table. Meg was on the offensive.

She leaped up like a snake shooting from the grass, her long fingers capturing the camera orb. This time she didn't smack it away. Instead, she grabbed the orb, her fingers somehow finding purchase on the metal, and pulled the orb close. Loul could see the muscles in her arms bunching as she fought with the operator to draw the camera close to her face. She didn't look into the lens. She pulled it in close to The Searcher, turning it so it stared into his face.

"Why Hatador has this? To see. To learn. Yes? Yes?"

"Yes." His face flushed deep red. "Yes. To learn the truth. To see the truth and tell it to the world. The truth you still haven't given us!"

Meg tossed the camera away from her grip and this time Loul was certain the camera operator fell over. The camera arm swung wildly up over the back of the booth as The Searcher banged his fists against the table.

"The people of Didet deserve the truth." He yelled into his microphone. "There are ships amassing in orbit over our planet. You have made inroads in our culture. It's a fact that you've interfered with communication all over the country as you raid our databases for information, so don't tell me that this is just some sightseeing trip to the country! Tell me the truth!"

Everyone jumped when Meg slammed her hands down flat on the table. For just a second, Loul thought she might strike out at The Searcher, smacking him like she'd smacked the camera. Instead, she blew out a loud breath and folded herself back down onto the seat and turned to Loul.

"Talk this."

"What?"

"This." She waved her hand over the text boxes. "Talk this. Talk this Hatador say."

Without a chance to catch himself, Loul barked out a laugh. It was the wrong reaction, he knew, but he couldn't stop himself. One laugh led to another, and in no time he was reduced to loud, huffing snorts. Hark and Reno Dado sat frozen, hands over mouths, Po looked pale enough to faint, and The Searcher looked within an inch of punching Meg in the face. Only Meg seemed undisturbed by Loul's reaction. Her eyes widened but she smiled, an easy smile, the smile she showed him a lot. She'd told him before that she liked his laugh. Apparently she liked it even when it was completely out of place.

"What the hell is so funny, Pell?"

Loul clenched his teeth, trying to rein in his nervous laughter before answering. "I'm sorry but could you repeat the question?" Po snorted out a laugh, followed by Hark. Reno Dado kept her hand over her mouth but Loul could see her smiling. "Maybe I didn't make this clear earlier. The Urfers don't actually speak Cartar. We're lucky to distinguish the difference between edible foodstuffs and pants. I appreciate the fact that you've got a show to produce, but if you want this to make any sense at all, you're going to want to keep the grandstanding to a minimum. It's wasted here."

Loul and his friends may have been amused but The Searcher most definitely was not. He leaned in close to Meg and shouted. "How many Urfers are coming?" Loul shot his arm out to hold the man back but Meg's light touch stopped him.

"One."

"Bullshit! How many Urfer ships are out there? How many are coming to Didet?"

"One."

The Searcher's face turned redder than his shirt. "How many Urfers are on the ship that is orbiting the planet? How many soldiers are you bringing? If you think I'm going to turn my world over to you and your goon squads, you can think again! I want an answer. You tell me! You tell the people of Cartar, of the world, how many Urfers are on that ship?"

The louder he yelled, the stiller Meg grew. She waited until he finished his last tirade to wipe the globs of spit off her cheeks with delicate fingertips. Making a show of drying her hands on her shirt and then folding them before her, she spoke in a soft, breath-filled tone.

"One."

The Searcher punched the table and pushed back. "This is useless. She's playing with us. They're all playing with us. Pell, you listen to me. You're going to go down in history as the man who let these monsters onto our planet. You understand that? Your name, your family's name will forever be associated with the ruin of Didet. Are you prepared for that?"

Loul swallowed loudly. It seemed Meg wasn't the only one with the ability to cut right to the core of Loul's thoughts. That was an unpleasant realization. He tried and failed to find the words to defend himself. Surprising everyone, Po broke in.

"Maybe she's telling the truth." Everyone turned to Po, who looked entirely comfortable with the attention. The Searcher scowled at him with a look that said such an idea was beyond possibility, but Po ignored him. "Meg said the Urfers want to see. They want to learn. Isn't that the underlying premise of, like, eighty percent of the Magagan comics? The urge for scientists to explore and discover? I mean, they flew through space! Space! They didn't just build some crappy telecom satellites and call it a day. They're like...they're like...maybe they're like the Sea Gods of the Skies. Did you ever think that?"

Po slid the scrapbook closer to Meg. Her eyes watched his fingers as he flipped through the pages. "Here." He pointed to a Magagan image that bore the wear and tear of frequent viewing. It was one of the older images in the book, cut from a classic edition of the Evanestas series where the reptilian Evanesta aliens invade Didet and spawn planetwide mayhem. Even non–comic fans like Reno Dado were familiar with the series since it had been the basis for multiple TV, Internet, and theater movies. The image Po pointed to showed a heavily armored Evanesta bracing itself on its spiked tail to draw back a whipping cane over a bent and bloody Dideto child. All around the alien, other Dideto children crouched cowering, locked together with thick chains.

Meg's eyes narrowed at the image. "This?"

"Do you really think she's going to tell you if that's what they have planned?" The Searcher spit on the ground. "You said it yourself. They're not stupid. They're not going to give us any advance warning."

Loul looked up at him. "You mean like sending a landing party to build a language?"

"If that's what they're here for. If you believe her."

"I believe Meg."

Meg must have understood the words because she turned to him and smiled. Then she pointed to the comic book picture. "This? Loul talk this?"

Loul didn't want to explain it to her. As much as he really desperately didn't want this to be the fate of Didet, even more he didn't want Meg to think anyone considered the Urfers capable of such dramatic violence. Face-to-face with Meg, a real alien who was no more reptilian than Reno Dado, the whole scrapbook concept embarrassed him.

"Some Dideto"—he waved his knuckles in the direction of the scowling reporter—"think…um, have thoughts…that this is why Urfers are here. Urfers do this."

"This?" She pointed to the whip. "To children? Why Urfers do this?"

The Searcher leaned in again. "For world domination."

Meg squinted at Loul. "Loul thoughts this?"

"No."

"Po? Po thoughts this?"

Po's mouth hung slack when Meg turned to him. "Not anymore."

"Hatador thoughts this. Yes, Hatador thoughts Urfers have not good/bad to children."

"Not just kids, sweetheart." The Searcher lined himself up for one of his classic confrontation shots. "I think you have plans for all Dideto. I think you're in collusion with the Cartar Administration, letting them think they can make deals with you. Trade technology for a higher ranking when you colonize the planet. You've done your little mind tricks on them, convincing them to sell out their entire race for bigger scraps of food and nicer cages to live in."

Reno Dado banged her fists on the table. "Do you even hear yourself? She's sitting right here. They've been here for, what, a week? Has anyone been hurt? Has there been even a single gunshot? I saw the footage. We're the ones with weapons trained on them. We're the ones with the army assembled. There are five of them. Why does everyone think that Didet is the center of the universe? What the hell are they going to get colonizing us? Dust?"

"They're going to get a planet full of free submissive slave labor!" He slammed a photograph onto the table. "If they're not invading, why are there ships amassing in orbit? Why has this image been redacted from national weather imaging? Why is the administration hiding the truth? Answer me, Meg."

Meg pulled the photo up from beneath the light screen. Loul heard her breathe out a quiet word and she dropped the picture. Her fingers moved through the text boxes, whipping through the database until a photograph appeared on screen. It was another Urfer in a stiff fabric overshirt staring unsmiling at the camera. This Urfer had black hair and black eyes but its skin was somewhat paler than Agnar's, the Urfers' leader.

Meg pointed to the picture and spoke a word. Over the din of the social center and The Searcher's muttered complaints, it took several tries before Loul could get it. "Rarenson. This is Rarenson."

She tapped her knuckles and then pointed to the ship. "Here."

Po traced his finger over the edge of the photo box. "Rarenson's on the ship? Just him?"

Loul leaned in to see the picture more clearly. "I think that's a female." He nudged Meg with his shoulder. "Only Rarenson on ship? One Urfer?"

"Yes."

"Bullshit. Nobody flies a mission with just six people."

Hark snorted. "And we know this because we've done so many missions. Oh that's right. We can't even get out of the atmosphere."

While The Searcher shouted directions to his cameraman to resituate himself, Meg flipped the light screen up once more, only this time she used it to wall the angry reporter away from the table. When he saw the light box swing up in his direction, his mouth dropped open. When Meg ran her fingers along the control slide, making the screen opaque, he growled.

"Meg no talk to Hatador. Hatador talk much...big." She smiled at the group.

Reno Dado smiled back. "He does talk too big. Too loud."

They could see his raised fists behind the screen. Loul snickered. "How long do you think it'll take him to figure out that the screen is just light? That he can stick his head through it? We've been moving through it the whole time."

"I'm not going to tell him," Po said. "It is kind of cool that he came, though."

"Mr. Pell!" The Searcher resorted to shouting as if from a deep hole. "Ask her how many ships there are. Ask her how they plan to disarm our military forces. Ask them how many of us they plan to spare? Ask her, Mr. Pell. See if she'll tell you the truth!"

"Can I?" Po leaned forward on his forearms to better see Meg's face. "Can I ask you a question, Meg? Will you tell me the truth?"

"Meg talk Po yes good/okay."

Po stared at her face, his eyes moving over her hair and the long, narrow cheeks. "Meg, can I see your ship?"

EIGHTEEN

MEG

Well that hadn't gone as planned. That Hatador fellow, whoever he was, turned the whole happy occasion on its ear. The weird thing was that she kind of liked the guy. *Liked* may not have been the right word. She kind of understood him. There was something familiar about him, about his attitude and his stance and his persistence. In the whirlwind of this entire experience, it had occurred to Meg more than once to wonder why Loul and his people weren't more curious about them. Sure, they had examined them and shared information. They had brought what looked like an entire army to guard them, or maybe to protect themselves. But even with Baddo and the black-shirt crews, with the generals and the press conferences, the Dideto as a whole were just so polite. It was kind of unnerving.

Meg kept thinking about Prader's comment that if their positions were switched, if the Dideto had approached from the sky, Earther forces would probably have shot them before they made landfall. Cho hadn't found the jokes about dissection and experimentation in the least amusing, and she knew it was because he didn't find the idea too far-fetched. At least not from an Earther standpoint. But here on Didet, five strange creatures had dropped from the sky with a sixth circling the planet, and only this Hatador fellow seemed inclined to shake his fist and demand answers.

Not that she wasn't thankful. Heaven knew she'd stretched the bounds of even Loul's wide trust by not telling him about Aaronson and the *Damocles*. But even knowing how shocked he must have been when Hatador told him about the ship coming into a detectable orbit, still Loul had trusted her. Still he had given her the benefit of the doubt. It sounded like even his friends did. Would she have done the same? A diplomat and protocol specialist, would she have stuck with her gut even when all the evidence pointed to signs that her contact had been hiding information? She didn't want to think about that.

What she had to face now was that Hatador wasn't going to hide behind that screen forever. (It did make her laugh that he couldn't figure out the barricade was nothing but light. He might be persistent and nosy, but clearly he was no genius.) Loul and his friends were discussing something, and now it looked like Po wanted to see the ship. The girl cut him off after that question and another hurried discussion arose. All four leaned forward on their arms, their thrums back in that mesmerizing harmony. She wished she could understand what they talked about. ProLingLang picked up a few phrases but she couldn't make sense of them. Family was mentioned. The generals came up, as did the wind truck. Hark seemed displeased when he mentioned *tut*, but one word kept tripping up the translation. It had to be a misunderstanding, a homonym of some sort, but it sounded like they kept referring to something purple.

She just couldn't be as polite as the Dideto. If the *Damocles* had been spotted, Captain Wagner and the crew were no doubt facing tough questions. She had to get back to the landing site. Plus, depending on how the Chelyan crystal was recuperating and how well Jefferson's quest for Class IV silicates was going, she might have plenty of time to chitchat with Loul and his friends, more time than she ever dreamed of having. So whatever purple thing they were discussing was going to have to wait.

"Loul." She put her hand on his wrist, stopping him midgesture. "Meg go back. Meg go to Urfers. Meg need/want go back." She pointed to the countdown clock on the screen. It wasn't counting down anything right now on her screen, but he knew what it meant.

Po leaned in close. "Meg? Po go with Meg to Urfers?"

"Yes."

Loul had a lot to say to that, his thrum hitching and his knuckles grinding into the table. From the way he punched the air toward the guards lined up behind the still-shouting Hatador, she guessed he thought they might not be keen to the idea.

"Why Po not go? Po and Loul Dideto? Yes? All go with Meg Loul."

She didn't need to see Loul's hand on the screen to see his maybe face. He drew into himself when he spoke. "Is not okay/bad to generals, no?" She heard the collective thrum soften, and to her untrained ear it sounded like a sigh. It wasn't a happy sound.

"Loul talk is good/okay. Loul need/want Dideto go with?"

He tapped his knuckles. Before he could start to explain why it couldn't happen, and Meg had a pretty good idea what he was going to say, she reached past him and drew back the light screen. Hatador toppled onto the table, his face and his lips shiny with spit.

"Hatador go with Dideto? Yes? See Urfers?"

Loul nearly choked, his thrum hiccupping, and Meg saw the gazes of his friends fall away. Hatador ground out something between his teeth, his tone rough. She picked out the words *generals* and *guns* and a reference to something black and purple. Feeling just overwhelmed enough to risk being cocky on Loul's behalf, Meg played her bluff.

"Loul talk okay/good is okay/good. Loul talk generals. Generals talk yes. Yes?"

All eyes watched her. Hatador seemed the first to get her meaning. Keeping her tone as matter-of-fact as she could manage, unnecessary since even Loul probably couldn't tell the difference, she explained the situation to Loul's friends the way she wanted them to see it, the way she believed it should have been anyway.

"Loul talk yes and generals talk no—this is yes. Loul talk no and generals talk yes—this is no. Yes? Loul talk. Generals hear. Urfers hear. Loul is—" She plucked at the front of her shirt the way she'd seen Loul do in the wind truck when he'd mentioned the black-shirt crews. She hoped she had it right, that the gesture meant important, not pompous or abusive. His three friends sat back a bit, their eyes wide. Hatador smiled another sharp smile. Loul seemed the last to absorb her message. She brought it home.

"Loul has wind truck. Loul talk all go is good/okay, all go. Is good/okay, Loul?"

Loul's mouth opened and closed several times. Hatador punched his arm softly, pushing him back into the booth. Loul gripped the table and then pounded his knuckles.

"Is good/okay."

LOUL

He didn't know how it happened or how he had pulled it off or what was going to be waiting for him when they landed, but somehow he found himself loading his friends and The Searcher onto the airvan, followed by Meg and only four of the guards who now had seats. He drew the line at the cameraman, insisting the outside media crossed the lines of security. The Searcher pulled out a small handheld box camera that Loul approved with authority that he came nowhere near possessing.

Everyone seemed to take it in stride, accepting his instructions and following his orders. The soldiers had balked at first, but with all eyes, including Meg's, on him, he'd held his ground and ordered the remaining guards to head back to the landing site by car. He did catch Hark throwing him a side-eye once or twice, biting back a laugh of disbelief, and he knew his best friend could sense that Loul was just in over his head. But bluffing or not, they were all in an airvan with armed guards and an alien flying over Cartar and heading for the spaceship at the Roana Temple as the sky turned bluer and bluer. Even Hark couldn't argue with those facts.

General Ada seemed prepared to argue, however, when they touched down on the edge of the landing site. He'd come out by himself to meet the airvan, the guards obviously having radioed ahead to prepare him. Anger flew off him like sparks as he bellowed "what the hell" and "are you out of your mind" at Loul multiple times in no discernible order. It was as if his rage had scrambled his meaning, overwhelming all need to communicate anything but loud bursts of sound. Loul knew he'd have enough of this to spare for possibly the rest of his life, so instead he concentrated on helping the still-smiling Meg from the airvan, followed by a grinning Hark, an opened-mouthed Po, the smirking Searcher, and, funniest of all, the lovely Reno Dado, who actually held up her hand to silence the general while she finished her phone call with her mother.

"Okay," Reno Dado said, turning off her phone and slipping it into her pocket. "Mom is making our apologies to your mother.

I told her that while the Purpling may happen only a few times in our lives, experiencing it at the Roana Temple with extraterrestrials was definitely a once-in-a-lifetime experience. She sends her love and said she'll save you a big bowl of *checha* soup, but only if you promise to take lots of pictures. You know Mom. She's a nut for her photo albums. What is that man yelling about?"

"That's General Ada," Loul said, leaning in under the pretense of being heard over the red-faced man's shouts. In fact, he wanted, as always, to catch a whiff of Reno Dado's skin. "He's one of the ranking generals on-site and he's a little pissed that I brought unauthorized civilians inside the barricade. You know, national security."

Reno Dado smiled at him with a slight tease in her eyes. "Well, Meg says you're the ranking figure on the site. Meg says they do what you say, right? After all, you're Loul Pell. You don't need a black shirt to be boss, do ya?" She bumped him with her shoulder, making him laugh. Her fingers brushed against the inside of his wrist. "I know I've always teased you about all this alien stuff. I mean with Po being Po how could I help it?"

She ducked her head and Loul thought the blush on the edges of her face might be from more than just the change in the light. "But part of me always sort of hoped you were right. I spend all day long doing these boring finance transfers, and when I would hear you all talking about it, when I'd hear all those ideas you had, I just…I'm just really glad you were right." She squeezed his wrist before stepping away and laughing. "Now let's go see that spaceship before Po pees in his pants."

Po charged ahead like a Pummel star, almost in full crouch from his excitement. He waved his fists and yelled out descriptions even though Loul stood less than five feet from him. When they cleared the inner barricade and the ruins of the temple came into sight, complete with the Urfers' spaceship perched atop it, even Po fell silent. Reno Dado gripped his arm, and Hark dropped into a deep, breathless crouch.

The Searcher broke the silence. "The Roana Temple. They had to have known where to land. This can't be a coincidence that they would choose to land on the Sea Gods' footstep."

"They haven't really explained why they landed here. I mean, they've barely explained why they landed on Didet at all." Loul watched the reporter gaze at the ship. "You don't really think they're trying to invade, do you? Not really, right?"

"I'll reserve judgment until I've had a chance to see for myself."

"I think you'll be surprised at what you see. They're very peaceful people." Loul walked closer to the site, more intent on watching his friends' reactions than noticing the change in demeanor of the workers around him. He had just noticed the Effans huddled together, rocking back and forth in distress when he heard one of the Urfers shout Meg's name louder than he'd heard any Urfer speak so far. Meg jumped at the sound, running ahead to her crew.

Po watched her run, making sounds of awe at the incredible distance her long, spindly legs could cover. "Look at that! How do they keep their legs from snapping at that speed? And what's that one doing? What's that tool? Is that tool? Or a gun? What's it doing? Why is it hitting the temple? Hey!"

His shout mingled with others who rushed forward toward the ship in outrage. One of the Urfers, Cheffson it looked like, was swinging a heavy metal bar over and over against the edge of the slab beneath the ship. He made a high-pitched, harsh sound as the metal made contact again and again against the tan rock, dust and pebbles flying everywhere. Cracks snaked across the surface of the slab as he continued to hammer with the bar. Two of Kik's crew rushed forward, shocked into action at the desecration of the sacred site. Mil reached the Urfer first, crashing into the alien at stomach level, sending the long-legged creature to the ground and the metal bar flying.

"What's happening?" Hark asked, or maybe it was The Searcher. Loul didn't listen but ran ahead, trying to catch up with Meg, who was being held by the leader. He held her in his dark hands, gripping the edges of her arms, shaking her hard, snapping her head back.

MEG

"Did you have a good time, Meg?" Wagner grabbed her by the shoulders. She could feel the strength in his hands. "Did you get some shopping done? Maybe stop for lunch? Did you make some new friends?"

"Captain, what? I told Cho. I just went to see Didet before—"

He stopped shaking her, holding her still and very close to his face. "Before what? Before we left? You shouldn't have hurried, Meg. Looks like you're going to have plenty of time to see the sights. We all are. All the time in the world."

They heard Jefferson grunt as the Dideto engineer tackled him. The wrench flew from his hands and landed near Cho's feet. Cho didn't move; he just stayed where he sat, legs crossed, elbows on his knees, eyes down. Jefferson used leverage and rage to dislodge himself from the heavy Dideto wrestling with him. When he saw Meg, he stopped.

"You."

With one word, Meg felt her knees threaten to buckle. The look in his eyes, the sound of that one word slipping from his lips made her wish that he'd punched her in the face instead.

"Will somebody explain to me what's going on?"

Jefferson spat on the ground, turning away from her. Wagner pulled in a deep breath and blew it out noisily. When he looked into Meg's face, he had a tighter rein on his emotions.

"The crystal is dying."

"But Aaronson said—"

"Aaronson said the crystal needs an injection of Class IV silicates, which we cannot find."

Meg tried to let the message sink in, but the words jumbled up in her brain, dropping in broken, unconnected pieces. "Aaronson. She's coming down?" Wagner shook his head. "But she has to. She'll…if she stays…"

"Yeah." Wagner's shoulders drooped. "She won't abandon the ship."

Prader looked up from the toolbox she'd been staring into, pointedly not looking at Meg. "It's a deep-space thing. You wouldn't understand."

"It's a ship thing," Jefferson said. "So we're pretty much in the minority in understanding that little bit of knowledge." His Galen drawl rolled the words out thick. He stalked away from her toward Prader, who handed him another heavy wrench.

Meg knew she should just walk away. She didn't understand what was going on but couldn't stop herself from asking. "Are you sure there aren't any of those silicates? Anywhere? Did the computer find—"

"Class IV silicates, Meg." Jefferson shouted, moving toward her with the wrench held like a club. "Officer Dupris." He spit the words. "It might behoove you to learn the proper terminology if you're going to be undertaking a mission of this scope. The Chelyan crystal needs an injection of Class IV silicates, a source of which I cannot locate on this godforsaken planet."

He held up his hand to stop her from speaking. "Oh, there are traces of it. God knows I've found traces of it in the rain runoff, in sediment. Dusty little sparkles of it all over the place, but at this point we need to find approximately enough Class IV to fill the cargo hold and the passenger deck to the walls. And if we found it and if Prader could get the sub to launch with the weight and if the crystal hasn't decayed to the point of no return, maybe, just maybe we could hump 'n' jump out of here. But there's really no point in worrying about that, is there? Because your boys here think they know where the silicates are. They're pretty sure they know where all these traces are coming from, but they can't be totally sure. You know why?"

Meg shook her head.

"Because they're in the ocean." Jefferson's voice dropped low as he leaned in close. "Yeah, they think the silicates are on the seafloor, but they're really not sure. You know why?"

She wished he would stop asking her that. "Because they've never been to sea."

Meg blinked, not understanding.

"You heard me. They have never been in the water. Never." Jefferson gripped the wrench with both hands like he planned to bend it, to wrap it around her neck. "A billion people on a planet that is seventy percent water and they have never thrown a fucking piece of wood into the sea and thought, 'Hey, we could float on that.' Never."

"Really?"

"Really. And since we have no submersible equipment on the shuttle and time isn't exactly on our side—"

Meg wasn't listening. Without her bidding, the sociologist within her tried to make sense of the bewildering revelation. "Didn't you say the land mass of the planet is an unbroken ring at the equator? Maybe that's why. Maybe they've never needed to cross it. Or maybe it's sacred. Maybe their mythology—"

"Don't you dare!" Prader sent her toolbox clattering to the
ground with a sharp kick. She ignored the mess as she stormed
over, jabbing her finger in Meg's face. "Don't you fucking dare
give us that protocol shit. Not now. Not when Aaronson is gone.
Not when these fucking monkeys could have saved her, saved all
of us, if they'd gotten off their fat, lazy asses and looked around
their own fucking planet."

"What are you talking about?" Meg felt her own temper rise.
"They've got a whole culture, a whole world. So they're not like
us, not exactly like us. What makes us so perfect? This is exactly
the kind of xenophobic shit that's been the cause of every major
war and holocaust, the Evang-jihad for fuck's sake, or have you
already forgotten that?"

"Don't you say that word." Prader shoved her with both
hands, but Meg caught her wrists, fighting the urge to twist them
and drop the smaller woman to the ground. "Aaronson lost her
husband in that attack. Aaronson lost everything in that, so you
don't get to talk about it."

"Me?" She threw Prader's wrists away from her, still tempted
to start punching. "What does that mean? Why is everyone pissed at me? How exactly is this, any of this, my fault?"

"Like you don't know," Prader said.

Jefferson snorted an ugly laugh. "She doesn't. She never
could."

Wary confusion overrode anger and Meg stiffened. "Don't
understand what?"

Cho spoke up. "Drop it, you two."

"Drop what?"

Prader stepped in close enough for Meg to smell the motor
oil in her hair. She looked up into Meg's face with cold eyes. "You
should never have been allowed on this mission. You have no
idea how the crystal works."

"Can it, Prader," Wagner said, his voice tired. "Leave it alone."

"No, tell me."

"It knew." The smaller woman nodded as she spoke. "It knew all along that you didn't want to be there. It knew you hated space. We all knew. We all knew how much you hated the black and how much you hated being out deep. And if we knew it, you can bet your ass the crystal knew it too."

Meg waited for any of this to make sense. When Prader said nothing more, she shook her head. "You have got to be kidding me. You think I caused the crystal to die? You think it read my mind and lost its will to live because I don't jump up and down and stick my hand down my pants every time we leave orbit? It's a propulsion crystal. It's a chemical reaction, not a mood ring. And you call these people stupid?"

She didn't think it was possible for Prader to get any closer but the smaller woman did, stepping so close to Meg that their shirts rubbed against each other. Meg couldn't believe any of this, couldn't believe she stood toe-to-toe with the engineer, seconds away from a fistfight over something so incredibly stupid. When Prader's arm shot up, Meg drew back her own arm, ready to defend herself. Instead of hitting her, however, Prader snatched the chain around Meg's neck, whipping her hand back and snapping the old clasp. She leaped back, taunting Meg with the locket dangling from her wrist.

"Give me that!" Meg's mouth went dry.

"Tell me something. Tell me the truth." Prader swung the locket, turning her body to keep it out of reach as Meg lurched for it. "In your heart of hearts, tell me you didn't want to stay here. Tell me you haven't been dreaming of spending the rest of your miserable life on this dry rock chitchatting with your little boyfriend, never having to step foot into the *Damocles* again. Tell me the truth, Meg."

"Give me that locket or I swear to God, Prader, I'll kill you."

"Who's in the locket, huh, Meg? A boyfriend? A girlfriend?"

"Knock it off, Prader," Cho warned, rising to his feet. "Give her the locket." But Prader ignored him, dancing backward, keeping her arm and the locket out of Meg's desperate reach.

"Is it Mommy and Daddy? Is that what it is? Mommy and Daddy who didn't love you enough, who weren't proud of you and made you run away to try to be a big shot? What did they do, Meg? Huh? Did they fight all the time and make you be the little peacemaker?"

Meg could hardly see through the tears that rose up as she jumped and clawed for the other woman's hand. "Shut your mouth, Prader."

"Shut it? But that's not what you want, is it? That's not what you do. You talk. You talk and talk and get other people to talk so that everybody is talking and talking and everybody's friends. Right? Because we're all supposed to be friends. We're all supposed to like each other and respect each other and be interested in each other because everyone has a story. Isn't that what you said to me once? Everyone has a story."

"Prader, please," Meg sobbed, needing the locket like she needed her next breath.

Prader's face was ugly with contempt. "Everyone has a story. Even short, stupid, hairy passive little monkeys like these freaks that we're stuck with." She hurled the locket over Meg's head, aiming for and hitting a wide-eyed Loul in the forehead with it. "You got your wish. You can sit and talk yourself to death with them now. Hear all their stories and tell them all of yours. Oh, but don't bother telling them the 'Three Men in a Tub' story or Jonah and the whale. They won't get it."

Prader turned away as Meg rushed toward Loul, sprawling on her knees in the dirt looking for the locket. Loul crouched down in front of her. Tears made her blind and she clawed at the ground uselessly. Her breath caught when Loul opened his fist, the dented locket resting on the tender pink pad of his palm. It looked so small there, so old and battered, that she could only sob. Tears ran off her cheeks as she dropped her forehead against the locket, pressing her weight into Loul's solid hand.

"Meg."

Meg raised her head, blinking away the tears to see Loul's worried eyes. His thrum was hushed and jagged, no longer in sync with his friends or anyone at the work site. Behind him, Dideto crews clustered, pressing against each other in anxiety.

LOUL

"Meg." He moved to brush his knuckles against her cheek and then changed his mind. Opening his fingers, he dragged the tender pads of his fingertips through the dampness of her skin. A lock of hair clung to her cheek, and he felt the fine strands tickle his sensitive pads. She put her head back down in his other palm, and he could feel the hard metal pressed between them. The littlest Urfer had ripped it off of Meg's neck, making Meg chase and yell for it. It looked like a game, a child's game, but even with the little he understood of Urfer body language, Loul knew this was no game. Something had changed.

Chaos surrounded him. The Effans, Kik and his crew, Olum, and all the work site crews crouched and muttered together, bewildered by the explosion of noise and motion from the otherwise placid aliens. Mil and two other engineers examined the fractured slab of the temple for damage from Cheffson's blows. The generals shouted orders that nobody listened to, and from what he could hear Po was on the brink of exploding from curiosity. Loul ignored them all, focusing instead on the delicate knobs of Meg's spine that arced beneath her thin shirt as she hung her head in his palm.

Feet shuffled, voices rose and fell, and he ignored them all until something metallic crashed close to his feet. Meg's head snapped up, the small ornament sticking to her forehead for just a moment before dropping back into his palm. To his right, Loul saw the broken frame of a box camera. Cho and The Searcher stood facing each other, the reporter's hands out and apart as if he still held the camera. Despite his thin frame, the Urfer loomed over The Searcher, hand drawn back up, ready to whip out with that unreal precision to strike anything else the man decided to point at Meg.

The Searcher stayed very still, eyes locked on Cho's wet stare. "They really don't like cameras, do they?"

As The Searcher lowered his hands, Cho relaxed, keeping an eye on the man as he folded his long legs down to Meg's level. Meg sat back on her heels, graceless. She took the round piece of metal from Loul's hand, her fingernails tickling the sensitive skin, and wiped her face with back of her fist. The ornament's chain bounced against her wrist as she smeared muddy streaks across her nose and cheeks.

"Meg." Cho spoke, his voice so low Loul wouldn't have heard it but for the earpiece he wore. Loul watched with a mix of worry and envy as Cho said words to her that made the water stop running from eyes. He heard the sound of Meg's name the way it was supposed to be spoken, the way his Dideto mouth could never manage. Cho's long brown hands feathered across her cheeks with a gracefulness only the Urfers knew, smoothing back her hair behind her ear, running a bony thumb over the fading imprint the ornament had left on her forehead.

Meg let Cho guide her to her feet. His long fingers tangled with hers, releasing the ornament. Slowly and with a precision Loul could only dream of, Cho maneuvered the ends of the chain, his fingernails catching on a release so small it was nearly invisible. Meg watched as he twisted and manipulated the fine chain until he achieved something that made Meg sigh. Cho held up both ends of the chain, the ornament hanging between them. Meg turned and Cho reached over her. When the ornament touched her chest, she pressed it to her, dropping her head, exposing the long line of her neck. Cho leaned in, staring intently as his fingers worked the chain until the two ends joined. When he finished, he put his hands on her shoulders and pressed his lips where his fingers had just been.

Meg looked at Loul, her eyes red, her pale skin blotchy and smudged. Her lips parted and she looked like she might speak, but she just drew in a shuddery breath. He wanted to step in closer to her. He wanted her to tell him what was happening, what that ornament was, and why, if it was so important to her that she would crawl around in the dirt for it, would she not have shown it to him before. He wanted to know why Cheffson and Agnar and Prader were vocalizing so loudly and harshly and why Cheffson had damaged the slab. He didn't get a chance to ask any of those questions because Po charged in, fists waving, face red from exertion.

"What the hell? What are they doing?" Po stared from Meg to Cho to Loul. "They're banging on the temple? They're going to get shot!" Loul shook his head, but Po punched his shoulder, pointing to the barricade. Soldiers were lining up with shields and rolling pom-cannons. The three generals stomped in uneven lines before them, shouting orders and listening to orders being shouted through radios. All eyes moved from the guns to the slab.

The Searcher grabbed Loul's arm. "Son, if you know what they're doing you'd better explain it to those soldiers right now. Once those cannons are activated, it's going to take more than diplomacy to turn them off. Can you think of any good reasons they'd be defacing the temple slab? Have they destroyed anything else? This isn't the time to be coy, Pell. If she's told you anything, you had better come clean or this is going to get ugly really fast."

"Nothing." Loul watched Cho lead Meg away toward their shelter. Prader had returned to her toolbox and Cheffson and the leader stood together talking and shaking their heads. Cheffson still wielded that heavy metal bar. "They've never shown any interest in the slab before. The ship did some damage when they landed, burned off the top edges, but as far as I know they've never even poked at it."

"Did anyone tell them it's sacred?"

"Sacred?" Loul punched his hips in frustration. "We can't even find the word for *lunch*. You think we managed to catch up on religion? I don't even know if they have gods."

The generals finished their tirade, stepping away from the now organized soldiers. The pom-cannons whined as their ignition switches activated. The Searcher sighed. "Well if they do have gods, any more damage to the slab is a good way to get back to see them."

NINETEEN

MEG

Cho kept his hand on the back of her neck. She sweated against his palm, the sun and her anger making her too hot, but she didn't move away. He felt solid and calm. He felt like he could single-handedly keep her world from blowing to pieces. She could feel the bent clasp of the locket chain pressing into her skin, and that little point of pain helped her focus.

"Meg."

Cho's grip tightened at the sound of Loul's yell. "This isn't the time, Meg. Trust me, it would be better if he gave us all a little room."

"It's not his fault."

"It's nobody's fault." He pulled her closer, turning her to face him. "It isn't. They're angry. They've been busting their asses trying to find that silicate. Jefferson's been a crazy person tearing through files. He's only half-hinged as it is, and when he found out the silicate might be on the seafloor, he just fell apart. It's such a stupid situation. To be this close to what we need and not be able to reach it. Boats. We came all this way through space and we're stopped because we don't have a boat."

"It's not their fault." Meg looked up at Cho, keeping her neck long so he wouldn't move his hand. "It's not my fault. You know this isn't how I wanted it to go, right?"

Cho sighed a soft laugh. "You mean do I think the crystal committed suicide because it read your mind? Of course not. But I'm not a deep spacer either, not like those three. Not like Aaronson. It's just…"

"It's just what?"

Loul shouted her name again and Cho squeezed his eyes shut. "It's just that you wasted no time getting in tight with them. You let them in."

"That's what I do. That's what my job is. That's why I'm here, why I made this mission in the first place. What was I supposed to do?"

"You left the site. You left the site on your own and went out with them when all of this was going down. We didn't know what was going to happen and you just left us, Meg. You took off with your little friend. You weren't here when Aaronson called in distress. You weren't here when she made her decision to stay with the ship. You came back here laughing and smiling like you'd just been to a party when—" Meg cut him off, dropping her head onto his shoulder. He rubbed her back, kissing the side of her face. "They'll come around. They have to, don't they? You're the only person the Dideto can talk to."

They heard Loul's breathless approach, the frantic hitch of his thrum as he stopped just a foot from where they stood. Cho muttered a curse as Meg lifted her head. They both knew she had to talk to him. He wasn't going to just go away. With a weary nod, he released her and she turned to her fidgeting Dideto friend.

"Meg." He waved his fists in either direction. To his left, he jabbed toward the slab where Meg could see deep cracks crisscrossing the upper edges. To his right, he pointed to the approaching line of soldiers pushing carts holding blunt tubes. "Meg, not good/bad. Very."

The rest of the crew noticed the organized approach as well. Prader took her firearm from the toolbox drawer and slid it into the pocket of her pants. She kept her fingers on the end of the weapon. Meg saw Wagner unfasten his own gun pocket, knowing he kept his weapon with him at all times. Jefferson kept his gun with Prader's. All he had was the heavy wrench that he gripped before him with both hands.

"Meg?" Wagner moved back a step, keeping in line with Jefferson, moving toward Prader. "Want to tell me what's going on?"

She saw Cho walking slowly backward to the shelter. He crouched down smoothly, reaching behind him into the tent for the gun she knew he stashed in a pocket by the opening.

"Everyone stand down."

"Fuck that," Jefferson said, hefting the wrench.

"Those are guns," Prader said.

"Let me find out what's going on. Everyone, just give me a minute."

Jefferson spat between his feet. "Yeah, because I'd hate to get any bad news today."

"Loul." Meg sidled up to him, keeping her movements small and her eyes on the soldiers. "Talk this to Meg. What the hell is this?"

Loul stomped his foot, obviously frustrated since he'd been trying in vain to get her attention. He jabbed his fist again toward the landing slab. "Not good/bad." His fist moved in a jagged pattern in the air. "Bad. Very."

"What's bad? The ship?"

"Cheffson." He banged his meaty forearms together.

"Jefferson?" She followed his hand again as his fists drew jagged lines in the air. He pointed to the slab and banged his arms together again. "It's the slab. We've damaged the slab."

"That pisses them off?" Jefferson asked with a harsh laugh. "That? That's what it takes to get these ugly monkeys pissed off?"

"Jefferson," Wagner warned, "this isn't the time."

"Shit." Jefferson spun away from the captain, letting the wrench swing free from one hand. "Time. Time is the one thing we've got boatloads of. I mean, oops! Can't say boatloads, can we?" His voice grew louder as he let the weight of the wrench spin him around. "We can't put boats in your fancy translation program, can we, Meg? Because they don't know what boats are. They've never built a goddam boat, and since they don't know how to swim, we don't get to get back on our little boat, do we?"

He stopped spinning, the wrench banging against his shin. "Hey, question for ya. If they don't know what a boat is, what word do you suppose they're using to say ship? Banana? Underpants? Lavender?"

"Jefferson!" Wagner moved closer to him, putting himself between the geologist and the slowly approaching soldiers. "Knock it off."

"Sorry, Captain, just free thinking, you know." His Galen drawl got thicker as he loosed a wide, stupid-looking grin. "That's what we're gonna hafta do, aren't we? Just like ole Meg there. Think outside the box. Think like we never thunk before, right Meg? Get inside those hairy little skulls since we're gonna be stuck here with them for the rest of our freaking lives."

Meg clenched her fists. "Shut up, Jefferson. Just shut your mouth."

"I will, Officer Dupris. I will stop talking and I will start reaching out to discover the wonder that is the Dideto." He exaggerated each syllable of that last word. "As a matter of fact, I'm gonna start right now, and I'm gonna find out just what it is about that slab that's got these boys so worked up. Whaddya think, Prader?"

Prader's laugh hissed in the coms. "I think that's a very scientific approach."

"Both of you," Captain Wagner said, "stand down now."

"Aye-aye, Captain," Jefferson said. "Let me just get rid of this wrench."

Meg didn't breathe as she watched Jefferson heft the wrench over his head, his long strong arms swinging the heavy metal bar over his head in ever-widening circles. She wanted to scream, to close her eyes, to shoot him, anything to stop him from what she knew he planned to do. But she couldn't do anything but watch as the wrench whipped out of his grip and sailed end over end, smashing against the upper edge of the landing slab.

Nobody moved. Nobody spoke. The soldiers stopped their approach and every thrum fell silent. The only sound was Jefferson's labored breathing. Until the cracking started.

At first it sounded like sand pattering to the ground. Then a crackling, grinding sound arose. A dark web of cracks skittered across the surface of the slab, racing out from the point of impact, stretching far past the nose of the ship. Everything grew silent once more for just a moment and Meg watched in horror as a dozen feet of the front of the slab disintegrated into rough chunks that crashed to the ground in a cloud of dust.

LOUL

Loul fell into a deep crouch. He wasn't alone. The Effans, Hark, Po, Kik and crew, even The Searcher dropped down low to the ground as an enormous section of the Roana Temple crumbled into pieces. The soldiers stopped their advance, stunned at the sight. Nobody could speak. Nobody could look away.

In that minute Loul didn't believe in anything. He had never really believed the temple slab was an actual footstep of the Sea Gods. He didn't even know if he believed in the Sea Gods to begin with. He realized he'd never truly believed in the ornate, complex structures theorists had depicted being built on the stone. He didn't believe that if someone ran across the surface they would be transported to one of the other six slabs around the globe. He didn't believe that inside the slab lay the remains of the Sea Gods themselves or that any ancient creature was chained beneath the stone waiting to wreak havoc among the living. He didn't believe science would ever explain the presence of the seven slabs and at that moment he didn't care.

What he cared about was the slab itself. All its mystery, all its history, whatever it was, it was a piece of his world, the world he'd been born into, the world he loved. Nobody touched the slabs. Nobody crossed them or defaced them or drilled into them. Nobody. When he had seen the Urfer ship perched on that slab, it had only driven the point home more solidly. The slabs, whether the Roana Temple or the Steps at Ga or twin slabs of North Her Mer, it didn't matter which slab it was, the slabs mattered. They were sacred. What kind of being, what kind of human being would purposefully and recklessly damage one? To what end? Another thick section of the slab crumbled, and in the rosy light filtering down through the dust, Loul saw the Urfers in a new light. They had never looked more alien.

The Urfers stood frozen. Meg's eyes were enormous, her hands clamped over her mouth. A sea breeze picked up, spinning the dust in little twisters through the work site, picking up as the sky color shifted. It was like the planet itself felt the damage to the slab. It felt like the wind was angry. Tiny pebbles thrown by the wind pinged against the metal cases on the work site. Another set of fissures widened, cracking loudly before separating into jagged boulders and crashing to the dirt. For one horrible moment, Loul found himself calculating how long it would take for the entire slab to disintegrate.

General Ada's radio crackled, breaking the stunned silence. All around him people broke into muttered sounds of protest and despair. Loul never thought he'd see anything harder to believe than the presence of an alien vessel on his world. The shattered corner of the ancient slab changed that forever. He heard Meg saying something low and urgent to the Urfers, something that made them break their stillness and move slowly toward the center of the site. They walked with the same careful precision they had used when they had first arrived. They moved like animal trainers frightened of spooking their charges. He almost laughed. It was a little late for that precaution.

Ada shouted an order and the soldiers settled back into their formation, the pom-cannons level and loaded. Loul saw the Urfers' hands moving toward their legs. That's where they had kept their weapons when they had landed. He thought they had put their weapons away. At some point they had all managed to replace them. Slowly, in rhythm, the five long-legged aliens stepped closer to each other, bony fingers flickering at the sides of their legs. It was like watching their arrival in reverse. It was like watching reality unravel.

The little one, Prader, stumbled over one of the tools she had kicked from her toolbox, and the sudden motion made two soldiers on the end of the line raise their shields aggressively. Agnar and Cheffson reacted quickly, drawing slender weapons from their pockets and aiming into the barricade. Someone barked another order, and the first pom-cannon ignition switch was opened. Loul felt a curious detachment. He'd never seen a pom-cannon fired before. He'd seen the aftereffects, the shrapnel and flaming debris; he'd even heard the roaring boom on tape. He wondered if it would hurt his ears to hear one go off this close.

The Urfers were talking, their voices low and hissing in his earpiece. He could hardly make out the sounds, and the translator made sense of none of the words. Prader picked herself up off the ground carefully, dusting rocks off of her hands as she righted herself. Not rocks, Loul corrected himself, pieces of the slab. Pieces of the Roana Temple that lay in crumbling mounds because one of the aliens had hit it repeatedly, hammered at it and smashed it like a waterbird pecking at a *loro* nut on a cliff-side. But a waterbird needed to eat. Why would anyone need to smash a slab?

His thoughts whirled and fizzled like the dust twisters blowing red and hot in the changing light. The Purpling. Maybe that was it. Maybe the changing suns had driven the Urfers insane. It wasn't impossible. How many stories had he read where the lowering light and the appearance of the pin lights in the sky had driven people mad? Loul ground his teeth, chastising himself. Stories, he shouted in his own mind. Stories. His whole world had been stories. This wasn't Magagan. This was real. Soldiers pointed pom-cannons at five aliens who had defaced the Roana Temple.

Not aliens. Urfers. Meg. Pom-cannons were pointed at Meg.

He rose from his crouch, his fists tight against his side. "Stop."

All eyes moved to him. He pointed his fists at the Urfers. "Stop. No." Then he pointed at the soldiers. "Stop with the cannons. This isn't the way to do this."

"Pell," General Ada yelled, "get out of the way. We've waited too long to get a handle on this and now they've gone too far. They're trying to destroy the Roana Temple."

Loul couldn't help but laugh. "And so what's your plan? To shoot pom-cannons at it? Those things can blow through buildings.

Even if you hit the Urfers, even if you blow them right out of their shoes, do you think you won't damage the temple?" He didn't know if the general was listening but Loul could see the doubt on the soldiers' faces. "It's already cracking farther down the length. Look. You shoot anywhere near the slab and it's going to crumble."

"Well what do you suggest we do, Pell?" Ada said. "Wait until they finish destroying it? Give them a map and see what else they'd like to attack?"

Loul saw Hark and Reno Dado watching him. Po stood beside The Searcher, eyes flying over every inch of the scene. "Who says they're attacking?"

"What the hell else would you call it?" Ada's voice cracked as he yelled. "What else could it possibly mean?"

He looked at Meg, whose hands he noticed were not reaching for her weapon. One hand rested near her throat, wrapped around the ornament that hung there. The other she held out away from her body toward the other Urfers, palm down. Holding them back. Waiting.

"Why don't we ask them?"

MEG

At that moment, Meg wanted to do a number of things. She wanted to punch Jefferson in the face. Prader too. She wanted to throw herself in front of Loul and beg him to forgive them. She wanted to find a quiet spot to rip off Cho's clothes and lose herself in his body. She wanted to invent a time machine so she could go back to her childhood and pick a very different path than the one that had placed her on an alien planet billions of years from home with no way of returning and a crew that blamed her because of some idiotic superstition. And she had to pee.

She did none of those things. She did nothing. She found she could do nothing but stand and stare as huge chunks of the landing slab slid to the dry earth, listening as the thrums of the Dideto around her rose and fell in harsh distress. Then those weird tube machines came rolling in, complete with teams of soldiers, and before she let out the breath she'd been holding, Prader was on her knees, weapons were drawn, and Loul was standing the middle of it.

Loul shouted to the generals. Wagner spoke low in the coms, asking Meg what was happening and what they should do. She resisted the urge to scream, "Now you want my feedback? Now you need me?" Because they did need her. Not that she was going to do any good to any of them. She had no idea what the significance of the landing site was to Loul and his people, but in her experience, enormous hunks of unique, shaped rock did not just lie around untouched because nobody had noticed them. The ground around the site had been maintained, if left empty. Nothing about the landing site seemed accidental.

Meg heard the word *ask*, and the tubes pointed at them lowered to the ground. Whatever Loul had said, the soldiers had listened. Maybe she hadn't been wrong in her bluff about Loul's importance. If it kept this situation from erupting into violence, she'd happily admit her mistake.

"Meg." Loul moved toward her, his movement steady, but she could hear the hammer of his thrum. "Talk this. Talk this." He waved his hand over the Earther crew.

"I'm sorry." It wouldn't translate but she hoped Loul could see the meaning in her face. She looked down at him, the reddening light picking up flecks of amber in the hair around his eyes. His inner eyelids rose slightly as the wind shifted. The enormity of what she had to say made her want to lie down on the ground and go to sleep.

"This." Loul jabbed his fist toward the slab. "This. Cheffson."

Meg nodded. "Jefferson is not good/bad. Jefferson thinks…" She sighed, ignoring Jefferson's huff of protest in the coms. "Earthers think…shit. This is pointless. You can't understand what I'm saying to you. I'm just talking and talking and it's not getting us anywhere." She closed her eyes and sighed. "And now that we have all the time in the world to talk I can't think of a single way to explain any of it to you."

She stood there, swaying, eyes closed, listening to the discordant sound of worried thrums all around her. She heard her crew breathing in the coms and tiny pebbles blowing against metal in the rising wind. Then she felt rough fingers brush against her hand where it hung limp by her side.

"Meg," Loul said, tugging at her hand as he dropped into a crouch. "Talk Loul." He crouched down low, looking up at her, his thrum now low and steady like this was any other day. Any other day with a team of aliens on his planet walking around like they owned the place. He crouched and waited for her to join him. So, surrounded by drawn weapons and a damaged landing slab, Meg folded her legs beneath her, sinking down to the ground to sit cross-legged, face-to-face, the way she had done when they had first met.

Loul didn't rush her. He waited while she searched for a way to reach him. She figured she might as well get right to the point. "The ship." She pointed to the sky above them. "The big ship. It's not coming. Earthers are not going." She saw his surprised smile start and shook her head. "Not good/bad. Meg talks about Aaronson? Yes?" He tapped his knuckles. "Aaronson is…Aaronson does not come to Didet. Aaronson does not come to the Earthers."

"Why?"

She smiled. It was such a big word for making such a small sound. It was a universal question in a breath. She picked up a clod of dirt in her hand and held it up for him to see. "The ship is…" She crumbled the dirt, letting the dust fall from her fingers. "Earthers not going. Earthers stay on Didet. All time."

Loul watched her face, shifting as he did in his crouch. He looked at the dirt scattered at their feet. Shifting forward, balancing on the knuckles of his right hand, he lifted his left hand and reached out for Meg. His fingers opened and he brushed the tender pads against her throat where a Dideto's thrum spot would be.

"Okay."

"Okay," Meg said, leaning into his hand.

In her com, she heard the sound of a deep breath being sucked in, and then Prader's voice hissed. "Son of a bitch. Son of a bitch! Jefferson, can you see this?"

The Earthers spun around to see Prader, who knelt on the ground in front of the damaged slab. Loul had heard her as well and rose from his crouch as Meg got to her knees to look behind her. Prader pressed at the seam of one of the deeper fissures that stretched to the ground beside her. Her fingers clawed at the crumbling stone, clearing room enough to stick her arm in up to the elbow. She climbed to her feet, pulling at the rock, ripping away chunks of crumbling stone.

Prader's voice was a whisper. "Meg, ask them where this rock came from."

Meg turned back to Loul, watching as the translator made sense of Prader's request. She didn't need to repeat it. He jabbed his fist at the slab. "This. From there." His arm swung toward the cliffs, toward the sea.

Jefferson ran to Prader and joined her in ripping off chunks from the already damaged slab. As the tan stone fell away they could see in the darkening red of the sunlight a wide ribbon of black rock speckled with rough maroon lines and flinty gray streaks. Jefferson pressed his cheek to the stone, his arm stretched long to caress the seam.

"Class IV."

TWENTY

MEG

Every muscle in her body screamed for relief. Her back twinged with effort, her arms trembled as she slid another pallet into the passenger hold. Her fingertips had bled and scabbed over so many times she could no longer feel them or tell where the black rock dust ended and her skin began.

Kik's destructive tendencies had turned out to be crucial to retrieving the silicate from beneath the slab's exterior. His natural inclination to break things translated into a cunning skill at unearthing the black rock. As he dug and chipped and broke away the slab, the Class IV silicate revealed itself not as a slab of its own but rather jagged mounds jutting up from the ground. The tan clay covered them solidly, making one solid slab out of a pile of black debris. Even as they excavated, Jefferson couldn't help but marvel at the precision with which the silicates had been covered.

"There are seven of these on the planet?" He kept asking the crews around him who just grunted their assent as they drilled and hauled the silicate out from its hiding place. "Why don't you have these in your database? Why don't you keep a record of them?"

"Maybe they do," Meg said after hearing his question a dozen times. "Maybe they just don't look at it like you do. Maybe it's more important just being what it is than for what it's made from."

Jefferson wiped a muddy hand across his forehead, leaving a streak across his orange-tinted skin. "Then why are they letting us have it? If it's so important, why just hand it over?"

Meg moved aside to let a crew of Dideto push a heavy wagon-load of the silicate to the cargo hold. "Because we asked nicely?"

Jefferson stared at her for a long moment and then laughed. "How about that?"

Of course it hadn't been as easy as that. Upon discovering the silicate, Jefferson had continued to hammer at the edifice while Prader yelled and waved her arms, holding off Kik and Mil and the rest of the Dideto ground crew nearby. Wagner had dragged over the geologist's test kit, and when the black mottled stone proved to be Class IV, Jefferson had held it up over his head as if its existence justified the destructive behavior. When the three generals marched forward, soldiers in tow, and shouted at the Urfers in a loud, barking chorus, Meg had tried to intervene. Loul jumped in with her, shouting and waving hands and generally adding to the chaos. It was Wagner who changed everything.

He had taken the sample, glowing blue in the testing fluid within the clear jar, and held it before the generals. "We need this." He didn't shout. He didn't threaten or tower over them. He held the jar out for their inspection, and when they looked back up at him, he waved his hand over the slab behind him. "We need this rock. To live. To go. Please." And with a grace that surprised even his own crew, Wagner sank slowly to his knees before the generals. "Please."

One by one, Jefferson, Prader, Cho, and finally Meg all followed suit.

"Please," Wagner said again. "Please."

The generals had turned to face each other in a small circle, their thrums rising and falling during their quick debate. It took less than a minute before the three turned back as one.

"Okay."

Jefferson had started to cry. Wagner nodded. "Okay."

They stripped the sub of every extraneous piece of equipment they could remove. Cho sealed a piece of Gro-Wall in an eco-pocket. The rest of the plants they incinerated, storing the ash in a vacuum tube beneath the pilot's seat. All but the most critical insulation panels, cargo walls, and floor panels were removed to make room for as much silicate as the sub could carry. Prader raged through fuel-to-weight ratio calculations while Wagner triangulated the course for Aaronson to rendezvous with the sub. Cho, Jefferson, and Meg worked with the Dideto to dislodge and haul the silicate into the cargo hold and passenger deck. By the time the sub was fully loaded, over a third of the landing slab had been excavated. The ship perched on a jagged circle in the middle of the demolition.

"That's all she can carry," Prader said, wiping blood and mud on her pants. "It's going to be close but it should be enough."

The five Earthers stood in their usual ring at the door of the ship. The Dideto hung back, resting from the hours of backbreaking labor they'd just completed. Wagner checked his screen although they all knew he didn't need to.

"Aaronson's moving into position. She's going to try to meet you a little lower to compensate for the weight drag while still staying high enough so that, you know."

"Yeah." Prader had agreed to fly the shuttle. She and Aaronson had the most experience with Chelyan crystals, and nobody knew more about pulling off the dangerous maneuver of jumpstarting the propulsion system. Plus Prader weighed less than anyone on the crew. That's how close the weight calculations had become.

"So I'm going drop the payload high," Prader explained as if anyone would question her. Nobody did. Just like nobody acted like they heard the tremor in her voice. "I'm figuring eight hours up, drop the load, and give Aaronson room to make the hump 'n' jump. All told we should know for sure in about ten hours, give or take." Prader cleared her throat and Meg could see her lower lip quiver. "If it's all right with you, Captain, I'm going to stay up there with her just in case the injection doesn't work."

Wagner nodded, his jaw muscles clenching. "Understood."

Meg spoke up. "If it doesn't work, are you going to bring her back down here?"

Prader, Jefferson, and Wagner shared a look she couldn't read. Prader's mouth twisted into a sad smile. "If it doesn't work, that crystal's going to blow us into stardust. If that happens, I just…I want to go with her, you know?"

Jefferson whispered, "Some of us want to see the stars…"

Prader and Wagner finished the line in unison. "Some of us want to be them."

Prader climbed into the shuttle, slipping into the narrow space between the silicate piles that led to the pilot's seat. She hesitated in the door and smiled. "Just for the record, when I get back here to pick you guys up, the trip back is going to be a bitch. We're not going to have time to put the seats back in. That means you're going be strapped to the floor. Just saying, put your big boy pants on."

"I'm gonna sit in your lap, sweetheart." Jefferson grinned.

Prader laughed and looked up at the red-and-blue-streaked sky. "All those suns are going to set, huh? Figures I'd be gone the one day this planet gets any fucking shade. Hey, Captain?"

"Yeah, Prader?"

Her smile stayed in place even when a tear dripped into her dimple. "Do me a favor. Don't run the clock, okay? Nothing good ever happens at the end of a countdown."

"Understood."

They stepped back, clearing the work crews back from the radius of ignition. The burners flared and for one horrible minute it looked like the thrusters would not lift the overburdened sub from the slab. But Prader knew her ship, and in seconds the heat around the slab became unbearable, more rock splintered under the thrust, and the *Damocles Sub 2* shot through the air.

LOUL

Loul had been born the year of a Purpling. His mother always told him that meant his life would be special. She'd told him that as an infant, his eyes had watched the darkening skies, and she swore that he'd been the first to spot the pinpricks when they'd appeared. At his second Purpling, he'd told his mother those weren't pinpricks in the sky. They were suns just like the ones that had set and that the sky was full of them, hundreds and thousands of suns just like theirs all through the universe, and that the only reason they couldn't usually see them was because the Dideto suns made too much light. His mother had laughed and asked him when he'd gotten so smart. He got the feeling that she didn't believe him about the pinpricks.

Now, with the Fa sun behind the ridge of the mountains, the Red Sun dropping into the water, and the rarely seen Green

Sun shining weakly behind him, he hoped his mother still didn't believe him. Now that there was proof, now that the satellite images had been confirmed by the incredible technology the Urfers had brought to the world, now that everyone knew there were billions of stars and that they could be charted and navigated by, now more than ever he hoped his mother watched the skies for the places where the Sea Gods had pricked the veil.

Prader had been gone for almost two shifts. The smudge log had burned down to embers and somebody had managed to get hold of a few tubs of *checha* soup. It wasn't as good as Reno Dado's mother's soup, but Loul couldn't be sure if that was because of the soup or because of the bitter taste in his mouth. The work site had been cleared and equipment packed up and stored in the lines of trucks. Now, instead of toolboxes and sample cases, the area within the barricade was filled with people lying out on blankets, propped up on backpacks and food bags, watching the wide streaking bands of colors as the Red Sun took the last of the light from the sky.

Mamu the archivist had cut long strips of purple fabric for everyone. According to Cartar tradition, everyone would wear something purple, and Loul had smiled as Meg and the Urfers had taken their pieces and wrapped them loosely around their slender necks. Everyone else draped the fabric across their shoulders as they dipped fingers into the embers and smudged soot over their cheekbones. Po offered to smudge the leader, Agnar, who had laughed and made a comment about black on black. Still, the tall alien sat still as Po rubbed the gritty stain on his skin. Loul smudged Meg, and the Effans took turns smudging Cho. Only The Searcher had the nerve to approach Cheffson, who struggled to sit still while his cheeks were blacked.

Bowls of soup were passed around. Meg ventured a taste. The way her mouth twisted made Reno Dado laugh hard enough to spit soup on her overshirt. The rest of the Urfers dined on piles of dried *tut*. As the sky turned from a kaleidoscope of colors to a wash of streaky blues and purples, conversations died down. Meg moved away from Cho, whose hand she had been holding almost nonstop since the ship had flown off, and moved to the blanket Hark had claimed for them. Hark and Po rested their heads on a duffel. Reno Dado lay beside Loul, her arms folded behind her head. Loul was beside her still propped on his elbows, scooting over to make room for Meg.

She folded herself down to the ground beside him, her long neck craning gracefully to watch the darkening sky. Her pale cheeks picked up hints of rosy lavender when she tilted her head back. "This." She waved her fingers over her head, moving across the sky. "This is good, yes? This is…big?"

"Yes." Loul spoke softly. "The Purpling. This is important."

"Yes."

The breeze from the sea picked up, whistling through shelters where the remaining equipment was stacked. Clouds skittered over the sea, reflecting the last of the Red Sun across the water. Loul knew if he turned around to look where the Green Sun had long set, he would see only rough shapes and shadows, the light gone from the southern horizon. Nobody looked that way though. The Red Sun was the father sun, the life sun. It would be the last to set and the first to rise, and all over the planet, the Dideto watched its journey.

He looked at Meg. The smudging hadn't done much to camouflage her in the shadows. The Urfers' skin didn't hold the soot well, and light still shone on their lips and cheeks and foreheads. Her eyes, though, were shadows, dark and strange.

"Meg, is this night?"

He could see her teeth white in the darkness and hear her soft laugh. "Yes, this is night."

"This is good/okay, yes?"

"Yes, Loul. This is good/okay. Very."

They still didn't understand exactly what was happening, where Prader had gone with the load of black stone they had excavated from the slab. When The Searcher had asked if the ship would return, Meg had let her hand waver between *yes* and *no*. Maybe. Loul could see the trembling in her delicate fingers. By unspoken agreement, the ground crews stopped asking questions then, choosing instead to focus on preparing for the Purpling. Nobody took the generals up on their offer to shuttle anyone home. The Urfers had been quiet ever since. None of them opened their light screens.

In the growing darkness, he felt Reno Dado shift against him, her skin warm in the cooling air. How long had he waited for this Purpling to tell her how he felt about her? She lay beside him uncovered, her hands now loose by her side, and he let his fingertips brush her wrist. She squeezed his fingers in return. "Talk to Meg." He could hear the smile in her voice. "I'll wait." He sighed when she lifted her hand, letting her fingertips graze his rose spot.

On the other side of him in the shadows, he could make out Meg and the long line of her spine as she bent over her lap. He heard a click and a slide and then felt something warm pressed into his hand.

"To Loul. Loul has this." Her fingers flitted near his, and the warm plastic in his hand glowed a pale red. "Loul has this." It was her wristband, where she kept the light screen.

"Meg, this is…I can't keep this."

"Yes. Meg to Loul has this. Loul thoughts to learn this. To see Urf. To learn." Her teeth and the whites of her wide eyes seemed to glow in the vanishing light as she brought her face close to his. "Meg go. Loul has this. Meg not go. Loul has this. Loul has this."

He felt her fingers as they ghosted around the band, and he wondered how she could see what she was doing. He thought she must know the device by heart as she pinched and drew the light screen out. She traced the edge of the screen and the light vanished to almost nothing. He was glad she understood the need for darkness.

Her breath was warm on the side of his face as she whispered to him. "Meg talk to Loul. Meg say this to screen and Loul learn this after. Okay?" She was going to tell him something, something the computer would have to translate, maybe even after she was gone.

"Okay," he said, pulling her hand to the earpiece in his ear. "Loul hear Meg talk. Meg. Not Dideto. Meg."

"Okay." Her fingers flitted over the screen and the translator program went off. He lay back on the blanket, one hand in Reno Dado's, one hand holding the wristband. He scanned the sky for the pinpricks and listened to the bell-like sound of Meg's voice in his ear.

MEG

They didn't need a clock to keep the countdown. They counted in breaths and heartbeats and stacks of equipment. They took turns dozing, unable to really sleep, and finally Cho offered them all a vitamin amphetamine shot.

"We'll sleep on board," he said. Nobody argued.

Maybe she was running out of time with Loul, but as the sky exploded in a color show like none she had ever seen, Meg wanted to be still. She wanted to sit with her crew. During the packing and loading, Prader and Jefferson both had made their version of a peace gesture, including her in the conversation and helping with the work. She appreciated the effort. Watching the Dideto smearing soot on their faces, tasting the sour, muddy soup, and watching them sprawl their bodies awkwardly onto their wide backs, Meg felt loneliness wash over her. She didn't want to translate. She didn't even want to talk. She held Cho's hand and accepted the peeled *tut* Wagner handed her. They watched the suns set.

When the last sun, the hot red one, began to sink into the sea, Cho released her hand. Prader would have reached the *Damocles* by now. The solar shields for the radio had been stripped for their weight. She might not be able to contact them until she returned to atmosphere. They might not know if she would return until they saw the burners in the sky. Whatever was going to happen, whatever they were going to learn, they would learn in a few hours. The crew didn't make any good-byes, not wanting to jinx the mission, but they understood that Meg had more to say than any of them.

"With your permission, Captain." She raised her wristband to him.

"Did you strip it?"

"Yes sir."

"All right."

She moved through the bodies on the ground to find Loul and his friends. The sky glowed warm lavender, making the scene around her look like a dream. As the suns set and the light dimmed, she heard the pulse of thrumming rise up on the breeze. All around her, the crews and archivists and soldiers reclined, watching the sky. They didn't speak, but their throats hummed, rising and falling in a rhythm that came together so solid, so in tune with the others, that Meg felt light-headed. She listened, picking Loul's thrum out from the throb of harmony, hearing it rise just slightly when the girl's fingers touched his wrist.

"Is this night?" Loul asked.

She turned to him and saw that his gaze fell near her but not on her face. The last sun had dipped below the water and the sky flushed a deep purple, but the sight was no darker than a late summer twilight. Still, she could tell that Loul and the other Dideto could barely see. They didn't know darkness.

"Yes," she said, watching Loul smile, "this is night."

Meg gave him the wristband. ProLingLang would continue to run translations and she had faith that Loul could figure out the kinks. As protocol dictated, she'd stripped the database of all weapons and military information. She put the library of comic books at the top of the access list.

"Meg talk to Loul. I want to tell you something, something the program can translate later. Loul can figure it out. I know you can." Loul put her hand on his earpiece. He wanted to hear her voice, not the translator. She was glad. The story was easier to tell to someone who didn't understand the words. She turned off the connection to her crewmates' coms so only Loul's computer could hear her and pulled the locket out from beneath her shirt. In the purple light she could make out two young girls with identical haircuts and identical dresses. Their faces would have been identical too except that one girl smiled with gap-toothed glory. The other's smile was closed-mouthed and shy.

"This is my sister, Maddie. My twin sister. Six minutes older than me and she never let me forget it. She bossed me around like a drill sergeant and I never questioned her, not ever. She had this way about her, this power. She had a million jokes, knew the words to all the songs. She could wear anything and make it look cool and she never left me behind.

"I was nothing like her. I know our parents must have wondered what the hell happened that they could have one vivacious firecracker and one backward paste-eater. Maddie always had a boyfriend. From first grade on she always had the cutest guy and another in the wings. And she always insisted they find a guy for me too. They must have hated that, having to find a date for Meg the Peg. That's what they used to call me, because I'd just stand there, afraid to speak up. I'd just stand there in Maddie's shadow.

"What people didn't get was that I liked it there. I felt safe there. I felt important because I was Maddie Dupris's twin sister. I got to see everything. When Maddie was around, people forgot about me and I could watch them. I could listen and see what made them smile, what made them mad. Maddie didn't care what people thought. She did what she wanted.

"She was careless, though." Meg flipped the locket closed, not wanting to look, but opened it back up. "She thought nothing bad could ever happen. That was the only thing she ever teased me about, that I would get scared and not want to do things that she wanted to do. She was so athletic. She could jump off a garage roof and not even get a bruise. I'd twist my ankle climbing out of the car. I got scared easily. She never did.

"We were fifteen. Out at our grandma's house in Kentucky. We loved it out there because we could wander in the woods for hours. Nobody worried about us because they all knew Maddie'd never let anything bad happen to me. So when that board broke, that stupid rotted board neither one of us saw, and we fell down that well, nobody thought to look for us. Not for hours. Not until dark.

"It was so black down there, Loul. It was the blackest place I've ever seen. Everyone thinks space is the blackest place but they're wrong. Earth is the blackest place. Under the earth. Under the ground, where there aren't even stars and the tiny patch of sky you can see just makes the blackness blacker and the small spaces smaller."

Meg's throat ached as she told the story she had never told anyone. She'd never told the mission evaluators or the psychiatrists. She'd never even told Cho. "They said maybe she'd have been okay if someone had found us right away. I tried. I tried climbing up that hole but it kept crumbling underneath my hands. I wasn't as strong as Maddie. I wasn't as coordinated and nobody ever said anything but I know they had to be thinking it; thinking that if our positions had been switched, if I had fallen first, Maddie would have been able to climb that well and get help. But Maddie always went first. Always.

"She woke up a week later and they were able to take the breathing tubes out. Mom tried to make me leave the hospital then, telling me that the doctors said she was stabilizing, but I wouldn't go. I just wrapped myself around the legs of the hospital bed and hung on. I hung on so tight two big interns tried to pry me off and couldn't do it. I slept in the chair next to my sister listening to the machines breathing for her. Then I slept on the chair next to her listening to her breathe on her own.

"What I was listening for was her to tell me everything was going to be okay. I didn't want to hear it from the doctors or our parents. I needed to hear it from the one person who had never lied to me, who had never lost patience with me or ignored me. I needed Maddie to tell me she was better and that it was okay I couldn't climb as well as she did and that it wasn't my fault I landed so hard on her when we went down that hole. I needed to hear it from Maddie. But she wasn't talking.

"They brought her home a month later. Said the brain damage was irreversible, that there were no signs of cognition, but I knew they were wrong. I could tell. I could see it in her eyes. She couldn't control her body and couldn't make her mouth work, but I could see it in her eyes. The doctors said they were just reflexive movements but they were wrong. I knew. I know. She was my twin. I knew."

Meg wiped at the mess running down over her lips, seeing the soot she smeared across her face. "She was home for two weeks when she started the hand gestures. Mom said they were just spasms but I knew she was trying to tell me something. We used to signal each other like that when we were on double dates or cheating in class. Her hands didn't work like they were supposed to, but I could tell she was gesturing to me. When the nurse saw the movements, she gave her a shot and Maddie got quiet again. The nurse told me I was upsetting her, that she needed quiet and rest. She told me if I wanted to stay in there with her, I had to be quiet too.

"The next time Maddie started moving, I shut the door to her room so nobody would hear her bed squeak. I unplugged the heart monitor so it wouldn't alert the nurse. I told Maddie what I was doing and why I was doing it. I told her I knew she could hear me and I wanted to figure out what she was trying to tell me. I told her I wouldn't let anyone give her another shot until we figured out a way for her to be understood. She smiled. The doctors told me later that it was just a spasm but it wasn't. She looked at me and her mouth turned up and I knew she was glad I was there. Her hand reached out and I took it and she squeezed so hard my knuckles cracked.

"She said my name. It's funny, she said it the way the Effans do, kind of sloppy and garbled but I heard it. I heard it. She tried to turn her head to face me but her muscles were twitching so I turned her face toward me and she said my name. She said it twice and it was the most beautiful sound I ever heard. The most beautiful sound I'll ever hear. I said to her, 'I'm here, Maddie, tell me what you want to say.' And she made this sound. She said something but I couldn't understand her, so I asked her to say it again and she did. She said it again, only this time she said it really loud, like a scream.

"Mom came running in the room. Maddie's back arched up and she got all twisted in the bed. Her hand kept reaching out over her head and I knew she was reaching for me, but Mom pushed me out of the way. She pushed me really hard and I fell back over the chair and then the nurse was there and they were giving Maddie a shot. They kept pushing me away from the bed and I saw Maddie's face, her eyes were so big and she looked so scared, trying to talk, trying to reach for me. And I couldn't get to her. I couldn't reach her."

Meg rubbed the locket against her wet cheek. "They said it was a blood clot. That it had just been a matter of time. Said it was a blessing, that she shouldn't have had to suffer like that. When I came home from the funeral Mass, I locked myself in our room. I didn't talk to anyone for a month. Didn't go to school. Dad left meals for me on a tray outside my door. I think they were probably glad to not see me. I think they loved me but I don't think they could bear to see my face without Maddie's beside it. My voice would never sound like Maddie's.

"I don't know what prompted me but I got on the computer and learned Cantonese. I'd never been much of a student before, never really applied myself, but all of a sudden languages just opened up to me. By the time I went back to school the next fall, I was fluent in Cantonese and could hold a decent conversation in Russian. After that, I just started collecting them—languages, dialects, codes. If it said something, I learned it. I'm fluent in nine languages, conversant in twenty-seven others, and I can read in half a dozen more. Hell, I'm even learning Dideto." Her voice broke as she tipped her head up to the darkening sky. "I can understand everyone in the universe but I couldn't understand my sister."

"Oh!" Loul sighed, his thrum rising. He stared straight up at the sky, his fist raised above him. All around the field, the Dideto followed suit. One after another, hands shot up, pointing to the sky. Meg followed his gaze. There in the darkening sky she could just make out the flicker of a star.

"Meg see this?" Loul asked. "This is night, yes? Urfer night?"

"Stars," Meg said. "Just like night on Earth."

Loul smiled even though he didn't think anyone could see him. "Good/okay."

"Very."

Seven more stars came out during the Purpling and the Dideto called to every one of them. They sang songs and banged their fists. Some of them rolled around on top of each other, "sexual intercourse Dideto style," Cho explained with a badly concealed grimace. For one night out of years of endless daylight, the Dideto moved in shadows. They weren't afraid of the dark. Meg could hear it in their thrums. It thrilled them. It happened so rarely it didn't occur to them that there could be any threat in the shadows. The Earthers wandered through the work site easily, finding their way in the dusky twilight, undetected by the Dideto. Like ghosts, Meg thought. Cho joined her, sitting on the dirt beside the blanket she shared with Loul and his friends. He didn't say anything but just sat down beside her as the sky began to turn rose.

When rose turned to pink, they stood together and moved back to where Jefferson and Wagner sat quietly, staring out over the sea. The breeze shifted up and around them, throwing a fine mist of sand and salt. Long lines of orange and pink streaked the horizon over the sea, not quite sunrise but coming close. They could hear the Dideto rising in clumsy form from their supine positions, could hear blankets and bags being dusted off as pale light warmed the mountains in the east.

"The Red Sun rises first," Wagner said. "Then the one they call Fa. Fa will come up and stay on the horizon for another ten years at least. Can you imagine that? Ten years of daylight?"

Nobody answered him. Cho pulled out the vitamin shots and they all wordlessly rolled up their sleeves. More than twelve hours had passed, they could feel it in their bones and their dry eyes and rumbling stomachs. Jefferson's eyes were especially bloodshot, and Meg thought he had probably spent the entire dark period watching the sky, as if he would see the explosion. Maybe he would have. Meg didn't know where the ship was supposed to be. She wasn't a navigator or an engineer. She wouldn't have known where to look.

The Red Sun broke the surface of the water and the sound of Dideto chattering rose. Someone broke out more food, and the log they had used to smudge their cheeks was broken up with rocks and scattered on the wind. Soldiers and work crews gathered the last of the boxes stacked up under the shelters and carried them toward the waiting trucks. Other workers began dismantling the shelters themselves. If the Earthers were staying, they weren't staying here. The Red Sun cast hard shadows on the broken slab, casting the holes and crevices in sharp relief until the Fa sun rose high enough to soften them.

Loul said something to his friends, leaning in to brush his cheek against the girl's face. She closed her eyes at the touch, her arm lifted to brush her fingers against this thrum spot. Meg smiled. Loul pulled away and looked over at her, finding her in the shifting crowd. It made sense. It wasn't like they blended with the Dideto around them. He smiled at her, short brown teeth catching the red dawning light. Wagner's hand felt heavy on her shoulder.

"You might as well talk with him, Meg. Find out what happens now."

"Yeah, okay." But she didn't move. None of them did. Cho, Jefferson, Wagner—they stood beside her watching the work crews doing what they did, busy with whatever they were busy with. They chattered among themselves, calling out to each other and laughing. Some leaned against each other, bonds having been formed in the privacy of darkness. With the translator off, none of the words made sense. It didn't matter. Nobody was speaking to them.

Meg rubbed her wrist, the bare skin an odd feeling without her wristband. She had others in her kit. They all did. She knew she'd have to clip another one on soon. The breeze shifted, coming in now from the south. In the greenish light, she could see the silhouettes of birds flying in a chevron toward the eastern mountains. They looked like geese with incredibly long legs that trailed behind them on the breeze. She watched them fly, their wings beating slowly, just enough to keep them afloat on the currents. She counted sixteen birds before they disappeared in the rising Fa sun.

When the radio crackled, the four of them jumped as one. "Would you look at that goddamn sunrise?" Prader's laugh cackled through the coms. "Son of a bitch! It's beautiful!"

TWENTY ONE

LOUL

The generals barked out orders as the convoys rolled out. A secretary appeared with a binder of documents that Ada kept insisting he sign. Black-shirt crews flooded the site, bagging debris and tagging damage done to the slab. Ada had handed over an Urfer wristband to a team of computer scientists, not Olum and the team who had worked with the leader of the Urfers, but a well-dressed team of black shirts. The leader, Agnar, had given it to Olum, but the general insisted he turn it over to the administration. Ada also insisted Loul turn over the one Meg had given him, but Loul refused. The Searcher had stood by him as the general raged, stating protocol and national security.

"If you give it to him," the reporter spoke in low, even tones as if the general weren't even present, "you'll never see it again. That information will go in a drawer in a locked room in a basement beneath the administration's headquarters. They won't use the technology. They won't study it or build on it or learn from it. They won't try to follow the star charts or figure out who the Urfers were. They'll hoard the information, gather it like *loro* nuts in a cliff nest."

Loul knew he was right. What the administration called research was just a filing system. They didn't value information as anything other than a currency, a stockpile of words and numbers. They didn't value curiosity at all.

"What about you?" Loul asked. "What would you do with it?"

"Me?" The Searcher said with surprise. "She didn't give it to me. She gave it to you. Of course, if you came to work for me, we could study it together. You could study it and share what you learn. What you choose to share."

Loul shook his head, working the flexible wristband in his fist. "Why should you trust me like that? Why should anyone?"

"Because Meg did. They all did. You're Loul Pell. You'll go down in history as the man who made first contact with the aliens."

MEG

Cho smoothed the wire netting down along her spine and waited while she lay back. The sleep sack shifted beneath her and Meg resisted the urge to poke her fingers through the netting. Her skin smelled like the antibacterial scrub that made her arms and legs tingle. When she grew still, he placed the adhesive dots underneath her nose and along her cheekbones, on either side of her mouth and one at the jut of her chin. Once she was deeply asleep, BESS would follow those dots to insert the life-support devices. Meg tried and failed not to shudder at the thought of the machine taking over her body once the tranquilizers took effect.

Cho read her mind. "I promise you, as I always do, that the sleep sack will not draw in until you are completely under. There are fail-safes. Trust me."

"I trust you." She raised her hand to stop him from injecting the first of the muscle relaxers into her leg. Cho pulled the injection gun back.

"It's time, Meg. We're going to hit maximum velocity soon. You don't want to be awake for that. None of us do."

"I know. I just..." A tear slid down into her hair and Cho brushed it away. "Is this what it's going to be like? Is this what we're going to do? Just go from world to world crashing in, breaking stuff, and blowing out like a tornado?"

"I don't know," Cho said, putting the injection gun beside her on the bed. "This mission, this whole idea is insanity. It seems like everything that could go wrong went wrong down there and we still made it out."

"And left them with what?"

"Information. Knowledge. Questions."

Meg sighed. "Who says that's such a good thing?"

"I do." Cho leaned over her and looked her in the eye. "You do too. We're agents of change. We're part of evolution. It's who we are. I want to show you something." He rolled back the sleeve of his sleep shirt and showed her a small tattoo on the inside of his wrist. She'd seen it a hundred times, kissed it half that many. Cho rubbed that particular symbol a lot when he was lost in thought.

"My great-grandfather was born in a concentration camp in North Korea, before the unification. He was a fourth-generation prisoner." Cho traced the symbol, two broken lines running parallel to each other, like two equal signs side by side. "He told my father that all he ever knew was food, fighting, and fucking. That by the time he was born the guards didn't even have to beat them, they were so ingrained as prisoners. He said the guards would tell them, 'Where will you go where you're freer than this?' and none of them could answer. The camps were all they knew."

Cho watched Meg trace her fingers over the tattoo as he continued. "When Japan fell, when the radiation couldn't be contained, he said refugees poured onto the shores by the hundreds, sick and poisonous. He said they'd watch videos of the soldiers shooting them as they staggered out of the water and it didn't mean a thing. They were nothing, these bodies piling up on the shore. They weren't part of the prison so they were nothing to them."

Cho sighed. "The refugees kept coming in such numbers that they needed more guards to protect the coast. They pulled a whole shift of guards off the gate one day, leaving the prisoners they thought they could trust alone, unwatched. Great-grandfather was one of them. He said the idea of escape had never even once crossed his mind, that he had believed that as bad as the camp was there was no place any better. But he said when he saw that gate unguarded, something moved inside of him. Something changed. He said he and eight other prisoners got up without a word and just walked out the door. They had no money. No shoes. Nowhere to go, but they just walked out the door and walked all the way to the border.

"None of them could read or write but they used symbols. He said that the old-timers had a saying, 'The gate is inside you.' This symbol, this is that saying. 'The gate is inside you.'"

"What does it mean?"

Cho picked up the injection gun again and Meg nodded, letting him shoot the warm chemical into her thigh. He rubbed the spot gently. "He told my grandfather who told his son who told me that at that moment he understood that the gate really is inside each of us. Each of us has a door to walk through, maybe a thousand, and if we don't walk through them, we aren't alive. We aren't human until we walk through that gate regardless of what's on the other side."

She reached for his arm and brought the tattoo to her lips, kissing it, feeling his pulse against her mouth. "I almost stayed."

He brought her fingers to his lips. "I know. I'm glad you didn't. Go to sleep."

"Okay."

He smiled at her. "Okay/good."

The lights dimmed slowly, and Meg took a deep breath, feeling the artificial relaxation moving through her system. Soon she knew the sleep sack would draw up around her, and fine needles would emerge from the sides of the bunk, following the signal in the electronic dots along the nerve netting. Tranquilizers and anesthetics would flood her system. Tubes would go into her body, and BESS would take over the living for her while the *Damocles* hurtled through the blackness of space.

She tried not to think of it as her eyelids drooped and her breathing slowed. With effort, she turned her head just enough to see the locket secured to the wall of her bunk, nestled against a thin swatch of purple cloth.

ACKNOWLEDGMENTS

Thanks as always to my agent and good friend, Christine Witthohn; to my editor, Terry Goodman, who has entirely too much faith in me; to the amazing team at 47North who work so hard, so fast, and make it all look so easy; to my family who have yet to cull me from the herd; to the fabulous Elizabeth Jennings and all my Matera peeps; and of course endless cheers to the best group of friends a writer could ever hope for: Gina Milum, Debra Burge, Tenna Rusk, Christy Smith, Angie Harp, Alecia Cole, Angela Jackson, Karen Karr, Debra McDanald, Gordon Ramey, and all the fearsome Book Thugs and Debra's Pictures Aficionados. It's good to be among my own.

ABOUT THE AUTHOR

S. G. Redling parlayed her degree in English from Georgetown University into various careers including waitress, monument tour guide, sheepskin packer, and radio host. She has leapt from a plane and a moving train, gotten lost in Istanbul and locked in the dining car of a midnight train through the Carpathians. She currently lives in Huntington, West Virginia, and is also the author of the thriller *Flowertown*.